THE
TURIN SHROUD
SECRET

THE
TURIN SHROUD
SECRET

SAM CHRISTER

sphere

SPHERE

First published in Great Britain as a paperback original in 2012 by Sphere

Image credits, in page order: © 2004 Topfoto.co.uk; © GL Archive/Alamy; © Mary Evans
Picture Library/Alamy; © The Art Archive/Alamy; © The Art Archive/Alamy;
© The Art Archive/Alamy; SSPL via Getty Images; Getty Images; © Camera Press &
© Alinari; © Mary Evans Picture Library/Alamy; © Mary Evans Picture Library/Alamy

ISBN B 978-0-7515-4714-6
ISBN CF 978-1-84744-523-0

Typeset in Bembo by M Rules
Printed and bound in Great Britain by
Clays Ltd, St Ives plc

Papers used by Sphere are from well-managed forests
and other responsible sources.

MIX
Paper from
responsible sources
FSC FSC® C104740
www.fsc.org

Sphere
An imprint of
Little, Brown Book Group
100 Victoria Embankment
London EC4Y 0DY

An Hachette UK Company
www.hachette.co.uk

www.littlebrown.co.uk

To Donna and Billy for your priceless gifts
of time and understanding

One by one the devotees remove bricks from the centuries-old sanctuary. They know they are unleashing a force that will kill most horribly, one that will either save everything they hold sacred – or destroy it for ever.

PART ONE

And Joseph bought a linen shroud and taking
him down, wrapped him in the linen shroud
and laid him in a tomb that had been cut out
of the rock.

English Standard Bible

1

There are many reasons why he kills. Why, right at this moment, he is about to kill again.

It is a need. A craving. An aching, gnawing compulsion. Like sex. When he's not doing it, he's thinking about it. Fantasising. Planning. Rehearsing. Killing to him is as necessary and inevitable as drawing breath. Only more pleasurable. Memorable.

This one is going to be easy. Perfect. The best yet. The unkilled always are. That's what he calls them. Not the living. Not the next victim.

The unkilled.

A quiet neighbourhood. A woman living alone. One not even aware that while she busied herself in that pretty rear garden he slipped into her life and home.

He's been lying in wait for hours, unnoticed like a dog in a favourite hiding place, his ears twitching as he follows

3

her sounds around the darkening house, his furtive mind imagining her every movement.

There's a thin clattering noise – she's tidying up after her dinner for one.

A soft *thump* – shutting the dishwasher.

Tumbling *clunks*. Ice from the dispenser on the tall fridge by the kitchen door. A glass of water to take to bed.

Click, click, click. Turning out the lights. Closing doors.

Bump, bump. Bump, bump. Footsteps. Coming upstairs. Heavy footed. Desperate to lie down on her big soft bed and sleep.

A soft *click*. A bedside lamp warms the big bedroom with a buttercup glow.

Running water. A shower. Nice and hot. A warm soak to make her clean for bed.

Fresh for death.

He waits. Counts off the seconds and minutes. Seven hundred and twenty seconds. Twelve long minutes. Now the whirr of a hairdryer. Best not to go to sleep with wet hair. Most unhealthy. The television mutters. Music. A film. News. She's zapping. Searching for something to distract her from the rigours of the day. *The Tonight Show. Conan. House.*

Click. The crackle of static on the plasma screen.

Silence.

A final *click*. The lamp.

Darkness.

He lies there. Beneath the bed. Savouring the floating

4

echo of the last sounds – like a sliver of communion wafer dissolving on the tongue.

Soon he hears the whisper of her breathing, faint sighs rising like soft light breaking the dawn sky. Sleep is gently preparing her for God and for him. He rolls out from his shelter. Slow. Graceful. Careful. A deadly animal emerging from cover. Exposed in the wild. Closing on its prey. Tingling with anticipation.

He puts one hand around her throat and places the other across her mouth. Her eyes flash open with shock. He smiles down at her and whispers, '*Dominus vobiscum* – the Lord be with you.'

2

THURSDAY MORNING
MANHATTAN BEACH, LOS ANGELES

It's November but still ninety out on the dunes. California does that sometimes. A golden fall to make up for a poor summer. Thirty-year-old homicide detective Nic Karakandez makes a visor out of his right hand and strains his blue-grey eyes at the sparkling diamond swirl of the Pacific. Dressed in faded blue jeans and a black leather bomber jacket, the big cop stands out on top of the sands.

He's staring hard and seeing more than anyone else.

Certainly more than the sand-crusted stiff that the ME and CSIs are bent over. Way more than the bobbing heads of swimmers gawping from the waves.

Nic sees the future.

A month from now to be precise. His boat heading out to sea, wind billowing in the sails, a reel or two hanging over the back and a time when jobs like this sorry floater are nothing but distant memories.

'*Nic!* Get your ass down here.'

There's only one woman in the world who speaks to him like that. He drops his hand and squints at his colleague and boss, Lieutenant Mitzi Fallon. 'I'm coming – give me a chance.'

The thirty-nine-year-old mom of two is twenty yards ahead of him, down a dip in the soft Californian sand. 'Hey Big Foot – are you the fast-moving murder police I taught you to be or have I got you mixed up with some pale-throated sloth?'

He can't help but laugh. 'I'm the fast-moving murder police, ma'am. What exactly is a *sloth?*'

'Short-necked, fat-assed mammal. Sixty million years old and spends most of its time sleeping.'

'I wish.'

Mitzi's been breaking his balls since his first day in the department more than five years ago. He pads alongside her as they head towards the fluttering tape ten yards from the ocean's edge. Pretty soon the crime scene will be gone. Washed away by Lady Tide, that ancient accomplice to so many murders.

6

They badge the uniforms guarding the area, slip on shoe covers and join the ME, Amy Chang, a second-generation Chinese medic with a brain as big as the state deficit.

'Afternoon, doc,' breezes Mitzi. 'Any chance your poor lady there died of natural causes? I gotta be at a soccer game tonight.'

The pathologist doesn't look up. She knows them both well. *Too* well. 'Not a chance. Not unless it's considered normal to go swimming fully dressed after you've just had two teeth pulled out, an eye removed and your throat slit.'

'Man, that's some careless dentist.' Nic leans over the body.

'Obama's got a lot to answer for,' adds Mitzi. 'He never should have messed with the health care.'

'He got Bin Laden, though – that gives him a Get Out of Jail Card as far as I'm concerned.'

Amy looks up and shakes her head in mock disgust. 'You two jokers got a single ounce of respect for what's going on here?'

Nic catches her eye. There's a spark between them. Small but it's there. He blows it out before she can even blink. 'Tons,' he says. 'We just hide it well. Black humour is the only way we know to protect our fragile constitutions.'

Amy stares him down. '*Sick minds* are more like it.'

The lieutenant rounds a CSI sifting sand for anything that might have come off the body and got buried or trodden on. She circles the corpse, staring at it from different angles, like it's a piece of modern art that doesn't yet make sense. 'Any ID on her?'

'None,' says Amy. 'Surely you knew you weren't going to get that lucky?'

'Just hoping.' She circles again. Slower this time, stooping to study the vic's hands and feet. 'Any idea how long she'd been in the water?'

Amy looks up again. 'C'mon, Mitzi, I need to check body temperature and tides – you're way too early to get a polite answer.'

Amy forces a thermometer through the eye socket into the brain. It will give her a window of about three hours on the time of death. She glances up at the pull and push of the waves beside her. Once she's consulted a tidal expert, she'll have a good idea of where and when the vic met her end. She notes the body temperature then uses scissors to cut off the fingernails and bags the clippings.

Mitzi is still hanging over her and she feels obliged to give the cop something. 'We're talking hours in the water, less than a day. That's all you're getting for the moment.' She straightens up, brushes off sand and beckons two orderlies who've been waiting with a marine body bag, the type that lets water out but keeps any evidence in. 'Okay, parcel her up.'

'What kinda freak could have done this?' Nic's eyes are scanning the raw, mutilated flesh.

'No mystery there.' Amy pulls off purple rubber gloves and snaps her metal case shut. 'Some bad son-of-a-bitch kind of freak – you know, the type that's done it before and will soon be doing it all over again.'

3

The food corner in the mall is a free-for-all. Shoppers and office workers jostle like cattle at feeding troughs. Stressed-out servers bark orders in the soupy air and pound labelled till keys.

An olive-skinned young man in his mid-twenties with dark hair and even darker eyes waits patiently in the thick of it all. An island of calm caught in a raging river of inhuman rudeness. Indifferently, he waits his turn, then pays for miso soup, a box of sushi and black coffee. It's a diet that renders him more slim than muscular – lean, if you want to be kind in your description – too small and skinny for women who like big broad-shouldered guys to hang on to. It's also landed him with the nickname 'Fish Face' at the factory where he works.

'Let me help you.' He moves quickly to clear chairs and tables so an old man can push his wife's wheelchair through the dining jungle and lay their food tray at a free table.

'Very kind of you.' The senior nods a thank you as they settle.

'No problem, you're welcome.' He takes his lunch to a table a few yards away. He smiles at the couple as he mixes fiery wasabi paste with soy sauce, stirs it with chopsticks and dips a tuna roll, then turns his attention to the tide of people flowing past. They fascinate him. All of them. No exceptions.

A teacher leads a crocodile of foreign schoolchildren, Chinese he thinks, in a two-by-two line, little cherubs all holding each other's hands. All wearing the same orange tops and caps and looking like dolls fresh off a production line. He remembers seeing a poster somewhere proclaiming that there are five times as many people in China learning to speak English as there are people in England. The world is changing. So is he. He can feel it. Sense it.

His eyes swing to a mature blonde in a business suit scrambling for a ringing cell phone in her small black leather bag. A cougar past her prime. Smart clothes and a good diet can't hide what age and the Californian weather do to your hair and skin. She finds the iPhone in the nick of time but doesn't look pleased. Not a call from her husband or lover, he guesses. More likely a wail of despair from a colleague – a cry for help from the workplace she's just left behind.

The young man smiles as she passes him. There's something familiar in her eyes. He snaps his fingers as he realises what it is. She reminds him of the woman he was with last night.

The one he murdered.

4

The ME's heavy morgue wagon, a white Dodge van with shaded windows, ploughs ruts in the litter-free sand as it disappears with its sad cargo. Crowds of rubbernecking bathers return zombie-like to towels and loungers as though nothing had happened. Life goes on – even after death.

Nic Karakandez steps out of the taped-off crime scene and walks the amphibious tightrope between sand and sea, the line where the dark water washes onto the white sand then mysteriously vaporises in a fizz of outgoing wave. A north-easterly wind is kicking up as he looks to the glittering horizon.

He's done with being a murder police.

Done with being any kind of police for that matter. His notice is in. The well-muscled six-footer made the decision years back, following an incident he doesn't talk about – the kind that would make most good cops quit. Since then he's been treading water, going through the motions, marking time until he got enough money together, nailed down his skipper's licence and finished the repairs on his little sloop. Thirty days from now he'll be sailing into the sunset to start a whole new life.

Mitzi looks back towards the disappearing tape and the uniforms she's just briefed to start canvassing the gawping

11

zombies. 'How d'you think Mr Freak dumped her? I mean, I didn't see any tyre marks back there and the sand's as soft as my gut.'

Nic points east to a band of black running from the coast road across the beach and out to a squat building some way off in the sea. 'Over there's the Roundhouse. I guess he drove down the pier as far as he could then popped his trunk and simply slid her body over the side.'

'I can see how that would work. From the looks of her, she didn't weigh more than eighty pounds. It'd be an easy drop.' Mitzi gazes out towards the end of the pier with its marine lab and aquarium, a big draw for the rich locals and their kids. Not hers, though. Her twin daughters are allergic to anything academic. They'd rather chase a soccer ball, play video games or bait the boys next door.

As she and Nic trudge towards the jetty, Mitzi gets a mental flash of the dead woman. 'You notice our Jane Doe was still wearing jewellery?' She twists the tiny wedding ring that's been on her finger for close to two decades and waggles it for Nic to see. 'She was carrying a rock big enough for boy scouts to camp on.'

'Certainly wasn't a robbery,' observes Nic. 'Given the brutality of the other injuries, our perp wouldn't hesitate to cut off her finger if he wanted that sparkler.'

'So what then? A kidnapping gone wrong?'

'Maybe, but I would have expected a ransom demand. Even if the husband – presuming there still is one – had been frightened into keeping us out of it.'

Mitzi thinks back to the corpse. 'Yeah, it doesn't follow. Kidnappers stiff their victim when the money talks are over, not before. By then the family's jumpier than Mexican beans and always come running to us. So if it was an abduction, we'd have heard something.'

As they climb the last stretch of beach to the pier Nic's thinking the kill bears the mark of a professional – albeit a crazy one. 'Last time I saw anything like this, it was Italians out in the valley,' he says. 'They cut up one of their own after he crossed them. Revenge, pure and simple.'

Mitzi frowns. 'You think she was mixing with organised crime?'

'Could be. Imagine, for a minute, that she's a mob wife and her old man finds out she's cheating on him.' He puts out his hand and pulls Mitzi up. 'At first she refuses to name the guy banging her, then, finally when she gives it up, said lothario turns out to be hubby's brother or best friend. Boom.' Nic slaps his hand. 'The boss gets all emotional. He feels he has no choice but to have someone mess her up and finish her off.'

'You've got one sick imagination.'

'It's how you taught me.' He looks beyond her, down the wide pier leading to the red-tiled angular building at the end. A four-bar metal rail runs either side, out over the water. It comes up to his chest. He was right. Drive a car out here, it'd be easy enough to tip a body over the side.

Mitzi drops into a squat. 'Lots of tyre treads down here.' She sweeps an indicative hand over the area just in front of her. 'And, thank you God, a nice layer of sand that's printed just about everything that's recently come and gone.'

'I'll get uniforms to tape off the pier and have CSI do the treads.' He pulls a cell phone and sits up on the rail while he makes the call.

Mitzi takes out the small camera she always carries and snaps off some shots. Sometimes the techies turn up too late and the evidence has gone. Better safe than sorry.

Ten minutes later a red-faced, overweight cop in a sweat-stained uniform arrives with a young crime scene photographer. While Mitzi briefs them, Nic wanders a few yards away to watch the surf breaking around the legs of the pier. There are pictures in the bubbling white froth. Abstract images, open to interpretation. Some people see galloping horses or Vikings or sea gods.

Nic sees the wife and baby son he lost.

They're lying in a sea of their own blood. Eyes rolled back like rancid scallops.

And every time he sees them – when their unexpected appearance breaks his heart – he does nothing to block them out, nothing to divert the blame from himself.

Carolina had wanted him to leave the apartment and push the pram a while. Max was crying and a stroll around the block always seemed to settle him. But Nic got stuck on the phone – a work call on his day off. She'd grown bored waiting and finally gone without him. Two blocks later she stopped at a grocery store. Had Nic been there it would have been different. He'd have known right away what was going down – the crackhead robbing the register, jittery and paranoid, a human timebomb bound to explode; the dope of a store owner playing hero by grabbing a gun taped beneath the counter and the shoppers panicking and screaming, ratcheting up the mayhem.

It had been Armageddon.

After the weapon came up from behind the counter, the junkie slaughtered everyone. Then he just stood there in a daze. He was still staring at the carnage when the cops came. One lowlife's moment of madness ended a dozen good people's lives and created a lifetime of misery for their families.

'If this was the killer's drop spot, he's not a local.' Mitzi is pacing again.

'What?' Nic's thoughts are still three years back.

'The *ocean*.' She points over the rail to get his attention. 'The water here is too shallow. The perp probably thought it was deeper. When he dumped her over the side, he must have believed the body would be gone for ever.'

'The tide might have been in,' says Nic, his brain and body finally reunited in the same time zone. 'Or else the guy didn't care. Could be he was only bothered about her being hidden long enough for him to skip town.'

'You're good,' she says with a smile that hints at why ten years ago every cop in the precinct made time to walk by her desk. 'I'm going to miss you when you're working as a crabber on *Deadliest Catch*.'

He laughs. 'Does the Discovery Channel have any other shows than that damned thing?'

15

'Not worth watching.'

They walk single file down the edge of the pier, close to the rails, so as not to disturb any more tyre tracks. He makes a slow circuit of the aquarium and marine lab, shielding his eyes and looking skyward. Eventually he finds what he's looking for.

'Surf cams.' He points out two small cameras at the tip of long poles. 'You can watch shots from these things online in real time.'

'Kill me before my life becomes so boring that I would even think about doing that.'

'Each to their own, Mitz.' He points to another steel pole, one topped with a security camera. 'Now this is more your taste.' He palm-gestures like a teleshopping host showing off some pile of crap that can only be bought in the next ten minutes. 'A channel exclusively available to good-looking and talented LAPD cops, featuring – *hopefully* – all the once-in-a-lifetime footage of Big Rock Lady's killer.'

5

LATE AFTERNOON

Amy Chang suits up, snaps on latex gloves and enters the newly equipped morgue. It's a cold vault of stainless steel, illuminated by pools of limpid green and blue lights. Steel body-fridges, sinks, carts, tables and tools crowd the central autopsy table with its inelegant taps and cruel draining holes, portals for the last of the deceased's blood and body fluids. There's far too much dull and deathly metal for Amy's liking. Another world away from the thirty-two-year-old's elegant bachelorette home, steel-free except for the knives in the pretty picture-window kitchen overlooking a small but well-ordered garden.

Less than a week old, the morgue already smells of Deodorx and Path Cloud cleansers. Amy looks sympathetically at the flesh and bones laid out on the slab. To her, the remains are still a person, a desperate woman in need of her expert help. 'So who are you then? What can you tell me, honey? What secrets do you have for us?'

Even at first glance it's obvious the victim suffered excruciating pain before she finally died. The injuries are all pre-mortem. Lips are split, teeth are missing and then there's the awful cavity where her left eye should be – a terrible testament to the level of torture she endured.

She clears space so she can work. Adjusts the ceiling-mounted dissecting light with its dual beams and slips on a tiny, head-mounted video camera for the close-ups. She wants to capture everything she says and sees during the examination.

'The victim is a well-nourished woman in her late forties or early fifties. She has extensive pre-mortem injuries to her face including the loss of her left eye and two upper middle teeth. There is evidence of recent plastic surgery,

17

nip and tuck scars still healing around the ears and neck.'

Her voice grows more sombre as she realises how the deceased must have hoped a more benign encounter with a blade would keep her looking younger and more desirable. 'Less cosmetic are the injuries to the left and right cheeks – these are consistent with a series of blows, probably from front- and back-handed slaps. She's suffered powerful blunt trauma to the left cheek, possibly from a fist. It's split open and the flesh exposed to the bone.' Amy moves down to the neck. 'The deceased has bled out through a horizontal three-inch wound that severed the vessels in the carotid sheath. A fatal cut. She'd have died from an air embolus even if she'd survived the wound.' Amy can't help but notice its precision. No hesitant stab. Just a confident and ruthless action.

She picks up the deceased's manicured hands. It's not the first time she's touched them. Back on the beach she clipped the nails for trace evidence and toxicology and then had fingerprints taken. 'No signs of major defence wounds but there are marks around the wrists, indicating she may have been tied up.' Amy uses tape to lift what she's sure are small fragments of rope twist from the grey skin. She stands back a little and surveys the whole torso, paying particular attention to the feet, knees, elbows and hands. 'No friction or abrasion marks on normal surface contact points. No indications of the body being dragged across any kind of surface.'

Next she examines the empty, red, raw eye socket. The killer used something to lever out the victim's eyeball.

What?

There are no gouge marks inside the cavity to indicate where any metal might have been forced in. She realises what has happened. He used his fingers. The attacker pushed his thumb into her eye socket and forced it out. He then cut through the exposed muscle and nerve attachments. It takes a special kind of monster to do something like that. She grimaces – something Amy Chang seldom does. In the corner of the woman's thin purple lips are abrasion marks, tell-tale signs that a tight gag stifled her screams.

A phone on the wall rings and flashes – then trips to the message service. Amy moves on. She considers the missing teeth. These probably had been extracted prior to the eye damage. She looks again into the woman's mouth. There are marks on her back teeth and upper pallet. Something was jammed in there to keep her jaws open while the guy went about his work. Amy angles the deceased's head back and swings down the overhead light. She uses tweezers to extract small traces of white plastic from the inside of the upper and lower back molars. Unless she's mistaken the killer forced a golf ball in there to be able to get at the front teeth.

Amy's seen a lot of nasty stuff on her table but her tummy turns every time she sees something like this. Something she recognises as the unique work of the worst kind of predator in the world – the serial killer.

6

The dark-haired man with thick eyebrows and olive-coloured skin makes sure he's locked the front and back doors and secured the windows. Burglary is not something he wants to fall victim to – the irony would be unbearable.

He walks through to the Spartan kitchen and opens an old larder fridge that only ever contains three things: UHT milk – the type that lasts six to nine months – a box of eggs and a tub of low-fat spread. If he's really hungry, he'll use everything and make omelettes. Otherwise, like tonight, he just drinks milk. Fish and soup for lunch, milk and eggs for dinner. That's his entire diet.

He feels somewhat strange as he moves through the house drinking straight from the carton. Edgy. Off balance. Nervous. Not that any of that surprises him. The day after is always like this – contradictory and confusing. It's a period of anxiety and elation.

The mood swings used to throw him but not any more. He's experienced now – understands that with every kill comes an aftershock. Like the physical recoil of a firearm. The bruising kick of a rifle against a shoulder muscle. Take a life and your psychological muscles take a pounding. The purple bruise of guilt surfaces first, then the yellow fear of capture and finally the ruddy red flush of conquest.

He's spent the day like he normally does, holding down a job that's beneath him, working for people who don't appreciate or understand him. Not that anyone does. Still, routine is important. A change of habit attracts attention if the police go nosing around. Besides, he's learned that right after a kill it's good to be with people, to stay in the stream of mindless fish flowing to and from homes and jobs. He likes the distraction, the filling of time. And he appreciates the camouflage of commonality, the necessary disguise that dreary everyday life gives him.

But now it's the night time. And the night is different. He feels different. Is different. It is a time of energy and power. A time when kills can be savoured. Darkness brings with it a justification, a validation of what he does and who he is. Throughout the day he longs for the dipping sun and the rising of the raw energy within him.

The rented house where he lives is plunged in blackness. It always is. The thick curtains are forever drawn. There are no bulbs in any of the light sockets. No electricity or gas. Instead, he uses an open fire for both warmth and what little cooking he does.

Pale light flickers from candles in his bedroom, as he strips naked and prepares for sleep. There is no bed. No quilt. No pillow. In the corner of the room are the few things he treasures. He opens up the folded handkerchief and removes the sacred wafer of honed steel and crosses his chest with it, then he criss-crosses the tops of his thighs and arms. Before the blood can really show, he wipes the blade. He kisses it and holds it aloft, like a priest showing the blessed host to his congregation. As his chest fills with red, he returns it to the handkerchief and refolds it in precise squares.

Flat out on his back, he presses his feet against one skirting board, his left shoulder and arm square to the other. Carefully, he tucks a single bed sheet under his heels and wraps it tight around himself until he's completely covered from the head to toe.

Snug. Tight. Secure.

Like he's wrapped in a shroud.

7

FRIDAY MORNING
77TH STREET STATION, LOS ANGELES

The squad room stinks of late-night burritos and looks like a summer-long frat party's just finshished. Mitzi Fallon's government-issue metal desk is an OCD island in the endless sea of male debris.

'*More* coffee.' Nic puts down the lieutenant's 'World's Best Mom' mug, bought for her two Mother's Days ago by her twins. 'What's with the hand?' He nods to the strapping around two fingers.

'Fat oaf of a husband fell on me when we were fooling around.' She tries to wriggle it. 'Celibacy might be a good idea after all.'

'Too much detail.'

She manoeuvres the mug to her lips. 'This has to be my last caffeine of the morning, don't let me have any more.' Her eyes swing back to the surveillance footage running on a flatscreen monitor at thirty-two times normal speed.

'You seen anything yet?' he asks.

'Yeah, my will to live – it went psycho and threw itself off that pier about three hours ago.'

Nic settles into a chair next to her. 'I just checked with the uniforms. They came up with diddly squat.'

'And that's news?'

'Guess not. I swear some of those guys down there are too young to cross the street on their own.'

She laughs. 'Listen to you – already the great veteran. You need to mind your manners, you're still too wet behind the ears to be calling the rookies.' She glances at the big clock on the wall near the captain's office. 'One more tape then I'm going for food. You comin'?'

'Sure, but no pizza. I need to start getting into serious shape for the big trip.'

'You *are* in serious shape – take a swim when you're out at sea and those momma whales are gonna come courtin'.'

'Funny ha ha.' He slaps the small dome where his six-pack used to be. 'Cut the carbs, hold the beer, skip pizza and I'll be okay. Famished and bored but *o-kay*.'

23

'*O-kay*'s not a good place to be. *O-kay*'s no man's land. You're caught in the crossfire between pigged out and happy and starved but gym–body hot. Only settle on *o-kay* when you're married.'

'You forgot – I've *been* married.'

'It was good for you once – it'll be good a second time.' She looks up at him, eager his old pain doesn't surface. 'I'm just jerking your string. You're still a catch. And not just for the whales. Don't worry about it.'

The phone on Nic's desk rings. He glides his chair back and reaches over an exploded volcano of paperwork to grab the receiver. 'Karakandez.'

Mitzi sips her coffee and watches him. Shame he won't start dating again. He'd make someone a good catch. Kind, modest and as honest as the day comes. Good looking but not so much of a pretty boy that he's gonna get hung up when things really slide south. She smiles. Yeah, when Nic Karakandez finally drags himself out of his shell some gal's gonna win the lottery.

He hangs up, takes the notepad he's been scribbling on and rolls back to her desk.

She nods to the pad. 'What you got?'

He holds it up. 'Look who our vic is.'

Mitzi stares at his spidery scrawl. 'Tamara Jacobs.' She shrugs. 'I'm supposed to know her?'

'Clerk in fingerprints said you might. She's a film writer. Some kind of a hotshot. Does big historic costume dramas – romantic stuff too, about ancient

24

Romans and British monarchs. Is that your kind of thing?'

'You kidding me? Harry Potter is as close to British costume drama as I get.' She pulls over her keypad and Googles 'Tamara Jacobs'.

A page from the *Hollywood Reporter* comes up with a head-and-shoulders shot of the deceased and a big block of bold text beneath it.

Nic leans back as he reads her screen. 'Her new picture's called the what?'

'*The Shroud*,' says Mitzi. 'She was working a flick called *The Shroud*. Maybe I'm gonna like her kind of movies after all.'

8

FRIDAY AFTERNOON

BEVERLY HILLS, LOS ANGELES

Stepford wives and Mad Men husbands watch from the safety of grand doorways as LAPD cruisers crash the calm of the quiet cul-de-sac where Tamara Jacobs lived.

The uniforms are locking down what could well be a crucial crime scene – one where the victim met her killer, was abducted or even murdered.

After an eternity of bell-ringing at the writer's six-million-dollar mansion Mitzi gets a couple of cops to bust open the back door. She and Nic step cautiously into a vast kitchen full of mahogany carpentry and marble worktops. Both have their guns drawn, even though they're 99.9 per cent certain the place is empty. Plenty of cops have been killed by that 0.1 per cent.

'Clear,' shouts Mitzi from around a corner.

'Clear,' echoes Nic as he moves through the living room.

The perp's been here. Nic knows it. Feels it tingle his blood.

They sweep the downstairs rooms first. There's no sign of a struggle. Next they check all five upstairs bedrooms, accompanying en-suites and a separate dressing room full of clothes, shoes and handbags. Nothing seems obviously out of place.

Mitzi slides open a wardrobe as big as a wall and stands back in shock. 'Jeez, Bloomingdales has less stock than this. I mean, how many clothes can one woman wear?'

Nic turns his back on the expanse of dresses, tops, skirts and blouses. 'I'm going down to the study. Writers are strange creatures. Let's see what's in her natural habitat.'

Mitzi takes one last envious glance at the glamorous gowns then follows him. A forensic team and photographer are in the kitchen. There's nothing to suggest a break-in before the cops forced their own entry. No jimmied frames, no drilled-out locks or broken glass. Maybe the killer wasn't ever here.

The study is even more of an indulgence than the upstairs dressing room. Ceiling to floor oak, a purpose-built desk, plush brown leather chair – antique by the look of it –

shelves packed with every kind of reference book. Nic guesses Tamara was old school, the kind who only relied on published books rather than internet sources, the type who wanted substantial proof behind her work.

It takes him a second to work out what's missing. There's a printer, scanner and a whole host of tidied cables and chargers.

But no computer.

That instinctive tingle that he felt grows a whole lot more as he pulls open a cupboard. No tower unit for a desktop PC either. Okay. Not so surprising, writers often favour laptops – they're slimmer and better suited to jotting down weird and wonderful thoughts as they travel. But there are no spare cables or docking station. He searches more cupboards and finds installation disks and guarantees for an eleven-inch MacBook Air. Nice. Much cooler than the old Dell buckling the legs of a table in *his* apartment. But something's still irking him.

Writers back things up. Professional ones back everything up. All the time. On multiple sources.

Nic searches but can't even find a single USB stick, let alone anything heavyweight or professional like an Iomega or Tandberg.

He's been here. He's cleaned her out.

'Nic – come see this.' Mitzi sounds more sad than excited.

Whatever she's found he knows he's not going to like it. He leaves the acres of oak and makes his way into a pasture of thick, white living room carpet.

'The cat's dead.' Her face just about betrays the fact she

had one as a childhood pet. 'Been killed by the looks of it.'

Tom Hix, a forty-year-old bearded CSI in a Tyvek suit holds the white Persian out at arm's length. 'Its neck's been broken. There are ligature marks beneath the fur and its eyeballs are dilated. I'd say it's been strangled with some kind of noose – maybe even swung around some.'

Mitzi shakes her head. 'Sick bastard.'

'But an *interesting* sick bastard.' Nic looks closer as Tom lowers it into a large paper bag. 'There aren't many people who carry rope with them and know how to kill with it.'

The CSI labels the bag. 'We'll pass it to our forensic vet, he's top notch. If there's any trace evidence or offender DNA, he'll find it and he'll figure out exactly how it died.'

Nic moves on and searches through a pile of mail, then checks a small cordless phone on a base by the window ledge. The display says there are fourteen missed messages. He lifts the silver phone from its cradle, examines the icons on the main body and finds the contacts book function. There are 306 entries, all listed surname first. He punches in Jacobs and it comes up with only one – Dylan. His eyes flash back to the mail stack and an envelope addressed to Mr D. and Mrs T. Jacobs. He picks it up and sees it's been opened. Inside is a hard white card filled with flowery gold writing inviting them to a charity ball. Nic holds the phone and card aloft for Mitzi to see. 'Looks like we've found Rock Lady's hubby.'

She drifts away from the CSI, the dead cat now forgotten. The husband of Tamara Jacobs is either her killer and knows she's dead or his life is about to be ruined. 'If you've got a number, call it.'

Nic picks up the phone again, finds the entry and presses call. The room falls silent. All eyes are on him as he listens to the dial tones roll out across the airwaves. No number is displayed, just the name Dylan Jacobs – he could be a mile or a whole continent away. Nic's heart thumps with anticipation.

The tones stop.

A deep baritone voice speaks. 'This is Dylan, I can't talk at the moment, leave your name and number and I'll get back to you just as soon as I'm free.'

Nic kills the call. 'Went to messages. I'll try again from the office where I can record it.'

Mitzi nods. 'Okay. Take that home phone away with you, check the callers and process it. I can do the rest of this search without you.'

He unplugs the telephone and waves a hand as he heads for the door. A thought stops and turns him. 'No pictures.'

She throws a frown across the room. 'Say again?'

'There are no pictures around the house of husband and wife. Not in the study, not in the bedroom or anywhere.'

Mitzi casts her mind back to the rooms upstairs. 'You're right. There were no male clothes in any of the closets either, no shaving gear or toiletries save female stuff. In fact, no trace of Dylan Jacobs ever being here.'

9

Twenty-seven-year-old Viktor Hegadus shifts uncomfortably on the edge of the sun lounger only feet from the private pool.

He has a lot on his mind.

No wonder he has a headache. The kind that will become a migraine. He just knows it will. His only hope is to take a snooze for a while – a little power nap – but he can't. Not with so many things troubling him. The builders arrive tomorrow and he's wondering if he should put them off until he's had another think about the plans for the extension – a separate guest wing complete with its own pool and courtyard.

The midday sun creeps over his feet. He gets up and adjusts the parasol so he's safe in the shade. He'd hate to burn. It would be awful to have red and dry skin.

The cell phone under the lounger next to him rings. He tries to ignore it, as he's done for most of the morning. A twinge of guilt finally makes him grab it. 'Dylan's phone, who's calling?'

There's no answer. Just a click and a clunk, like the call is being transferred.

'Hello,' Viktor scowls into the phone.

'Is Mr Jacobs there please? I need to talk to him.'

'Not possible. Who is this?'

'My name is Karakandez, Nic Karakandez. I have some important business to discuss with Mr Jacobs. Can you please put me through to him or tell me what number I can get him on?'

'He's meditating at the moment. He doesn't want to be disturbed.' Viktor abruptly finishes the call, turns the phone to mute and throws it angrily beneath the lounger.

If Dylan can't spare the time to *be* with him, then he's certainly not going to let him spend it talking to strangers.

10

77TH STREET STATION, LOS ANGELES

The Trakscan software on Nic's terminal generates a pop-up window showing the call was received at a private villa off Tower Street in Gordon's Bay, New South Wales. He searches the computerised Interpol directory and finds details for the New South Wales police. He toggles through until he pinpoints the area covering Gordon's Bay and then dials the contact number.

'Chief Superintendent Hawking – how can I help you?'

Nic tells him exactly how.

Thirty minutes later, armed police slip into position around the multi-million-dollar villa overlooking the tropical waters of the Tasman Sea and Nic receives a call back.

'You're good to go, Detective,' says the Chief Super. 'Your fella hasn't left in the past half-hour and now he has nowhere to run but into the welcoming arms of my officers.'

11

DOWNTOWN, LOS ANGELES

The dark-haired young man zaps open his old Ford Explorer and dumps his tired frame behind the well-worn steering wheel. He's just finished a full day of hard work. Factory work. Good honest labour. His place of graft is ten miles from his last kill site – his home even more miles in a different direction. He thinks of these things and is comforted by them as he starts the engine and heads off for a long drive before turning in for the night.

Driving is good. He likes to get to know new neighbourhoods – study the unkilled walking around with their children, dogs and loved ones as he cruises past.

He imagines what their lives are like. What their deaths would be like. How sweet and merciful he could be to them – given the chance. Some years back a cop on the TV news described him as a reptile, a cold-blooded killer with no feelings, no emotions and no morals. The cop couldn't have been more wrong. What he does is out of love. God's love.

He turns on the radio and tunes in to the news as he drives. Listens out for himself. There's nothing. He's relieved. It means no manhunt, no interference in his work. Anonymity is his protective shield, God's way of showing approval – a blessing, if you like. He puts it down to his MO. Modus Operandi – his *method of operating*. Strange how Latin phrases still exist in the modern day. Fragments of a past civilisation blown across the centuries and continents, turning up on the blood-soaked streets of the City of the Angels.

The young man slows as he passes his local church and makes the sign of the cross. Instinctively, he mutters more Latin: '*In nomine Patris, et Filii, et Spiritus Sancti.*' The rhythm of the words comforts him. He turns them over and over like a fascinated child might with a smooth stone in his palm. And then his favourite, *Dominus vobiscum* – the Lord be with you. He says the phrase differently.

The words have to be pronounced softly, clearly, slowly, reverently. After all – they're the last his victims ever hear.

12

When Nic makes his next international call, it's 8 p.m. Friday night in California and 2 p.m. Saturday afternoon in Gordon's Bay, Sydney. As he dials, he taps up a Google Earth map. On the screen he zooms along the beautiful Australian peninsula, past the striking ocean frontages around Dunningham Reserve and Bundock Park and then down the northern headland that showcases the select homesteads of multi-millionaires.

This time Dylan Jacobs answers his own phone and it doesn't sound like the meditation and sunshine have done much to relax him. 'Jacobs,' he snaps, irritably.

'Nic Karakandez, Mr Jacobs.' The cop's voice is calm and friendly. 'Just to be clear, you are *Dylan* Jacobs, the husband of Tamara Jacobs the Hollywood writer?'

'Why do you want to know, Mr Karikeez?'

'Karakandez – *Lieutenant Kar-a-kan-deez* of the LAPD.'

'I *am* Dylan Jacobs. Tamara is my wife.' The aggression has gone from his voice. 'Why are you ringing me, Lieutenant?'

'I'm afraid the body of a woman has been found at Manhattan Beach. From photographs we've obtained it appears to be that of Tamara.'

'Dear God. It can't be—'

'Mr Jacobs, I apologise for calling you like this, but I'm a homicide detective and we're treating the death as suspicious.'

Jacobs struggles to speak. 'This isn't real. It just can't be. You're certain it's Tamara?'

Nic weighs up the voice down the line and decides the shock is genuine. 'We're as sure as we can be without next-of-kin identification.' One thing is bugging him, though, something he just has to mention. 'Mr Jacobs, I've listened to all the messages on your wife's home answerphone and despite her being missing for more than twenty-four hours, none of them are from you.'

Jacobs lets out a long sigh. 'We don't talk much, Detective. Maybe once a week. Sometimes less. We're estranged, have been for years. I have a home out here in Sydney with my partner – I believe you spoke to him earlier.'

Now Nic gets the picture – a rich married man approaching the autumn of his life comes out of the closet. Probably, for his wife's sake he agrees to maintain a veneer of heterosexual respectability for as long as possible. 'Mr Jacobs, in a moment an officer from the New South Wales police will knock on your door and show you a photograph we've scanned and emailed to him. We need you to officially confirm it is your wife – do you understand?'

'I do. Is there, then, a chance you could be wrong?'

'We really don't think so. The ID is more of a formality.'

'Oh.'

'I'm very sorry for your loss and for the fact that we have to do this. I'd also like the policeman to ask you a few questions, to see if you can help us find whoever was responsible for your wife's death. Are you able to do that for us?'

Your wife's death. The words stun Dylan Jacobs into silence. He and Tamara have been apart for some time but he can't imagine never seeing her again. Never wondering about her. Never hoping she's forgiven him and is having a good life without him.

'Mr Jacobs, did you hear me?'

He's still struggling as he nods at the phone. 'Yes,' he manages finally, 'I heard you.' He places the receiver back on its cradle feeling hollow.

His world has changed. His wife is dead. He is no longer a married man.

13

SATURDAY MORNING
INGLEWOOD, CALIFORNIA

Eight a.m. and Nic rolls out of bed more tired than when he got in. He crashed in the early hours then woke four or five times. Insomnia has been habitual since Carolina and Max's deaths. He turns on the TV as background noise – virtual company – and because his apartment is so small he can still listen in the shower.

He's towelling dry when his cell phone rings. Without

looking he knows it's Mitzi. She's the only one who ever calls at weekends and as it was too late last night to update her on his conversation with Jacobs. She's probably itching for info.

'Morning,' he says, still rubbing his wet hair. 'I'm fresh out the shower and was going to make coffee then call you.'

'You mean I caught you naked? Lordy lordy. Please answer yes, even if it's not true. You know how us married women need a little harmless fun.'

'Butt naked and in all my athletic glory.'

'Enough, now I'm having flushes. How'd it go with Jacobs?'

He drops the towel and dresses with one hand as he talks. 'Husband turns out to be gay and living with a partner half his age in Sydney, Australia.'

'No way.'

'Every way, by the sound of it. Aussie cops tell me he and his wife split several years back after he admitted to his homosexuality, but they never divorced.'

'Why so?'

'Bit vague. Dylan said Tamara didn't want everyone laughing at her and as he always worked away a lot he just went along with the story that he was always travelling and working.'

'But now he has a *home* in Australia?'

'Yeah, and the South of France and Bali. He's a property guy, sells top-end stuff to the rich and famous, gets a few bargains for himself along the way.'

'Sweet deal.'

'Cops in New South Wales were really helpful. I wired a photo that one of our CSIs recovered from Tamara's house and Jacobs ID'd it as Tamara.'

'Where was Mr Property Tycoon when she was killed?'

'Sydney, where he's been for the past month. His story checks out. He couldn't have done it.'

'No motive?'

'Don't think so. He gave us his lawyers' details so we called them. Dylan Jacobs signed an agreement more than a year back giving his wife the LA property and dividing stocks, shares and savings. Seemed a strange but amicable affair.'

The sound of teenage girls shouting at each other spills down the phone. 'Keep it quiet!' Mitzi with a hand over the receiver. 'Don't go annoying your father, he's trying to sleep.' She waits for them to shut up then speaks to Nic again. 'Sorry, I gotta go, they both have parties today and they're wound up already. You heading boatward?'

'You read my mind.'

'Have a good one.'

'You too. Hope the girls have fun.' He hangs up and pictures Mitzi bundling Jade and Amber into the family's beat-up station wagon while her lazy no-good bum of a husband stays in bed and sleeps off another Friday night bender. She could do so much better.

Nic makes instant coffee and thinks a while more about Mitzi's old man. She said he hit her once. Slapped her after he saw a male neighbour coming out of the house when he rolled home drunk from a bar crawl with the boys. The idiot put two and two together and made five. Mitzi had kicked his ass back and that had been it. But Nic wonders now if the strapped-up fingers he saw in the office were really the result of another fight. He pours OJ and eats a cup of granola without any milk – a quirk dating back to bachelor days when he was always running out of everything except cereal. If Mitzi's in trouble, she'll tell him. And if she is, then it'll be his pleasure to go and straighten her husband out.

It's a little after nine when Nic shuts his front door and begins the thirty-minute drive to Terminal Island, just east of San Pedro and west of Long Beach. The Al Larson Marina on Seaside Avenue is leased from the Los Angeles Harbor Department and has more than a hundred slips, for vessels between twenty and fifty feet long. Slap bang in the middle is Officer Karakandez's pride and joy. The one thing that's kept him sane.

Reunion isn't a yacht that turns heads. In fact, the nine-ton Hillyard sloop is a real Ugly Betty of a boat. No bikini-clad supermodel or playboy prince will ever be seen near her, let alone on her. But after his wife and son's deaths, Nic fell in love with the rust bucket and saved its cast-iron keel and white oak ribs from the breaker's yard. The process of renewing something was good for his soul, if not his pocket. Every spare dime he's made has gone on repairs – reframing and caulking, a new centre cockpit with wheel steering, three cabins refurbished in mahogany, fresh fibreglass over thick pine decks.

Nic passes the morning tending her thirty-four-foot mast and adding varnish to the back decking. Around 1 p.m. he steps ashore to get a bite of something hot. Across the quayside he catches sight of someone he thinks he knows. It needs a double-take, though – he's never seen her dressed in anything like jeans and a sweater.

'Dr Chang?'

Amy Chang turns from the water's edge. Her jet-black shoulder-length hair bounces, there's a flash of ice-white teeth beneath soft pink lips and a sparkle in her green-brown eyes. 'Detective Karakandez.' She says his name warmly as she walks towards him, hands in front pockets, a gentle rock of the hips against a large camel-coloured bag slung over her shoulder. 'Little birdie told me you had a boat down here.'

He tracks her way. 'Little birdie's right. But I'm certain *you* don't sail. Do you?'

'No, not at all. Never been to sea in my life. Unless a ferry ride in San Francisco counts?'

'It doesn't. So what brings you to the water?'

She smiles. 'Fresh air. Clear my head. Forget work for a while.'

'It sure is a good place for that.' He nods towards the metal whale occupying the slip to his right. 'That's mine. Quite a looker, eh?'

She smiles ironically. '*Distinctive* may be a better word for it.'

He laughs. 'I'm going to grab coffee and a sandwich. You got time to do that?'

'Sure.' She falls in comfortably by his side as a flock of seagulls break from the deck boards and scatter skywards.

He turns to her as they walk. 'That little birdie who told you I had a boat down here – its name wasn't Mitzi, was it?'

Amy puts a finger to her lips. 'Detective, you know better than to ask someone to betray their sources.'

They're both still smiling when they walk into The Deli on the Deck. It's as busy as hell on Judgement Day. Filled with families drawn out by a splash of decent weather and the lure of a weekend by the water.

Fortune smiles on them and they grab a newly vacated table right at the back, from where they order coffees, tuna melts and a bowl of fries to share. Despite Amy's stated desire to get away from work, it's the only common ground they have, so she can't help but update him on his case. 'I called a tidal expert. Turns out your lady on the beach went into the ocean in the early hours of Thursday morning. He reckons around 2 or 3 a.m.'

'Any idea *where* she went in?'

'From the pier. Perp probably thought she'd be dragged out to sea.'

'Could you fix a time of death?'

'You know how these things work, Nic. TOD isn't a precise call. From the body temp I get about a three-hour window, so you're looking at one, one-thirty, to four, four-thirty. Given the tidal pull and where she ended up, I'd say we're nearer the one-thirty mark.'

He pulls off a string of browned cheese from the edge of the melt. 'She's a writer from over in Beverly Hills.'

'*Was* a writer.'

'Was.' He licks grease from his finger and points to the heavens. 'Maybe still is. Perhaps she's working with Shakespeare and Orson Welles as we speak.'

'Be nice to think so.' She dips a fry in mayonnaise and ketchup. 'Was she killed at the house?'

Nic holds off on his food. 'Living room, by the look of it. I couldn't see any trace when I was there but criminalists found blood spatters on the ceiling.'

'Same type?'

'They've not run DNA but it's the same grouping.'

Amy gives a knowing nod. 'But no spatter on the furniture, floor or walls?'

'Apparently not.' He can read her thoughts. 'Yep, we guess the killer came prepared.'

'Whoever invented plastic sheeting has a lot to answer for.'

'You're telling me.' He sips coffee. 'We found her cat; the perp had wasted that too. Did they send it your way?'

She nods and picks another fry from the bowl. 'In the freezer. Something for the forensic vet to look at first thing on Monday.'

'Tell me, does all the death ever get you down?'

'Sometimes. Aside from your writer, I got another seven bodies this week. Three road fatalities, a suicide, a drive-by shooting, a rape–murder and a homicide that could be part of a serial.'

He wipes his fingers on a paper napkin. 'I can't wait to get away from these slimeballs. Get all those serial killers, gangsters, dopeheads and rapists a million miles out of my life.'

She studies him more closely. 'So it's true. You're really handing in your badge?'

'Already done. End of the month I'm history. Then me and that big lumpy boat you saw back there, we're off to get married and start a new life together.'

'I hope you'll both be happy.' She smiles softly. 'Shame, though, I always thought I'd date someone who didn't work in the job.'

He shifts uneasily. 'Doc, when I'm not in the job I hope I may be ready to respond differently to a line like that. Right now, I'm still. . . ' He struggles for the right words.

She says it for him. 'Screwed up. I know, the little birdie told me.' She puts her hand on top of his. 'No pressure, Nic. Just remember me – if and when that time comes.'

14

SUNDAY

CARSON, LOS ANGELES

It's still early but neighbours are already out in Renton Street. They're washing cars and windows, cleaning blown trash off lawns – making the most of what little they've got.

The man in the rundown fixer in the corner of the cul-de-sac takes the short walk from his front door to the rusty green mailbox at the end of the drive. It's a chore he does just once a week. Always straight after breakfast on his way to church.

The mail in the box is addressed to John James. It's the pseudonym he changed his given name to legally. James is the most common Christian name in the US, followed by John. With his desire to blend in, it seemed appropriate to combine the two.

JJ lives alone and is a creature of habit. Habit is important. It is close to ritual and akin to sacrifice. He never misses work and never misses Latin Mass on Sundays. Dedication and devotion are two of the most important things in his very strange and unusually private life.

St Patrick's is one of the few churches where the tradi-tional Catholic service can still be heard. He always sits in the same place. Centre aisle. Right at the back. It's the perfect place. He can be last in and first out from there. Gone before the others mill around him and block his way.

For a moment he sits in his car and watches the unkilled mixing and talking to each other, kissing and shaking hands, waving and smiling as they go their separate sinful ways.

Liars. Cheats. Deceivers. He sees them for what they are.

JJ starts the Explorer's engine and drives away, scripture rolling round his mouth, like a child with a hard-boiled sweet he's trying to make last for ever: '*Hóstiam puram, hóstiam sanctam, hóstiam immaculátam* – a pure victim, a holy victim, a spotless victim.'

The neighbours are still cleaning and washing when he gets back. He ignores them, goes inside and upstairs to the bedroom. Straight to the razor blade. He stands naked. Naked before the eyes of God. Slowly, he cuts the skin of his chest, legs and arms in an intricate pattern of crosses. The steel slices deep enough to draw blood but not so far that it opens a wound that needs stitching.

It wasn't always like that. During the early days of his devotion he caught a femoral artery and almost died. Now he's more practised. More careful. It would be awful if he died before his time. Died before he'd completed his duties. In front of a long mirror screwed to the back of the bedroom door he inspects the patchwork of bleeding wounds. '*Omnis honor et glória* – all honour and glory.' He whispers the words over and over. Deliberately. Slowly. Heavy pauses between each one.

As the mantra fills his mind he takes a long white sheet and wraps it tight around himself. It's a divine feeling – the crispness of the cloth, the smell of the soap, the sight of blood soaking slowly through the heavenly whiteness.

JJ curls up on the bare wooden floor and imagines that he's dying – that he's going straight to heaven.

15

Ten a.m. and the Californian sun is comic-book bright. An end-of-the-world ball of blistering orange energy that's already scorching everyone and everything beneath it.

Nic is giving 'little birdie' Mitzi a hard time as they drive to the film studio where Tamara Jacobs worked. 'I don't need matchmaking. It was so embarrassing her turning up out there.'

'No, it wasn't.' Mitzi flags a hand at him. 'You're an idiot. Amy's single and likes you enough to have travelled across town on an off-chance. You won the lottery then ripped up the ticket rather than collect. You're the dumbest asshole I know.'

'You shouldn't mess with me like that.'

'Apparently.' She glances his way and shows her disappointment. 'Nic, wake up and smell the beans – Amy Chang is nice *and* bright – *beautiful* – and available. I've known her since she came here. She's a friend, a wonderful woman, believe me there aren't many like her around.'

'Look – I know she's nice, but plee-eze just leave me be.'

'By the time you've reached "be" you'll be past your

46

sell-by date and too old to *be* anything or *be* with anyone. You need a good push – that's my job. I'm your pusher.'

'Not out of work it isn't.' He almost says she's the last one who should be dispensing relationship advice but stops short. Mitzi means well, no matter what she says or does, her heart is always in the right place. 'Three weeks.' He slaps a hand on the dash. 'It can't go fast enough. Three weeks and I'm a civilian.'

'Thanks,' Mitzi takes it personally. 'I'll miss you too.' She'd lay into him some more, point out what an ungrateful SOB he is, but they're already at the lot. She lifts her shades and shows her badge to the gate guard at Anteronus Films Inc. He raises the red-and-white-striped security pole and waves them in.

The two cops park and wait in the bone-warming sunshine, thinking about how much they need a quick end to a case that's already threatening to do the unthinkable and turn itself into a major inquiry.

A uniformed security guard turns up and breaks their concentration. He ushers them into a cream-coloured electric kart and drives to a corporate red-brick building surrounded by immaculate lawns.

A shiny elevator of polished brass and streak-free mirrors takes them to the plush blue carpet of the executive floor, where they're shown through a set of hand-carved walnut double doors to meet the company CEO.

Brandon Nolan is a sixty-something Hollywood exec who made his name thirty years ago as a fierce agent and brilliant film financier. Barely five-six in his stockinged feet, he's one of the biggest names in Tinsel Town. The media make much of the fact that he never dates women more than half his age or less than five inches taller than him.

'Detectives, come in, sit down. How can I be of assistance?'

'Mr Nolan, one of your writers turned up dead on Manhattan Beach.' Mitzi curses her bandaged fingers as she drags out a copy of a photo they took from the vic's house. 'Tamara Jacobs.'

Nolan seats himself behind a giant desk, steeples his hands together and looks thoughtfully at the picture. 'I didn't know her.'

Mitzi raises an eyebrow. 'How can that be?'

'We make fifteen, maybe twenty pictures a year. All the directors I know – all the stars I know. The writers? Only the clerks in accounts know who the writers are.' He puts his hand on a telephone. 'Were you offered coffee?'

'We're fine.' Already Mitzi can tell the guy doesn't care about anything other than the bottom line. 'Articles we pulled says she was working a movie called *The Shroud* – what's that about?'

'Ah, okay, that's hers, is it?' Nolan replaces the phone. 'It's a religious thriller, set around the Turin Shroud.'

Nic's interested. 'What's the plot?'

Nolan smiles. 'Buy your ticket and popcorn, you'll find out.'

'Not much chance of me doing that. Will it still get finished without her?'

'Sure. Writers are a dime a dozen. It'll get finished.'

'Did Tamara have an office here?' asks Mitzi. 'Any desk she worked from? Any place she kept research notes, diaries, that kind of thing?'

Nolan scratches an eyebrow. 'I don't know. I'll get someone from Human Resources to talk to you.'

'Only she had no computer at home,' adds Nic. 'I guess a writer has to have a laptop, or tablet, or netbook or such like.'

The CEO nods. 'I'd expect so. Anything else?'

'We'd like a copy of the script she wrote,' says Mitzi. 'Plus copies of any more footage that's already been shot.'

'Is that really necessary?'

'I don't know, not until I've seen it. Might be a complete waste of time, might be a big break for us. Please just make sure I get it.'

He lets out a disgruntled sigh. 'Very well.'

'And her colleagues,' adds Mitzi, like she's remembering things for a shopping trip. 'We need to interview any work colleagues she had. I guess the director and entire cast.'

Nolan grimaces. 'Is there any hope you can do all this discreetly and in the staff's own time? Maybe after work so the picture isn't disrupted?'

Mitzi smiles. 'Sure there is. There's Bob Hope and No Hope. Which do you prefer?'

16

An uncomfortable fifteen minutes pass before there's a knock on the CEO's door. A pencil-thin young woman in a light-brown suit steps in and looks to Nolan, who nods towards the two cops. 'Sarah Kenny,' she says. 'I'm from production and I'm here to take you to the set.'

As they walk out, Mitzi sees she's red-eyed and guesses she's been told the news. 'Did you know Tamara well?'

'Not before the movie. She was always very nice to me.'

The well-dressed graduate doesn't say much more as she drives them half a mile across the lot to a security barrier, where she shows her ID to a guard. They drop the kart and walk towards what she proclaims is the studio's biggest stage – a vast space the size of three aircraft hangars, housing an historic landscape.

'Sheesh, it looks like the whole of the Middle Ages just fell through a time tunnel and ended up here,' says Mitzi, feeling like a tourist.

'Thirty-three AD to be precise,' says Sarah, still sounding sad. 'You're looking at Pilate's house in Jerusalem. Mr Svenson had a team of historians in here for weeks supervising the build just to ensure accuracy. He's such a perfectionist.'

50

Nic reads the signs. 'You got a thing for him?'

'No.' She blushes a little, then motions off-stage to an area filled with drapes, dead-eyed lights and unmanned cameras.

'Sure you have,' Mitzi insists. 'Honey, be careful what you do. Tongues wag like you'll never believe. Things you do, *people you do*, right at the start of your career – they have a nasty habit of coming back and biting you in the ass.'

Sarah turns bright red. She reaches across a table filled with scripts and pulls over a copy each for her guests. 'The scene about to be filmed is just after the execution of Christ.'

They hear a male voice shout 'Action!' and dip their heads to the script.

EXTERIOR. Pilate's House. Night. Building illuminated by strong torchlight in plush green gardens. Centurions pacing on guard duty.   Scene 31

HIGH CRANE SHOT, SLOW ZOOM IN TOWARDS GRAND PILLARS. CUT TO –

INTERIOR   Scene 32

PONTIUS PILATE sits on an ornate red and gold chair on an elevated platform as befits his position. He looks anxiously (camera left) as an out of vision SERVANT makes an official announcement:

SERVANT
Nicodemus of the Pharisees and Joseph of Arimathea, my Lord.

51

PILATE gets to his feet and forces a business-like smile as he
steps from the podium. He glances towards the SERVANT.

    PILATE
    Leave us. Clear the room.

PILATE walks towards the two men and embraces Nicodemus,
a man he knows is a powerful figure, capable of causing him
immense problems – or doing him considerable favours.

    PILATE (continued)
    Nicodemus, guiding light of the Sanhedrin, always a delight to
    see you – though I suspect it is *not* pleasure that brings you to
    my home in the dead of night.

    NICODEMUS
    Indeed it is not pleasure – but it is the dead that have me
    disturb you at such an irreverent hour –

(He gestures to his right)

    – this is Joseph of Arimathea. You have heard of him?

    PILATE
    I have.

PILATE cautiously considers the baby-faced man in rich robes and
extends his arm. They grasp each other's wrists in Roman fashion.

PILATE (continued)

You are a relation of the man we crucified – Jesus the
Nazarene. The uncle of the woman claiming to be both a virgin
and his mother.

JOSEPH (defiantly)

I am.

PILATE

Then I need not explain to you the difficulties I have had – the
problems your kin have thrown in my way.

JOSEPH (pointedly)

Under Roman law the body of an executed man must be laid
in a common grave for a year before the family is permitted to
collect it.

PILATE

That is the custom.

JOSEPH glances to NICODEMUS for support.

JOSEPH

I wish to *break* with custom. I wish to take the body now and
hold it in my own tomb.

PILATE (shocked, responds in ironic tone)

Of course you do. How could I have the audacity to imagine

that this man might stop troubling me just because he is
dead?

JOSEPH (ignoring the outburst)
I have money, power and influence. All of which you know you
will need in abundance in the nearest of future. I beg you to
reconsider.

NICODEMUS (touching Pilate's sleeve)
You would do well to listen to him. It is nothing to you to give
up the corpse of this man.

PILATE (pacing away)
It is plenty – and you know it, Nicodemus.

JOSEPH (following PILATE)
It is a favour I will never forget – one I will gladly repay.

PILATE (hand to chin)
This is what is possible. You may have your crucified Jew, but
he must remain in your tomb until a year has passed. Only
then may his family take his body.

'Okay – cut. Cut there!'

The instruction comes from an unseen male with a
Scandinavian lilt in his voice. 'Tack själv – thank you. Stand
down, please.'

Sarah Kenny looks like she's just witnessed a real-life

54

miracle. 'I'll get Mr Svenson now.' She bounces away, chasing the Swedish echo.

'Look at her, Little Miss Bright Eyes.' Mitzi's gaze tracks the assistant. 'So loved-up it almost hurts.'

Nic fakes a frown. 'I thought you were on a quest to get everyone *loved-up*?'

She glares at him. 'Not everyone – just dumb partners who are living too much in the past.'

17

DOWNTOWN, LOS ANGELES

Twenty-four-year-old Emma Varley stares in the mirror over the row of cracked and filthy sinks in the staff washroom. Like a zillion women before her, she wishes things were different.

She peers in particular at a thumb-sized strawberry birthmark in the middle of her left cheek. Her mom always told her it looked like a cute dimple. If she ever earns any decent money, she'll have surgery. Until then she does her best with cheap concealers and powder.

Now that she's been tricked into looking at herself, she finds other things to hate. Thick brown hair that won't grow a decent length without frizzing and eyes that are so damned short-sighted they need itchy contacts or bottle-lens glasses.

She wishes her nose were smaller, her chin longer, her cheeks less fat.

Even retreating from the mirror has its dangers. As she stands back she's reminded that her breasts are too small, her waist too big and legs too short. Her mom says looks aren't everything – but in LA it sure as hell feels as though they are.

The girls at work bully her, make her life unbearable. They're such douchebags they even make the manager's life hard. They flirt with him and mock him, tease him with flashes of breasts and legs then ask him about the girlfriend they know he doesn't have, possibly never has had. They call him Fish Face.

Emma leaves the washroom the way she always does – angry and depressed. Head down and hand self-consciously over her birthmark, she veers towards the exit and the prospect of some fresh air.

'Hey, watch what you're doing!'

She's barged into Fish Face and made his day as bad as hers. She's knocked a cup of piping-hot black coffee over his pants and shoes. Now he's dancing like a scalded cat.

'Oh God, I'm sorry!' She takes the cup from his left hand and a soggy clipboard and papers from the other. 'I've got some tissues. *Sorry.*' She puts his things down and pulls a wrap pack of Kleenex from her purse. 'What a mess. I'm so—'

He turns and walks away. Leaves her hanging. Strides angrily towards the men's room.

'God almighty!' Emma stamps her feet. She'd scream the f-word and pull her ugly hair out if it was in her character to do that. But it isn't. That's not how she's been brought up. She takes deep breaths and tries to calm down. If she gets fired, she gets fired. It's a crappy job anyway.

18

When Matthias Svenson appears, Mitzi immediately understands why Sarah Kenny and probably every other female on the film lot has fallen for him. Late thirties, he has a thick mane of sandy hair, stands a good six-three and was undoubtedly a Norse warrior in a previous life. His glacial blue eyes and amazing white teeth have clearly evolved from a stealthy predator, a wolf-like beast with primeval sexual needs that she's sure he indulges regularly.

'I'm Matthias,' he extends a warrior hand and well-learned Hollywood smile. 'I'm the director.'

Mitzi loses her fingers in his cavernous palm. 'Lieutenant Fallon – LAPD. This is my partner, Detective Karakandez.'

Nic just nods.

Mitzi looks at the director with heightened curiosity. 'Are you European, Matthias? I couldn't quite place your accent.'

He laughs. 'Most people can't. I am Swedish but my name is German – it means "Gift of the Lord".' He reads her thoughts. 'It's not a name born out of vanity. It is because my

57

parents lost several children before birth and had me late in life.'

Mitzi could warm to this guy. Oh yes. Given a time machine to take her back to a pre-marriage epoch, a chalet in the snow-capped Scandinavian mountains and a rug in front of a log fire, she could warm to him in a very special way. She glances towards Sarah. A sisterly look of approval. Female consent for her to feel free to make a fool of herself in whatever manner she wishes.

'I'm afraid we have some very bad news, Mr Svenson,' Nic cuts in, anxious to get to the purpose of their visit. 'Your writer, Tamara Jacobs, is dead.'

'Tammy?' Svenson looks genuinely shocked. 'Dead? How?'

Mitzi adds some detail. 'Her body was found in the ocean, down on Manhattan Beach.'

'Oh my God.'

'Do you know if she has any close friends, family?'

He pauses to think. 'She and her husband split up some time ago. That's confidential. Amicable break from what I know.' He struggles for the words. 'I think he spends a lot of time out of the country – with his *new* partner.'

Nic notes the emphasis. 'When did you last see her, Mr Svenson?'

'Me?' He looks puzzled. 'Wednesday, I think. Yes, I'm fairly sure it was.' He glances from one cop to the other. 'I remember now, it was early afternoon and we sat outside the set with a coffee and talked about the script.'

'What time exactly?'

'Of that, I'm not sure.' He holds out his bare wrists to

58

indicate he doesn't wear a watch. 'I'm an artist, I don't believe in being manacled like that. It was after lunch. Maybe three, four o'clock.'

'We broke for lunch at one,' says Sarah, eager to assist.

'Then it was nearer four,' adds Svenson. 'I was late getting off set. I had lunch with the studio publicist, then I looked at some rushes with the assistant director. After that I met Tammy and we decided to grab coffee outside in the sun and talk about the end.'

Mitzi needs him to be clearer. 'The end of what – the movie?'

'That's right. She still hasn't delivered the final scenes. We have a fallback of course, but there was an agreement that she could keep the ending secret. All I know is that it is set in the Holy Land.'

'That's a lot of scenery to build.'

'It is indeed. Thank God for green-screen technology.'

'Were there any on-set problems, Mr Svenson? Arguments between Tamara and any of the characters?'

'The actors, you mean? No – not at all.' He seems almost amused. 'Tammy wasn't interested in actors, just words and screenplay. The only time she came on set was to see me and offer rewrites.'

'Who did she have most contact with?' asks Nic.

Svenson nods to the assistant. 'Me and Sarah. When I wasn't around she'd pass notes through Sarah and she would help her with much of her admin.'

'There's lots of it,' says the assistant with a smile.

'I really have to go now – is that all right?' Svenson motions to the set behind him.

'Sure.' Mitzi pulls a contact card from the inside of her jacket. 'But I need a full copy of the script – or at least the fullest that you've got – and please don't leave town without calling me first.' She smiles at the delivery of the corny old line.

Svenson takes the card and crinkles his cool blue eyes. 'I won't, Lieutenant. You can bank on it.'

19

DOWNTOWN, LOS ANGELES

The wall bell rings.

Clocking-off time. A cheer rolls like a wave across the factory floor. Raucous female voices replace the relentless rumble of old machinery. Emma stays at her machine and keeps her head down as the coven file out.

'Blotchy, hey douchebag.' The shout comes from Jenny Harrison, the worst witch of all. 'Bring my limo round the front, I'm 'bout ready to split.' She draws giggles from her cronies.

Varley tries to ignore her. Bullies bully more when they see the pain on your face – she learned the lesson a long time ago.

'Useless bitch, I oughta sack your blotchy ass.' Harrison clips Emma's head as she struts past.

It takes several minutes for the room to empty, the mocking laughter and insults to disappear.

Silence. Peace. Dignity.

'Emma.'

She looks up. Her boss is stood there. Fish Face. The man she spilt coffee on.

'Time to go.'

'I hate them.' She doesn't mean to speak, the words in her head just tumble out. Her face contorts. 'I wish Jennifer Freakin' Harrison would get caught in one of these machines and—'

'She's not worth it.' Fish Face walks past her. 'Forget about her and go home.' He starts to check all the machinery has been turned off.

Emma clears her things and heads to the door. A thought hits her. She turns around and walks back to him. 'I just wanted to say sorry again for this morning.' Her eyes drift down to the dark stain on his trousers. 'I'll pay for cleaning – if they need it.'

He looks away from her. 'They don't.'

'Okay. Well, if they do – if you change your mind – then I'll pay. You can dock it from my money.'

He turns off the banks of strip lights covering the factory floor. 'They won't.'

'Right. Goodnight, then.' She still feels bad as she visits the restroom. It's a long way home, two buses and a

61

twenty-minute walk. She doesn't want to get caught short. She hates the winter months. It's dark at six when she leaves and dark at six when she gets up. One day she'll have enough money for a car – like her mom says, only the poor in LA have to walk. She clocks out at the front door and fastens her coat against the chill.

'Hey, hold up.'

She turns on the steps and sees Fish Face behind her, door keys in hand.

'You want a lift? I go right past your place.'

Normally she'd say no. Most nights she'd be too shy to accept. Tonight she's exhausted and needs the company. 'That'd be great. Thanks.'

He smiles and finishes locking the door.

Maybe spilling coffee on him wasn't such a bad thing after all.

20

GARDENA, LOS ANGELES

Away from the snarl of rush-hour traffic, Emma's boss takes Harbor Freeway south until the Gardena junction then the western slip to Artesia Boulevard. She doesn't say much and neither does he. Mostly they listen to the radio channels he keeps switching between.

She breaks one of several awkward silences. 'You like to listen to the news and talk stations?'

'Sometimes. Good to know what's happening in the world.'

'Bad stuff. That's all you hear on the news.'

He almost argues the point but instead hits search on the radio again. It rolls off the news and parks in the middle of a talk show.

'KKLA 99.5. This is a Christian station.' There's a laugh in her voice. 'I come across it sometimes. You'll find this funny, but late at night, when I find it, I leave it on. It's just nice to hear folk talking kindly to each other rather than shoutin' and swearin' like shock jocks.'

'You just like the station or are you Christian as well?'

'I'm not sure how to answer that.' She gives him a quizzical look. 'Suppose I am. Let's put it this way, I ain't a Muslim or Jew, so I guess I must be Christian.' She points through the windshield. 'You need to pull a right here, straight after the warehouse store on the corner.'

He flicks on the indicators and turns the Explorer into South Normandie Avenue.

'You can drop me here, if you like. I'm only a couple of blocks down.'

'It's not a problem.' He smiles at her. 'Would be unchristian not to take you to your door.'

She smiles back. 'Thanks, it's West 169th. You'll see it coming up on your left.'

There's a line of working trucks, old motor homes and

campers parked out on the blacktop, early signs of the kind of neighbourhood he's driving into. She's obviously dirt poor and from dirt-poor stock. These days it's tough to own anything but clapboard unless someone's given you a headstart up the ladder.

'I'm just after the telegraph pole.'

He slows and pulls over outside a wooden throw-up that's more shack than house. A scrub of weeds and bald lawn lie in shame behind a tiny fence of rotting, bare wood.

Emma can read his face. 'Not much but it's still home. I rent it. No point spending money on what's not yours, right?'

'Right. Mine's the same. Needs paint and money that I haven't got.'

She unbuckles and grabs her bag from beneath her feet. 'Thanks for the ride . . . ' She almost calls him Fish Face '. . . Mr James. You wanna come in?'

Instinctively he scans the street. Out of sight, somewhere else, he can hear the siren of an LAPD cruiser.

A bad sign.

'Not tonight, maybe some other time?'

Emma is disappointed. He seems a nice guy. Would be good to have a friend at work, especially one who's your boss. 'Then thanks again. See you tomorrow.' She leaves him with a smile and swings the door closed.

'Sleep well,' he says to her retreating back.

He watches her through the gate and smiles when she looks back and waves at him. The houses around are all jammed in tight – there must be a hundred windows for people to watch from. She's safe here.

For now.

21

By 11 p.m. the Homicide and Robbery squad room is close to deserted. Only the dregs remain. Nightshift rookies working their way up and weathered old wasters who've fallen so far down they're stuck in the sediment of the system.

Nic Karakandez is stuck too. Stuck in front of footage from the security camera at Manhattan Beach. It's his turn at the monitors. Not much of an ordeal really. He'd rather be here than home alone with the memories that won't go away.

He drinks cold coffee and watches the speeded-up images as noise boils in the corridors around him. Women's voices. Coarse. Shouting. Swearing. Hookers pulled in by vice being milked before being processed then cut loose to start all over again. He's seen it all during his time here – the girls get arrested and fined then returned to the streets where they have to turn tricks to earn the money to pay off the fines. The proverbial vice circle. He heard someone once worked out that if the women all got handouts of

$500 a week, they wouldn't need to sell themselves, could avoid pimps and the state of California would be more than a million dollars a year better off. He doesn't know if it's true or not but he wouldn't be too surprised to find out that it was.

He glances at his watch. Another hour and he'll call it quits. Leave just after midnight, maybe by then he'll be tired enough to sleep a little when he gets home. The screen in front of him shows the black of night at the beach, faint ocean waves crashing unheard on the silent footage. Yellow security lights vaguely illuminate part of the aquarium and marine lab where he and Mitzi looked around. He watches a few couples walk down the approach and lean against the rails to fool around a little. A couple of drunks turn up to light a cigarette and one takes a leak in the ocean. The other is so wasted he curls up in the lab doorway and starts to sleep.

Nic speeds the images up some more, thirty-two times normal speed, then a flash of light on the screen makes him take notice. He glances at the time log. It's just after two in the morning – 02.09:15 to be exact.

The hood of a car comes slowly into shot and he feels his heart jump. No way should a vehicle even be down there and the driver knows it. The headlights aren't on – the flash Nic saw was of security lighting bouncing off the vehicle. He leans close to the monitor and watches every pixel as it comes to a halt. He can't see the front or back plate, nor can he work out the make. It's an SUV of some kind. Not a big one like a Land Cruiser or Range Rover, something smaller.

The security lights are so yellow and the camera lens so poor it's impossible to guess whether the car is black, blue or green. The driver's door opens. A thin shadow of a man slips out. Nic recalls the height of the rails around the pier edge and where they came up to on him. The driver looks about his size. Six foot, no more. He goes to the back of the car and pops the hatch.

Nic almost bangs his nose against the screen.

The guy leans into the vehicle and lifts something out of the back. The shot's not close enough or clear enough to see what he's carrying in his arms but it's draped across them and looks long enough to be a body.

What else could it be?

The shadowy figure struggles to the end of the pier and slides his heavy burden into the dark waves of the Pacific.

22

TUESDAY

Mitzi never makes it to work before Nic. That's the agreement they have. She takes Amber and Jade to school while he gets in early and checks what has come in overnight and been thrown in their tray. If something big is going down, he calls her. Otherwise she usually rolls into the squad room somewhere between nine and nine-thirty. In return, she brings coffee from Starbucks and on Tuesdays donuts or muffins. Today it's muffins.

'So my little night owl,' she waggles a paper bag from her bandaged hand as she approaches his desk, 'did you come up with anything to deserve your treat? I have a choice of stem ginger or skinny blueberry to go with your steaming Venti Americano.'

Nic doesn't even look up. 'What I've got for you deserves much more than anything you've got in that little bag of yours.' He taps a printout of timecodes and notes made from viewing last night's footage. 'We have a lead.'

'You serious?' She puts the bag on his desk, slips her jacket and shoulder bag over the corner of her chair. 'You got lucky?'

Now he turns to her. 'Luck had nothing to do with it. I watched every damned frame of that footage.' He cues up the material on his monitor. 'This is just before ten past two, the light flash is a car coming into shot. Watch what happens now.' He sees her drawn to the screen, hypnotised just as he was by the shadowy figure getting out of the vehicle, going to the rear and then carrying something heavy to the far side of frame and dropping it over the rails.

'Yes!' She slaps the desk with excitement. 'Play it again.'

He hits rewind and uncaps his coffee.

She watches even closer the second time. 'Any other footage? Any idea of what make that car is?'

'It's a Lexus hybrid. A four-by-four. Security cameras picked it up travelling east towards the pier.'

'Plate?'

'Don't be greedy. These are night-time shots, ma'am. You should be grateful for what I'm giving you.'

'Women always want more – especially ones my age.'

'Four-door plus hatch, no sunroof. RX 450h in Argento Ice.'

She frowns. 'In what?'

'Argento. I looked it up on the car company's website. It's a kind of pearly creamy white that's really hard to make out beneath sodiums. Came up clean, though, on some of the wider footage.'

'How many Lexuses – do you say Lexuses, or Lexi, are there in LA?'

He pulls a face. 'You're looking at America's bestselling luxury crossover in the SUV market. Close to a hundred thousand a year.'

She tilts her eyes to the ceiling. 'Why God, why us? We're good people – we just seek to serve.'

'This is the latest hybrid. There are fewer of those around.'

'How many fewer?'

'Lexus shifted ten thousand across the country last year. Figures down badly after the quake and tsunami in Japan snd of course the recession back home.'

'Oh, that makes life much simpler,' she says, sarcastically.

'Only a couple thou' in LA and just a few hundred in this spec.' He glances at his watch. 'I've begged a little extra manpower.'

'Let me guess, Sandra and Denise in Robbery?'

He smiles. 'They seem willing.'

'I'm sure they are.'

'Listen, with *their* help, come midday we'll have covered body shops, rentals and insurance claims.'

Mitzi thinks of another angle. 'You sure it's not the vic's own car? Tamara's second vehicle?'

'I checked that already. No.'

She rips open the paper bag and hands him the stem ginger muffin. 'You're getting good, you deserve this.' She shifts to her own desk with her coffee and blueberry muffin. 'I'm going to finish this shitty low-cal apology of a treat then head back to the film studio to see the archivist. You wanna come or you gonna need to stay here?'

'You go.' His eyes are fixed to data searches coming up on his monitor. 'I want to finish the Lexus trawl then I'll catch you later. Okay?'

'Fine. Trace that hybrid before our debrief with the captain at the end of the day and you could maybe take Sandra and Denise for a drink.'

He laughs. 'We're going to fall out if you keep this up.'

She raises her palms in surrender and pulls open the cake bag. 'Just saying, that's all.'

23

The thirty-seat executive viewing room is the most luxurious cinema Mitzi Fallon has ever been in. The place is bathed in a perpetual twilight, the temperature is T-shirt warm and it's so acoustically perfect you feel like you're wearing noise-cancelling headphones.

Executive Assistant Sarah Kenny rides a stream of super-soft blue carpet down rows of calfskin leather reclining chairs. Mitzi caresses the tops of the chairs as she follows. 'Jeez, this is so plush I could live in here.' She looks up and halts as the screen flickers into life. 'What's that? They going to show something?'

Everything's moving backwards. A tape is being rewound in vision. 'It's a sequence from *The Shroud*.' Sarah points beyond the screen, to the side of the auditorium. 'There's a projection room back there – it's where we're headed. The archivist must be preparing your footage.'

Mitzi dips into a row and with all the enthusiasm of a small child on a party outing takes a seat. 'Let's watch a minute.'

The assistant gives her a disapproving look.

'Just this bit.' Mitzi sinks down in her recliner and snuggles her head against the top cushion. 'C'mon. Take the weight off.'

Sarah has no choice. She tucks her stylish white midi dress around her tanned model legs and flips a muting switch on the end of her armrest. Giant recessed speakers engorge with a torrent of rich sounds – rolling thunder and a crack of lightning against a pale sky. The camera cuts to a hillside and slowly zooms in to two centurions standing sentry by the rock face.

She rolls the volume knob down to a more comfortable setting and leans close to Mitzi. 'Remember the take of Joseph of Arimathea asking for Christ's body to keep in his family tomb? Well, this is the next scene – at the tomb in Golgotha.'

A male narrator's voice speaks over her – '*When it began to dawn towards the first day of the week, came Mary Magdalene to see the sepulchre.*'

'That's just a guide track. The words are from Matthew 28,' whispers Sarah, proud to add the religious insight.

'*And behold there was a great earthquake,*' continues the narrator. '*For an angel of the Lord descended from heaven, rolled back the stone and sat upon it. His countenance was as lightning and his raiment as snow. And for fear of him, the guards were struck with terror and became as dead men.*'

The screen fills with fleeing centurions and blinding light. The camera cuts to a close-up of a broken Roman seal lying in the dirt besides the giant rock and the open entrance of the tomb. Sarah points a perfectly manicured finger at the screen. 'The seal is significant because it bore the authority of the Emperor of Rome. It was a really big thing back then.

Breaking the seal on the tomb of a crucified felon was showing disrespect to the Emperor and running the risk of execution.'

'My boss is the same with his coffee mug – anyone uses and breaks that, they may as well hand in their badge and go kill themselves.'

Out of the swirling dust two frightened women appear. They huddle together. Mourning robes are pulled tight around their bodies and faces. An angelic voice is heard off camera: '*Fear not you, for I know that you seek Jesus who was crucified. He is not here. For he is risen.*'

Mitzi shrugs. 'Takes a similar miracle to raise my old man.'

On the big screen, a naked and shapely angel appears. Her long golden hair and feathered wings just enough to pass the scrutiny of censors. She beckons the terrified women. '*Come and see the place where the Lord was laid, then go quickly and tell his disciples that he is risen.*'

'Jeez, why don't they do something original and have fat angels for once?' Mitzi turn to Sarah. 'Or a black angel, or Hispanic or Mexican – why always the naked white chicks?'

The film freezes and saves the assistant trying to answer. It goes into high-speed rewind and then the screen turns black. 'They're changing spools,' she explains. 'After this Mary goes into the tomb and finds the sepulchre is empty. There's just the burial cloth lying there.' She stops abruptly, almost as though she's said too much already and gets to her feet. 'We should go now and collect your copies.'

Mitzi struggles out of the comforting hug of the seat and follows her. 'What happens next?'

'We go through the back – to the rooms behind the screen – I'm taking you to meet the archivist.'

'I know that. I meant in the movie. What's next?'

'I've been instructed only to talk to you about what's been shot and what you are being given copies of.'

'Say *what*?'

The tone is enough to add speed to Sarah's stride. She pushes through a soundproof back door into a passage with restrooms off to the left and a storeroom to the right. In front of her is another heavy door marked 'John Kaye Snr, Chief Archivist'.

'Hang on,' protests Mitzi.

Sarah escapes into a large, cool room almost entirely filled with ceiling-to-floor shelves stacked with cans of film. She gestures towards the far end, to a worktop desk and a tiny old man perched on a stool in front of three viewing monitors. Big headphones are wrapped around his completely bald head. 'That's Mr Kaye,' she whispers. 'He suffers from dwarfism and his hearing is not good – but he's a really nice guy.'

Mitzi grabs Sarah's arm as she sets off again. 'Be sure of one thing, when we're done here, Miss Smarty Pants, you *will* tell me everything. Even if I have to drag you by your slim little ankles across the parking lot and haul you downtown.'

The young assistant is shaking as she takes the final steps

to where the archivist is working. 'Hello – Mr Kaye,' she says loudly. 'This is Detective Fallon.'

'*Lieutenant* Fallon,' Mitzi offers a hand.

Kaye shakes it but looks away. He's either embarrassed or more interested in the screen than the policewoman. 'You've come for the rushes. I'm just copying them.' He glances at a clock high up the wall in front of him. 'There's about twenty minutes left to go on the transfer.'

'We've burned them onto DVDs for you,' explains Sarah trying to build a peace. She dips into her large Gucci shoulder bag. 'There's also an NDA, a non-disclosure agreement, for you to sign.' She fumbles with two copies of the document. 'As the material has not yet been transmitted it makes you responsible for ensuring it isn't copied, pirated or lost.'

Mitzi takes the paper and looks it over. It's full of legal mumbo-jumbo that make her and the LAPD responsible for zillions in damages. 'I'll sign when the copies are done.' She peers at the desk monitors. 'Is this the movie?'

He nods. 'What there is of it. They've only cut together thirty minutes – about a quarter.' He points to the footage. 'These are rough cuts made by the assembly editors, they won't make a master cut – a *fine* cut – until the entire film has been shot and the director has had time to consider any changes.'

The screen shows modern-day Italy. A busy street crammed with cars and scooters, Italian signs, shops, stylishly dressed men and women.

'What's this? What happened to Pilate's house and all that old stuff?'

The assistant doesn't answer.

'It's Turin,' explains Kaye. 'It's where one of the contemporary protagonists is introduced.' He glances towards Sarah, unsure if he should say anything more.

She tries to pull off the impossible task of not too obviously shaking her head.

'C'mon,' snaps Mitzi. 'Why all the secrecy?'

Sarah colours a little. 'Truth is, we all signed confidentiality clauses specifically prohibiting us from talking about the movie, its content, or anyone associated with the creation of it, and we've all been issued with memos reminding us of the pledges we took.'

'I'm a goddamned police officer,' fumes Mitzi. 'Confidentiality doesn't apply to me, especially when I'm investigating the death of the person who wrote your damned movie.'

'Please understand, we could get fired,' says the archivist.

'You could get arrested long before you get fired.'

There's a mechanical click and beep from under the worktop. 'They're done,' he says, apparently thankful for the distraction. 'Your copies are ready. I'll case and bag them for you.'

'The NDA, Lieutenant Fallon, could you sign it now, please?' Sarah holds out the papers and a pen.

Mitzi draws a giant cross through each page of legal text, flips a sheet over and scribbles on the back: *I promise to do my best not to lose or show this movie film to bad people. Honest.* She scrawls her name and shoves the paper back in Sarah's hand.

'Now cut the secret squirrel shit and tell me exactly what's going on.'

24

Force Press Officer Adam Geagea perches on the edge of Nic's desk while the detective finishes a call. He knows he's an unwelcome guest. Cops like to keep cases quiet and his job is to tell the world what's happening. Chalk and cheese.

Geagea is nearly fifty and would love to have been a cop. The only things that stopped him were a shortness of height and a dubiously foreign surname. If he had a dollar for every time he had been forced to spell it out or tell people it's pronounced *Zhar-zhar*, he'd be a billionaire. Only the well-educated recognise he shares the same family name as Samir Geagea, the notoriously ruthless Middle-Eastern Christian freedom fighter. It's not something he draws attention to.

Nic finishes his call and stares accusingly at the man sat on his desk.

Geagea is fiddling with a flip-over calendar. 'What is this, Detective, some kind of IQ question?'

Nic's not in the mood for small talk but tries to be pleasant,

'One a day – it's a vitamin supplement for the brain.'

The journo examines a sheet and reads it aloud. 'What do the following have in common – Chairwoman, Peruse, Anomalies, Antiperspirant?' He looks across the squad room as he thinks. 'I give up, what's the connection?'

'It's for clever people, Adam. Best you leave alone. What do you want?'

Geagea takes the insult in his stride. 'I've had *Variety* and the *Hollywood Reporter* on the phone after quotes on Tamara Jacobs's death.'

'How do they even know she's dead?'

'They're reporters. It's their job to know things like that.'

'I get it, but how? I mean, it's got to have come from someone – so who?'

'Not me.'

Nic smiles. 'Didn't say it was. Then who?'

'Morgue. Coroner's office. A dozen people on the beach when she was fished out. Colleagues at the studio. You want me to go on?'

Nic surrenders. 'There's no statement prepared. Mitzi is over at the studio right now. Tell the media the usual – we're awaiting the ME's report, no comment until then.'

'These flies won't blow away so easy, Detective. In LA, dead film writers are newborn celebrities.' Geagea shrugs. 'Hollywood press doesn't give a damn about them when they're alive, but dead – well, that's different, they become *saintly*.' He says the word with irony as thick as grease. 'The hacks are going to be swarming tomorrow.'

Nic's desk phone rings. 'Tomorrow's tomorrow. Are we done for now?'

Geagea levers himself off the desk as Nic snatches the phone from the cradle. 'Karakandez.'

'Nic, Tony Peach. I've got news on your car tyres.'

He reaches for his notebook, eyes flicking back to Geagea who's still hovering near his desk. 'Shoot.'

'You're looking at Maxxis MA-S2 Marauders. High-performance tyres, not cheap, probably around a hundred and fifty bucks a pop.'

'They fit a Lexus Hybrid?'

'Sure would. They'd go on standard eighteen-inch wheels. From the pattern, tread width and depth, we're talking new shoes here. These babies haven't run more than two to three thousand miles.'

'Time-wise, how does that translate to a normal amount of motoring, T?'

'Average Joe does twelve thou a year, not as much as they used to because of gas prices. So these babies would probably have been levered on back in September, maybe mid-August. Could be they were a production-line fit or a recent change up. For a rental car, story's different. Rents can easily burn a thousand miles a week. One other thing – you don't usually find these treads on a rep's car, so you maybe want to push salesmen to the back of your filter.'

'You're a star, buddy. I've got some cops in Robbery doing a little phone-bashing for me. I'll get them to hit rental companies first, run down new Lexus hybrids or ones with tyre changes in the last month. I owe you.'

'I'll hold you to it. You fixed your leaving drinks yet?'

It's something Nic hasn't even thought about. 'TBA. I'll come back to you.'

Peach laughs. 'Better still, I'll call Mitzi. Take care, man.'

'You too.' Nic hangs up and stares at Geagea, who's still there.

'Sorry, Detective,' the press officer points to the quiz-a-day calendar. 'Before I go, give me the answer will you? Otherwise, it'll eat me all day.'

'Okay. All the words hide countries – Chairwoman contains Oman, Peruse Peru, Anomalies Mali and Antiperspirant . . .?' He pauses to give the hack one last chance to grab a little respect.

Geagea looks blank.

Nic shakes his head. 'It's your part of the world, buddy. Iran. As in Ante-persp-*Iran*-t. Now get out of here.'

25

ANTERONUS FILMS, CULVER CITY

Sarah Kenny makes her wisest decision of the day. She takes Mitzi to a quiet corner of Plunge, an in-studio coffee franchise, where she starts to spill the beans on *The Shroud*.

'Tamara was very secretive about the script. Not even Mr Svenson knew what the ending would be.'

'How can that be?' Mitzi looks confused. 'I mean, the actors *have* to know, don't they? How can they play their parts unless they have the lines to learn?'

'They were all given an outline script—'

'Which I'm still to get a copy of by the way.'

Sarah ignores the pointed remark. 'All the cast were warned the ending would be rewritten. They were told it was so secret a copy wouldn't be circulated until the day before the shoot and even then only to the few actors taking part.'

'Why? What's all the fuss about?'

She scans the coffee shop nervously. 'Tamara had a contact in Turin in Italy – someone called R. Craxi and he'd given her certain facts about the Shroud that have never been disclosed publically.'

'And this film discloses them?'

'The studio's marketing department expects all the film's final publicity to be driven by public disclosure.'

'Disclosure of what? What are the *certain facts* you mentioned?'

'I really don't know. I haven't seen anything scientific of any kind. I guess they're to do with the authenticity of the Shroud.'

'The ending that *was* circulated – what did it say about the Shroud?'

'It didn't commit. The whole modern-day section – the

81

reveal, if you like, was missing. I heard Tamara telling Mr Svenson he would need a scientific setting, a CSI-style lab for some scenes.'

'For carbon dating or DNA testing?'

'I don't know. Maybe both.'

'But there were no results in the script?'

'Not in any version I've seen.'

Mitzi thinks it through. The best outcome for the writer would be the most shocking. So Jacobs's new ending would have had to be explosive – something that rocked church or country to the core. Which is fine – providing it's only fiction. But what if it was based on fact? That would be different. Totally different.

Suddenly, the death of Tamara Jacobs starts to make some sense.

26

77TH STREET STATION, LOS ANGELES

The sixty-year-old estranged husband of the dead writer is dressed in a black suit with white shirt and neatly fastened black tie. Dylan Jacobs's hair is silver and cut elegantly short and despite crossing continents, he is clean-shaven and alert. His partner Viktor is sat beside him in the police reception area reading a day-old newspaper. He is wearing cream jeans, a glittering Dolce and Gabbana T-shirt and gold silk jacket.

Nic clicks open the security door and looks across to them. 'Mr Jacobs?'

Tamara's husband rises wearily to his feet. 'Yes.'

'Nic Karakandez.' He extends a hand. 'My sympathies for your loss.'

'Thank you.' Jacobs shakes and motions to the man next to him. 'This is Viktor. I believe you spoke on the phone?'

'We did. Please both come through.'

They follow him up a couple of sets of stairs and into a dull interview room that has a table, six chairs and a wall bearing a large blue LAPD crest, complete with American flag, scales of justice and the motto 'To Protect and to Serve.'

Nic motions to the seats. 'Can I get you drinks? Coffee, soda, water?'

'Black coffee, thanks,' Dylan Jacobs settles in a chair with his back to the crest.

Viktor takes a seat alongside him and holds his hand under the table. 'Just water, please.'

Nic ducks outside for drinks then returns and shuts the door. Hands out the coffee and water. 'When did you get into town?'

'Yesterday.' Dylan rests his elbows on the table and rubs tired eyes. 'We went to the morgue and then finalised the funeral arrangements. We're told Tamara's body can be released now.'

'That's right. The ME has concluded her examinations.'

Jacobs grimaces. 'We've fixed a cremation service for next week—'

'I didn't go to see her,' interrupts Viktor. 'Tamara and I didn't get along that well. I don't think she approved of me.'

Nic can't begin to think how she possibly could have. 'Mr Jacobs, we're trying to pin down a reason for your wife's murder. Is there anything you can tell us that may be of assistance?'

He looks a little confused. 'She was a writer, Detective – not a gangster or a drug dealer. Tammy mixed with good people, mainly of our age and of artistic and gentle natures.'

'Good people sometimes carry grudges or harbour hatred. Rich, educated people are every bit as capable of doing bad as poor, uneducated ones. It's usually just a question of motivation, morality and means.'

'I take your point but I'm sorry, I can't think of any reason why anyone would want to hurt her.' Jacobs suddenly looks much older than his sixty years. His voice breaks a little. 'Tammy's face was partly covered when I saw her and the medical examiner said she'd suffered some deep wounds. What had been done to her?'

It's the kind of question only innocent men ask. Nic measures his answer carefully. 'We're not certain, Mr Jacobs. We're still piecing things together.'

'But you must have some idea, something to go on?'

'We're working hard on that. What I can tell you is that your wife was not randomly murdered. She was deliberately targeted.'

Dylan Jacobs looks from the cop to the table, then down to the floor. He can't help but imagine Tammy in her open-plan kitchen with its black granite tops and biscuit-coloured wood units. He can see her cooking her favourite salmon and linguini, a glass of crisp white wine at hand and piano jazz playing from her favourite radio station.

He looks up and his eyes are wet. Viktor takes his hand and holds it openly on the table now. 'Thanks,' Jacobs says and pats the comforting hand. He looks at Nic. 'My life is with Viktor now but Tammy and I were *once* very close. We spent fifteen years together as man and wife, trying to make things work. Even when it didn't, we remained good friends, the very best of friends. She was a wonderful, kind and loving woman. Even when we split up, she tried to be understanding.' He looks at the wall, remembering for a second when he told her he was leaving her not for another woman but for a man. 'I think she knew about my homo-sexuality even before I did. She had an instinct, a way of picking up on things. I guess that's what made her such a good writer.' He manages a half-laugh. 'Of course, all her compassion didn't stop her and her lawyers taking me for a fortune.'

'You paid her too much,' interjects his new soul mate. 'Much more than you needed to.'

'It's only money, Viktor, only money.'

Nic takes a sip of coffee. 'Mr Jacobs, if you and Viktor could take some time and list your wife's acquaintances for me – maybe with a short note saying how long she'd known them and how she was connected to them – that would be a real help.'

'Now?' Jacobs looks troubled.

'No, not now, but it would be good to have it some time tomorrow. Do you know anything about this movie that Tamara was working on, *The Shroud*?'

'Oh, *that* thing?' says Viktor, his tone sniffy. 'Is that what she was in the middle of?' He gives Jacobs a strained look.

'Yes, I think she was,' Dylan answers, wearily.

Nic spots the tension between them. 'What about it, Viktor?'

He hesitates.

'Go on,' says Jacobs. 'You might as well say it.'

'Well, it was asking for trouble, wasn't it?' He lets go of Dylan's hand and becomes animated. 'I mean, suggesting that the Shroud didn't come from Jesus, it's bound to upset all those extreme groups in the church, isn't it? It's blasphemous really.'

'Viktor was brought up a Catholic,' explains Jacobs, patiently. 'He reads too many mystery books and imagines hooded killers are running around everywhere.'

'They are,' he insists.

'Not in Hollywood, Viktor, not in Hollywood.' Jacobs pats his hand. 'Isn't that so, Detective Karakandez?'

'Well,' says Nic. 'I've seen plenty of hooded killers, but they were interested in drugs, guns and two-hundred-dollar sneakers, never religion.'

Dylan Jacobs manages a smile. 'Find him, Detective.

Please give me your word that you'll catch whoever did this.'

Not likely.

The detective doesn't say it, but it's the truth. Because a month from now he won't even be around to take a progress call. Instead, he does what he's always done, what he's always delivered on. 'I give you my word, Mr Jacobs. I'll find him.'

27

Captain Deke Matthews isn't the kind of cop you want to keep waiting. He's a big guy in every sense of the word. Big physically. Big in the department. Big on making his detectives' lives hurt. He sits behind his office desk waiting impatiently for Fallon and Karakandez, his barrel stomach wrapped in a blue shirt battened down with braces as red as his jowly face.

'Sorry boss.' Mitzi breezes in with Nic in tow.

'Fifteen minutes late, Lieutenant. D'you have any idea how burned good food can get in nine hundred seconds? How mad Mrs Matthews will be if I am the reason said good food is burned?'

'I get the message, boss.'

The captain drums all ten of his chubby fingers on his desk, like he's waiting for a plate at Thanksgiving. 'So what have you got? Let's be having it, with luck I may still make it before the charring starts.'

Mitzi thumps down a thick wad of folders and pulls out some photographs. 'Tamara Jacobs, screenwriter, mid-fifties, found dead in the water at Manhattan Beach. Unsub had tortured her – taken out her left eye and some teeth, ligature marks around the wrists. To finish, he cut her throat. Kill scene seems to be her home, nice spread in Beverly.'

'Why so?'

'Forensics matched blood spatters on the living room ceiling to the victim.'

Matthews glances at the post-mortem pictures then picks one up between finger and thumb like he doesn't want to be dirtied by what's on it. 'What we have here, lady and gentleman, is something straight from the sewers.' He slaps it down on his desktop. 'Why didn't the perp leave the old girl in her own home after he'd killed her? Why drive out to the beach and dump her in the ocean?'

'Buying himself time.' Nic slides over a pack of surveillance-camera shots from the beach. 'He was most probably an out-of-towner and the driver of this rented Lexus.'

'This one of those 4×4s?'

'Yeah, pricey metal, a hybrid.'

'Nice.' He takes the photograph. 'What pins your guy to this car?'

'Tyre treads in sand on the pier match those of one rented from LAX. Could be he flew in for the hit then flew straight out again.' Nic gets out the documents his helpers from Robbery traced.

'Our flyer got a name?'

'Agne.' He passes over a rental agreement.

Matthews frowns. 'Agnes – a girl?'

'No, Agne – that's the last name the driver entered on the paperwork. First name "Abderus". Take a look.'

'*Abderus?*' He stares down at the photocopy. 'This for real?'

'Probably not. I Googled both names. They're Greek and common. Abderus was an ancient hero, of dubious parentage.'

'It figures.' Matthews pushes the copy back. 'Nothing good came from the Greeks. Their economy is down the pan. Their food is crap. There's a reason you don't see Italians smashing plates at the end of meals.'

'Civilisation?' suggests Mitzi. They both frown at her. 'I hear rumours that came from the Greeks.'

He ignores her. 'So we got a Greek hitman – possibly flying in to torture and kill a writer from LA. This make any sense to you two dinner-spoilers?'

Mitzi pushes over a copy of the script she finally prised from Sarah Kenny. 'This is the movie Jacobs was working on. It's about the Turin Shroud and we believe it makes some startling claims about whether it really was the burial cloth of Christ.'

Matthews glances at the clock. 'Do people really give a shit about this?' The comment stuns his detectives. 'I mean, have you even seen a good movie with religion in it?'

'*The Exorcist*,' says Nic.

'*Bruce Almighty*?' suggests Mitzi. They both frown at her. 'That was sort of religious.'

The captain shakes his head. 'Okay, I concede God can be box office. But tell me, who in real life cares so much about this Shroud? Catholics? Greeks?'

'Them and maybe others.' Mitzi sifts through the stack of folders as she talks. 'An assistant at the studio we spoke to said Jacobs paid researchers in Italy to work for her – maybe provided data on the Shroud.'

'What data?'

'Can't be sure. There was going to be a lab scene, so perhaps scientists do carbon dating or take DNA from blood on the Shroud. Maybe they come up with proof of whose body was under it.'

The captain wags a finger at the files she's still rifling through. 'Are you just spitballing or is there something in there that makes you look smart?'

She finally finds the papers she's looking for. 'These are copies of confidentiality agreements that everyone working on the film had to sign.' She passes several over. 'And here's a copy of a memo from the publicity department to Tamara Jacobs, asking if she wanted *New Scientist* and *National Geographic* added to the press day launch. These kind of publications would never normally be at a movie bash.' She opens another folder. 'And here's an IBAN number of the bank account of an Italian Tamara was paying in Turin. It belongs to an R. Craxi.'

'*Excellenti*, it sounds like you have several leads already.' Matthews pushes his chair back and glances again at the clock as he walks to his jacket hung behind the door. 'I'm off for dinner. You two had better get yourselves to the canteen – you've got a long night ahead.'

28

Dust motes billow in the yellow light from the desk lamp as Crime Scene Investigator Tom Hix drops his report on Mitzi's block of wood in Homicide. He's just heading back out as she and Nic roll in from Matthews's office. 'Little treat,' he says, as she approaches.

'What's that, Tom?'

'The vet finished examining the Persian cat from the Jacobs house. Kitty scratched someone deep and it's not her owner's flesh.'

'Really?' Mitzi reaches for the file.

'He found traces on the left claw and ran DNA. It's definitely not from Tamara Jacobs.'

Nic asks the obvious question: 'So who is it from?'

'The eponymous Unsub. Nothing on Profiler or the other databases. Whoever the cat clawed doesn't have a record.'

'At least not in the US,' Nic qualifies. 'We linked the perp to a rental car from LAX.'

'Driver hired it under a Greek name,' adds Mitzi, 'and there are Italian connections too. We'll check international record systems.'

Hix takes this as a good moment to exit, 'All yours now.'

He musters a fresh smile for Mitzi. 'If you want to grab coffee and talk about the case, you know where to find me.'

'I sure do.'

They watch him leave. Nic gives her a knowing look. 'You do realise that coffee is not all he wants you to grab?'

'Shut up! He's harmless. Besides, a little attention never hurt anyone.'

'So, how are we going to divide the pain? You do forensics, I chase down Tamara's family and friends – see if there are skeletons in the closet?'

'Deal.' She flips open the report that Hix just left her. 'You think the killer is European? Flew in, flew out – left us with only a false name and a speck of DNA that doesn't ring bells in any law-enforcement office on the planet.'

Nic lets out a long sigh. 'We're in trouble if he is.' He corrects himself. '*You're* in trouble, that would make for a really long job – and I'll be long gone.'

She tries not to think about him leaving and focuses on her growing hunch. 'Makes sense, though. Kill and run. Cross a continent and just vanish.' She looks up from the DNA report. 'You think Matthews would sanction a trip to Italy to find this guy Craxi, the researcher getting wired money from our dead lady? He always says that if there's money involved in a murder, you should chase the dollars.'

Nic muses on it. 'Clear-up rate is down. He needs a result on a high-profile case like this. Why, d'you fancy a trip?'

She shakes her head. 'No. But you do.'

29

JJ is surprised to see Emma Varley hanging back as the shopfloor clears at the end of the day. She smiles when she spots him. Looks him straight in the eyes with her baby blues. 'You locking up?'

He jangles the keys in his hand. 'That's what they pay me to do.'

'Want some help?'

He figures she's angling for another ride home. 'Sure, I'm always in the market for unpaid overtime.'

'Well, there's a surprise.'

He waves to the rows of distant machines: 'Can you just check that they're all off? Operators usually leave one or two on. They don't realise, or don't care, that it burns out the motor. Wastes a lot of energy as well.'

Emma doesn't give a damn about energy. All that crap about greenhouse gasses and ozone layers doesn't affect her. You don't worry about stuff like that when you haven't got enough money to run a car or put the heating on if you're cold. Given the chance, she'd burn three times as much energy as she does.

JJ turns off the lights and for a moment the two of them stand in a quiet darkness broken only by the pale spill and hum from overhead tubes out in the corridor.

'How romantic,' jokes Emma.

Too many random thoughts are trying to connect in his mind. The darkness – a woman alone – the excitement he feels rising inside him. He has to control himself. Mustn't get carried away.

She senses his arousal – goes with her impulse and leans close. The kiss is gentle, hesitant, uncertain. She's giddy, treading the tightrope between rejection and acceptance.

JJ feels strange. Magnetised to her. Physically unable to pull away. Her sexuality has a powerful hold on him.

She shuts her eyes, takes his face in her cool hands and kisses him more deeply.

He feels his heart jump as he breaks for breath. Without thinking, without censoring his thoughts, he finds himself pulling at her sweater, lifting it over her head. He must have her naked. Her hands fall to his belt and pull at the buckle. 'Stop.' He puts a hand to her face – thinks of covering her mouth – then he gently touches the strawberry birthmark with his thumb. 'Wait. Let me lock up. I don't want anyone to walk in on us.'

Emma Varley kicks off her shoes and smiles as he disappears in the darkness.

She leans back on the long workbench behind her and gets ready to offer herself to him.

30

Mitzi has the same bedtime ritual every night. She goes into the girls' room and turns out their light. And usually the TV, which they've fallen asleep watching, even though they've been told not to. She kisses them and pulls their quilts up snug, kisses them again and slips out the door, making sure she leaves it open just enough for Amber and not too much for Jade. Sometimes she wonders if boys would have been less fussy.

She uses her own en-suite bathroom, slips into a modest black nightdress and then sits at a small dressing table with a tiny book-sized mirror and takes off what little make-up she ever wears.

The blow to the back of her head sends her sprawling face down on the bedroom floor. It catches her by surprise, even though it wasn't totally unexpected.

'Do you think you can treat me like shit? Like I'm one of your bum collars?' Alfie bends low and throws another sweeping right-hander that smacks her ear and sends bells peeling through her shocked brain. 'I oughta kick some respect into your cheap fat ass.'

The attack is her husband's response to a scolding she gave him an hour ago. A bawling out for not finding work or doing anything around the house other than sinking beers. He slides the leather belt from around his waist and lashes wildly at her. 'You don't think I'm a man, do you?' He's slurring his words. 'Cos I can't get work doesn't mean I'm still not a man.' He folds the belt in two and this time when he hits her raises a crimson welt on her thigh.

Mitzi tries to get to her feet but he lays into her with the leather, slashing hard at her arms and legs, his anger fuelled by her cries and the sight of the deep red marks he's creating. Finally, she catches the belt. She slides towards him as he pulls, and slams her left foot into his ankle. He tugs harder and she drives the flat of her right foot into his balls.

Alfie drops the strap. Staggers backwards. Falls.

She's standing and he's flat out now. There's no room to aim a kick at his head. No way to land a meaningful punch in his face without him getting hold of her. Mitzi grabs the chair she'd been sitting on, flips it and jams the top of the seat across his windpipe.

Alfie clutches at the wood. She can see fear in his eyes. She leans down on the chair and watches his face redden. Alfie gasps for air. She presses harder. Knows what she's doing. Knows that within a minute she can end it all. End Alfie.

He kicks with his legs. Thrashes for his life.

'Mommy!'

Amber at the door. Watching her mother choking her father to death. Mitzi drops the chair like it's electrified.

'It's all right, baby.'

The look in her child's eyes says it isn't – it never will be again.

'Come on.' Mitzi pushes her daughter towards the bedroom. 'Go back to bed. Mommy will be there in a minute.'

Alfie's still on his back. He's holding his throat, making gasping, choking sounds, struggling for breath. Screw him. Mitzi sweeps a hand under her side of the bed and pulls out her force-issue Smith and Wesson. She checks the magazine, points it at her husband and looks down the barrel. 'If you know what's good for you, you'll get your shit together and get out of here. Come into the girls' room or even still be here when I come out and I'll blow your damned head off.'

31

CARSON, LOS ANGELES

JJ feels unusually excited.

He's never brought a woman home before. Never even considered doing so until Emma came along and boldly suggested they go back to his place. He could tell from the sparkle in her eyes that she was the one he could take a chance on. Full credit to her, she's special. More than special – she's *blessed*.

He closes the front door and carries her carefully up the dark stairway. He's crossed a threshold, created a spiritual

97

bond. Breathless, he reaches the top of the stairs and the creaking wooden boards of the landing. Being with Emma, 'Em' as he's going to call her from now on, has made him realise that he's been lonely, isolated, cut off from the big wide world. It's not healthy. Not what God would want.

In the flickering candlelight of his bare bedroom his thoughts run fast as he tenderly undresses her, his excited fingers drifting over her smooth, cool skin.

Em is beautiful. Even more beautiful dead than she was alive. God had told him it was her time but he can't leave her yet. Can't be without her. His mouth greedily finds hers. The hot breath of passion passes from space to intimate space until he breaks for air.

She lies still beneath him, her eyes shut, lost in another world, as he marvels at her. His attention falls on her distinctive birthmark and he smiles. It's not a blemish. Not a fault, not a mar of perfection as the rest of the world may see it. It's nothing of the sort.

He knows what it is. He alone understands its importance. She had been marked out. Chosen for him. JJ's never felt anything like this before. Never felt so complete. In the calmness and silence that follows he reaches to one side and pulls a long linen sheet around them both. He makes sure she's well tucked in. He doesn't want her getting cold. Not colder than she already is.

He leans over her and kisses her neck, then whispers in her ear, '*Dominus vobiscum*, my sweet darling. *Dominus vobiscum.*'

PART TWO

God is dead! And we killed him!

Friedrich Nietzsche

32

Beyond a thick grove of giant cedars, hidden in the shadows of the snow-covered slopes of Mount Lebanon, a kiln master performs a job passed down his family line for centuries.

His name is Ziad Keffy. He is forty years old, bald and fat. His skin has been roasted chestnut brown by the scorching sun. As he nears the opening of the blistering furnace his bare, sweat-glistened stomach looks like it is about to pop. Keffy's decades of expertise tell him the kiln's temperature is at the level he needs, and the clay inside begins to shimmer like molten gold. He stands in front of the fire and watches.

Periodically, he quenches the monstrous oven with water to produce the surface glaze that will protect the bricks. Each of them has been hand-crafted by his team of uniquely devoted workers, who have engraved their own personal marks on the precious blocks.

Keffy turns from the kiln to check on the labourers. It's

a brief escape from the broiling heat. Some are mixing clay with water and others are driving oxen over a fresh mix and trampling it into a thick slurry. Soon they'll scoop it into wooden frames, then use wire-strung bows to cut the bricks before they're moved to his kiln ready for firing.

It's hot and dirty work. Toil that drains you and dries up your organs from the inside out. You're never more than a few seconds from being desperately thirsty. Behind him Keffy hears his brother's voice. 'They are ready for you. They say it is time for you to come.' Dany, younger than him y ten years, tall and slim, so unlike Ziad it is hard to believe they are related.

The kiln master uses a filthy cloth tied around his waist to wipe the sweat from his forehead. 'Then they shall be obeyed,' he says. 'Don't let anyone near the fire.' He lives in fear of someone ruining his work or injuring themselves. If they did, there'd be hell to pay.

There's no bounce in his stride as he ducks under a small brick archway and descends a steep set of cold, stone steps into the thousand-year-old building that dominates the grove. The hairs on his arms prickle. Partly because of the change in temperature. Mainly because of the task he's about to carry out.

Just as Ziad is the only one entrusted with firing the bricks, so he is the only one ever called upon to supervise their use. His leather sandals make thin, echoing slaps as he walks the narrow slit of an underground passage, lit by fire torches on the walls. He shakes his head as he goes, unable to understand how people can spend any time down here, how they can live as they do.

The passage opens into a large subterranean square. The only light is from the candles placed around the central fountain. In the middle of the constantly pooling water is a statue. It's a tall figure, with a stern face. The founding saint of the monastery. Ziad makes the sign of the cross and dips his head respectfully as two black-robed monks approach him. The older of the two holds a sledgehammer in his liver-spotted hands, the younger – a youth of no more than eighteen – three stone chisels. The kilnsman wonders why the teenager didn't do the heavy lifting. Perhaps even here men are still keen to demonstrate their masculinity.

'Is it the same one?' he asks, fearfully.

The elder doesn't speak but his eyes confirm it. The old man never speaks. That is to say, he hasn't spoken for more than half a century. Ziad purses his lips and relieves the monk of the hammer. 'Please lead the way, Brother.'

He follows behind them, his thoughts turning to the job in hand. How best to strike the first blow. How to do minimum damage to the tiny but sacred structure he only just erected. Most of all, how not to injure the beast of a man they so recently sealed inside it.

33

It's 3 a.m. and Mitzi hasn't slept. She's sat bolt upright in Amber's bed, her two daughters finally asleep in the twin bunk beside her.

The Smith and Wesson dangles from her strapped-up hand. Her legs and arms are still red and stinging from the strapping Alfie gave her and her hearing is clouded with a constant buzzing from the blow to the ear. But she is oblivious to the pain. Her eyes are fixed on the bedroom door she's barricaded with a chest of drawers.

A while ago she heard a door slam, a car start and then squeal away. Hopefully it was him. Please God let it have been him. She still won't put the gun down – not until she's certain. In the darkness she's been thinking about the girls – the fights they've seen – the damage that's been done. Strange thing is, he's not been a bad father. Far from it. He adores them and they adore him. He's never raised a finger to *them*. Only her. *For her own good. To teach her a lesson. Because he loves her and he's scared she'll leave him.*

Mitzi's heard all the excuses and made them all to the girls – even told them it's normal, said that all parents fight from time to time. She remembers how, battered and bruised after a

104

fight, she'd let him hug her while they'd both tell the kids how much they loved each other and loved them. The most sickening thing of all was they'd meant it. Really meant it.

Crazy. She'd been certifiably insane.

She creeps out of bed, slides the chest of drawers slowly away from the door, picks her gun back up and takes a deep breath. Very slowly she prises the door open and heads back towards the bedroom where they fought. Maybe she should have called the cops when she'd floored him. Put up with the inevitable humiliation, the wagging tongues at work – what the hell. Come to think of it, she should have called them a long time ago. Right after the second time he punched her and then turned into a cry baby and asked her to forgive him.

She swings her gun around the doorframe and takes a shooting stance.

Empty.

Even in the soft glow from the bedside lamp she can tell he's gone. She backs out onto the landing and wonders now how she fell for all the old baloney he's given her. Sure, love stretches a long way. Love and two adorable kids stretch even further. But she should have known better.

Mitzi walks tip-toe down the stairs, gun out in front, clutched in her professional but still slightly shaking hands. She doesn't switch on a light until she gets to the kitchen. Then she wishes she hadn't.

The brightness falls like Judgement Day. A bolt of lightning straight from the hand of God rocks her head. She sweeps the gun around to see if the monster in her life is lying like a whale on the sofa.

He isn't.

Thank God for small mercies.

Five minutes later Mitzi is sure she and the girls are alone. She bolts the doors and sits at the kitchen table staring at the place where Alfie used to sit. Where he'll never sit again. In front of her is a bottle of whisky, a glass, the gun and a whole scary future.

34

CARSON, LOS ANGELES

She's cold now.

Colder than JJ thought human flesh to be. It fascinates him. Cops on TV call it the death chill, the stage of decomposition scientists know as algor mortis.

Poor Em.

Every hour her body temperature has been falling by one and a half degrees and right now it's barely that of the unheated room she's lying in. Her room. Her resting place. He strokes hair from her ghostly white face and tenderly wraps an arm around her. Strange noises surface. For a moment he thinks she's breathing. Rising from the dead. He places an ear to her heart and listens for a beat. Nothing. He moves down her torso, hands on her slim hips, cheek against her smooth abdomen. Now he knows what it is.

Gasses and liquids inside her. She might be dead but there are things living inside her – organisms feeding in her intestines – little parts of Em that are still alive. Life after death. He wonders if there are thoughts still in her brain moving like the bacteria, twitching in their final throes. Do memories just vanish like a heartbeat or do they hang around after the final breath and putrefy over hours, days or months? He knows the brain can be kept alive when all other organs are dead. Perhaps that's where the soul is.

He slides up alongside her and looks into the empty eyes and says something he's never said before. 'I love you.'

It feels good. Saying it. It's what God wants. God is love. God has brought him Em. She is his. He puts his mouth close to her face. 'I do, Em. I love you. I really do.'

35

VATICAN CITY

Two Swiss Guards accompany the special advisor through the Cortile de Sisto V, the courtyard of Sixtus the Fifth, the former swineherd turned Pope. Their boots clatter as they briskly climb stone steps to the top floor of the Apostolic Palace. Since the seventeenth century the ten rooms in front of them, including a medical suite, have formed the *appartamento nobile,* the official winter residence of the Supreme Pontiff.

The papal secretary shows Andreas Pathykos through the vestibule and leaves him in the small study. The earnest Greek has known the Holy Father for thirty years. He is his eyes and ears in the outside world. Andreas paces until the doors open and his old friend enters.

'Your Holiness.' He bows, then adds, 'I trust you are well.'

The old Pontiff smiles. 'As much as a mere man of eighty ever will be. You told my secretary you had urgent news?'

'I did.' His demeanour changes. 'It is not good, I am afraid.'

The Holy Father eases himself into a high-backed chair. 'Urgent appointments seldom bring good tidings.'

'The lady writer – she is dead.'

The Pontiff looks shaken. 'God bless her.' He makes the Sign of the Cross. 'Under what circumstances did she pass?'

'She was found in the sea close to where she lives in America. It was not an accident. We are reliably informed that the Los Angeles Police Department is treating her death as murder.'

The Pope lowers his head in solemn contemplation. Later he will pray for her soul. And he will pray that the worst of his imaginings is not true.

The advisor does not add any more details, certainly not the bloodier ones that he knows – the loss of an eye, the torture. His Holiness looks up. A pale blue gaze that has seen

108

much sin and witnessed much wisdom falls upon his trusted servant. 'Andreas Pathykos, if you have any information that can help the police catch this lady's killer, you must inform the authorities.'

'I understand, Your Holiness.'

'The Church has done much to unite the factions, the modernists and the orthodox, but we cannot be the friends of extremists.'

'Holy Father—'

The Pontiff stops him with a raised palm. 'They mean well but are overzealous. History has taught us this much.'

'Indeed, Your Eminence.'

'And the other matter. Is the book now closed on that?'

Pathykos flinches. 'I think not. I am afraid to speculate that it is just the opposite. This unfortunate death is most likely to keep the pages fixed open – for some time.'

36

WALNUT PARK, LOS ANGELES

At 5 a.m. Mitzi begins her new life.

She puts away the whisky, brews fresh coffee and sorts through bills that can't be put off any longer. The soul-destroying sift reminds her that the girls are going skiing with the school at the weekend and the final payment for the trip is long overdue. She can't afford it but she'll find it somehow. It feels important that they're away from home right now. A break down at Mount Baldy could be just what's needed.

She opens up the household laptop and starts a trawl for a locksmith and a lawyer. All the barrels on the doors and windows have got to be changed. It won't be cheap, but she can't think about that. And she needs to make an appointment with someone who can take care of all the nasty official things – the divorce – and the inevitable battle to hang on to what little she's got.

Alfie has taken her self-respect, she's damned sure he's not taking her home as well.

She goes upstairs and checks on the girls. They're still sleeping. Good. Maybe the deep rest will erase some of the horror of the night. She pads barefooted to her bedroom and pulls down a dusty trunk from the top of the wardrobe.

Twenty minutes later she's sat on it, squashing in as many of her husband's clothes, shoes and personal belongings as she can. She'll bag the rest and dump it in the garage for him to collect when she's not there. One thing for certain, he's never coming in the house again.

In the bathroom she sweeps his razor, foam, deodorant and clutter into a wicker bin and steps into the shower to wash off the dirt of her experience. A clean start. Never has there been a truer phrase. She towels dry and examines each of the fiery whip marks on her body. They'll fade. Given time they'll all go and so will the memories, the

110

nagging doubts and the fear that right now are eating her.

She dresses for work. Bright colours today, nothing but bold statements and certain steps. A buttercup-yellow blouse, saturated blue trousers and matching jacket. Too strong, she knows. Too summery, too gaudy. No matter. She needs the power of the colours around her, a halo of energy to see her through the day. There are still a couple of hours before she needs to take the girls to school so she settles at the kitchen table and surfs the internet. First the headlines. Then the gossip. Bored with the same old same old, she finds herself entering 'Turin Shroud' into the search engine.

Half a million entries pop up in a ninth of a second. Impressive. If only they made men as efficient. Give a man a whole day and he can't even find where he put his wallet, let alone four hundred and ninety-nine thousand other things. Search engines must be female.

There are numerous quasi-religious pages and the artefact has its own website, plus offerings from the usual suspects –Wikipedia, BBC and CNN. She opens Wiki and looks for the first time at the haunting image that so obsessed Tamara Jacobs.

From the accompanying text she learns the photographs were taken in 1898 by an Italian called Secondo Pia. She's blown away by how much clearer the negative is than the sepia print. It's hard to believe they're the same image.

Mitzi goes to a kitchen drawer and finds a pen and spiral notepad. On a fresh page she makes bullet point jottings, jumping from site to site.

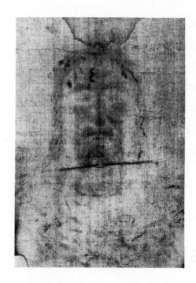 

- Shroud is a large linen cloth seemingly bearing marks of a crucified man.
- Kept in special chapel at the Cathedral of Saint John the Baptist in Turin.
- 1978 a detailed examination was carried out by a team of American scientists called STURP (Shroud of Turin Research Project). They found no reliable evidence of forgery and said it was a mystery how the image had been formed.
- 1988 radiocarbon dating was performed by universities of Oxford and Arizona and the Swiss Federal Institute of Technology. All independently said the Shroud originated in the Middle Ages, between 1260 and 1390 – all concluded it couldn't have been Christ's burial cloth.

Mitzi sits back from the screen more certain than ever that the answers to her murder lie in Turin. She looks at her watch and realises she's been so engrossed in the mystery of the Shroud that she's lost track of time. It's eight in the morning. Face the girls time. Time to tell them that last night wasn't a dream. That she really has kicked their father out and is not having him back.

Not ever.

37

VATICAN CITY

Andreas Pathykos leaves the Papal Palace and walks the five minutes to a café in the Piazza del Sant'Uffizio, off the southern curve of Piazza San Pietro. He's been coming here for years. So has the man he's about to meet.

He orders a large plate of pastries, espresso and water then watches the door for his guest. He doesn't have to wait long. Father Nabih Hayek jangles the overhead bell of the front door as he walks in. His thin face lights up as he spots his old friend at a table.

Hayek is in his late fifties and Lebanese. He can trace his family back to the early days of the Maronite Syriac Church of Antioch, a unique Catholic order that retains its own liturgy, discipline and hierarchy. Antioch has a special place in Catholic hearts. It is here that followers of Jesus were first called Christians and after the destruction of Jerusalem in AD 70 it became a centre of the faith.

'It is still cold,' grumbles Hayek as a greeting. He embraces the papal adviser. 'I long for spring.'

'Have this coffee, I'll order us some more.'

'*Grazie.*'

The visitor warms his arthritic hands around the small cup as Pathykos signals to the barman to bring refills. He lifts a *Pasticiotti* from the mound of pastries and places it on Hayek's plate. 'This one I got just for you.'

'What's in it?' Hayek pulls the plate towards him.

'Vanilla and chocolate,' he declares, almost sinfully. 'Enjoy.'

Hayek bites into the tender pasta frolla pastry cup and relishes the rare indulgence.

The following ten minutes are spent talking food, drink and the frivolities of life. Then Pathykos cuts to the chase. 'I have informed His Holiness of the difficulties that are unfolding in Los Angeles.'

'And?'

'He expressed his concern.'

'Explicitly?'

The Greek takes a moment before answering. 'He demands that if I have knowledge then I should share it with the authorities.'

'How would His Holiness define "knowledge"?'

'Justified true belief.'

'Ah, the Plato definition.' He licks cream from a finger.

'The great man said, *for someone to have knowledge of something, it must be true. It must be believed to be true and that belief must be justified.*'

'It is what most epistemologists accept, and according to such a definition then I have knowledge.'

Hayek is not so sure. 'You have *supposition*, dear friend. You have supposition not unequivocal confirmation, and therefore, as a consequence of having only supposition, you do not have truth.'

'I suppose you are correct.'

'I know I am correct.' Hayek looks pleased with himself.

'Now Andreas, in accepting you do not have truth – in admitting that you do not irrefutably know what has happened, you must also accept that you do not have *justified true belief* and therefore you do not have knowledge.'

The papal adviser sips his espresso and absorbs the argument. He puts the tiny white cup down. 'If asked, I will tell the Holy Father I have no knowledge in the truest sense of the word. If he instructs me to share more than knowledge, then I will tell you.'

Hayek nods in agreement. It is the most he could hope for. He returns to his pastry and considers how much more to tell the Greek. Until today it has been easy to be open about these somewhat delicate matters. Given the discussion of the last few minutes, that may no longer be the case. 'You have a contact in Los Angeles. Perhaps it would be better if from now onwards I dealt directly with him?'

Pathykos understands the implication behind the offer.

This way he can avoid any question of *future knowledge.* He can take action now to distance himself from things. But there is a price to pay for such a convenience. Loss of control. The Greek knows that once he hands the reins to Hayek, he will never be able to get them back again.

The two men sit in coffee-fuelled contemplation for several minutes, both weighing up the possible consequences of Hayek's request, not just for their churches but for themselves.

Pathykos finally calls for the check. He settles in cash and writes a name and phone number on a napkin, then passes it hesitantly across the table. 'You realise we must not meet again. Not for years. Perhaps not ever.'

Hayek takes the napkin. 'I do.'

Both men stand. They embrace and kiss each other on the cheeks before leaving and going their separate ways. The Greek walks back to the Papal Palace knowing one day he will need to seek forgiveness for what he has just done.

38

WALNUT PARK, LOS ANGELES

Mitzi is red-eyed and so exhausted that she almost calls in sick.

Amber and Jade cry their hearts out over breakfast, then

shout and blame her. Then they cry some more. Eventually everyone holds each other and says how sorry they are before falling silent with dark thoughts about life as a broken family.

Mitzi gets her shit together. 'Life goes on,' she tells them. 'No one has cancer. No one is dead. And you're still going skiing.'

The bribe works. But only for now. She drops her key with a neighbour so the locks can get changed, drives the girls to school and heads into work.

She's trying to act like nothing has happened. Like it is a normal, boring everyday kind of day. Only it isn't. It's a terrifyingly different kind of day. It's her first day as a single parent. Her first day as a woman who's about to start divorce proceedings. She calls the number of the lawyer she found online and makes an appointment for next week. She'd prefer one sooner but he's all booked up. For some reason her hand touches her gun, the Smith and Wesson she aimed at her husband last night.

Would she have shot him?

Damned right she would.

Tried to kill him or wound him?

A more difficult question.

Just struggling to answer it makes her realise that under all the layers of hate, all the scars, bruises and contusions of abuse, there's still the gossamer of true love, a thin link back to the good times. She swigs from a large mug of black coffee, and starts up the computer. Some day she'll cut down on the beans, maybe do a complete detox and drink the daily bucket of water that apparently all good girls do. Not today, though. Today

Mitzi is already doing ninety in the outside lane on caffeine superhighway and that's where she's planning on staying.

Now she wishes she'd called Nic in rather than have him chase down Tamara's family and friends. She could do with his energy around her, some positive momentum to keep her going. Then again, in a way, it's a good job he's not here. If she told him about Alfie, he'd probably go crazy and do something regrettable.

Her desk is a mess. Piled with paperwork and files. Surely not as she left it. She's usually much tidier than this. She must be cracking up. Or else someone's been rooting for something, and gave up part way through. The surface is covered with forensic reports, interview statements, bank accounts, bills and records pulled from Tamara Jacobs and her estranged husband Dylan. Plus all the goodies she finally shook out of Sarah Kenny – Tamara's memos, notes and some USB sticks. From the storage devices she's managed to print a paper tower of early scripts – numerous different versions, marked numerically and chronologically – 'The Shroud Draft (1) Jan 10', 'The Shroud Draft (10) July 26', etc.

She forgets the nagging worry that someone's been prying and starts reading from the beginning. The first copy may be the roughest but may also be the most valuable. Later drafts might have things taken out, refined away, covered up. She swings her legs around and puts her heels up on the desk, then slides down a little in her chair with the manuscript until she's comfortable. It's a long time since she read anything other than a paper or magazine – that's something else she's going to put right in her new life. She leafs through the pages and tries to follow the layout and stylised flow of screen directions and plot development.

THE SHROUD

By Tamara Jacobs

<u>**OPENING TITLES**</u>

BLACKNESS.

FROM THE DEPTHS OF THE NOTHINGNESS THERE IS THE **SOUND OF A DESERT WIND** BLOWING AND HOWLING.

THUNDER.

THE THUNDER TURNS INTO THE **SOUND OF NAILS BEING HAMMERED** INTO WOOD. MORE HOWLING WIND. THE WIND FADES INTO THE **SOUND OF WOMEN WEEPING** AND SCREAMING.

STILL THE BLACKNESS.

A TENSE MUSIC UNDERSCORE BUILDS.

SUDDENLY A MONTAGE OF BLACK AND WHITE IMAGES SPLATTER THE SCREEN. POSITIVE AND NEGATIVE SHOTS OF THE FACE ON THE TURIN SHROUD.

BIG CLOSE-UP OF THE SHROUD'S DARK EYES.

MUSIC POUNDS.

QUICK CUTS OF IMAGES THAT LOOK LIKE THE CROWN OF THORNS.

SHARP, JABBING MUSIC ON EACH PICTURE CUT.

IMAGES APPEAR – RIPPED, SHREDDED, SCRATCHED LIKE OLD BLACK-AND-WHITE FILM BEING SHUTTERED THROUGH AN ANCIENT PROJECTOR.

119

BLOOD SPATTERS THE SCREEN. DISSOLVES INTO THE FABRIC OF
THE SHROUD, THE CLOTH SOAKING IT UP AND IMAGES FADING AWAY
AS CENTURIES PASS.

CLOSE-UP OF LOWER PART OF THE SHROUD. CAMERA TRACKS
ALONG THE CLOTH WHERE THE PALMS OF THE HANDS AND THE FEET
WERE COVERED – WHERE RED BLOOD NOW SEEPS THROUGH.
CAMERA DRIFTS FROM THE BURIAL CLOTH INTO BLACKNESS.

SOUNDS OF DISTANT CRYING. THIS BECOMES MIXED IN A FADING
ECHO WITH THE **NOISE OF A VICIOUS WIND** RISING THEN DYING.

LIFE AND TIME HAVE PASSED.

THE SCREEN TURNS BLACK AGAIN.

CUT TO

OPENING SCENE

FROM PREVIOUS BLACK FRAME WE SEE A STARRY SKY. CAMERA
PULLS OUT TO REVEAL WIDE SHOT OF NIGHT SKY, THEN SLOWLY TILTS
DOWN TO SHOW MODERN DAY TURIN, ILLUMINATED BY CITY LIGHTS.

CUT TO

WIDE EXT GV OF THE CATHEDRAL OF ST JOHN THE BAPTIST

(SOUND OF CHURCH BELLS)

CUT TO

CRANE SHOT OF CATHEDRAL ENTRANCE

OLD ENTRANCE DOORS SUDDENLY BURST OPEN. A NOISY

CONGREGATION FLOODS OUT. PEOPLE ARE FASTENING COATS, PULLING ON HATS, HOLDING HANDS OF CHILDREN. THEY SOUND HAPPY. RENEWED.

INTERCUT WITH

OLD PRIEST WANDERS INTO SACRISTY AND CHANGES OUT OF HIS VESTMENTS. ALTAR BOYS COLLECT HYMN BOOKS, BLOW OUT CANDLES, STRAIGHTEN KNEELERS.

THE CHURCH EMPTIES. THERE IS BLACKNESS.
SOUND OF A KEY TURNING IN THE LOCK OF THE BIG HEAVY FRONT DOORS. **FOOTSTEPS HEARD** DISAPPEARING DOWN THE STONE STEPS OUTSIDE.

THE FACE OF A MAN APPEARS IN A SMALL POOL OF FLASHLIGHT. THE BEAM FLICKS DOWN ONTO THE TILES OF THE CHURCH FLOOR. WE **HEAR HIS FOOTSTEPS** AS HE WALKS AND WE FOLLOW THE BOUNCING BEAM. IT STOPS AND RISES OVER THE PLACE WHERE THE TURIN SHROUD IS LOCKED AWAY. THE LIGHT FOCUSES ON THE LOCK TO THE CASE HOLDING THE SHROUD. A LATEX-GLOVED HAND INSERTS A KEY AND TURNS IT.

WE HEAR A DOOR CREAK OPEN. LIGHT FALLS ON THE SHROUD. NOTHING HAPPENS FOR A SECOND OR TWO.

NOW WE SEE A GLINT OF A KNIFE IN THE LIGHT.

IT LOOKS LIKE THE SHROUD IS ABOUT TO BE RIPPED. DAMAGED. DESTROYED. THE LIGHT CARESSES THE SHROUD – SMUDGES AND STAINS APPEAR (IMAGES REMINISCENT OF THOSE WE'VE JUST SEEN IN THE TITLE SEQUENCE).

121

THERE IS A LOUD BANG. THE TORCHLIGHT IS QUICKLY
EXTINGUISHED.

                                                        CUT TO

EXT GV

TWO YOUNG BOYS OUTSIDE HAVE KICKED A FOOTBALL AGAINST THE
CHURCH WINDOWS. THEY GRAB THE BALL AND RUN AWAY SCARED.

INTERIOR

IN THE SHADOWS WE SEE THE FACE OF THE MAN WITH THE KNIFE,
WAITING PATIENTLY.

WHEN NO MORE SOUNDS DISTURB HIM, HE RESUMES HIS TASK.

CLOSE-UP

THE LENGTH OF THE KNIFE'S BLADE SCRAPES SLOWLY BACK AND
FORTH ACROSS THE SURFACE OF THE OLD CLOTH, LIKE IT'S BEING
METHODICALLY SHARPENED ON A WHETSTONE.

THE KNIFE DISAPPEARS FROM VIEW. THERE IS A SHORT PAUSE.
STICKY TAPE – THE TYPE CSIS USE TO LIFT FINGERPRINTS – IS
PRESSED DOWN AND PEELED AWAY.

Mitzi studies the crossed-out lines and sees a handwritten
notation a little lower: *too sensitive/rw

She guesses *rw* means rewrite. She pulls apart the tower of
drafts and after some rooting finds the next version of the
script. It reads:

THE KNIFE DISAPPEARS FROM VIEW. THERE IS A SHORT PAUSE. A CREAM ENVELOPE COMES INTO SHOT FROM LEFT OF FRAME. THE SHROUD IS LIFTED BY A HAND BENEATH IT AND GENTLY FINGER-TAPPED. TINY PARTICLES OF SCRAPED CLOTH AND BROWNISH DUST ARE SEEN TO FALL INTO THE ENVELOPE. IT IS NOW SEALED.

Mitzi is wondering why Tamara changed the text. What was wrong with the original version? She compares the two. The only significant change seems to be the dropping of the first draft's reference to 'the type CSIs use to lift fingerprints'. She swings back and forth in her chair, almost in the hope that the motion will dislodge a jammed thought, a clogged intuition.

The cell phone on her desk rings. 'Mitzi Fallon,' she says, still staring at the script, still wondering about the changes.

'It's me.'

The words make her freeze.

Alfie.

Her heart pounds. She pulls the phone away from her ear and glares at it. He's still talking as she cuts him off.

Somehow disconnecting the call is not enough. Mitzi makes sure the phone is completely turned off. She knows she'll have to talk to him. But not now. Not until she's really sure she's strong enough.

39

Factory manager John James stands in the open doorway of the machinists' workroom as the claxon sounds for the eleven o'clock tea break.

'Wait! *Wait!*'

He has to shout loudly above the cacophony of chair legs scraping back over the wooden floor. 'Hold on. You need to hear this before you go.'

The noise dies down to a grumble. The expectant faces of thirty women stare at him. Some are desperate to go to the washroom, others to get coffee, soda or cigarettes.

'Emma Varley handed in her notice last night and isn't coming in any more.'

The news raises a couple of whistles and even some bored clapping.

'It means we have a vacancy for a machinist. If anyone knows someone who needs work, let me know. Applicants need to provide references. That's it.'

The wave of noise rises again and the exodus resumes. JJ steps to one side and lets the tide of women flow past.

'Good freakin' riddance,' says Jenny Harrison as she approaches him. The thirty-year-old's brunette hair is tied back in a greasy bun and her face is heavily made-up.

'Bitch was no good anyway, dragged the rest of us back.'

JJ feels compelled to defend her. 'Em not being here is a big loss to this company.'

Harrison stops in front of him. '*Em?*' Her voice crackles with excitement. 'Was *Em* teacher's pet, then?'

JJ says nothing. Inwardly, he's already scalding himself for the slip of tongue.

'Aw, you gonna miss her, Mr J?' Harrison reaches out and grabs the arm of one of her passing cronies. 'Hey Kim, you think the boss was soft on Blotchy?'

Kim Bass, a platinum blonde, not young but not old either, stares baldly into her manager's face. 'He looks embarrassed to me, Jen.' She chews gum nonchalantly as she looks him over. 'Yeah, maybe he was. Or maybe he wasn't soft on her, he was *hard* on her.'

They erupt with laughter. Hold on to each other as though the joke was so funny they'd collapse if they didn't.

'Get out of here!' JJ waves them through the door. 'Take your break or get back to work.'

Harrison is too bold to be talked to like that. She's eaten men twice the size of Fish Face for dinner and spat out their scales and bones before breakfast. She steps close to him, so close her breasts brush him and her cheap perfume makes him cough. '*We* could be your pets, now Mr J. Kim and I here could show you things you never even imagined.'

Bass follows her lead and leans against his shoulder, pressing her body up against him. 'That's right, boss. Treat *us* properly and we'll really treat you.'

His temper snaps. He jams a hand across the blonde's mouth. Anger surges through him. Images flash to mind. He has to fight to keep his other hand at his side, use all his willpower not to grab her throat and squeeze the life out of her.

'Hey!' Bass pulls away. 'You just assaulted me.'

'Get your stuff. You're both fired. Get out of here.'

Bass no longer has a smart look in her eyes. 'You can't do that.'

'I've done it.' His heart is racing. 'You're *both* fired. Clear your things and get out of here. Now.'

The women look at each other uncertainly.

'It was just a joke, Mr James.' Harrison almost sounds apologetic. 'We're sorry if we wound you up.'

'Get out.'

'Please,' begs Bass. 'Dwayne will beat me stupid if I tell him I've lost this job.'

JJ couldn't care less. 'You're stupid already. Get your things and leave or I'll call the cops and have you thrown out.'

They can see he isn't going to change his mind. Harrison's face fills with fury. 'You sexually assaulted her.' She points at Bass. 'I saw you. You felt her up.' She turns to her friend. 'Didn't he, Kim? He grabbed at you, didn't he?'

'Yeah. You're a sex maniac. You've been pestering me all the time. All the girls have seen ya.'

They see the smug look slip from his face. Poor bastard doesn't know what to do now. Doesn't have a clue. Harrison taps him on the cheek as she walks away. 'We're takin' our break now.' She glances at her wrist. 'Only we'll be a bit late coming back, cos you kept us talking for so long.'

40

Deke Matthews' office chair creaks ominously as he rocks back and forth, weighing up Mitzi's unexpected plea to send Karakandez to Turin.

If the beach corpse was only a street bum, he'd say no. He'd send her away with a flea in her ear for even suggesting such a thing. But a Hollywood writer is a different thing. Very different since this morning when he had the mayor riding him hard for progress reports and reminding him that elections are just round the corner.

He rights the chair and gives his verdict. 'Okay, send him. Only do it cheap. Get him on a parcel plane or bucket airline. Strap him to a flock of pigeons or have him swim. No overtime, no fancy meals.'

'Thanks, boss.' She starts to leave.

'And send him now. Today. *Tonight* at the latest. I need a result on this Fallon and I need it quick.'

'You got it.' She makes for the door.

'Good. In fact, make it even quicker than quick.'

Mitzi dials Nic as she heads down to her car and out to

her next appointment, a catholic scholar and expert on the Shroud.

'Karakandez.' There's a lot of noise on his end of the line. 'Where are you?'

'Cruising coffee shops near the studio lot.' He mimes a thank you to a young assistant he's just finished interviewing. 'Thought Tamara might hole up here for brunch – or whatever it is writers have.'

'Any luck?'

He gazes across the dull faces he's been showing his badge to. 'Not so far.'

'Then get yourself home and pack a case. Admin is booking you on a flight to Turin to go find Craxi.'

'No way, Mitz. I've got one foot out of the door. It's too late in the day for me to be crossing the Atlantic.'

'It's not a request, it's an instruction – straight from Matthews.'

He doesn't speak for a minute, just stews on the news. He knows Mitzi has two kids and a drunk to look after at home. There's no way she can go and there's no one else senior enough to send. 'You owe me for this, big time.'

'Remind me when you're done sailing the seven seas.'

He ends the call as he heads out of the coffee shop.

Mitzi wishes she wasn't landing the load on his desk. Not just because he deserves a soft landing as he jumps from the squad, but because if the case isn't wrapped by the time he leaves, then she's going to have brief someone new on everything Nic's been doing.

Just after midday, she parks up and rides an elevator in an ugly concrete tower off West Temple Street. The office she enters is covered in old brown carpet tiles that long ago stopped being wipe-clean like the guarantee promised. A grey metal desk with three drawers and two moulded plastic chairs takes up half the room. The other half is dominated by a wall-mounted three-foot crucifix with a disturbingly lifelike figure of a bloodied Christ.

Rising from his seat to shake her hand is Father Patrick Majewski of the LA Archdiocese. The ruddy-faced cleric is the distilled product of spirited generations of Irish and Polish grandparents filtered through Gdansk and Belfast. His short but thick white hair fuses into a similarly short but thick white beard.

'Please sit down,' he settles back into his chair, 'I hope you don't mind – I'm still finishing lunch.' He gestures at a shallow bowl of watery broth on an old wooden tray on the desk.

'Not at all. Go ahead. Enjoy.'

'Would you like some brought for you?'

Mitzi's seen more appetising dishwater. 'I'm good, thanks.'

'Your loss.' He gives her a benign smile and tucks a white napkin into the top of his black cassock. Each spoonful is slowly savoured. No greedy slurping. Nothing rushed. Not a drop wasted.

After what seems an eternity, the good father places the spoon noiselessly in the bowl, removes the napkin and pats his lips. 'Absolutely delicious. You missed something of a treat.'

'I'm told denial is good for the soul, Father.'

'Not so good for the stomach, though.' He laughs. 'Now, you've not come here to talk soup. You said on the phone that you want to discuss the sacred Shroud of Turin.'

'I do.' She hitches forward on her chair. 'The Diocese press office said it's your area of expertise.'

'It certainly is. I've spent my life fascinated by it. I'm told this is in connection with a criminal investigation. May I ask what kind?'

'The *ongoing* kind. I don't want to be rude, but I really can't say anything more at the moment.'

'I understand. What exactly do you want to know?'

'If you believe the Shroud is authentic.'

'I saw the Sacra Sindone when it was last exhibited in Turin. Just being in its presence made me realise it was our Lord's.'

'How so? How could you be so certain?'

His face brightens. 'As a servant of Christ, I just knew.'

She opens her notebook. 'Give me a second. I wrote some things down, stuff from the web.' She flips a page and then another. 'Here we go – scientists who carbon-dated the cloth insist it can't be Christ's because it's from the Middle Ages. I'm quoting here, "undeniably between 1260 and 1390".'

'They're wrong. They carried out that dating almost thirty years ago. Back then the process wasn't nearly as accurate as it is now. It was somewhat flawed.'

'Really?'

'Really. You'll find several examples of carbon dating being out by hundreds of years.'

'Being out by more than a thousand is unlikely, though, isn't it?'

'Wrong is wrong, Lieutenant.' He licks a taste of soup from his front teeth. 'If in court you presented forensic evidence – DNA, blood-typing, fingerprinting – and that was even fractionally wrong, a judge would throw your case out, wouldn't he?'

'I guess he would. But even today the university scientists who tested the Shroud – all big kahunas from Oxford, Arizona and Zurich – they still say it was accurate.'

'Of course they do. They're protecting their reputations. Look, X-rays were invented in the nineteenth century, it was an incredible thing, an ability to see inside the human body and cure what was wrong. But those early machines are nowhere near as accurate as the ones we use now – they missed thousands of medical problems and illnesses. Carbon dating is just the same. It's in its infancy and in this case it's as innacurate as a nineteenth-century X-ray machine.'

Mitzi's face says she still isn't convinced.

'There are other factors as well – many of them.'

'Such as?'

'For a start, they took the samples from the wrong area of the Shroud.'

'How can there even be a wrong area?'

'Easily. The cloth is large and old. Fourteen feet six inches

131

by three feet nine inches. Over time it has become worn – damaged by folding, by water staining and, most notably, by a fire at Sainte Chapelle in Alpine Chambéry in France, where it used to be kept. So, over all those centuries, the scorched, stained and frayed fabric has been repaired – fresh weaves integrated into old weaves. The carbon testing, I am afraid, was done on a repaired area, not on the original cloth.'

'The scientists didn't pick up any of the old cloth in doing it?'

'Apparently not.'

'I'm sorry, I guess I'm just being stupid, but I don't see how a mistake like that could have happened.'

Now he looks stumped. 'I don't understand.'

'Well, from what I've read, it was the Church that determined exactly where the samples should be taken from, not the scientists. And if the Church knew of these patched-up parts, why didn't they have the samples taken from an area of original cloth?'

Majewski looks annoyed. 'The Holy Shroud wasn't patched up. It was expertly repaired using seamless and near invisible weaves of new yarn into old. The Church did not mislead anyone. It simply had not realised beforehand that these areas were those that had been repaired.'

Mitzi is intrigued. 'You mean, there are no records to prove this repair was carried out in the Middle Ages?'

'No.'

'Aw, c'mon.' She can't hide her incredulity. 'This is the

132

most famous religious relic of all time and no one kept a note of what was done to it and when?'

'If you'd kindly let me finish.' He glares at her. 'The lack of documentation is not strange at all. Over two thousand years, things get lost, they get destroyed. It is a sad fact that many records and testimonies that relate to the Shroud, and other important religious relics, have disappeared over the centuries.'

'In my experience, Father, important records only go missing or get destroyed when people want them to.'

He sounds offended. 'We are not common tax dodgers, or fraudsters, Lieutenant.'

Mitzi's unimpressed by his show of indignation, 'Forgers are forgers. Doesn't matter if they're presidents, politicians or priests.'

He lets out a weary sigh. 'We know from reputable documented reports that after the French fire in 1532, four nuns from the Order of Poor Clare made sizeable repairs. And we can similarly prove further work was carried out in 1694.'

'I don't want to upset you, Father, but those sixteenth- and seventeenth-century tags are nothing to do with thirteenth-century work.'

He turns away from her and tugs open the top drawer of his desk. His fingers trip along the top of the hanging green folders inside and stop about halfway along. He plucks out a thick folder. 'Have you seen any good-quality photographs of the cloth?'

'Only what's online.'

133

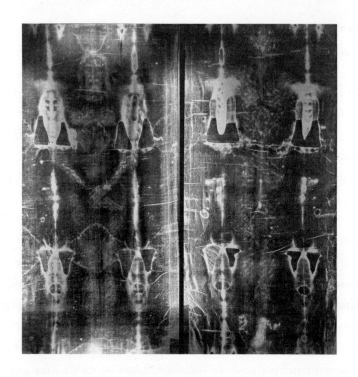

'They'd be low definition.' He opens the file. 'Here.' He hands over a set of prints. 'These are high-definition prints made with Church approval. The one on the left shows the front of the Shroud, the one on the right, the back.'

Mitzi handles them as she would a deck of crime-scene stills. She takes a quick glance, then goes back to the first to examine each in detail.

He pulls his chair closer and runs his finger down the crossed arms of the corpse in the left-hand picture. 'This mark on the wrist is where they hammered in one of the iron nails – not, as many thought, in the palm of our Lord, but between the bones under the ridge where the wrist meets the hand.' The cleric's finger moves to the torso. 'These faint criss-cross marks are where the soldiers scourged him with their flagrums—'

'Flagrums?'

'Whips, leather tongues embedded and tipped with metal barbs.'

Mitzi clearly sees everything he's talking about. The incredible detail is compelling.

Majewski can tell she's being drawn into the mystery – the miracle. 'It's hard to explain, isn't it?'

'It is,' she concedes, shifting her focus to a new image, a close-up of the head and face. 'It all looks chillingly real.' She thinks hard but can't remember ever seeing or hearing of a corpse transferring its features to any cloth or fabric.

The old priest leans close to his visitor. His breath is warm and still smells of soup. 'Lieutenant, I have no idea what your investigation is about, but I urge you to run it with the greatest of care.' He gently touches the photograph on her lap and speaks in the authoritative tone of the confessional booth. 'Your eyes rest upon the face of Our Lord. Remember, one day His will rest upon you. I pray that He, in His mercy, will judge you then on how you judge Him now.'

41

JJ can't look at the women as they file out of the factory at the end of the shift. Their noise disgusts him. The whole seething, heaving mass of them turns his stomach. At the heart of their stupid babble, he can hear Harrison and Bass calling him names, taunting him.

He wanders away from the machine room, back down the corridor to his office. It's like being back at high school. He remembers the bigger, older boys, baiting and brutalising him. He feels the acid-sharp reminder in his stomach.

JJ settles behind his desk, closes his eyes and lowers his head. He knows what is going on. They are evil. Wicked. Sent to test his resolve. Put on earth to stand in his way and to destroy all he stands for, all he has to complete. Well, they won't. He won't let them.

There's a rap on the window in his door. He looks up. Harrison's face at the glass. Her foul, mocking mouth is open wide. Her right hand making obscene motions. After a few seconds of staring at him she laughs and walks away.

JJ is unable to move. She's humiliated him again. Harrison and Bass are going to make his life hell. He just knows they are.

He gets up from the desk and heads back out to the floor.

He turns off all the machines, then closes the windows, checks the taps are off in the washrooms and the kettles and appliances in the small kitchen area have all been disconnected. After switching off the lights, he returns to his office and opens an old metal filing cabinet buried under a dead computer and a stack of papers in the corner of the room. He sifts through the personnel files until he finds the two he's looking for – Harrison and Bass.

Good news – they live close to each other. Not far from work. Not far at all. He makes notes of the addresses and home phone numbers, then returns the files. He turns off the last of the lights and locks up. His spirit lifts as he drives away into the dark of the night and the even darker plans he has for his troublesome employees.

42

77TH STREET STATION, LOS ANGELES

The rest of Mitzi's day gets chewed up fixing permissions for Nic's Italian trip and dodging Matthews, who's being hounded hourly by everyone from the mayor to the commissioner and back again. Poor guy looks like he's going to blow a gasket.

Tonight she's planning to treat the girls to a takeaway, whatever they want and some good ice cream. They can pig out together on comfort food. A girlie night in before they go skiing. God knows they all need it.

On her way home she calls Nic and braces herself for a torrent of abuse.

'Hello?' His voice crackles through the speaker in her car's hands-free.

She clicks the volume up as she answers. 'Shouldn't you be saying *bonjour* or something like that?'

'Very funny. I think the Italians say *buongiorno.*'

'Guess you're gonna find out soon enough. You all packed?'

'Just loaded the car and I'm leaving in a minute. Thanks for this, Mitz. Just what I needed to see me out – a ball-breaking trip of several thousand miles to chase shadows.'

'Hey, had there been someone else I would have sent them. Had I been able to go myself, I would have. Believe me you were my last resort.'

'Last resort, eh? You sure know how to make a guy feel good.'

'Enough of the complaining. Did you manage to make contact with the Carabinieri?'

'Only just. They say they'll have a liaison officer for me. I've got an FBI buddy reaching out to find me a friendly face too.'

'Make sure we don't have to pay for it. Matthews will have my badge if you run up anything more than a coffee bill.'

'Great. A bitch of a trip and full radar on what I spend. How was your day?'

'I've had better.'

'How so?'

She almost tells him, then pulls back. What's the point of passing on the poison? He's minutes from heading out to LAX and has a murder case to run. 'Been driving myself crazy reading those damned scripts you left behind. I ended up over at the Catholic Diocese this afternoon consulting a so-called Shroud expert.'

'God bless you. Make you any the wiser?'

'Some.' She beeps her horn as an asshole in a Tahoe cuts her up. 'Forensically, there doesn't seem any proof this Shroud is really Christ's, and that might have been what Tamara Jacobs was driving at. I'm gonna call Amy tomorrow and get her opinion as a pathologist. Maybe she could tell if the markings on the cloth match those of someone who's been crucified.'

'You know what, I'm not sure Amy's ever worked a crucifixion.'

'Weird shit goes down in LA, dumbass, you never know. You should try to see the cloth while you're over there. I checked out some HD photographs today. It's certainly amazing.'

'In what kind of way?'

'In the way that you just can't explain how the whole body image got there. I mean, I just don't understand it. From what I've read and heard, there's no evidence to say it was painted or rubbed on. The one thing that's real is that it's a mystery.'

Nic looks at his watch. 'Mitz, I got to run, that's if you want me to make check-in?'

'Go. I just called to wish you luck. Mail me an update when you can.'

'Sure. I'll touch base as soon as I'm settled, okay?'

'Fine.' She pauses. 'Take care.'

'You too.'

He's gone in a click. She switches on the radio but doesn't really listen. She drives the rest of the way on autopilot, wondering what kind of day the kids have had, whether they've done their homework, how they're going to be with her when she gets in.

She turns into her driveway and steps hard on the brakes.

Alfie's car. Smack bang in its usual place in the carport.

She unbuckles the seatbelt, her heart hammering, then gets out and slams the car door. She's so angry she almost kicks her own front door in rather than opens it.

'Hi,' he says, bold as brass, sat with his daughters at the family table around a big bucket of KFC. 'I brought chicken, so you don't have to cook.'

43

It says Boyle Heights on the map but locals call it Paredon Blanco – 'White Bluffs' – a hilly neighbourhood on the eastern banks of the Los Angeles River. It's a main gateway to the city for new arrivals. The place where an Irish immigrant called Andrew Boyle settled, back in the days when California was more Mexican than American. He went on to become mayor and built much of the infrastructure that led to the place becoming a modern-day melting pot for Latinos, East Europeans, Japanese and white minority Americans.

JJ is parked up just south of St Mary's Church and west of Promise Hospital watching the front of a big five-bedroom home that was once a highly desirable residence and no doubt housed a good, God-fearing family. Now it's old and rundown and is staggering to the end of its life as a cheap stack of one-room rentals. This is Jenny Harrison's address, though from where he's staked out, he has no idea in which part of the building she rests her sorry butt in.

A glance at the clock on the Explorer's dash says he's been here for more than four hours, painstakingly watching a whole army of people troop in and out. Harrison's friend Kim Bass arrived about three hours ago and hasn't come out

141

since. Maybe she's staying over. If not, she has a walk of less than a mile to her own place. A farewell walk.

It took JJ a while to figure out what was going on. At first he guessed there was a party in the offing, then he realised none of the male visitors stayed for long and none brought any bottles or gifts with them. It's a whorehouse. He should have expected it. Harrison and Bass are low-life. That's why God pointed them out to him, that and the fact they made Em's life hell. And hell is exactly where he's going to send them.

An S-Class Merc pulls up and two muscular Hispanics get out and disappear inside the house. Twenty minutes later they strut onto the decking near the screen door, blowing cigars and counting cash. They half-jog down the front steps and then out of the gate to the sleek limousine.

Lights start to go off in the house. The girls are calling it quits for the night. They've earned enough.

JJ wonders what it's like in their darkness, to lie at the bottom of their private swamp and move in on them.

Easy meat.

He pictures the layout of the house. How to enter and exit. Which way to drive off when it's over. When Harrison and Bass are dead.

44

Mitzi drops her bag and jacket in the hall. Tells herself to stay calm but her heart is trying to kick a hole in her ribcage.

She walks back to the front room and looks at her daughters. Jade offers the explanation before her mom even asks. 'I let him in.' She sees the anger and adds, 'He's still my dad.'

Amber backs away a little from her father and sister. She wants to be close to her mom if things kick off.

Mitzi glares at her husband. She can't believe this is the man she gave eighteen years of her life to. The man she once thought she wanted to spend every breathing second of her existence with. 'We eat this then you go.'

'We need to talk, Mitzi. You know we do.' He says it like he's the smart one, the reasonable one, the one showing them the safe path across the crazy dangerous ground facing them. He picks up the chicken tub. 'How about you get some plates and I dish out the good stuff?'

She feels rage rising. How dare he breeze back in here like last night never happened – as though it was nothing out of the ordinary.

'I'll get them.' Jade jumps to her feet and heads to the kitchen. She knows her mom is close to breaking point.

'We're done talking, Alfie. I've hired a solicitor and I'm

143

'divorcing you.' Mitzi says it with cold determination but part-way through feels a stab of regret, a sting of sadness that her dream of love has turned into a nightmare.

'Don't do that, Mitzi.' His voice is soft and reasonable. 'I know I screwed up. I screw up a lot, eh? But you know I love you. I love you and the girls more than anything in the world.' He gets up from his chair and creeps around the table towards her.

'Don't!' She raises a hand. 'Don't even *think* about coming near me, Alfie.'

He stops beside her chair, stranded, lost.

She looks away from him. Her eyes pass from Jade in the kitchen doorway, a second away from tears, to Amber at her side, gripping her hand and shaking with fear. 'Sit back down, Alfie. Sit down or leave.' She can barely breathe as she speaks.

He stays where he is. Still hoping to close the gap between them. 'I'm asking for you to forgive me. Give me another chance to fix things, to make us all a family again.'

He's been drinking. She hadn't noticed it at first but she smells it now – yeasty and stale. When Alfie drinks, anything can happen. Suddenly she stops fumbling around like a scared wife and mother and starts thinking like a cop. He could get violent. The girls could get hurt. Mentally and physically.

She has to take control. Mitzi smiles across at her daughter. 'Come on, Jade, don't just stand there – get those plates sorted or we're all going to starve to death.' She looks up at Alfie and tries to sound submissive. 'Sure we'll talk, Alfie, but not until we've eaten, okay? I've had a hard day and the girls are tired and hungry. *Please*, sit down.'

He doesn't move for a second, then edges back to his seat – his usual place at the family table.

'Anyone want a drink?' She looks towards her husband, her soon to be *ex*-husband. 'You bring any soda?'

He shakes his head. 'No.'

She rolls her eyes. 'Thought not. I'll get some. What do you want, Amber?'

'Coke.'

'Coke what?'

'Coke please, mom.'

'That's better.' She heads to the kitchen. 'You want coke or beer, Alfie.'

'Beer.' His tone is as sour as his breath.

Mitzi takes cans from the fridge as Jade heads back to the table with four white plates. There used to be six but Alfie broke two along with a dozen other pots when he lost his temper one night. She puts the drinks down on the table. 'You girls washed your hands?' Their faces confirm they haven't. 'I didn't think so. Go get scrubbed.' She pushes the bucket of chicken towards her husband. 'Dish it up, will you?'

'Sure.'

'I need to wash as well.' She shows him the palms of her hands and drifts into the hall. 'Come on, kids, hurry up, food's going cold.' She says it loud enough for him to hear, loud enough to disguise the fact that she's already dialling 911 on her cell phone.

Damn the humiliation. She's going to get the no-good son-of-a-bitch locked up once and for all.

45

A glint of light draws his eyes.

The door is open. Two people are there. Someone's leaving.

He can see more clearly now. Jenny Harrison is out front, in a short skirt, boob tube and high heels. An amber bottle of Bud dangles in one hand as she waves goodnight to someone. Kim Bass's big blonde hair blows back as she picks her way down the decking and out onto the worn pathway. JJ hesitates for a moment. He'd imagined he would kill Harrison first. God knows, she deserves it. But now he feels directed towards Bass. The woman is out on the street. Alone. Vulnerable. There for the taking. There to be punished.

He starts his engine and drives with the lights off. Her home is a fifteen-minute walk – if that – down past Hollenbeck Park across East 4th Street then right past the garage at the corner of South Cummings. He can make it in less than five.

A thought hits him as he pulls a right onto South

Chicago. She might cut through the park. It would be the perfect place to take her. Twenty acres of rolling grassland. And a lake. He turns again and takes South Saint Louis along the edge of the green sprawl. It's too busy. Skater boys jerking around the kerbside. Falling about and laughing, slugging beer. Further down he sees stoners hanging out in the entrance to the Recreation Centre, weird music pounding out from some boombox.

A voice inside his head tells him to stick to what he does best. Stay on plan. Do things the way he's done them before. He parks on the forecourt of a disused gas station, right opposite the Subway sandwich franchise, the kind of place he wouldn't be seen dead in. He looks around for cameras as he zaps the car closed. There aren't any.

Thank you, God.

Bass's building is a three-storey brown stucco block behind a small chainlink fence and a couple of token patches of rubbed grass. He walks calmly to the entrance door and is pleased to see it has been wedged open. The interior lights come on as he steps inside. An empty boxy corridor, blue-painted walls, blue polished floor. No central mailbox unit, no way of knowing who lives where. Just three doors. There are numbers on the doors but no names. He walks back outside to look for a bell box. There isn't one. So he comes in and looks around. The apartment doors are old style, British, with mail slots cut into the wood – a lot of places have started using them because it cuts down on crime, especially identity theft and card fraud. Next to each door is a vertical strip of frosted glass, a vain attempt to let in a little light.

The stairwell is narrow and too open for him to hide anywhere. She'll be here in a minute. There isn't long.

He considers just knocking on the door to his left and asking where she lives. As he looks at it he notices it's wider than the one to his right. It's been altered for wheelchair access. He examines the other one. It has flowers painted around the door handle. A stencil. Bass wouldn't do that. She doesn't have an artistic or cultured bone in her. There's a light glowing behind the third door. He steps close and listens. Deep male voices laughing, a TV playing.

JJ moves upstairs. The first landing has another three doors. All in darkness. He walks up to the top level. Three more apartments, two with lights on. He kneels in front of the darkened door and opens the mail slot. It smells musty inside. Earthy, like no one lives there.

It's the second floor. He's sure it is. Kim Bass lives on the second floor. He can feel it. God is telling him that's where she will go. He unbuckles his belt and makes a noose out of it. Sits like a shadow on the top step of the block's stairwell. Waits motionless. Listens in the darkness and tunes into the noises.

Clunk. The gate being closed on the small metal fence.

Click, click. Click, click. Heels on the concrete path.

Cough. A throaty female hack, sign of a smoker, signs of someone coming up the stairs.

He stands and stretches the looped belt between his hands.

46

It looks like old times. The best of times. Happy times. Four plates of picked-clean chicken bones, kids licking spicy fingers.

Only this is the new time. An unforgettably bad time. Mitzi wipes her mouth with a KFC napkin. 'Help me clear the table, girls.'

The twins are glad to. Anything other than see mom and dad fight. They push back their chairs and sweep up the takeaway tubs and plates.

Only Mitzi hears noise outside. Only she has been expecting it. She follows the girls, closes the kitchen door behind her and leans against it. Her daughters dump mess in the trash and don't see the look on her face. Right about now uniformed cops are piling through the front door she left open.

She hears Alfie shout, 'What the fuck?' Her heart jumps.

Amber's running hot water in the sink and can't hear a thing. Jade wipes her hands on a tea towel and sees her mom with her back to the door. She knows something's wrong. 'Mom, what's happening?'

Mitzi's face offers no comfort. 'Something that has to happen, baby.'

It has to be her dad. He's in the front on his own. Jade tries to push past.

'Leave it, honey, leave it.'

Amber's backed up against the sink, staring at them both.

Mitzi wants to hug her and hold her. Tell her baby that it's all okay. Everything will soon be all right.

There's a meaty thump on the wood behind her head.

'Ma'am, we need to speak with you.' The voice is male, full of street grit and a West Coast drawl.

Mitzi swallows and opens up. Jade flies past her. There are two cops in the room. Big black guys who could play offense for the Lakers.

No Alfie.

The furthest cop grabs Jade. 'Slow up, Princess. Hang on there.'

Mitzi is with her in a flash. She holds her by the shoulders, looks her straight in the eyes. 'Take your sister and go to your room. Don't argue with me.' The instruction is more cop than mother. The teenager does as she's told.

Mitzi stands in the room with the cops and the consequences of her actions. It's for the best. If things had turned nasty tonight, it could have been her being hauled away with her hands behind her back – and Alfie being carried out the back door in a body bag.

'You going to be okay, ma'am?' The question comes from Officer Logan Connor, six-three and two-twenty pounds of raw LAPD uniformed muscle.

'I'm fine,' she lies. 'Just fine. Thanks for your help.'

'You're welcome.' He gives her a respectful head tilt and

follows his partner to the front door. 'We'll sure take *good* care of your husband, ma'am.'

'Hey! I don't want anyone going Tyson on him. Please just get him downtown and book him. You've got my statement. I'll be in Homicide in the morning if anyone needs anything else.'

'Understood.' He looks at the swelling to her ear. 'Might be worth having if you had the doctor examine you and photograph any injuries.' He sees her open her mouth and prepare to bawl him out. 'I know you know your job, ma'am, and I'm not trying to be smart. It's just if we are to press charges, every bit of evidence helps.'

She knows he's right. These cases are messy. 'Thanks. I'll think about it. She eases him outside. 'Please don't let anyone cut up rough on him.'

'You got it.' He nods and heads to the squad car.

Mitzi shuts the door. Whatever Alfie's done in the past she doesn't want him roughed up now. She needs a clean conscience over whatever's going to happen next.

Prosecution.

If she goes through with things, he's going to get processed, land a criminal record and have what remains of his life ripped up. Can she really do that to him?

She climbs the stairs and goes into the kids' room.

Jade is red-eyed and angry.

'Honey—'

'Leave me alone.'

Mitzi's heart sinks. The kid needs space. The apple of her

father's eye, she's going to take some time to get used to things. It'll take everyone some time. This certainly isn't the moment to bawl her out about letting Alfie in the house. Amber is sat silent on the end of her bed, looking blitzed by the whole affair. Mitzi sits down and puts an arm around her. 'We'll be okay, baby. Everything will be fine in the end. We just have to get through this bit.'

The thirteen-year-old snuggles tight and relaxes a little as her mom finger-brushes hair from her face.

'I love you, sweetheart.' She kisses the girl's forehead. 'And I'm always going to be there for you and your sister, you know that, don't you?'

'I know, Mom – I know.'

47

BOYLE HEIGHTS, LOS ANGELES

Kim Bass has drunk too much vodka and smoked too much weed. But hell, a girl has to have some fun. She's thinking about the laughs she's had and the extra money she's made, as she fishes for the apartment door key in her purse. She wants to get inside, take a leak, shower and sleep. Grab a little rest before life starts all over again.

She pushes open the front door then stumbles over the mat as she steps inside. The door slams behind her and she sprawls face down in the dark. A sharp pain erupts in the back of her head. Her hair is yanked violently and a terrific force presses painfully into the middle of her back and bends her upwards. If she could scream, she would bring the place down. But something tight is around her throat choking her. She grabs at her neck. Her head smashes into the floor. An even more horrific weight crushes her back. She can't breathe now, let alone scream.

Blood pounds in her heart. Someone is choking her. Panic churns in her chest. For a split second the agony stops. She can breathe. Cool air fills her lungs. Whatever is around her neck has gone slack.

Unseen hands turn her over. She pants for breath. He's above her, in the darkness of her own home, she can sense him. A heavy weight hits her chest. His knees are on her. She can smell him now.

Fish Face.

The boss at work who always smells of his fish lunches.

'Em sends her love.'

One of his hands is tight around her throat. The other is across her mouth. He bends low and whispers so close his breath mists her skin. He says, '*Dominus vobiscum*.'

PART THREE

Woe to those who are wise in their own eyes
and clever in their own sight.

Isaiah 5:21

48

No one knows how old he is. Not even the man himself. All he is certain of is the name he's been given. His parents didn't choose it. It was passed down from generations of monks. A name men have grown to fear.

Ephrem has never celebrated a birthday. Ephrem has never celebrated anything. He has no social security number, mortgage, bank loan, or any manner of insurance, assurance or medical or legal agreements. As far as the world is concerned, he doesn't exist.

A doctor or dentist would look at his skin, eyes, bones and teeth, and hazard educated guesses that he's in his forties. But Ephrem has never been to a doctor or dentist and never will. Nor has he ever been to school, university or any other institution that might have entangled him in the mechanical record-keeping of growing up. No official papers bear his name despite his four decades on earth.

It is for all these reasons that the tall, youthful and Arabic-looking man is a little anxious as he presents the passport at border control, then from an ATM in the airport terminal withdraws three hundred euros from an international bank account set up to serve his purposes.

Ephrem's true vocation is even stranger than the mysteries surrounding him. He is an anchorite. A hermit. Part of an orthodox sect, withdrawn from secular society. He lives without trace in a monastery hidden on the slopes of Mount Lebanon. Isolated. Barely consuming anything.

Ephrem is the most trusted member of a highly secretive and revered order inside the Maronite Church and is the one devotee who the Patriarch and esteemed advisers like Nabih Hayek can trust.

It's on Hayek's orders that he has come to Turin. Mixing in society is painful for him. He would rather be bricked in his cell in the Lebanon, his only link to life the hagioscope, the shuttered slot through which he receives his food. But this is a necessary sacrifice. As night falls he sits cross-legged on the floor of the cheap room he has rented near Turin and thinks about who he is, where he came from and what his duties are.

His DNA is half-monk, half-warrior. His blood courses with that of the Brothers slain by the Monophysites of Antioch and with that of the Crusaders who slaughtered the sons of Islam on the borders of the Byzantine Empire. He remembers well standing in the crowds when the Holy Father visited his homeland and declared, 'Lebanon is more than a country, it is a message.'

158

Ephrem has learned he is more than a man, he is the hand of God.

A hand that is clenched.

One that will deliver divine retribution.

49

WALNUT PARK, LOS ANGELES

It's something o'clock.

An indeterminate time in the dead of night when you should be asleep but you're not. A time so horrible it doesn't deserve digits. Mitzi hasn't been to sleep. She's been lying in the dark for hours churning things over in her head. The bed is big and cold and empty. Alfie was a pig and a bully but he was a warm one. She's been reminding herself that despite the tears of Jade and Amber, she's done the right thing – should have done it years ago. He didn't hit her until the second year of their marriage. A backhand slap when they'd both been drinking and she'd been busting his balls because he'd lost his job. The next morning she got round to thinking it had been her fault. Maybe she'd been too physically confrontational and had pushed him into it. She'd grown so used to fighting hard-asses in the street that a scrap at home didn't seem so off the scale to her.

Then he hit her when he was sober. A full-blooded blow

in the stomach that knocked the wind right out of her. She left for a week after that. Made him crawl through broken glass to get her back.

The beatings stopped when the babies were born. Or at least they did for a while. Then, because she was too tired to do anything but sleep at night, rows over sex, or more accurately the lack of it, often ended with fists flying. Then they made up. Made up and swore it would never happen again. Made up like the world was going to end and only the greatest sex ever might save the planet.

She knows now how foolish she's been.

At *way past* something o'clock she climbs out of bed, finds her robe and checks on the girls. They're sleeping like angels. Maybe they'll get through this all okay. Maybe she will too.

50

CARSON, LOS ANGELES

JJ sits in the chilled dark of his bedroom trying to compose himself. The kill is only an hour old and his adrenalin is still pumping.

He breathes in slowly, the sweet smoky smell of burning candles a balm for his raw emotions. This one felt different. Less spiritual. More visceral. More human than divine.

He looks at his hands. Marvels at them and their power of

life and death. Until tonight God had always controlled them, guided them to the mouths and throats of the unkilled. But not tonight. Tonight he made the choices. He *was* God. The thought troubles him. A tiny speck of doubt, like a tear in the corner of a baby angel's eye. Perfect, but somehow wrong.

The sight of Em lying before him, just as he left her, shakes him out of his reflective moment. She looks so beautiful. Lovingly covered from head to toe in the long, clean sheet of expensive linen he stole from work. He touches the cool, soft cloth. Em's shroud. He unwraps it, like an archaeologist discovering an Egyptian queen.

Queen Em.

He kneels alongside and whispers proudly in her ear, 'One of them is dead, my sweetheart. That piece of trash Kim Bass – her Day of Judgement came and went.' He moves the candles on the floor around her. There are odd smudges on the inside of the shroud. Marks so clear that he can see the outline of her face. Maybe the smudges have come from the last of her make-up, sweat, or even speckles of blood.

Darker stains follow – leakage of urine and faeces. He's not shocked. Nor revolted. No more so than a parent in the first days of handling a newborn.

JJ leaves her on the floor and wets a flannel in the bathroom. He wipes her gently then pats the skin with a towel. Just like a baby. Now he's done they'll sit together and hold each other in the first light of a new day. He and his love. His queen. Together for ever.

51

Lock-up is not the place you want to have spent the night.

From a whole corridor away Mitzi can smell the drunks and the down-and-outs who've passed the hours of darkness sweating off their addictions and stewing in the fear-soaked, overheated, overcrowded bullpens. There's no denying it, she's feeling guilty as hell as she heads into the hole to see what kind of hell Alfie Fallon endured following his arrest.

'Morning, Bobby,' Mitzi's smile masks her embarrassment. 'Guess you know why I'm here?'

'Whole station knows, Mitz. Come here.' Custody Sergeant Bobby Sheen opens his big arms to hug her.

Mitzi gladly gives herself up to the bear hug. 'Thanks.'

He answers her unasked question. 'Been a model lodger. Not a peep out of him since they shut the cage door.'

'Was he ... ' She just can't say it. 'I mean, you know ... did any of the guys ... '

'No. They would have liked to, but none of them laid a finger on him. Logan Connor put out the word – wasn't gonna be anyone crossing him on that.'

She nods as she remembers the big black beefcake who turned out to her house.

162

Sheen reaches over the reception desk and presses a button. 'Look at screen four.'

A black-and-white feed of Alfie's cell fizzes up on one of six video surveillance monitors. It breaks her heart. Despite everything he's done and said, the sight of him bent forward on the edge of a bolted-down bunk with his head in his hands rips her apart.

'Hey, now don't you dare go feeling sorry for him,' says Sheen, putting a hand on her shoulder. He's close to retirement and has seen every drama of life acted out in his cell blocks. 'A night in the pokey never harmed no one.'

'Jeez, Bobby, just look at him.'

He clicks off the monitor so she can't. 'You want a cup of Joe?'

She nods. 'Just black.'

'You got it. Watch the shop for me.' He pads down the corridor, keys on his belt jangling until he turns a corner to find the hotplate where the coffee bubbles all day.

Mitzi wonders what happened to her life. How come she let things slip so much that Alfie ended up in the bullpen?

Sheen returns with coffee in mugs so chipped and dirty they'd get a restaurant closed down.

'Thanks.'

He clunks his pot against hers and gives a reassuring wink, as he's done a hundred times before when they've worked together. 'So what do you want to do?'

Mitzi puts her hands around the mug and is comforted by its warmth. 'You didn't charge him yet?'

'He thinks we did, but no.' The custody sergeant points to the admin book on the countertop and the ugly black pen dangling on a steel chain. 'Logan and I didn't write him up. Far as we're concerned, there was a call-out but your man ain't never been in here.'

'Appreciate that.' She knows the risks they've taken. If there'd been an incident – if Alfie had got physical, hurt himself or someone else, then the proverbial shit and fan would have come together.

'If you want him in court, I need to get someone go through your statement with you and have you examined and photographed.' He stares into her eyes. It's the concerned look of a friend as much as a colleague. 'Did he mark you, Mitzi? Have you still got bruises that'll show?'

She feels ashamed. It's not her fault but she feels like crying because of what she's let him do to her. Their dirty secret. 'Yeah. I got stuff to show.'

He nods. This isn't the time to push it. One word from this angel and he'll personally see the bum behind bars gets every one of his no-good bones broken.

She sips her coffee and weighs up the dilemma. Alfie gets charged then he sure as hell stays away from her and the girls. If she cuts him a break, he could get the wrong idea and think their marriage is still alive.

'I don't know what to do, Bobby.'

He wants to help but knows the dangers. 'Got to be your decision, Mitz. Way I see it, you're damned whatever you do. We process this guy, he gets a record, then, shit, you know how hard it is to get a job after that.'

She nods.

'We don't put him through the system, then he's coming right back at you.'

The old-timer bangs a fist against his heart. 'Go with this, Mitz. If your brain's run out on you, then go with whatever you feel in here.'

'Emptiness, Bobby. That's all I feel right now. Emptiness.'

52

DOWNTOWN, LOS ANGELES

It's worth it just for the look on her face.

JJ has to fight back a smile as all of the women settle at their machines and Jenny Harrison looks around for her friend. He can see her glancing repeatedly at the empty seat, wondering if the absence is due to oversleeping, overindulgence or overdosing.

'Anyone seen Kim?'

She's asking the silly bitches either side of her. How sweet. How nice to be concerned about her co-worker – her co-bully. What a shock she's going to get when she finds out the truth.

Harrison puts a hand in her jeans and pulls out a pink cell phone.

'No phones,' he shouts across the room, walking towards her. 'You should have left that in your locker.'

'I won't be a minute.'

'You won't even be that. You know the rules – no phones in the machine room. Give it to me. You can have it at the end of the day.'

Her mouth is open. A white worm of chewing gum lies on a pink floor. 'Did Kim call in, Mr James?'

Mr James. How quickly they learn. Amazing what the fear of God can do to mannerless little whores like this one. 'No, she didn't. Phone, please.' He holds out his hand.

She gives it to him. 'I think she's sick. She was coming down with something last night. Said she thought she had a dose of flu.'

Liar. She's just covering for her. 'No show, no pay. You all know that.' He's only said what they'd expect him to say. No reason for him to treat Bass's absence with anything but annoyance. He's one down. Productivity is falling.

JJ takes the phone to his office. Sits at his desk with the door shut and scrolls through her messages. Most are to Bass. The ones that aren't are to a guy called Marlon. Probably her pimp. They're short and not at all sweet.

MARLON WEN U DUN?

JENNY: 20

MARLON: U GOT LESS THAN 2 AN U GET CUT UP
BITCH

Seems that given time Marlon might well carry out JJ's wishes for him. But he has no intention of waiting. He turns off the phone and puts it on the edge of the desk.

Jenny Harrison won't be missing her friend for long.

53

Alfie Fallon sits alone in the holding cage like an abandoned mongrel dog. Life as he knew it is over. That much he gets. The motley mob he's spent the night with have all been processed through the system and like an unwanted stray he's the last one waiting for his name to be called.

The air is sharp with the sting of industrial-strength disinfectant, the floor freshly mopped after hours of people vomiting and relieving themselves. He'd give anything for a hot shower, a walk outside and a decent breakfast.

A distant noise makes him look up. When you're in the pen you know someone is coming long before you see them. The lack of carpets, curtains or anything soft for that matter, means sounds from far away skim down the hard corridors until they hit your ears. After an hour or so you're an expert on identifying everything from a lock opening to a van of new arrivals backing up in the yard outside.

Someone's coming. And they can only be coming for him.

Buzzers sound. Metal doors slide open then clunk closed again. Feet slap on hard floors. His time is up. Alfie puts his hands on his knees and rolls his head side to side until it cracks the stiffness out of his neck.

The outer gates of the pen slide open. Mitzi. His hopes rise. The little old guy who scowled at him last night is with her as well. They've both got blank faces – hard faces – cop faces. Mitzi rests her hands on the inner gate, 'They're going to charge you with assault, Alfie. Most likely you'll be in court in a couple of hours. I've talked to my lawyer and he'll be serving you with divorce papers as soon as they cut you loose.'

'Mitzi, listen—'

'No, Alfie. *You* listen.' Her voice is calm and without a hint of the fear and dread racing inside her. 'I've got to do what I've told every other woman over the years to do. You have to be dealt with properly, then life goes on. Whatever it is, whatever mess is left, life goes on.' She turns to Bobby Sheen and touches his arm. 'Thanks for looking out for me. I'm gonna go.'

'Mitzi!' Alfie is at the bars now. '*Wait.*'

Mother of two, wife of a decade and a half, LAPD hard-ass Mitzi Fallon is four steps away from moving on with her life. No looking back. No regrets.

'Mitzi!'

She stops and turns.

'I still love you.' His face says he does. Really does. He'd give anything for this not to be happening, for his life not to have disintegrated like this.

'And I still love you.' Her feet are glued to the spot. 'But not as much as I did. And I love the girls too much for this to go on any longer.'

Now she goes. Walks head held high. Heart beating like the drum at the front of the Macy's Day Parade. With any luck she'll make it to the washroom before she breaks down and wonders how she's going to cope for the rest of the day, let alone the rest of her life.

54

ITALY

It's the middle of the night in Turin. The bed in the rented room is still made, pristine. The monk hasn't sat on it, let alone slept there.

Ephrem is naked as he kneels and prays inside the single wardrobe. The door is closed tight and he feels comforted in the claustrophobic and airless space. He longs to be returned to the seclusion of the monastery where the unblinking kiln master will watch bemused as he bricks him into the sanctuary.

The hands that are joined together have taken many lives. Not so many that he can't remember each and every one but too many for all but a soldier – a crusader – to live with.

He prays, first in Aramaic, then in French and finally in Latin. He prays for God's strength and guidance for what he is about to do. Just before twilight he opens the wardrobe and spends half an hour stretching away the pain of motionless devotion. He focuses his mind. Then he clenches his fists and adopts the press-up position. His knuckles glow white with the weight of his body as he lowers and raises himself so slowly that the movement is imperceptible. Each press-up takes more than five minutes to complete. By the end of the hour his naked body is bathed in sweat. His abdomen, thighs and shoulders are muscular coils of writhing, sinewy snakes. He wants to collapse and rest on the floor, wants to rest and recover, but he knows it would be a personal indulgence and personal indulgences are sinful.

Ephrem takes a freezing cold shower, towels dry, then drinks a litre of bottled water. It's all that will pass his lips. He eats only every other day and today is the fast. He dresses in black, the traditional colour of his order, in T-shirt, sweater, trousers, socks and long wool overcoat, and pulls on a tight, black hat that covers his dark, close-cropped hair. He touches the hidden tools concealed about him within the layers of clothing – two knives, a garrotte, a spike and a coil of razor-thread no more conspicuous than a dental floss container.

The first pink light of dawn breaks over the rooftops. In the shadowy, night-frosted street he walks quietly from his hotel, clears the windshield of the rental car and patiently begins his day's work.

55

The call takes Amy Chang by surprise.

It's been a long day and she's just scrubbed up after dealing with a fatal RTA. Her secretary says Mitzi Fallon is waiting in her office. She glances at her watch – it's almost six-thirty. She wonders what her friend wants so late in the day and why she didn't call to say she was coming over. The two women go back a long way. Mitzi was on the first case Amy dealt with and since then they've grown close. A friendship born out of professional respect and common values.

The detective is sat on a moulded black chair, busy frowning at her phone when Amy walks in pulling a small jacket over her shoulders. 'So, Lieutenant Fallon, to what do I owe this unexpected pleasure?'

Mitzi looks up. Seems her bad news hasn't reached the morgue yet. 'Passing through. The girls are staying over at a friend's after soccer – I just found out they won two-nil. I hoped maybe you had time for a drink or some dinner?'

Amy's face brightens. 'Both sound good.'

'Both it is, then. My treat.'

She nods to her glass-walled office. 'Give me a minute. I need to grab some work.'

A few minutes later they walk out arm-in-arm and even

while they're making small talk she knows something's wrong. But she says nothing. Mitzi will tell her in her own good time. They drive separately to Amy's favourite Asian-Cuban place. It's more bistro than full-on starched-cloth restaurant. It has warm woods on the floor and walls and they both like the fact the waitresses are real waitresses not would-be actresses.

After a couple of margaritas and a starter of Tunapica with cucumber salad, Mitzi downs her fork and unburdens herself. 'Alfie and I had a fight. A big physical one.' She turns her face so Amy can detect the bruise beneath the concealer.

The pathologist stops eating.

'I threw him out. When he came back I called the cops and got him processed.' Mitzi downs the rest of her cocktail. 'I think I'm going to need more of those.'

Amy's in shock. 'How long's this been going on?'

'Jeez. How long hasn't it?' She catches the eye of the waitress. 'Two more peach margaritas please – the big ones.' She waits until she's gone. 'On and off he's been beating on me for something like a decade.' Shame rises like backwash.

'Oh, Mitz, I'm so sorry.' Amy reaches across the table and touches her arm tenderly. 'You did the right thing.'

'I know. Should have done it years ago.'

'It's never that simple, though – what with the girls and everything.'

'Nope. Funny, you hear about domestic violence and say that'll never happen to me. No man would *dare* lay a hand on me. But it's different when he does. You get so screwed up in your head you blame yourself. You kid yourself that it wasn't deliberate, it was a mistake. Life's full of mistakes, eh?'

'Tell me.'

The new drinks arrive and Mitzi dives in straight away. 'I may get wasted tonight.'

'Go for it.'

They clink glasses and the lieutenant smiles for the first time in days.

56

TURIN

The disused church is exactly where they told Ephrem it would be. At the end of a windy little street, behind a broken fence, hiding a small, cramped graveyard overrun by grass and weeds. The headstones are mould-green and long-forgotten. Like ancient teeth that have decayed, they lie at twisted angles in soft, subsiding plots.

The monk walks the perimeter. Church stone that was originally the colour of honey has been blackened by time and dirt. Someone has smashed most of the handcrafted stained-glass windows that bore the Stations of the Cross. Gang graffiti has been spray-painted over the rusted metal, symbols and names that he doesn't understand and doesn't give much thought to as he levers off the panels that bar the ancient front doors through which centuries of worshippers walked.

The inside is dark. Hardly any light penetrates the boarded-up windows and time-weathered holes in the unrepaired roof. Most people would struggle to see more than a few feet. But Ephrem has spent most of his life in total darkness and sees right into the furthest corner. The smell is of damp, rotting timbers and the faeces of rodents that have made this place their sanctuary. But the monk, as no one else could, can still smell candle wax, the incense of High Mass, the fresh soap on the skins of those who washed themselves knowing they would come and kneel in the presence of their Lord.

He moves past the broken pews and the empty space where the altar once stood. He turns to his left and finds what he came for. With a little work it will be perfect.

Just perfect.

57

BOYLE HEIGHTS, LOS ANGELES

'Kim? Hey Kim, you in there?'

Jenny Harrison shouts and squints through the mail slot of Kim Bass's apartment. Her friend can be such an idiot sometimes. If she does too many pills or hits on a half-decent guy, Jen doesn't hear from her for ages. Over Christmas she went on a binge with a cabbie and disappeared until New Year.

Odd for her not to turn up for work, though. She's broke and needs every dime right at the moment. 'Kim, if you're in there, stop messing around. It's Jen, I need to talk to you.'

Harrison lets the slot snap shut and bangs the flat of her hand on the door. Goddamn it. She spends half her freakin' life chasing after this girl. She walks away, calling her friend's cell phone as she does. It rings for a long time before going to the answerphone. 'Okay, Kimmy, if you don't get your sorry ass to call me, this best friend is soon going to be an ex-friend. It's Thursday night and we're supposed to be meeting those delivery guys. Call me or else.'

She stomps down the stairs, turns the corner and almost bowls over an old man levering himself up by the handrail.

'*Shi-it*! Mr Dobbs you nearly give me a heart attack.'

The bald-headed seventy-year-old is Kim's next door neighbour. Leroy Dobbs looks as shocked as she does. He keeps himself to himself and as far as seniors go he's okay. The girls even bummed cream and coffee off him one Sunday when they had hangovers so bad they couldn't crawl to the store to buy any.

He puts his hand to his bony chest. 'I'm the one should be cursing. You shouldn't come flying round the corner like that.'

'Sorry, Mr D. Hey, you haven't seen Kim, have you? She didn't make work today. Have you heard her knocking about?'

He looks cross. 'I mind my own business, I do. I don't go spying like some people around here. I ain't seen her.'

'I didn't say you were spying.' Harrison nods to the apartment upstairs and behind her. 'It's just the walls are thin and Kim says you like banging on them if she watches TV in her bedroom.'

'That's because it's so loud. I might be old but I'm not deaf.'

'Did you hear her?'

'Not last night, I didn't. I didn't hear no TV at all last night.'

Harrison thinks back to standing in her own doorway and waving goodbye to her friend. Kim was pretty wasted when she went. Both of them were. Crazy bitch had done too much blow.

'Can I get past now?' Dobbs is staring up from two steps down, frail fingers clutching the rail.

She weaves her way round him and over the remaining steps. Outside she lights a cigarette and walks the rest of the way home. Something's wrong. She feels it deep inside.

By the time she reaches her own porch, Jenny Harrison is sure she knows what it is.

58

Tonight Mitzi's only answer is drink. Drink to forget. Drink to lose consciousness if necessary. Drink to wipe out the memory that she pulled a gun on her husband and almost shot him.

She and Amy leave their cars at the restaurant and catch a cab back to the pathologist's place, where a bottle of cold white is uncorked before they do anything else. After shuffling the iPod into oblivion, Amy grabs blankets and pillows and makes up the sofa. One day she'll buy a two-bed place but not for a while – probably not until she gets herself a long-term man, a stayer. 'So where's Tricky Nicky?" she asks her friend.

Mitzi grins drunkenly from a chair she's slumped into. 'Italy. Turin.' Her wine glass wobbles. She wisely decides to hold it by the bowl rather than its elegant stem. 'Poor schmuck has been flying almost all day.'

'Oh.'

'*Oh?* That all you were thinking when you mentioned him?'

Amy smiles.

'Or maybe you were thinking, I wish I was in Italy with Nic. Quite a romantic country, Italy. Poetry. Violins. All that stuff.' She raises her glass. 'And really great wine.'

'It crossed my mind.'

'Course it did, sister. And so it should.'

'He's a bit uptight, though, Mitz. I know he's been through a lot but it seems his head is still a mess.'

'Probably is. Give the boy time.'

Amy remembers their afternoon at the boatyard together. 'I think he's going to need months – maybe years.'

'Could be.' Mitzi slugs a jolt of the cold, crisp Sauvignon. 'Worth waiting for though. He's a good guy.' She tries to blot out thoughts of her husband. Damn him. Alfie had been a good guy once. Damn the hell out of him for going from good guy to bum so easily.

'Why is Nic in Italy?'

'Long story. To do with Tamara Jacobs, that writer you had on your slab.' Mitzi sits up out of her slouch. 'Seems she's involved somehow with the Shroud. That's why Nic's there.'

The pathologist is left frowning at the sudden switch in conversation. 'Shroud? As in Shroud of Turin?'

''Less you know of another? Anyways, what do you think? Real or not?'

Amy suddenly feels exhausted. 'Mind if we do the brain-teasers tomorrow? I'm feeling beat and really need to turn in.'

'Sure. No problem.'

Amy gets up and switches off several lamps. 'Do you want me to fetch you some water before I go?'

Mitzi raises her glass of wine in one hand and the open bottle in the other.

'Okay, I get the message. Take it easy, though.' The medic walks over, leans into the chair and hugs her friend. 'Hope you get some sleep.'

'Me too.'

She heads to her room. If Mitzi had been sober, Amy would have asked her. Asked if there'd ever been anything between her and Nic. There'd been rumours, but then of course there are always rumours when men and women work closely together. But she still wonders.

59

FRIDAY

TURIN, ITALY

The morning sky over what was once Italy's first capital city is a magnificent mural of kingly gold and cardinal red.

Nic Karakandez stands hypnotised at the bedroom window of the cheap hotel he's booked into. He watches the dark chrysalis of night turn into the exotic butterfly of day. Somewhere out there, among the mysterious shapes, beneath the rows of red-tiled rooftops and within the swollen domes of ancient churches, lies the reason he's travelled thousands of miles. He showers in a bathroom so small it could make an ant claustrophobic, then dresses in black jeans, white shirt and a purple wool V-neck that somehow still smells of the deck oil from his boat. He sits on the saggy bed and takes a minute to go over the main lead Mitzi has him chasing.

Money.

To be more specific, a series of international bank transfer payments Sarah Kenny made on Tamara Jacobs's request to a man they know to be Roberto Craxi. The pieces of paper spread out before him show deposits of $5000 a month for eleven months, plus two lump sums of $25,000. Close to $100k in total. That's a nice amount. The kind of cash for which many people would be willing to break the law.

The next leads come from the writer's visits to Turin. Receipts found in her home show she made four trips in the past two years. Two in the last six months. One six weeks before she was killed. Nic is hoping the hotel bills, and restaurant and taxi tickets will help him retrace her steps. Then there are the last quarter's cell phone records showing more than thirty calls made to different Turin numbers. As he looks at the digits he has a bad feeling. She may well have had security on her mind. If that's the case, the numbers may well be street phones and untraceable calls.

He takes breakfast in a damp and draughty room that's being warmed by fan heaters at the foot of peeling cream walls. He hand-wipes condensation from the window by his table and looks out across frosted lawns to a paved courtyard, bordered by flowerbeds and potted Cypress trees. In summer this place might well change identities and pass itself off as quaint and delightful.

180

A young waitress, maybe the daughter of the owner, brings him cappuccino, a near-perfect brew of strong roasted beans topped by a thick, sweet creamy froth that you could stand a spoon in. He collects OJ from the small buffet table and takes a couple of homemade pastries.

Full and happy he goes to his room, scrubs his teeth, grabs a loose black leather jacket and walks back downstairs to wait for his allocated Carabinieri contact. He sits on an old couch in the tiny reception and tries to make sense of a copy of today's *Corriere della Serra* newspaper. Bad idea. Beyond Chianti, Quattro Formaggio and a few curses from *The Sopranos*, he can't make out a word.

An elegant woman in a navy blue jacket and matching knee-length skirt hesitantly interrupts his stilted reading. 'Signore Carry-can-diss?'

He looks up. 'Ka-ra-kan-dez. Yes, that's me.'

She's a couple of years younger than him, has short dark hair and intense blue eyes. 'Luogotenente Cappelini. Carlotta.' She confidently offers her hand.

He's surprised. Even annoyed with himself, for automatically expecting the liaison officer to be a man. 'Nic – very pleased to meet you.'

'Welcome to Torino, Nic.' She can tell that he expected her to be male – most people do. 'Are you ready to go?'

'I am.' He refolds the newspaper and places it on a well-worn wooden table.

Carlotta leads the way out. 'First we go to my office, we can talk confidentially there. Then we go wherever you need. My capitano says you have phone numbers and a man called Craxi you wish to have traced. I have people ready to help with that.'

'Music to my ears.'

She doesn't understand. '*Scusi?*'

'Sorry, just an expression. That would be great.'

The streets are wide and cobbled, blocks of stone intercut with steel channels for trams. Overhead a black cobweb of cable wires sag beneath the now dull grey sky. As they walk Nic spots the butt of a gun belted discreetly under her jacket. 'Do you always carry a weapon?'

'*Si*. Always. I am a soldier, I have to.' She touches it. 'But I like to, also.' She smiles. 'I like shooting.'

'What do you like shooting – things or people?'

'No.' She laughs. 'Shooting people is not what I like.'

'Not even the bad guys?'

She can tell he's teasing. 'No, this I have never done. But shooting on the range, then yes, that I like very much.' She makes a pistol out of her fingers and lets off a pretend round. 'I am very good at the shooting.'

He's sure she is. Probably much better at the shooting than at the English. Not that he should judge – he can't read an Italian newspaper, let alone speak a sentence.

'And you, Nic, you shoot the bad guys?'

'Sometimes,' he says. 'But not as many as I'd like to.'

182

60

As a small child, Ephrem learned to be silent. The monks would scourge the backs of his hands if they could even hear him breathe during their lessons. They educated him in the fine art of listening – how to concentrate first on what others said and only then respond.

When he was growing up they taught him about pain. How to endure it. How to turn off his thoughts while the white heat of a branding iron sizzled his skin. And he was schooled in how to *inflict* pain. How to use it as an instrument. How to use the threat of physical agony to do God's work.

As a man, he has learned transparency. How to walk among the ignorant as one of them. How to look at them and smile at them in ways that don't attract attention, create affection or leave any kind of memory. He learned the art of being instantly forgettable.

All those years of training and discipline surface in Ephrem as he parks the rental car about a mile from where he's been told the target will be. Jacket turned up against the wind and showers, he walks head down along the roadside, certain motorists flashing past in the rush-hour traffic will never remember him.

The monk is doing what he does best. He is becoming a sleight of hand. An illusion. Someone no one ever saw.

61

There is a stench inside the house. One like nothing else on earth. An odour few have ever been exposed to. He should have bathed her last night instead of just cleaning her with a flannel. He'd been too tired to do it. Too exhausted after vanquishing the tormentor Kim Bass.

Now Em needs him. He kneels on the boards of the bedroom floor and is shocked by what he sees. She is changing. Her eyes are covered in a thick milky veil, her flesh is discolouring. Even in the low light he can see the greenish tinge to her skin.

JJ reaches out to her face and strokes the dark birthmark, the sign from God that drew him to her.

Gravity has taken its course. Blood has drained from her heart and pooled in her buttocks, back and legs creating a layer of putrid purple and red. Bacteria is spreading through the body and it is beginning to marble. Hair is coming away and gasses and fluid ooze from her orifices into the fetid air of the room. He stands and backs away. He may have to give her up. Find a separate resting place for her. But not yet. Not until he absolutely has to.

62

Through the top-floor window of Carlotta Cappelini's city centre office, Nic can see the strange soaring spire of the city's famous Mole Antonelliana, originally a Jewish temple built in the 1800s, now a national cinema museum.

His attention has wandered because for the last ten minutes the Carabinieri lieutenant has been jabbering away in bullet-fast Italian on the phone. What's also distracting him is the realisation that the more progress he makes here, the less chance there is of him setting sail for a new life in just a couple of weeks. Trace a killer and the district attorney heaps a hill of paperwork on your head. Trace one on another continent and he drops a mountain on your skull.

Carlotta finishes the call and sees he's troubled. 'Is everything with you okay?'

Her mangled language helps him shake off the depression. 'Yes. I'm sorry. Everything with me is very much okay.' He reaches inside his jacket and produces a folded sheet of paper. 'These are the numbers we mentioned to your boss. Once we've got a trace, I want to meet the phone owner immediately. I'm guessing that Craxi is at least one of them. I don't want anyone asking questions until I'm face to face with him.'

'I understand. You are afraid he may run.'

'Very.'

She points a slim finger tipped in a very light shade of pink nail polish. 'These numbers here is – how you say . . . ' She struggles. '. . . *cellulare o cell*?'

'Cell phone?'

'Ah, yes.' She points again. 'And this here – they are public phones, ones in the street.' Her eyes move down the lines. 'But one or two numbers are private lines. Craxi is a common name - like your Smith or Jones.'

She pulls over the keypad of her computer terminal and expertly touch-types an instruction into the command terminal. '*Finito*. They will be traced very shortly.'

'*Grazie.*'

She smiles. 'You speak any Italian?'

He smiles back. '*Si.* I'm fluent in *grazie* and *prego*. Oh, and parmigiano and pesto.'

'*Va bene*. These are good words to know.' She glances at her monitor. 'Your victim, I read she was a famous writer.'

'Scriptwriter not author. No books to her name. I'd never heard of her before, but apparently she was big in Hollywood circles.'

Carlotta frowns. 'Do you have idea why she was killed?'

'We're working on it. Maybe something to do with the project she was writing.'

She puts a hand on a two-page document. 'I read the briefing you sent – you mean the movie about our Shroud?'

186

'Seems that way. Has anything particularly unusual happened to it recently?'

'Nothing ever happens to it. It is in a sealed case in the Duomo di San Giovanni in the darkness.'

'But it does come out regularly, right?'

She shakes her head. 'No. Last time the Church exhibited it was in 2010.'

'In the cathedral?'

'*Si,* but with big protection.' She draws a huge square in the air with both hands. 'They build a giant box of bullet-proof glass. In it they put the Shroud – a sealed case filled with nitrogen.'

'And a lot of people came to view this?'

Carlotta laughs. 'More than one hundred thousand people a day – *every* day. For five weeks they queue.' She pauses while she tries to remember more about the last exposition. 'I read that in those weeks, three and a half million people come. This is more in weeks than visit the grave of your John F. Kennedy every year.'

Nic is amused by the comparison. 'I wasn't aware the two were in competition.'

'It is good they were not. The Shroud would have won. Easily. Catholics will always win these kinds of things. Death and religion are very important to us.'

'I'll keep it in mind. So I guess it is no longer on display?'

'No. Displays are very rare. It is kept in a permanent case, closed within an alcove of the Duomo, where visitors can come to pray. The church has some private security – they

187

do not tell us exactly – and of course we have our own people watching the cathedral all the time.'

'So it could never be stolen or damaged?'

She shrugs. 'This you cannot say. In 1997 there was arson. Firemen had to break into the cabinet. They use their axes and sledgehammers to smash through the glass, thick bulletproof glass – then they had to pull it from the flames.'

'Was it damaged?'

'No, not that time, but before, yes. A long time ago, in the sixteenth century there was another fire – again arson – and, yes, that did damage it.'

'In the same church?'

'No. Back then it was in France, in the Saint Chapelle Chapel in Chambéry.'

'What was it doing there?'

'I believe it was in possession of the House of Savoy. In those days there was much theft and looting. Today, here, security is very good.' She says it with confidence and reassurance. 'These days you cannot get anywhere near the Holy Shroud.'

'Really?' He nods to the computer. 'While we're waiting for those telephone traces, why don't we give it a try?'

63

He tests the water with his wrist – like a parent does for a baby.

Not too hot. Not too cold. Blood temperature. He squeezes washing-up liquid into the water and stirs it until a layer of bubbles covers the surface.

JJ puts down the plastic bottle and returns to the bedroom. His knees crack as he crouches. Carefully he scoops Em's naked corpse into his arms and carries her across the room. In a mirror he glimpses himself with her. It's a powerful sight. Heroic. Like a firefighter carrying a woman from a blazing building. Like an angel of God saving a sinner from the fires of hell.

He carries her to the bathroom and lowers the love of his life into the soapy tub. Water sloshes over the side. It pools around his bare feet and sinks into the wooden boards. There are candles around the bathroom, on the floor, shelves and window ledge. Diamonds of golden light dance in the water. It makes him think of a baptism font.

She looks heavier somehow. Almost as though death has been good to her. Fattened her up. Fed her well. And peaceful too. He's never seen anyone look more at rest than Em does.

JJ strips and steps into the lukewarm water. He grimaces as suds splash over the side. He wants this to be perfect. Nothing must be wrong. They have so little time together.

He lowers himself further. Manoeuvres his body under hers. Wraps his arms around her breasts and holds her close for one final time.

64

A gust of wind irreverently shoves Carlotta and Nic down the hallowed and brutally open approach to the Duomo di Torino e Cappella della Sacra Sindone.

The cathedral has a near-white Renaissance frontage, newly cleaned, and is itself incongruously dwarfed by the spiral sprouting dome of Guarini's Chapel of the Holy Shroud.

'*Buongiorno*,' calls Carlotta to the small thin man clad in black robes waiting in the shelter of the front entrance. 'This is Lieutenant Karakandez, from the Los Angeles Police Department.'

The robed man politely dips his head of steely grey hair as he shakes hands with the big detective. 'Dino di Rossi – I am, what I think you say, is the verger.' He glances side-ward. 'Luogotenente Cappelini wishes that I accompany you and answer any questions about the building and the Shroud.'

'Good to meet you. Thanks for doing this at short notice.'

Nic follows Carlotta and the verger up the cathedral steps and through giant eighteenth-century wooden doors. Above his head he sees a copy of Leonardo's *Last Supper* and to his left – much to his surprise – a stall selling books, postcards, DVDs and cheap prints of the Shroud. A long nave spills out in front of them and down the side are two giant wall-mounted TV screens showing footage of the Shroud. The commodifying of the relic extends to plastic, electrically operated offertories, where pilgrims are encouraged to drop euros through a slot in return for the right to say a prayer and light a plastic candle. Far ahead is the more impressive transept and sacristy.

'This architecture – it touches your soul, no?' says di Rossi, in a hushed voice, as they walk the marble-tiled floor. 'It conveys to the devoted, the experience of entering death and of reaching the light of divine glory.'

Nic wouldn't go that far; but the altar, flanked by massive marble statues and a startling central crucifixion scene, is certainly something.

'The sculptures are of Saint Theresa and Saint Christina.' Di Rossi gestures to them. 'Made in Rome in 1715 by the Parisian sculptor Pietro Legros. The great wooden statue of the crucifix was carved by Francesco Borelli.'

'And the Shroud?' asks Nic, almost impatiently. 'Where is that kept?'

Di Rossi sighs as he leads him through the pews and past a stack of hard, brown metal chairs. 'Here,' the verger points to a strange roped-off area in the far corner of the cathedral.

To Nic's untrained eye the chapel looks like a couple of theatre boxes stacked on top of each other. The upper one has wide, gold columns, a gold balcony and above it a giant ornate centrepiece of what looks like golden angels plus a huge crown and a red shield with a white cross on it.

'That is the Royal Tribune.' Di Rossi's fingers flutter skywards. 'Carved by Ignazio Perucca in 1777. The Kings of Piedmont and Sardinia stood there. It has been graced by Carlo Emmanuele III, Carlo Alberto of the Savoy-Carignano line and the first King of Italy, Vittorio Emmanuele II.'

Nic's eyes drop to the lesser looking box under it. One with stone pillars and a bulletproof glass window.

'The lower tribune is where the royal pages sat. This is now the home of the Shroud – the cloth in which the body of our Lord Jesus Christ was wrapped after his death on Calvary.'

65

CARSON, LOS ANGELES

JJ curls his toes around the metal chain and pulls the plug. He lies there savouring the final moments as the soapy water drains off him and his queen. The noise of the bath emptying is irritating. Inappropriate.

He stays motionless. Plays dead. Doesn't blink or twitch a muscle as he concentrates on lowering his heartbeat and slowing his breathing. Water trapped between their bodies slowly pours away, creating the sensation that Em is touching him. The bathroom grows cold. The chilly air and metal of the old tub rapidly cool his flesh. He knows that if he stays as he is, his body temperature will soon match hers. They will become as one. United in death. Together for ever.

'One day, my love.' He kisses the back of her neck. 'One day I will join you.'

She is difficult to move without the buoyancy of the water. The wetness of their bodies seems to glue them together. Finally, he stands outside the tub, shivering in the candlelight. His feet make prints on the boards as he takes a towel from an old wooden rail and dries himself warm.

Warm – the difference between him and his love. The difference between life and death. He leans over the tub and pats her dry as best he can. Getting her out is harder than he imagined. The old-fashioned bath is too deep for him to be able to lift her without falling forward. In the end he stands opposite the taps, grips her beneath the armpits and pulls. Her skin feels like it's moving. Slackening and shifting as he touches it.

He lowers her to the floor and dries the parts he missed. She smells clean. Clean and fresh. He's too tired now to move her further. Too emotionally drained and distressed by the thought that his time with her is running out. He takes talc from a recessed shelf behind the bath and shakes the scented powder over her body. Smooths it out. Covers every inch. Until Em is as white as an angel.

Now he does the same to himself. Makes sure he is dusted from head to toe. Shrouded in white. He lies next to her. Two ghosts in the twilight. He pulls towels over them to keep warm. Snuggles up. Presses close and shares his warmth with her.

66

TURIN

Behind protective glass the casket sits covered by a dull cloth bearing a central red stripe and a crucifix. Above it is a bizarre tangle of giant thorns. Over the brambles, a cheap digital blow-up of the face of what Nic calls Shroudman hangs on a dark and dusty curtain. The unlikely home of the world's most famous religious relic.

'The Holy Shroud, like the Veil of Veronica, is a unique scientific, historical and religious artefact.' Di Rossi points as he explains. 'We now believe it was also shown far across the Middle East. History records it once being given to Abgar, the King of the ancient city of Edessa, and it is said to have cured him of illness. The Orthodox Greeks hold the image in the highest respect. They call it *Acheiropoieton* – an Icon Not Made by Hands.'

Nic feels he's being whitewashed. Just as surely as if he'd caught a spaced-out Westmont gangbanger trawling on Sunset. 'You said Veronica. Who was she and what's special about her veil?'

Di Rossi puts his hands to his face and mimes drying it with a towel. 'As Christ carried the cross on the way to Calvary, he wiped his face on a cloth given him by a woman called Veronica from Jerusalem – now Saint Veronica. After he had gone, the image of his face appeared on the cloth. The Church has venerated this event by marking it as one of the Stations of the Cross.'

'I'm going to burn in hell for asking, but the Stations of the Cross?'

Di Rossi's face registers shock and disappointment. 'They are the fourteen key historical Christian moments, marked usually in paintings or statues or stained glass. They show the stages of Christ's journey from when he was condemned to death to when his body was taken from the cross on Mount Calvary and sealed in the tomb of Joseph of Arimathea. The incident with the *sudarium* – the sweat cloth – is the sixth Station.'

The verger glances at his wristwatch. 'I realise, Signore, that you have many questions – and many doubts – but I am afraid I am now late and must go.'

'I'm very grateful for your help,' says Nic, aware he's being brushed off. 'One thing before you leave.' He nods to the glass and the cloth-covered casket. 'I'd like to see the Shroud, the actual cloth.'

'I am sorry, that is not possible. The Holy Shroud is locked and sealed in a metal and glass container.'

'Seals can be broken. I'd like it opened please.'

'I am sure you would but it is not possible. Only the Pontiff himself can order an exposition of the Holy Shroud.'

Nic's face reddens. 'You mean only the Pope can break the seals and open up the container?'

Di Rossi tries to keep anger out of his reply. 'No. The Holy Father is not the custodian of the keys. That is not what I told you. But he is the only one who can command any viewing of the Sacra Sindone.'

Nic looks to Carlotta. 'I guess that's not true – the Carabinieri could order the Shroud to be opened up for inspection, couldn't they?'

She looks nervous at being put on the spot. 'I think this is not even something I could request. It would have to come from our Generale.'

Without asking, Nic knows that would be a drawn-out route. He turns back to the verger. 'So if the Pope isn't the keeper of the keys, who is?'

'This I cannot tell you.'

'Cannot or will not?'

'Signore.' He sounds exasperated. 'Security is of utmost importance to us. I act under instruction from the Archbishop, and he in turn from the Pontiff himself.'

'Then I need to see him.'

'His Eminence is not in Turin at the present. I will pass your request to his secretariat.'

Nic's had enough of being jerked about. 'Then I'd like to speak to him on the phone. Today. *Now* if possible.'

The verger's eyes turn as cold as the statues around him. 'I regret this meeting is now over. I have tried to be of assistance. Give your details to the Luogotenente. I will pass your request to His Eminence.' Di Rossi's black cloak swirls as he turns and walks away, leaving Nic staring at the bulletproof glass separating him from one of the biggest mysteries of modern times and maybe the answer to his homicide case.

67

Beneath the leaden sky of Piedmont's capital, eighteen kilometres of arcades cover the sidewalks and shelter innumerable cafés. The sit-and-watch-the-world culture is a legacy from the time Turin was ruled by the House of Savoy and established as one of the arts capitals of the world.

In a bar populated more by locals than tourists, Ephrem realises the target he's been following since the man parked an hour ago is about to make his first mistake.

He's heading to the restroom.

The monk could take him there. It would be messy but possible. His hand finds the dental floss container in his pocket and he imagines the thin wire it conceals being stretched around the throat of the man he's hunting. Too risky. Too impetuous. Too public.

He dismisses the thought. Patience is a virtue. He must wait.

After a few minutes the man emerges. Ephrem slips from the cover of the arcade entrance directly opposite where he's been pretending to make a phone call. The target moves cautiously, like he senses he's being watched, like he knows this is the time anyone tracking him would have to break cover and fall in behind in order to pick up his trail. Ephrem is impressed by the caution – the confidence – the casual and controlled way the man walks about, looking around without any discernible effort, taking in all three hundred and sixty degrees of his environment without being obvious. He too shows no sign of hurry or nerves. They are worthy enemies.

The monk varies the distance he tracks from, sometimes coming within touching distance, often hanging so far back the target is just a dot in the distance. He swaps his black woollen hat for a green baseball cap, reverses his coat to change from black to green.

Over the course of an hour Ephrem becomes at least four different people, each with their own different way of walking and holding themselves. He is tourist, businessman, shopper, late-for-a-date boyfriend. Anyone other than who he really is.

A trained assassin closing in on his prey.

68

Nic and Carlotta take a table at the rear of the Baratti and Milano café with a view into the grand marble-floored atrium of a high-class shopping gallery. She hands him a menu across a table topped with fresh flowers and a crisp cotton cloth of burned orange. 'Di Rossi – he is only following instructions. It is best to remember the Catholic Church is a law unto itself.'

He takes the menu. 'No, it isn't. Nothing anywhere in the world is a law unto itself. This guy is not even going to talk to the Bishop and ask for me to see the Shroud, is he?'

'Archbishop,' she corrects him. 'Why is this so important for you?'

He lowers the menu. 'Where I come from making cases means finding out what people don't want to show you. When someone snow-blinds me like your verger did, I know there is some kind of a cover-up going on.'

A waitress arrives and Carlotta talks in Italian, occasionally pointing at Nic. The girl gives him a studied look and then slips away.

He realises Carlotta just ordered for him.

She smiles almost mischievously. 'This place, it is famous for espresso and hot chocolate. I also order their *tramezzini* –

small sandwiches of ham, mozzarella, salmon, tuna and vegetables. And the *Torta barattina*.'

'Tart of the House?'

'Very good.' She laughs at him. Another time, another place, he might even be fun to be with. 'Thick chocolate tart, with cream and raspberries.'

'You think I have a sweet tooth?'

'There must be *something* sweet about you. I am hoping the food will change your mood. In Italy when men are sour-tempered, we feed them things to make them sweet.'

'I think I have good reason to be sour-tempered.'

'Perhaps.' She notices he's playing with the wedding band on his finger, twisting it round and round. It's a chance to change the subject. 'You and your wife have any children?' She nods at the ring.

Nic stares through her. He heard the question but at the back of his mind he's still processing information about the verger. The guy's behaviour was odd. Not quite right in some way, but he doesn't yet know exactly why.

'Children,' repeats Carlotta, wondering if she mispronounced the word. '*Bambini* – do you have any babies?'

'No. I had a son, only a few months old. He was killed with his mother.'

'Oh.' She can see pain in his eyes. 'I am sorry. I feel stupid for asking.'

He twists the wedding band again. 'I can't bring myself to take this off. Probably never will.'

The waitress arrives with their food but Carlotta can tell

200

that for once the sweetness on the plate isn't going to alter the mood of the man opposite her. 'Turin,' she says, changing the subject, 'is divided into two cities. The place where the Shroud is kept we know as the Holy City. Not far away, under the Palazzo Madama is what we call the Satanic City.'

'Sounds like tourist claptrap.' He picks a dainty sandwich from the fine china plate. 'From my experience, true evil doesn't advertise itself. It stays hidden and moves like a criminal on the run.'

'It is not an invention to part foreigners from their money, it is a piece of our heritage. Beneath the ground are the Alchemist Caves in which during the first century Apollonio of Tyana, a great occult wizard, hid a powerful talisman. The scientists of Savoy thought it was the Philosopher's Stone and even Nostradamus came looking for it.'

Nic stops eating. 'And apparently didn't find anything. What's your point?'

She sips her hot chocolate. 'Turin likes to keep its secrets. We have a long history of it. Just be aware that your search may be as fruitless as theirs.'

69

Amy Chang yawns as she opens the curtains. She pads across the living room in her short white robe and takes a prod at the heap on the floor by the couch.

Mitzi groans.

'Morning. Just checking you're alive. So many of the bodies I find on a floor aren't.'

'I *aren't*.'

'Then stay dead a while longer. I'll make coffee.'

Mitzi willingly does as she's told. Just thinking about moving her head is a terrible proposition. She closes her eyes and runs a mental replay to see if she needs to apologise for anything. Save finishing a bottle of wine on her own, she thinks she's in the clear.

'You want some water too? Maybe breakfast?' Amy turns on the coffee machine. The sound of the beans grinding is enough to make Mitzi pull the covers over her head.

'Just coffee. *Quiet* coffee.'

'Anything *in* the quiet coffee?'

'Just black.' Mitzi sits up and pulls the covers back. 'What time is it?' Blood floods her head and she feels like she's on fire.

'Seven-fifteen. I'm afraid I'm an early riser.'

Mitzi struggles to her feet and staggers to the bathroom in her bra and knickers.

She uses the loo, then swears at the sink, an elegant designer bowl with a mixer tap and no obvious way of turning it on. She twists the tall gold tube, feeling like she's strangling a chicken. It suddenly spurts cold water so forcefully into the basin it splashes over her bare stomach.

She pulls a towel off the edge of the bath and dries herself. In the mirror she sees her sorry reflection. Beneath tired eyes and alcohol-flushed cheeks are the scars of her marriage – marks from Alfie's belt. Shameful purples, browns and reds spread across her stomach, arms and legs. Hands dangling by her side, she stares at herself. 'Shit, girl, how did you let all this happen?' She examines a couple of welts in close-up, turning one way and then another. No wonder she nearly killed him. She'd kill someone who treated a dog like this, let alone another person.

She straightens up. Cautiously fills the basin and washes her hands and face. Towels dry and avoids the mirror. She'll sort her hair out later. Amy's busy in the kitchen area when Mitzi reappears. 'Coffee and chopped fruit on the table. Be good if you eat something.'

'Yes, Doctor. Thanks.' She pulls on her clothes so her friend doesn't see the bruises. 'How about I eat some Ibuprofen with this?'

'Not on an empty stomach.'

'I *need* it.' Mitzi holds out a hand.

'Pathetic. You get any sleep?'

'First straight six hours I've had for a while.'

'Good.' Amy passes over a foil strip of tablets and a glass of water. 'Here you go.'

Mitzi pops two pills and swills them down with water. 'Thanks for being there last night.'

'No problem. I'll always be there.'

'I know. Me too – should you ever need me. Not for this kind of shit, though. I'll kick your ass if you let any guy mess with you like I did with that jerk.'

'You're going to move on, right?'

'You bet. Today is the first day of the rest of my life.'

The pathologist smiles. 'An oldie but goldie.'

'You gotta believe it.' Mitzi takes a sip of newly poured coffee. 'Did I mention the Turin Shroud to you last night?'

'Sort of. You said it was why Nic was in Italy but you didn't make much sense after that.'

'Okay. Here's the thing – we think the Shroud has something to do with the Tamara Jacobs case and we can't yet figure out what.'

'So how can I help?'

'Not sure. We're just opening every door and seeing what's behind them. One thing that keeps coming up is whether the Shroud really was Christ's. If I send you some high-def pics, could you tell me whether you think the marks on the linen are consistent with crucifixion injuries?'

'Wow.' The request takes Amy totally by surprise. 'You want me to PM the Son of God?'

If Mitzi's head didn't hurt so much, she'd laugh. 'Sort of. You're bigging up your part a little.'

'I know. But I still get to file a report marked "Jesus Christ". How many medics can say that?'

70

TURIN

The desk jockeys in Carlotta's office link one of Nic's numbers to the apartment of a Roberto Craxi in a block off Piazza Castello near the Quadrilatero. It's in the historic heart of the city, inside the perimeter of the ancient Roman *Castrum*, and bears the same address as several restaurants he found receipts for in Tamara's apartment. It takes a junior lieutenant called Fredo Battisti five minutes to drive them to the place and twice as long to find a parking spot on the busy cobbled streets.

They may as well not have bothered. Not only is Nic's main lead not there, but according to neighbours, he and his wife haven't been around for more than a month. Apparently they just vanished. Never said goodbye to anyone. Simply disappeared.

Carlotta and Fredo question neighbours on other floors while the landlord, Paolo Llorente, shows Nic around the empty apartment. Llorente, who is almost eighty-five, is dressed in unironed black trousers that hang four inches short of his shoes and a crumpled white shirt and saggy blue cardigan. Hip and knee replacements mean he shuffles more than walks but despite his appearance, his mind is still sprightly. 'In my youth, I had many American girls,' he says, flashing a nostalgic grin. 'I worked in Venice as a gondolier.' He mimes a punting motion. 'American girls drink a lot and they teach me bad words and good times.'

'I'm sure they did. Lucky you.' Nic pushes open the door to the living room.

The place is empty. Not a stick of furniture but spick and span. Polished oak floors, clean white walls and large patio windows lead to a neat balcony filled with terracotta pots and plants. Two bedrooms are similarly denuded and sparkling clean.

In a small but spotless kitchen Nic opens cupboards and finds them bare. No pots, pans, cutlery or crockery. It's like no one has ever lived here. All trace of the Craxis has been wiped away.

'Signore Llorente, do you rent the properties furnished or unfurnished?'

The former gondolier leans on a worktop to take the weight off his strained legs. 'Unfurnished, but if a tenant asks for beds and things, then I buy.' He grins again. 'I buy and put a little extra on top.'

'So the Craxis took everything with them when they went?'

'*Si.*'

'They didn't leave *anything* behind at all?'

The old man shakes his head. 'No, nothing.'

'Did you see them go?' Nic gestures to the empty rooms. 'I mean, it looks like they cleared the whole place out, so they must have hired a van and I guess workmen to carry furniture downstairs.'

'This I did not see.' Llorente touches a discreet hearing aid, a small transparent curl of plastic tucked behind his left ear. 'I am old and sleep a lot. At night I would not hear a bomb.'

'What about the rent?'

'They pay in advance. By the bank.'

'And they didn't default? They paid the last payment okay?'

'*Si*, they pay. They were good couple.'

Nic smells something. Something sharp and clean. White spirits? Paint? His eyes roam over the walls and woodwork. He gets it now. The place has been redecorated, ceiling to floor. Not a doorframe or window ledge isn't freshly glossed.

'How long have your other tenants on this floor been here, Mr Llorente?'

The landlord needs time to think. 'The Tombolini family three years. Then the Mancinis, only six months, I think. Luca Balotelli moved in five years ago – he divorced from his wife, and—'

Nic cuts him off. 'Could I trouble you to look at the Mancini place? Is it like this one?'

The old man frowns. '*Si*. It is just the same as this.' He

realises that's not exactly true. 'Except their living room faces the opposite side.'

'I understand.' Nic follows him out of the Craxi place.

Llorente rings Mancini's bell and knocks on the door. When he's sure the family isn't in, he opens up and stands to one side to let the detective in.

Nic opens every door and scans the place from top to bottom. It's exactly as he thought it would be. Feared it would be. It bears all the wear and tear of a place the land-lord should have decorated two years back. 'Thanks,' he says, stepping back outside. 'I'm done in there.'

71

The tram journey is unexpected.

Ephrem berates himself for not being more alert. He knew Turin had more than a hundred miles of overground network and should have anticipated the target would use it at some point. The man he's following has jumped on board and he's been forced to slip onto the tram at the last moment.

Just a carriage away.

In a confined space like this it's too close for comfort. Much too close. The monk consoles himself with the fact that three other people climbed on when he did. There's a reasonable chance they masked his movements. Ephrem doesn't look up from his seat and doesn't stare intently towards the target's carriage as he is itching to do. He's made a mistake and what happens next is going to be a gamble. At the next stop he has to be first off. He has to disembark like he's late for a meeting and then walk confidently in one direction. If he hangs back, his cover will be blown.

The bell rings and the old tram hisses to a halt. Ephrem jumps off and walks slowly away. Doesn't look back. Doesn't even think about it. It could be that the target is still on board and he lost him, but he doesn't think so. Crowds of people block his way. They're squeezing into the biggest open-air market in Europe in the Piazza della Repubblica. Ephrem sees the signs to a metro station.

His heart thumps. If the target goes down there, he could easily lose him.

The Porta Palazzo Market or the metro?

He gambles on the metro. It's where he would head. Maximum distance in minimum time. It makes perfect sense. To the best of his knowledge there are more than twenty stations but only one main line, running east to west between Turin and Collegno.

He trots quickly down the stone steps. He doesn't have a ticket and the target might well have. At the cashier's window he asks for a *biglietto*. As he pushes the money through the slit he turns and sees his man descending into the darkness below.

'*Rapidamente per favore!*'

The old man doling out change and tickets isn't bothered by the cry of urgency.

By the time the monk reaches the bottom of the escalator he can hear a train thundering away, eastbound.

The platform is empty.

72

Mitzi takes a long shower, more painkillers, fresh coffee and a short walk before a queasy cab ride to collect her car. It'll be a while before she hits the bottle like that again. It was worth it, though. Six hours of glorious sleep and for a brief passage of time no thought of Alfie, the girls or what a mess her life was becoming.

Was – past tense.

In the future – starting right now – it's going to be fine. She's going to finish this case, book a holiday for her, Jade and Amber, sell the house and start anew. Somewhere with no memories. Everything will be just fine.

Mitzi is parking in the station house when her cell phone rings. 'Fallon,' she answers, closing the car door and walking away.

'Logan Connor, Lieutenant.' There is a pause on the end of the line, then he adds, 'Sergeant Sheen gave me your number, said I had to call.'

'Go on.'

'I've just come from the courthouse, ma'am. They processed your husband's file.'

The comment stops her in her tracks. She had no idea his case was being heard so quickly. Someone must have pulled strings for her. 'Appreciate you reaching out. Tell me.'

'He plead to battery and his attorney cut a deal with the DA to avoid a full trial. He got thirty days.'

Mitzi feels numb. She can't work out whether it's good news or bad. Most cases land the minimum thirty. For what he did, he should go to the pokey for a year or more. Despite the lenient sentence, she also knows the die has been cast now. He's a jailbird. You can never get that particular tattoo lasered off. He's a convict. 'So he's being processed now, already in the system?' It's a rhetorical question, she knows what's going down.

'Yes, ma'am. Judge also set release conditions, prohibiting him from coming within a hundred yards of you, the family home or any family member without supervision and spousal consent.' Connor clears his throat. 'If you ask me, I think the court should have—'

'I didn't, Officer, and I really don't want to know what you think.' She's about to cut him off when she remembers her manners. 'I appreciate your call and how you've handled all this. Your discretion is duly noted. You ever need a favour in Homicide, one's waiting on my desk.'

'No need, ma'am. I'm just glad to have helped.'

She shuts down the phone. Thirty days. How the hell is she going to tell the girls?

73

JJ spends most of the day closeted in his office. But his mind is elsewhere.

It's with Em. She's all he can think about. He wants to be with her for ever. Even wishes she was still alive. But that was never going to be possible. He'd been sworn to secrecy. And he's obeyed. Always has. Always will.

He knows he has to move her. Let her go. But where should she rest? He's never disposed of a body before. Never done anything so unkind in his life. All those he has helped into the next world he has left in their homes.

Home. That's it. He must return Em to her home. It is where she will be at rest. It is the right thing to do. Unconsciously he puts a hand to his stomach and rubs an itch, one caused by the fresh cuts he made before coming to work. He undoes the buttons of his white shirt and looks at the livid criss-cross wounds opened by the razor blade. He lowers his chin to his chest and blows on the skin to soothe it.

A knock lifts his head. The sound of the door opening makes him close his shirt quickly. Jenny Harrison stares at him. Only she doesn't look as bold as usual. Hasn't done since her friend disappeared.

'Can I have a minute?'

212

'It's not convenient.' He finishes straightening his clothes.

She comes in anyway. 'It's Kim. Did she call you today? To say she was sick or anything?'

He wishes now he'd dealt with them both. If he'd gone back for Harrison after he'd finished Bass, this wouldn't be happening. 'I haven't heard from her. If she's not in by Monday, I'm giving her job to someone else.'

Harrison flinches. 'I think I know what's happened to her.'

JJ doubts it. 'What?'

She hesitates. What she's about to say could cost her friend her job. 'A year back Kim got pulled by the cops for making out in a car with a guy. They got it all wrong and charged her with prostitution. She did five days in prison, with a warning that if she got caught again, she'd go down for longer.'

'Prostitution?' He tries to sound shocked.

'Yeah. Like I say, it was a mistake. A *misunderstanding*. But Kim's always got lots of admirers and I figure there might have been another misunderstanding – do you know what I mean?'

'You think she's been arrested?'

'Yeah.' Harrison moves to the edge of the desk and puts on a helpless look. 'Mr James, could you ring the cops and find out if they've got her somewhere? I called the local station and they said check with Hollenbeck but they'd never heard of her. Maybe they'd do more if you called.'

The last people in the world that JJ wants to ring are the police. 'Leave it with me, Jenny. I'll see what I can find out.'

74

What disturbs Nic almost as much as the fact that Roberto Craxi and his wife have disappeared is that Carlotta and Fredo don't seem that bothered. Policing in Italy is a whole different ballgame to that in the States. Too laid back and far too sloppy for his liking.

He's still biting his tongue as Fredo drives them to Craxi's bank at the south-eastern end of Via Po, near the giant Piazza Vittorio Veneto. While it's not that unusual for people to change homes five or ten times in a lifetime, they seldom switch banks on more than a couple of occasions. The manager should be able to give them a new address.

Carlotta is sat in the back with Nic and can tell that he's churning things over in his mind. 'Something is troubling you?'

'Yeah, it is. Don't you think it strange that none of the neighbours back there saw the Craxis leave and none of them were friendly enough to have a forwarding address?'

She shrugs. 'It happens. In apartment blocks like that, you come, you go, you don't see many people. I live in one very like it.'

He's looking out the window as he talks. 'Those stairs were tight. You couldn't get furniture out without making a noise, scraping walls, being noticed.'

'The landlord, Signore Llorente, did you ask him about the relocation? Maybe he knows?'

'I asked. He doesn't.' He turns to face her. 'Something is wrong, and I get the impression that because this is an out-of-town case, you and the Carabinieri don't really care that much.'

'*Scusi?*' She reddens a little. 'I don't understand.'

'Come on. We get the brush-off from that verger friend of yours, then the Craxis have vanished and their apartment – well, their apartment is the only one to have been freshly painted – and you don't seem to be the least bit interested in that.'

She's offended by his tone. 'Maybe it was painted to attract new renters.'

'Maybe you're not trying hard enough. I bet if you sent a forensic team into that apartment back there, you wouldn't find so much as a fingerprint from Craxi or his wife.'

'He has left,' she throws up her hands in annoyance, a flash of Latin temper. 'The landlord says he has paid his rent, so for us there is no crime here in Italy to investigate.'

'Maybe not for you, but in LA we have a mutilated dead woman and she's directly linked to your missing Italian.'

'He's not missing. He just left. He just moved house.'

'We are here.' Fredo pulls the Alfa to the kerb.

'Thanks,' snaps Nic, pushing open the back door and getting out.

Carlotta stomps past him and into the bank. She walks by a queue of customers and shows her ID at a window. A senior

215

clerk eventually materialises and lets them through an electronically locked door into a passageway and then upstairs to the first floor to an office at the back in the corner. Seems big guys the world over always want the corner space, the one with double windows and the best street views.

Fabrizio Gatusso comes out and shakes Carlotta's hand. The silver-haired fifty-year-old looks every inch a bank manager – blue pin-stripe suit, white shirt and tightly knotted blue tie.

'He says to come in,' explains Carlotta, her voice showing she's still mad with Nic. 'He does not speak English but I will translate.'

Nic takes a seat beside her on the brown corner sofa, the kind that comes in movable sections. Gatusso settles on another square piece of it opposite them, behind a glass table stacked with paper and leaflets. The banker hands a file to Carlotta and she in turn passes it to Nic with an explanation. 'These are copies of Craxi's accounts for all the time he was a customer. Also his wife's.'

'Was? W*as* his customer.'

'*Si*. They closed their accounts a month ago.'

Nic feels his anger bubbling up again. Precious time is being wasted. 'So who do they bank with now?' His tone becomes almost derisory. 'Usually when customers move banks, the old bank and the new one work together to switch standing orders and exchange debit orders and things. Please don't tell me it doesn't work like that in Italy or that I need special permission from the President or the Pope or someone.'

She stares angrily at him. 'I ask for you.'

As she does, Nic opens the file and scans the statements. They show the sequence of payments from Tamara Jacobs – sums of €3600, the equivalent at the time of $5000. He flicks through and sees the bigger amounts as well – two deposits via international bank transfer of €18,179 – twenty-five grand.

Carlotta turns back to him. 'Signore Gatusso has no idea what bank the Craxis are now with.' She reaches across him into the file and searches for a moment. She finds a copy of a final statement. 'This is the bank's last link. When the Craxis closed their accounts, they took all their money in cash.'

75

77TH STREET STATION, LOS ANGELES

Sergeant Bobby Sheen has been expecting the call. He just hopes Mitzi isn't mad at him. He'd prayed Alfie Fallon would get prison time but it was always going to be a long shot. With a spiralling state deficit, first-time offenders are pretty much given a telling off and a free ride home these days. 'Hiya, Mitzi, how you doin'?'

She's stood in the ladies' restroom at work. 'I'm holding up, Bobby. Holding up. Connor rang me – said you told him to.'

'I did. Look, I'm sorry they were so chicken-assed. I

hoped the judge would have been a bit tougher, you know?'

She leans in the corner against the cold white tiles near the hand dryers, 'No need to say sorry. Who was it?'

'Kent. Justice Joe Kent. Should have retired the useless bastard ten years ago.'

'Should have been a woman.'

'Kent *is* a woman. He certainly doesn't have any balls.'

Mitzi smiles. Bobby's always been a hardliner, ever since she first met him. 'What was Alfie charged under? Two-seven-three or two-four-three?'

'Seven-three. The photographs we took of you were sufficient to prove physical injury.'

She has an embarrassing flashback of Bobby leading her down to the doctor after she'd seen her husband in the bullpen and all her injuries being noted and snapped.

'You okay, hon?'

'Not yet, but I will be when all this is over.'

'Soon. At least this is out of the way now.'

'I know. Bobby, thanks for pushing things through. I realise you were looking out for me. Don't go feeling bad about the sentence.'

'You're a star, Mitzi. Rise above this crap and shine again. Call me if I can help with anything.'

'Will do.' She clicks off the phone and glances in the restroom mirror as she heads to her desk. 'You're a star, Mitzi – just you remember that.'

76

Confession is good for the soul.

Admitting your mistakes. Repenting. It's how Ephrem has been raised. And right now he fully accepts his failings and is trying to make up for them. He was vain and conceited. Thought he had the better of the man he had been following – and he hadn't.

Pride before a fall.

He knows the teachings, the proverbs – *when pride comes, then comes disgrace, but with humility comes wisdom.*

Ephrem looks at the empty train platform and mentally chastises himself. When his mission is complete he will inflict agonising pain on his vain body to ensure today's lesson is learned and never forgotten. The only thing comforting him is the knowledge that no matter how frail and fallible he is, his opponent will have inadequacies at least equal to his own. Right now he is sure the man he is tracking will be feeling confident, safe, sure of his actions.

Pride before destruction. The monk abandons the chase and returns to the target's car. There's a chance that his enemy has abandoned it but that would be a big sacrifice for someone in his position, especially as this man has others to protect. No, Ephrem feels sure he'll come back here. All he has to do is wait.

Before his downfall a man's heart is proud.

77

Amy Chang spends the morning working a routine overdose case. A seventy-five-year-old woman living on her own decided to take a month's worth of anti-depressants and check out of Hotel California once and for all. Who can blame her? The City of Angels is hell on earth for anyone who isn't young, beautiful and hooked up with someone who loves them.

She scrubs her hands and arms, changes from morgue greens into a brown Peter Pan tunic top over comfortable black Jersey skinny trousers. Back at her office desk she opens up mail from Mitzi containing high-def pics of the Shroud of Turin. She's seen some of the photographs before but never really paid much attention to them. The big close-up of the face is the most recognisable of all. Even through the grey-black haze it's unmistakably an image of Christ that people recognise the world over – beard, long hair and the crown of thorns. She flicks through them until she finds a larger and more interesting body shot.

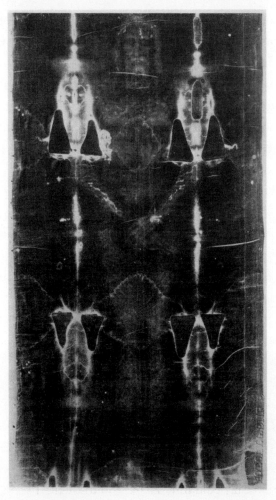

There's something about the image that instinctively feels wrong to the ME. Her eyes are drawn to the hands, especially the right one and its fingers. In proportion to the rest of the body they just seem too big. She types out a memo, attaches the print and sends it to Gunter Quentell at the FBI.

He's a world expert in photogrammetry – the forensic practice of determining the geometric properties of objects from photographic images.

Before Amy makes her own scientific evaluations she seeks some artful insight into the mysteries. She searches the online databases and the best she can come up with is the sixteenth-century oil by Giovanni Battista depicting how the body could have been wrapped. It shows the linen loosely looped over the head with the open end at the feet.

She glances again at the body print made on the Shroud and the two don't seem to tally. To leave such definite marks around all areas on the corpse would be impossible unless it had been bound tightly, not covered flimsily as painted by Battista.

Amy hits zoom on her monitor and examines the Shroud section by section, top to bottom. It takes an hour. Her findings are fascinating and frustrating. The body parts seem out of proportion to each other. They seem more like they've been drawn than traced. And the more she stares at the face the more she is both enchanted and confused.

The forehead looks too short for the rest of the skull. Remembering that the victim was supposed to be lying on his back, his hair should also be hanging away from, not over his head and face. She looks again at the full-length shot of the corpse. The man has no neck. At least she can't see one

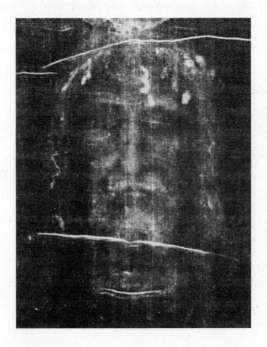

in the print. She searches for signs of the cloth having been cut and reattached, so possibly excluding part of the neck, but can't find any.

Another aspect of the Shroud worries her. Wrap linen around a corpse and it gets creased – deeply creased. But not in this case. There's no evidence of any twists in the cloth, only the lines where it's been folded for storage.

Amy searches police files and forensic image banks on wounds and torture marks. There's nothing comparable. A case in Canada in which a serial killer crucified his victims looks promising but it turns out he used execution methods totally unlike those performed by the ancient Romans. She turns her attention once again to the Shroud's positive and negative plates. The difference between the two is astonishing. In the positive plate the body image is virtually invisible. In the negative one, it jumps right out at you. It's like spraying Luminol at a scene that looks wiped clean only to see blood appear in all its glorious chemiluminescence.

The phone rings and makes her jump. 'Doctor Chang.'

'*Guten tag, schöner mediziner.*'

'Gunter!' She's genuinely delighted he's called her. 'Fantastic to hear your voice. How are you?'

'Me? I am very happy because you send me a note. Even if it is only to pick my giant German brain.'

She laughs. 'If I picked anything else, your giant German wife would have me roasted for dinner in her very fine restaurant.'

He sighs. 'She would indeed. But in another life we will

be lovers, of this I am sure. Now why are you looking at the Turin Shroud and asking crazy questions?'

'Are they crazy?'

'Of course they are. You ask are the hands and head proportionate to the body. The answer is no. Nor is the length of the corpse appropriate. This man would have been way over six feet tall – nearer seven feet. Jesus may have been the son of God but he wasn't a giant. Or if he was, no one ever bothered to comment on it.'

Amy inspects one of the shots that Mitzi sent her. She sees what he means. 'How do you know all this, Gunter? Did you do your own studies?'

'No need. There has already been a lot of work done. There are no external coordinates to compare the corpse with but the dimensions of the Shroud itself are good baselines. Another thing, if you measure the length of the image on the back of the cloth, it is two inches longer than on the front.'

'Maybe it stretched and distorted the image? That would also explain the over-large hands.'

'Good to see you are still so open-minded. There is an English professor you should talk to. I will go through my files and ask that he call you.'

'Is he an open-minded believer or non-believer?'

'Believer. Very big believer. Even though I am not, it is important that you talk to him and also to STURP, the Shroud of Turin Research Project. Speak to them, then use your own intelligence to decide that it's a fake – a fakety-fake-fake.'

She laughs. 'So I guess what you're saying is that you think it's a fake, then?'

'I have no doubts. No questions at all. I can even tell you who the faker was.'

'Go on.'

'Not so quickly. It will cost you dinner next time I am in LA.'

'Sure – but I get to call Astrid and tell her where I'm taking her husband.'

'An unnecessary offer.'

'So who faked it?'

'Open your email. I just sent you a document.'

78

TURIN

By 6 p.m. Nic's had it. He's done with Carabinieri inefficiency. With struggling around a foreign city where it's impossible to park. With the whole damned Tamara Jacobs case.

For the past two hours he's chased down addresses linked to Craxi's logged calls and all he's got for his troubles are a pounding headache and enough dead ends to fill a road atlas. Fredo drives them back to the station house parking lot in Via Beato Sebastian Valfré. From there, Carlotta walks Nic to the hotel and tries to make peace. 'I am sorry things didn't work out – that we didn't find Craxi.'

He's too angry to respond.

'I will make some more enquiries when I go back to the office. You should get some rest, you look tired. Tomorrow we will find Roberto Craxi, I am sure.'

He seriously doubts she could find milk in her own fridge.

'I pick you up at nine again in the morning, okay?'

'Fine.' He tries to be nice. 'I hoped for more – something quick, a strong lead to build on. I'm sorry if I've been gnarly. I know you've been trying to help. *Grazie.*'

She smiles at his first stab at Italian, '*Prego*. You have my numbers. Don't forget, if you want anything, call me.' She waits a beat then adds, 'If you feel better a little later and want to see some of Torino, I will be in the office. Like I said to you, I still have other crimes on my desk.'

'Thanks again.' He turns away, feeling a little guilty. He knows what a pain it is to babysit a cop from another country and do all the ferrying around and legwork on a case that isn't yours.

Nic collects his room key at reception and heads upstairs to sink into his swampy bed. No sooner has he kicked off his shoes than his cell rings and flashes up Mitzi's desk number.

'Pronto,' he tries to mimic Carlotta's accent. '*Signore Carry-can-diss* here.'

She laughs. It's reassuring to hear him cracking jokes. 'Glad you've still got your sense of humour, Signore. So how's it going?'

'You mean aside from the jet lag, crappy weather and major runaround I'm being given?'

'Yeah, *aside* from all those exotic treats, how's it going?'

'Just great.' He pushes the pillows back and leans against them. 'I went to Roberto Craxi's apartment. He wasn't there but I tell you Mitz, that place was so clean – fresh paint everywhere, new units in the kitchen, the works – it was like someone wanted to erase any trace that Craxi or his wife had ever set foot in the place.'

She toys with the phone cable and wishes he was back in the office with her. 'Sounds like a professional wipe-down – maybe after a shooting or at least some kind of bloodshed.'

'I thought the same, but there are no signs of a crime. No signs of anything. The Craxis just vanished – *poof*, gone!' He jams the phone between his neck and ear as he pours water from a bottle on the bedside table. 'I went to his bank as well. Account's been closed – all the money withdrawn in cash.'

'How much?'

'In euros, about a hundred and fifty thou'. What's that – about two hundred thousand dollars?'

'Guess so. However much it is, it sounds like he and his wife ain't coming back.'

'Yeah, sounds like it. But why?'

She sips coffee. 'Usual reasons – avoiding something or somebody. I'll check emigration, they might have left the country. Or maybe you can have the Carabinieri do that?'

228

'Ha, some hope. I've been assigned a beauty queen who couldn't investigate a crime in her own house.'

'You being a little sexist?'

'I don't know, Mitz. She's a *loo-geo-ten-ente* or whatever the heck they call it out here. So she certainly ranks big enough to know the ropes. It's just that everything takes an age in Italy and she really doesn't seem so bright.' He wonders for a second if he's being fair or whether his irritation is just the product of not understanding the unhurried pace of the culture. 'I went to see the Shroud – that was a waste of time as well.'

'How so?'

'I got more BS from the cathedral's verger than you got from Matthews last time you asked for a raise. The relic is locked in boxes inside boxes and only the Pope can fix for anyone to see it.'

'Do you think we're chasing down blind alleys, Nic?'

'If it wasn't for the money, I might think that. But Jacobs paid out more than a hundred K to this Craxi guy for some kind of information about the Shroud. What was the info and why was it worth so much? It's important, I'm sure it is.'

She trusts his instinct. It's one of the things that have made him such a good cop. Instinct. That's something she's certainly been lacking in her personal life. God knows she screwed things up with Alfie.

Nic thinks he's lost the connection. 'Mitz, you still there?'

'Yeah, I'm here. Just . . .'

'What's wrong?' He can tell from her voice that something is wrong. Can tell from that one lonely word hung out on its own.

Just.

'Nothing. Well, something, but it's only personal shit that I have to sort out.'

'Personal shit called Alfie?'

She nearly laughs – that instinct of his really is good. 'Yeah, but hey, what the hell, we all have to deal with our own crap, don't we?'

He shifts position on the bed. 'You want to talk about it?'

'Nah, get some sleep, and solve this case for me. I don't want you hanging around at work longer than need be, you've got a boat to sail. Bye.'

Nic smiles at the disconnected phone. His boss is a class act. Deserves better than that bum of a husband she's stuck with.

79

CORONER'S OFFICE, LOS ANGELES

The iMac cursor glides over the Adobe PDF icon and clicks it open. Amy Chang's jaw drops in astonishment. 'You are kidding me.' In front of her are more than four hundred pages from Gunter Quentell suggesting the Shroud of Turin was faked by one of the world's most talented artists, sculptors, writers, mathematicians and inventors.

Leonardo da Vinci.

Ridiculous. Then again, he was also a scientist and intellectual prankster. He conceptualised tanks, helicopters and solar power, and created the most reproduced religious painting of all time, the *Last Supper*, in which he inserted Mary Magdalene as the companion of Christ. Maybe not so ridiculous an idea after all.

Gunter's document claims that just as Leonardo allegedly modelled the *Mona Lisa* on his own face, he did the same with the Turin Shroud. Amy studies three shots – the Shroud print, a portrait of da Vinci and the Mona Lisa. There are similarities – in the eyes and even nose – but she struggles to be completely convinced. For a start, the great painter was born a hundred years *after* the disputed carbon dating. And multiple scientific examinations have recorded no sign of any oil or watercolours on the linen cloth. Could

Leonardo really have invented some form of photography hundreds of years *before* others claimed more widespread recognition for the technique? Not impossible.

At the bottom of the electronic document are copies of newspaper articles from 2011, detailing claims from an Italian art expert called Luciano Buso that the Shroud was created not by Leonardo but by Giotto di Bondone, who lived in the thirteenth and fourteenth centuries.

Amy scans them. It seems Giotto was a master of painting figures – especially Christ – and was allegedly chosen by the Church to create a replica of the cloth because the original was in such a poor state. He is said to have concealed the number '15' in the painting to denote the year he completed the work.

Further down the PDF there are several other articles completely dismissing Buso's claims as totally without foundation. Amy turns back to the images of the Shroud. Fresh questions arise. The cloth appears to show markings made by blood, sweat and tissue. Contrary to popular belief, bodies *can* still bleed after death, after the heart has stopped pumping, but it would be extraordinary for one to have done so in a way that left such vivid marks.

Another thing is disturbing her. Putrefaction. A corpse left for days, even inside a closed cave, would undoubtedly putrefy. If blood were visible on the linen, then other bodily excretions should be too. They aren't.

Her telephone rings. It's her secretary. She just missed a call from a professor in England. He left a message saying he wants to speak to her about the crucifixion of Christ and why he's convinced the Shroud of Turin is genuine.

80

It's 9 p.m. when Nic finally gets the phone call he'd been waiting for all day.

'Are you alone?' The voice is male and Italian. A voice he has heard only once before.

'Just me and a TV that doesn't work properly.' He drops the remote on the quilt and sits on the edge of the bed.

'Leave your hotel and cross the road. At the corner turn left and you will see a Fiat Bravo. I will leave the side lights on.'

Nic wriggles his swollen feet into shoes that have somehow shrunk since he kicked them off. 'You have some good news?'

'I have news.'

The line goes dead.

Nic locks his phone, ties his laces, gets up and grabs his jacket and keys.

It's dark and raining softly as he leaves the stuffy heat of the old hotel for the crispness of the November night. There's a drizzle falling, the kind of rain you can't really see but can feel all the time – an icy mist that surreptitiously soaks you and leaches your body heat. He turns the corner and within a couple of steps sees the parked Fiat.

He's never met Fabio Goria but the guy has come strongly recommended. He works for a premier private investigations company and came courtesy of a friend in the FBI.

He slips into the PI's Fiat Bravo, shuts the door and offers a hand. 'Nic Karakandez, good to meet you.'

'Fabio.' Goria is gravelly-voiced, unshaven, in his mid-thirties, broad-shouldered and smells of cigarettes.

'So what have you got?'

Passing car lights play on the investigator's stubbly face as he talks, his pinched blue eyes focused on either the windshield or rear-view mirror. 'You asked me to find Roberto Craxi for you and to keep a trace on him until you came to Torino. This I have done.'

Nic is more impressed than he is about to admit. 'Where is he?'

Goria doesn't answer immediately. He glances from the mirror into the detective's eyes. He has to be able to trust this man. There are things he needs to know – things he has to be certain about – before he tells him anything. 'I spoke to Special Agent Burge. He told me you are a good police-man, so I help you. But before we speak about Craxi and where he is hiding, tell me what you know about him.'

Hiding. The word makes Nic's heart quicken. 'I don't know much. He's Italian and the recipient of a sizeable income from a murder victim in LA. Oh, and the Carabinieri couldn't find him.'

234

Goria's smile is barely visible in the half-light.

'Craxi worked for the Carabinieri until only a few years ago.'

'What?'

'He was a member of the Raggruppamento Operativo Speciale – the ROS. You know what this is?'

'Special operations group?'

'Exactly. One of their main bases is here in Turin. It is the arm of the Carabinieri that deals with organised crime and terrorism. It reports directly to the Carabinieri general command. Not much is known about it.'

Nic starts to put the pieces together and it doesn't make for a pretty picture. In none of his calls from LA or the meetings today did any of his Carabinieri contacts mention that Craxi had been one of their own, let alone a special operative.

Goria can tell what's on his mind. 'Your pretty lieutenant wasn't of much help, was she?'

'No,' says Nic, 'And now I know why.'

The Italian lights a cigarette and winds down an inch of window to blow out the blue-grey smoke. 'Craxi wasn't only ROS, he was *un'ombra* – a shadow. He was part of a black ops team.'

'You mean she might not have known Craxi was part of her own force?'

'It is possible. The Carabinieri is a big organisation, with both military and policing functions. They overlap at times and are entirely separate when it suits them. The executives will know. They probably figure you are here for two or three days at most and will then have to go back to Los Angeles, so they assign someone to show you around a little and frustrate you.'

'They're certainly doing that.'

Goria grips the cigarette between his lips and digs inside his jacket. 'Take a look at this.' He hands over several long lens photographs of a man in a raincoat crossing a street.

'Dino di Rossi. This is the verger of the cathedral. I saw him earlier.'

'I know you did. We took these straight afterwards. One of my team has been watching you all day.' He takes the photographs back. 'But this man you met, he is not the verger of the Duomo.'

'Then who is he?'

'His name is Pausini. He is also from ROS, an undercover specialist. He is good, no?'

'I guess he is.'

'I don't know all of the details of your case, Nic, but I do know a little about the ROS. You don't want to upset these people. They are trained to kill. If they are involved in your inquiry, then I advise you to leave. Go home to America. Burge told me that you like to sail. Good. You should do that. Go home, sail as far away as you can from all this.'

Nic shakes his head. 'I can't do that. Much as I'd like to. There's been a murder and—'

'And there will be more –if you don't leave.' The statement hangs as unpleasantly as the fug of smoke around him.

'I can only help you so much, Nic. Only so much, then I am gone. Understand?'

81

Being called to Matthews' office is never good news.

Especially on a Friday afternoon. Mitzi thinks over the cold hard facts as she heads down his corridor. There are two times a week a boss will most likely lay you off, fire you or bust your balls. If he's a nice guy, he does it first-thing Monday morning. That way you've already had your weekend in blissful ignorance and most likely you're in for an extra week's pay if he takes your badge. If he's an asshole – or the timing's just plain bad – you catch it Friday afternoon. This way he gets the weight off his mind and the weekend ahead is a nice one for him but not for you.

She knocks on the upper glass part of his door, twists the dull brass knob and edges it open enough to stick her head through, 'You called for me, sir.'

'I did.' He's behind his desk in blue-checked shirtsleeves, cuffs rolled to his elbows, feet resting on the edge of a chair and a pile of financial papers spread over the vast curvature of an ample midriff restrained by black braces. 'Sit down and adopt a mood of joyous opportunity and stoic professionalism.'

She takes a seat the other side of the desk. 'I'd try to do that if I had a clue what stoic was.'

He takes his feet off the chair, spins round and drops his meaty forearms on the desk. 'Stoic: noun. A person who can endure pain or hardship without showing their feelings or complaining.'

'Ah, now I get it. Doesn't sound much like me, Captain.'

Matthews smiles. 'LA's most abused liver just checked itself into rehab and has taken Homicide Detective Jordan Lynch with it.'

Mitzi gives him her best so-what's-that-got-to-do-with-me look.

'Meaning Tyler Carter needs a number-two on his serial case.'

She drops her head into her hands. 'Boss, I've got Nic Karakandez in Italy on the Tamara Jacobs killing and he's only a week away from sailing off to God knows where. And— ' She stops herself. No. She's not going to say she has personal problems, he probably knows already.

'And what?'

From the look on his face he doesn't know. Even Matthews isn't so mean as to make fun out of the mess she's in. 'And nothing, sir. I was just having trouble transitioning from pissed and rightfully letting-off steam to professionally stoic.'

He slaps his hands on the table and smiles. 'No problem. You did it real well. Get Carter to give you an extra pair of hands to cover the Jacobs case until you crack it or it falls down. We'll run another week and then review. This way you can work both, okay?'

Her face says it's not but her mouth has learned to be compliant. 'Yes, sir.'

'That's all.' He swings his feet back up on the spare seat and reaches for the financial papers he had been worrying over when she came in. 'Stoicism suits you, Fallon.'

'Thank you, sir. Would you like your door slammed hard enough to come off its hinges or just sufficient to break the glass?'

82

TURIN

Fabio Goria chain-smokes as he drives. 'We are not going far. Across the river, about six kilometres south-east, into the forest. Craxi and his wife own a holiday lodge – a place to hide. They put it under her maiden name.'

It's raining heavily now. As he looks out of the window, Nic can't see much beyond the edge of the highway. 'You said they were hiding. What or who are they hiding from?'

Goria looks his way. 'I hoped you could tell me that.'

'The Carabinieri?'

'Possible but unlikely.' The PI takes a last draw of his cigarette and flicks it through the window slit, a tumbling red firefly crashing and bouncing in the blackness. 'If I were hiding from the Carabinieri, I would not do it on my own doorstep at a place they could easily trace.'

'Then I don't know. Things don't add up at the moment. But my instinct tells me Craxi is connected to my case and to the Shroud.'

'The Sacra Sindone has more than its fair share of mysteries. You have learned a little about it?'

'Only from a fake verger. So I have a trust problem.'

'Ill seldom comes from trusting strangers too little.'

'Is that a wise old Italian saying?'

'My father's.'

'And is he wise and old?'

Goria laughs. 'Not really. He died in his forties of alcoholism, but he left his impressions, like most parents do.'

Nic looks out of the window at the flat fields rushing past. The last of the city lights have gone. The car is picking up speed down a dual carriageway heading into the countryside. 'Given what you said about Craxi and his service record, is it a good idea to go surprising him in the dead of night?'

'You are right, even though Craxi is almost sixty, he could snap your neck and bury you in the dirt like a dog does a bone. So we will not be alone and not giving him that opportunity.'

'Glad to hear it.'

Five minutes later the Fiat turns off the Corso Chieri and down a tight, winding road heading to the Strada Communale di Valpiana. Goria kills the headlights as he slows almost to a halt and then eases the car onto a bumpy stone track running off to the right. 'We stop here and walk.'

Nic unbuckles his seatbelt, gets out in the misty rain and closes the door as quietly as possible.

As they trudge into the woods, the Italian takes out a cell phone and sends a short pre-written SMS to one of his team. A minute later the phone vibrates in his hand. He stops and turns to Nic. 'Now I make a call. The person who answers will be Roberto Craxi.'

Nic looks surprised.

'One of my men slipped a phone through a window vent when Craxi went out in his car this evening. When he finds it he will not touch it. Only when he is sure that it is not an explosive, will he pick up.' Goria makes the call.

As expected it rings out without any answer.

'The tone is distinctive,' says the PI, almost mischievously, as he calls again. 'You know the Pink Panther?'

'Of course. Henry Mancini – you picked it because he's an Italian composer?'

'No.' The call fails once more and he dials for a third time. 'No, not Italian – Mancini was American. His family, though, come from Abruzzo, as do Roberto's.' Suddenly he pulls the phone from his ear and thrusts it at Nic. 'It's him.'

Nic grabs the handset. 'Mr Craxi, please don't hang up, I'm—'

The line is already dead.

'He's gone.'

'Keep trying. Press redial.'

Nic tries again and listens to the call connect.

He's picked up.

'Mr Craxi, my name is Nic Karakandez.' He tries to cram in as much as possible to stop him hanging up again. 'I'm from the LAPD and I have to talk to you.'

This time the line doesn't go dead. Nic can tell the connection is still live. There's an eerie silence broken by the crackle of electronic static. 'I need your help. I have to talk to you about Tamara Jacobs and your relationship with her.'

There is still no answer.

Nic ploughs on. 'Please. I know you are there. I know you are listening. I've come all the way from Los Angeles to talk to you and I'd like to meet with you and ask a few questions.'

Still nothing.

'Mr Craxi – Signore – will you see me? Can we meet somewhere?'

Just the hiss of cyber-silence.

Nic looks worried. He glances at Goria. 'I'm not sure he's there.'

'Keep the line open,' says the Italian. 'We walk down here and in a few minutes you will see his lodge and my men.'

Nic keeps talking as they weave their way through the trees and down a soft, slippy embankment of wet soil and rotted leaves. Through the wood comes the sight of yellow boxes of light. Windows. Goria reaches for his belt and unclips a military-standard walkie-talkie, the type that scrambles signals and allows you to talk to people up to five miles away.

Nic watches as he whispers in Italian. Watches as he repeats the message and waits. Watches as his face gradually changes.

'There's something wrong,' says Goria. 'Very wrong.'

83

77TH STREET STATION, LOS ANGELES

Tyler Carter is either a wizard or an asshole. The Homicide Unit seems divided on the issue. A year-on-year record of turning in the best clean-up rate in the state means the smart money is on him hitting captain within the next few years. What's beyond doubt is that the thirty-three-year-old is arrogant, introverted and disrespects almost everything and everyone.

Carter comes from banker wealth and can't help but stand out from the crowd. He was supposed to tread the gold road like his daddy and his granddaddy before him. Only he had other ideas. He wanted a badge and a gun, not a briefcase and diversified share portfolio. Even Daddy and his millions couldn't stand in the way. Wall Street's loss turned out to be the LAPD's gain. Everything is going well. Or at least it was – until eight months ago.

Until the Creeper.

The Creeper is the name of the serial killer he's hunting, a moniker the cops hope the press never get hold of. To date, the perp has ten kills notched on his bedpost and there isn't anyone on the task force who would be surprised to find at least another ten down to him.

Mitzi Fallon sits at Carter's desk learning what she's let herself in for.

'The nickname comes from the fact the guy's never been seen—'

'Never?'

Carter flashes her a steely look. 'I don't like interruptions. If you need clarification, wait and ask at the end.'

'Pardon?'

'Let me finish and you won't need to ask unnecessary questions. The perp has never been seen. He creeps into the homes of women living alone and kills them in their sleep.'

Mitzi's about to ask how but decides to save it.

'Always the same MO. He pulls a bed sheet or quilt tight around their arms and legs so they can't struggle. He kneels on them and chokes them manually.' Tyler guesses what's in her mind. 'Left-handed, always only one hand. ME says there's evidence in some cases he put his right hand over their mouths.'

Mitzi wonders if the victims bit him, if there was a chance of DNA.

'We got genetic fingerprints from the first and third victims – first and third we know of, that is. I'll give you files.

First was hair and saliva. Shin hairs and wool sock fluff – caught on the side of the bed when he climbed up on the vic. Third was flesh and blood from a bite when he put his right hand over her mouth. Before you ask, yes, we ran database searches. The guy has no record and the FBI drew blanks as well. I even checked with Canadian police. You can ask questions now.'

She looks across and takes him in – the chiselled, well-shaven face, clear blue eyes, immaculately cut short, dark and grey-free hair, beautiful black suit and crisp white shirt. Perfect. Too perfect. 'Do you ever laugh, get drunk, jerk off or have any vices?'

'No.' His voice is as cold as his eyes.

'Good. Only I'd hate to think there was anything normal about you.' She gets up from her seat.

'Where you going? I'm not finished.'

'Tampon. I have a particularly heavy period at the moment and I need to change my sanitary product as quickly as possible. I'm using the super-strength version – maximum protection it says on the box – to absorb as much of the menstrual flow as possible for as long as possible. You can ask more when I'm done.'

His perfect jaw drops.

Mitzi turns and smiles pleasantly as she opens the door. 'I'll bring us both coffee on the way back. Then maybe we can round off with a summary of exactly what you want me to do and I can tell you exactly how I need to be treated in order for you to get me to do it.'

84

The two men hurry to the bottom of the steep embankment. Nic drops back as Goria jerks the black butt of a gun out of his belt.

In the soft earth and rotting leaves in front of them is the body of a man. Motionless.

Then slowly moving. Alive not dead, but certainly injured. Goria drops to one knee beside the prone figure. He points his gun into the half-light spilling from the lodge twenty metres away. Then he shines a torch into the injured man's face. 'Are you okay?'

'Someone hit me.' The man's fingers go to the back of his head. 'I'm sorry.' He struggles to his feet and looks dizzy.

The private detective steadies him, gives him time before pressing him for more information on the attack. Nic moves towards the log cabin. He hears a sudden sound. A rustle in the open, over to one side of the building. Like an animal caught in bushes trying to shake free. He steps closer, stands off about five metres.

'Fabio,' he whispers.

The Italian looks round and slides away from his injured colleague.

Nic points towards the thick shrub and says, 'In there.'

246

Goria takes a breath, swings over his light and gun. The beam picks out a scratched and bleeding face. A human face. A woman's face.

85

77TH STREET STATION, LOS ANGELES

Mitzi puts two mugs of black coffee on Tyler Carter's desk. 'I figured you didn't do cream or sugar.'

'You figured right.' He takes the drink nearest him. 'Matthews said good things about you.'

She takes it as a thawing of the ice. 'Nice to know. He mention anything about a raise, promotion or early retirement?'

Carter almost smiles. 'Not that I heard. Jordan's illness has come at a bad time.'

'For him or for you?'

'Both. I'm not as cold as I look. He may be a drunk but he was a better cop than most. Jay gave a hundred per cent effort a hundred per cent of the time. Point is, our killer is due. Overdue for that matter.'

'You know I'm still working the Tamara Jacobs case?'

'Matthews said. Out-of-town hit by the sound of it. Help me out on this – really help me out – and I'll give you men and brains to clear up your file.'

'Deal.'

Carter reaches behind and grabs two handfuls of manila files. 'Forensics, psych profiles and crime pattern analysis on the Creeper. Read and digest.'

'You said he was *over*due.'

'Kill pattern shrank from nine months to six, then to three. Held at twelve weeks for two kills, then we had another last month and one more just twelve days ago.'

'He's escalating.'

'Probably doesn't know it, probably thinks he's got everything under control and is feeling at his most powerful.'

'But he's not?'

'You worked a serial before?'

She shakes her head. 'A double murder, but both killed at the same time. Two serial rapes. One with more than a dozen attacks to the bastard's name.'

'Similar and not similar. Rape is usually about power and sexuality, the offender often goes to excess to control – ropes, bindings, verbal threats and there can be signs of rage on the victim's body. Serial murder can be a host of things. Our perp isn't sexual and there isn't rage.'

'Attacking a woman in her own bed at night isn't sexual?'

Carter nods at the files he's just given her. 'No point to this conversation right now – you're not properly informed. Read the profiles, then we'll talk more.'

A knowing smile starts to crease her lips. 'C'mon, you're holding back. If you need a hundred per cent effort, you've got to give me a hundred per cent information.'

He weighs her up. Seems every bit as smart as Matthews said. 'Okay, but listen, this isn't public knowledge. When the Creeper kills his victims he strips them, puts them on the floor and covers them.'

'With what?'

'He takes a sheet off the bed. Drapes them head to toe. Tucks it behind the back of the skull and lifts their feet. They look just like they've been wrapped in a shroud.'

86

TURIN

Erica Craxi is still shaking. And with good reason.

Goria leaves the fifty-four-year-old with his colleague Dario, while he talks to Nic. 'Her husband is not here.'

The American looks worried. 'The phone call, did I—'

'No. It wasn't that. He'd gone before you called. His wife says he heard something and went outside with his gun to investigate. He told her to go out the back door and hide in the woods until he came back.'

Nic nods towards Goria's colleague. 'What did Craxi hear, your man moving around?'

He shakes his head. 'No, not him. Dario heard something too but didn't want to break cover. He saw Craxi come outside and he went to follow him. Someone cracked him over the head and stuck a sedative in his neck. Now he thinks I will sack him for being useless.'

'And will you?'

'Probably, but not tonight. Tonight there is still much work to do.'

'So where's Craxi now?'

'The wife doesn't know.'

'And your men – your team – they didn't see anything?'

'Doesn't seem that way.' Goria falls silent. He's been outwitted. Made to look foolish. Now the LAPD officer with powerful FBI friends will start questioning his value. 'Let's go inside and speak to the signora. Maybe she can help us.'

Nic wonders who answered his call, who was listening to him when he thought Craxi was on the line. Goria uses his walkie-talkie to call the rest of his team out of their surveillance positions. The lodge is small and basic. Bare board walls and scatter rugs are warmed by a wood-burning stove that cradles the last charcoal embers of what an hour ago was a blazing fire. Two sofas covered with thick red blankets face off across a low, junk wood table covered in tabloid magazines and old paperbacks.

Erica Craxi settles in a dent on a sofa and Nic can tell this is her usual place. A lipstick-marked mug of almost-finished coffee on the floor by her feet confirms it. Goria sits next to her. She wraps a blanket protectively around her knees and tries to control the shaking as he talks softly in Italian. Right now she looks much older than her fifty-four years. Grey hair is clumped and matted with soil and shredded leaves.

250

Her eyes are darkened by tears and smudged mascara. Dario appears from the kitchen with a glass of water and a wet hand towel to clean the scratches on her face.

Goria keeps his voice low as he briefs Nic. 'The signora says Roberto was convinced there were people closing in on them. He thought he saw something moving outside, took his gun and went to look. He told Erica to hide in the woods until he returned because he knew she'd be a sitting duck if anyone entered the lodge. Anyway, after he'd gone she hesitated.' Goria half-laughs then whispers even more quietly, 'She wanted to go to the toilet first. While she was in there, she heard a phone ringing. The one we'd dropped through a window. It frightened her, especially when it went for the second time and she heard someone's footsteps inside the lodge. The phone rang again. She stayed tight and listened to the intruder walking with it through to where we are now. That's when she made a break for the woods and when we arrived.'

'So we just missed whoever was here?'

'Sounds like it.'

Nic turns his attention to the wife of the man he's tracked thousands of miles. 'Signora, I came here to speak to your husband about a Hollywood writer called Tamara Jacobs – do you know who I mean?'

She doesn't speak, just looks at him with frightened eyes and nods. It's a small gesture, but Nic feels a wave of relief wash over him. 'Mrs Jacobs is dead,' he says. 'She was murdered.'

Erica Craxi holds a tissue to her nose. Her trembling

fingers close around the Saint Christopher locket hanging from her neck.

'Your husband Roberto received a series of substantial wire payments from Mrs Jacobs. Do you know what she was paying him for?

Erica dips her eyes. 'I know exactly what he was being paid for.'

Nic's heart thumps. 'What was it?'

She shakes her head. 'Not with these people here. Ask them to leave and I will tell you.'

Nic nods to Goria and the Italian ushers his men outside. Erica takes a deep breath and looks trustingly to the American. 'My husband was on special assignment, part of a detail to protect the Holy Shroud, when it was last exhibited in public.'

'Back in 2010?'

'Si.' She needs a beat to compose herself. 'Roberto was persuaded by a scientist he knows . . . ' She gives a sad laugh. '. . . A so-called friend, to scrape blood and fibre from the cloth.' She hangs her head in shame. 'He did this – he damaged the cloth and passed on samples to be tested.'

Nic waits until she looks up and faces him. 'I need to know who that scientist is, Signora – why he wanted to test the Shroud and what he did with the results.'

Her face crumples. 'I am afraid.' She reaches behind her neck and unclips the chain holding the locket. She puts it to her mouth, closes her eyes and begins to pray.

87

JJ isn't surprised to find Jenny Harrison hanging around the factory floor after the rest of the mob have headed out into the Friday night blackness to begin their weekends.

She walks between the machines and gives him a hopeful look. 'Did you manage to find out anything about Kim?'

His face says he hasn't. 'It was like you said, Jenny. No one in the station has any record of her being arrested.'

She bites nervously on a fingernail. 'Who did you talk to?'

The question throws him. He hasn't talked to anyone and has no intention of doing so. 'Sorry, I can't remember their names. There was the woman who answered the phone, someone in custody and then someone else in the investigations unit. They're not very friendly or helpful, are they?'

She huffs out a sarcastic laugh. 'No cops ever are. Did you call East First Street? Was it an Officer Reed?'

'Might have been. I didn't make a note of his name. Didn't want to ask too much in case I got your friend into trouble.'

The comment silences her. Kim Bass has piles of trouble stacked in every corner of her life. She sure doesn't need anyone like Fish Face tipping them over by asking the wrong questions to the wrong people. Harrison slings her bag over her shoulder and zips her jacket. 'Thanks.'

He watches her head to the door. She's going to cause problems. He knows it. It's what women like her do. 'Jenny, wait.'

She turns around.

'I'll make some more calls tonight. Give me your cell number. If I can find anything out, I'll call you.'

She hesitates. 'Like you say, maybe it's best not to dig around too much.'

'Okay, but give me your number in case anyone calls me back and says she's in a lock-up somewhere.'

She swings her bag round, finds a pen and scrawls the number on the end of a cigarette pack. 'Call me at any time. I don't care how late.'

'I will.' He almost leaves it at that, then remembers it's not how he should act. 'Take my number too. Let me know if you hear anything.' He reaches into his back pocket and produces a business card.

'Thanks.' She looks at it, then wanders off again.

This time he lets her go. God has helped him. Having her phone number is a blessed surprise. If he rings it when he's inside that big old house of hers, he'll know exactly where she is. One call – that's all it will take to stop Jenny Harrison being a problem.

88

Roberto Craxi is feeling all of his fifty-nine years and it's annoying the hell out of him. He's gathering his thoughts as he regains consciousness, piecing together how he's been attacked and so easily beaten.

There was a time when no man was his match. In his prime, he could outsmart, outmanoeuvre or outmuscle the biggest, quickest and most savage of opponents. But things have changed. The metal garrotte someone pulled tight around his neck had been a sure sign those days are over. He never even saw his enemy.

Right from the start he suspected the sounds outside the cabin were a trap – but what choice did he have? Sit there in the dark with his guns cocked hoping his wife didn't get caught in the crossfire? No chance. And what fears had the night held for Roberto? None. Darkness was his friend, an old companion with whom he'd shared long battles and much bloodshed. It was in the darkness where he felt most alive.

Until tonight. Until he met his match.

The man holding him captive had known exactly what he'd do. How he'd slip out low and silent from the cabin and circle it clockwise – unhurried, meticulously, ensuring his wife was safe before disappearing into the undergrowth parallel to the main approach.

At first he thought he'd just brushed against a hanging branch, at worst a wild, straggling rose growing in the thicket. Then it had snapped around his neck. As soon as the high-tensile wire gripped his windpipe he realised he was in trouble. One swift pull and he was dead.

'Don't move and I let you live.'

He'll never forget the man's first words. It's what he would have said. What he *has* said, more than a dozen times. A clear, professional instruction from someone who is already in control and knows it.

But of course Roberto had moved. He'd tried to grab his attacker but the garrotte was unlike any he'd ever known. Instead of the wire being tethered to two small wooden handles, it was more like a lasso attached to the end of a long metal rod. Roberto couldn't even get near his attacker, let alone fight him off.

The man in the shadows had simply held tight at the other end, hauled him choking to the floor and jammed a sedative in his neck.

The painful memory of the attack races through Roberto's mind as he lies on his side in a small, black, cramped space. He doesn't know where his enemy is, but he's damned sure he knows what he wants and what he's prepared to do to get it.

89

JJ understands what he has to do the minute he opens his front door. The smell of the decomposing corpse can't be allowed to get any worse. It's going to attract attention.

He doesn't even take his coat off and hang it on the round post at the foot of the stairs like he normally does. He goes straight to the bedroom. The smell up here is stomach-churning. JJ has created death. Seen death. Handled death. But he's never smelled death. Not the brutal rotting stench that only death can bring.

He steps gingerly across the floor and covers his mouth as he gets close to the white linen sheet in which he's wrapped his precious Em. A part of him aches to look at her but he's frightened of what he might see. Best perhaps to remember her as she was that first night when he brought her home.

He sits on the edge of the bed and considers what to do and how to do it. Her home is overlooked. Even with the keys from her purse, returning her to the house is going to be risky. But she's worth it. She deserves it. She must be put to rest.

90

Erica Craxi tells Nic everything she knows about Tamara Jacobs, why the payments were made to her husband and who he was working with.

The revelation shocks him. He goes over the details several times. It's the kind of information you have to double-check. You do everything you can to make sure you're not going to make a dreadful mistake. Finally, after repeated assurances, she agrees to allow Goria in the room so Nic can make sure he has not misunderstood anything.

He hasn't. By the time she's done she feels exhausted and anxious – very, very anxious. 'What will happen to me now?'

Nic watches her bite on a nail as she waits for his reply. He looks towards Goria and the Italian's eyes give him the answer he's looking for. 'We can protect you. *We* being the LAPD, along with this man's men. I told you I trust him, and I do. We will make sure you are kept safe.'

'No Carabinieri.' She looks frightened.

'No – no Carabinieri. I promise. Fabio and his team will keep you safe until we find your husband.'

The PI crouches, takes her hand and says something in Italian that makes her smile briefly. She glances down at her cell phone then at Nic. 'Can I call Roberto again?'

'Of course.'

He watches as she speed-dials her husband and nervously paces the room while her call goes unanswered. She dials again. Nic knows the chances of Craxi returning safely have all but disappeared. His wife of twenty years closes the phone and walks to Nic. Tears are rolling down her cheeks as she takes both his hands and looks into his eyes. 'Please find him – don't let Roberto die.'

He squeezes her hand. 'We'll do our best.'

She puts something in the palm of his left hand and whispers, 'It is Saint Christopher, the patron saint of all travellers. May he guide you to my husband and all that you've come for.'

91

Ephrem works quickly. Methodically. He knows his task is far from complete. Under the pale moonlight and falling temperature he busies himself hiding the car he moved his captive in. He's covering his tracks. Laying traps for anyone who might be on his trail.

The untraceable cell phone in his pocket vibrates. 'Hello.'

'Do you have him? Is he still alive?'

'Yes.'

'*Molto buono*. You have served the Lord well. You know what to do – what is expected of you?'

'I am in no doubt.'

'Good. The Americans have sent a lieutenant from the Los Angeles police force to find Craxi. He is called Karakandez. When this call is finished I will send you a photograph and details about him. Be careful. He is very experienced and determined.'

'The man will not be a problem.'

'Don't make the mistake of underestimating him. He is from Homicide and has crossed continents to be here. He will not want to go home without a result.'

'Is that all?'

'It is.'

The monk finishes the call and waits patiently for an image to materialise on the screen of the phone.

Moments later, the face of Lt. Nic Karakandez appears. Ephrem takes a long look at it. It is the face of the man who called the cell phone in Craxi's lodge – the face of his enemy. He closes his eyes and imagines the man in front of him. Visualises what must be done to complete his mission. He takes one final look at the detective's eyes – the window to his soul – then he deletes the photograph.

Ephrem will meet Nic Karakandez, he is sure of it – and God will guide his hands as he kills him.

92

Amy Chang sits in her office chair, herbal tea in hand and listens to the very English voice of Professor Alexander Hasting-Smith on the other end of the line. She tries to picture him. Maybe public-schoolboy neat and tidy like the British Prime Minister or perhaps crazily hairy like that big bearded bishop who married Kate and William?

Professor Alex is nothing like either. He's late forties and barely five-nine, lives in baggy shirts and corduroy trousers and despite being an expert in anatomy and biology, is only a fried breakfast away from being clinically obese and a year or two away from being bald.

'Dear lady,' he says, stretching out the *lay-dee*. 'The comparable tests I undertook were exhaustive. I can categorically assure you the marks on the Shroud are not only consistent with having covered a man who suffered the ignominious end of crucifixion but are also identical to those endured by the body of Jesus Christ.'

'What do you mean?'

'Well, take the iconic spear wound. The cloth shows blood staining in alignment with a wound in between the right fifth and sixth ribs. The lower and inner part of this wound is approximately two-fifths of an inch below the tip

261

of the sternum and about two and a half inches below the midline. Entirely consistent with the hole made by the spear that the Roman soldier plunged into Christ. The staining on the Shroud is also corroborative in that it contains clear fluids as well as blood.'

'I didn't see any fluid markings.'

'You won't have done. Not unless you inspected the cloth itself. But it is there. I assure you.'

It's been a long day and she takes the point without rancour. 'And the fluid flow?'

'Down across the body. Consistent with the wound from the spear being made on a person in the upright – crucified – position.'

She puts her tea on a desk coaster and opens a folder on her Mac containing the high-definition Shroud photographs. 'Forgive my ignorance but exactly *what* tests did you do, Professor?'

'Goodness. What tests *didn't* I do? Are you aware of Pierre Barbet's work in this field?'

'I'm afraid not.' She suddenly feels out of her depth. 'Until very recently I hadn't even seen pictures of the Shroud. This really isn't my normal area of interest.'

'Oh, I see.' He sounds disappointed. 'Then why was I called and asked to contact you by the FBI?'

'Dr Quentell thought your knowledge about the Shroud could help with an ongoing investigation here in Los Angeles.'

'Ah, very well – then I'm happy to elucidate.' A little energy seems to return to his voice. 'Barbet was a French surgeon interested in the Shroud and had the good fortune to examine it in pure daylight. I'm going back to the 1930s now. Thirty-three, I think. Anyway, being a surgeon he had access to cadavers and amputated limbs, so he reconstructed the crucifixion of Christ. He nailed a dead body to a giant wooden cross and found the marks on the corpse perfectly fitted those found on the Shroud.'

'And you did the same?'

'Yes. I wish to be unambiguous about that.'

'Could you talk me through exactly what you did – and what you found?'

'With the greatest of pleasure. Some of it was debunking filmic myths. In Hollywood crucifixions you see nails hammered through the palms of hands. A completely inadequate way of holding a man upright. The movement and weight of his sagging body would soon tear the flesh. That certainly wasn't the method employed in the case of the Shroud.'

'It wasn't?'

'Not at all. Barbet discerned that the suspension nails had been driven through Destot's Space.'

Amy knows he means the gap in the wrist bounded by the hamate, capitate, triquetral and lunate bones. 'I can see that could certainly be strong enough.'

'It is. I assure you.' He sounds almost offended. 'If you look at the Shroud, you'll notice that the thumbs are not visible. Can you see that, do you have a photograph to inspect?'

Amy enlarges the shot she has onscreen. 'Yes, yes I have one onscreen.'

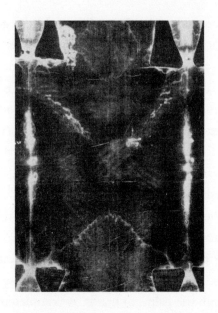

'Good. Well, as a pathologist, you'll know that a nail driven through Destot's Space would damage the Median nerve and that would almost always result in the thumbs turning inwards.'

Amy glances at the photograph and it seems to comply. 'What about stigmata marks – they're always in the palms of hands, aren't they? I've never seen religious paintings of people showing their wrists bleeding.'

'Not a question for me, Doctor, I am not a theologian, I am a scientist. Though I do believe stigmata take various forms and are not confined only to Catholicism.'

'I didn't know that.'

'Indeed. You'll find evidence of stigmata in Buddhism and

even in polytheistic religions, particularly ones with tutelary deities.'

'Professor, I'll have to take your word for it.' Her eyes go to the HD prints again. 'I'm looking at the feet and I can't see any images indicating how they were nailed to the cross.'

'An excellent observation. You can't see any because it's very blurred. There is a possibility, a thin one I believe, that the nails were inserted between the metatarsal bones.'

'Would that have been sufficient to hold a grown man?'

He becomes animated again. 'I think not, which is why I pinned my cadaver through the ankles. Entirely adequate. Again, if you examine any good stills, you will see dark patches indicating a spillage of blood around the ankle regions.'

Amy's not sure she can discern such detail but she doesn't want to debate the matter. 'Professor, is it possible for you to mail me a summary of your findings?'

'Certainly, Quentell gave me your details.'

'Thank you. One thing, though, before you go – I've been wondering about blood spillage and decomposition. Hours after death, wounds don't bleed enough to transfer perfect outlines of their shapes onto cloth. A body kept in the open air for days will putrefy and there will be signs of loss of body fluids and matters. The Shroud shows no evidence of that. How can you explain it?'

'Easily,' he says. 'It's a miracle.'

93

TURIN

It's 2.30 a.m. Saturday when Nic and Fabio Goria have settled Erica Craxi in a safe house guarded by the investigator's men. As they leave, rain beats hard on the windshield of Goria's speeding Fiat – too hard for the worn wipers to make clean sweeps of the heavy downpour.

The lateness of the hour, the warmth of the car and the rhythm of the rain are testing the detective's ability to stay awake. Boy, does he need some shut-eye. He drifts off as he listens to the repetitive rasp of the tyres on the wet road and the rain hitting the windows. He's miles away. Out on the open sea, his old boat cutting white water as it picks up speed towards the sun shimmering on the horizon. He turns towards the laughing voices on the back of the boat. Carolina and Max are there in red life-jackets, wind in their hair, the joy of life all over their wonderful faces.

Nic wakes. His heart is hammering with the pain of remembering them. He winds down the window and lets the cold air and beating rain pound his face. Not long now. Not long until late nights and murder cases like this are problems for other people. Gradually, familiar city centre sights smear themselves across the rain-streaked window. Goria kills the engine and headlights as he draws up to the kerb around the corner from Nic's hotel. 'Here you are. Now you can have a proper sleep.'

He yawns as he unbuckles his seat belt. 'Thanks, I certainly need it. Given the circumstances, Fabio, you and your guys did okay tonight. Erica Craxi certainly gave us plenty to follow up on.'

'*Grazie.* I will come for you at eight. I'm sorry we lost her husband. My men will find him, I promise you.'

'I hope so – for his sake and hers.'

Goria grabs Nic's arm as he reaches for the door handle. 'Be careful. The Carabinieri may be watching your hotel. They could have night sights on you from a kilometre away and we would not know. I will stay here until you get inside and have settled. If they are around, they will move closer and I will see. It is better we are safe than sorry.'

Nic steps from the car, nods goodnight and turns up his jacket collar against the rain. Save for the cars parked at odd angles all over the place, the streets are deserted. The neighbourhood's shops and bars are filled only with blackness.

He shakes off the downpour as he heads past reception and rides the lift to his room.

He freshens up in the bathroom and notices his toothbrush and razor have been placed neatly in a glass on a shelf by the sink. The maid must have been in. It's the kind of thing he'd expect in a four-star hotel but not this dive. He turns off the light and walks back to the main room. There's something different, maybe something wrong. He can sense it, in the same way he senses clues at a crime scene.

The bed has been turned back for the first time since he checked in. And it's not been done in the professional, neat way a maid does. It's been done by someone wanting to make it look like a maid's done it. Someone poking around.

There's been a stranger in his room.

94

CORONER'S OFFICE, LOS ANGELES

Amy Chang had been hoping to go home early – end her Friday night by cooking a light dinner and sinking a glass of crisp white or two, maybe even put her feet up on the couch, play a little soft music and forget a week's worth of cold flesh and sterile steel.

But it's not to be. What's pinning her to her office chair is the Shroud of Turin. Alexander Hasting-Smith's call and the subsequent reports he mailed have left her head buzzing so she may as well try to finish the report she promised Mitzi. Amy spends a good hour trawling the internet, pulling up pages, searching through dedicated Shroud websites, diving deep into religious discussion groups and social network blogs. She discovers Shroud universities, multiple Shroud shops and dozens of different video streams dealing with not only the carbon dating of the Shroud but also 3D renderings of its image, microscopic analysis and digital enhancements. Along with all the pictures come countless conflicting opinions about the cloth's authenticity.

Around 6 p.m. her tummy grumbles a reminder that all she had for lunch was coffee and a salmon bagel. The ME sits back from her Mac, twists her head from side to side to ease the tension from being hunched and reviews the notes she's made.

HISTORY (dates are approx)

AD 30: The Death of Christ. There are no immediate independent and indisputable reports of a shroud being discovered and being imprinted with Christ's image. There are similarly no such reports of it being stored, guarded or transported to a place of safe-keeping.

Seems strange that something so important wasn't acclaimed at the time!

AD 40: Reports of a King Abgar V of Edessa (now Sanliurfa, eastern Turkey) viewing a cloth (no dimensions) imprinted with the face of Jesus. Said to lead to conversion to Christianity (there are also later reports of a letter Jesus sent to Abgar promising to protect his country from foreign invaders).

AD 50–500: No reliable mentions of Jesus cloth, then suddenly stories about it resurface.

544: Persian army repelled at Edessa's walls. The Jesus cloth and letter are credited with affording protection to the city.

679: Edessa hit by earthquake. The cathedral where the Jesus cloth was allegedly kept is damaged – cloth said to be moved to Jerusalem.

690: Iconic bearded images of Jesus, identical to that on the cloth start appearing throughout Middle East.

944: Jesus cloth is said to have travelled length of what is now Turkey and is afforded its own feast day (16th Aug). Interestingly, there are no reports of public showings, only private ones. Cloth is said to have been stored in the Pharos Chapel of Constantinople's Imperial Palace.

1130: Reports in Western Europe (including monks in Normandy) about the Jesus cloth and how it contains an imprint of Christ's body.

1146: Edessa conquered by Turkish Muslims – mass

270

slaughter of its citizens (so much for the protective cloth and letter!)

1203: Reports attributed to French Crusader Robert de Clari say he saw a cloth in which Christ had been wrapped in the Church of St Mary in Constantinople.

1204: French crusaders ransack Constantinople and churches are looted. Robert de Clari denies the French took it.

1287: Reports say a knight called Arnaut Sabbatier, on being received into the Order of the Knights Templar in Rousillon in France, was taken to a secret place by the brothers and shown the shroud of Christ.

1307: Friday the 13th October (allegedly this is where the legend of the date being unlucky springs from) King Philip the Fair issues orders to arrest all the Knights Templar on heresy charges for worshipping the image of Christ. Many, including the grand master Jacques de Molay, are burned at the stake.

Amy decides to take a break. She goes to the washroom then brews a fresh cup of herbal tea and raids her small office fridge for one of the emergency Hershey bars she keeps there.

Back at her computer she taps the space bar to click off the screensaver. Nothing happens. The machine has locked up. She tries ESCAPE and then reluctantly reboots, sipping the tea and eating a square of milk chocolate while the machine gets up to speed.

Her document has gone. She searches the file folder.

Searches the cute little wire trash basket at the end of the shiny steel dock bar. Nothing. She's lost everything.

'No, no, *no*. This can't be.' Amy tries to stay calm. The Mac backs things up every couple of minutes. All her work will be somewhere.

It isn't. She searches every conceivable storage space, then searches it again. An hour later she fearfully opens her mailbox. Empty. Some kind of virus has penetrated the firewall and destroyed every document, image, file and presentation on the computer.

95

Nic takes a long, slow look around his hotel room.

He knows he's exhausted and knows tired people often don't think straight but he's sure someone's been in here snooping around. He opens the wardrobe and stares at the shirts and a sweater dangling from plastic coat-hangers. Are they really as he left them when he'd unpacked?

He doesn't think so. They're strung out across the silver hanging rail. Spaced almost evenly. Neat and tidy. Not at all his style. He has a longstanding habit of hanging things only on the left side of the bar. It's what he always does. Carolina used to hang her stuff on the right and even today he still leaves space. He can't help it. He certainly didn't leave them like this.

He lifts out the suitcase from the shallow well at the bottom of the wardrobe and drops it on the bed. The combination is 8634 – the same as his credit card pin. He always spins the numbers to 7523 to lock it – one digit back on each reel. He remembers the numbers precisely because in his mind he has a permanent picture of a clock in heaven (rhymes with 7) that's stuck at five (5) to (2) three (3) – the time his wife and child died and went to heaven.

The numbers don't read that any more. They read 1870. Someone has either opened the case and spun the locks randomly or tried to open it. He enters the combination and flips the locks. The inside is a mess. A gym kit and trainers he'll never get round to using, enough socks and underwear to dress an army, a camera that needs new batteries and copies of all the case papers he could carry.

He sits on the bed and lifts out the documents. There are so many he can't remember the order of the files stacked in there. He shuts his eyes and tries to recall what he last looked at. *Craxi's bank accounts. Carlotta had shown him the final withdrawal when they were in the bank together. He'd closed the file with that page facing up at him.*

He opens the document folder. It's as he left it. Despite the reassurance he doesn't feel satisfied. Maybe he's imagining things. Tiredness and stress can make you edgy – even paranoid. He needs a long, deep sleep. Another thing occurs to him. He flicks quickly down the stack of files and finds the crime-scene photographs showing Tamara Jacobs's body on the beach. He stares at the bundle not sure whether he feels relieved or not.

They're there. They're not missing. But they are back-to-front.

He'd arranged them in the order a psychological profiler does – pictures that set the scene first and then shots of the victim.

But that's not how they are. They're now in reverse order. He'd never do that. He's as messy as a teenager when it comes to leaving clothes and crockery around the house, but not work things, never professional stuff. Someone has been through all the photographs. But who? The Carabinieri? That doesn't make sense. He would gladly have shown them the photos if they'd asked. Until a few hours ago, until meeting Goria and talking to Erica Craxi, he'd have shared anything and everything with them.

If not the Carabinieri, then who? Tamara's killer? He looks down at the crime-scene prints. Is it really possible that the man who tortured her to death had held these photographs? Had admired his own handiwork in this very room? Nic looks around the room and finds a pad of complimentary paper and a couple of envelopes bearing the crest of the hotel. He slips the photographs inside one of the envelopes and seals it. It's highly unlikely the murderer left his prints behind but even hitmen make mistakes.

As he seals the envelope he thinks of the killer being in his room – being in the lodge and listening when he'd called Craxi on Goria's cell phone. The man comes and goes like a ghost. A tingle lifts hairs on the back of Nic's neck as he realises the killer knows more about him than he does about the killer.

96

CORONER'S OFFICE, LOS ANGELES

Barney, the emergency IT guy, finishes examining the Mac and gives Amy an expression that says he's almost at the end of his shift and she's screwed.

'I'm sorry, I just can't fix this.' The bespectacled geek repositions a fall of shoulder-length black hair behind his blue denim shirt. 'We're going to have to take your machine away, hook it up and run diagnostics.'

She doesn't like the sound of that. IT is a graveyard. Few loved machines come back from there alive. 'What about my files? They'll be backed up on the server, won't they?'

'Should be. You might have lost stuff you've been working on today. We did the last dump around midnight last night.'

'Shit.'

'That's the way it goes. I keep telling the Chief that he should give you guys portable back-ups. It's the only way to stay safe.'

Amy shakes her head. 'So how long? How long do you think it'll take to get me fixed?'

He looks at his watch. 'I should have been gone an hour ago. I'm afraid your Mac won't even get seen until Monday now.'

'*Monday*. That's a lifetime away.'

'Sorry. Overtime was cut for us as well as everyone else.' He peers at the computer as though it just whispered to him. 'Hold on. Let me just take a look at something.'

Barney settles in her chair, pounds keys and exposes parts of Amy's computer that she didn't even know existed. Administrator's privileges. Something akin to a surgical examination of her Mac's innermost and most private parts.

'Whoa. I don't believe this.'

'You can fix it?' Amy bends close to the screen.

'No way.' He sits back and folds his arms, staring at a mass of codes with apparent admiration. 'It's a zombie.'

'A what?'

'Some smart ass has infiltrated the firewall, downloaded everything from your computer and has been using it remotely.' He reaches round the back and snaps out the cable. 'Best get this quarantined and cleansed ASAP.'

Amy feels violated.

'Our guy will know we're on to him.' Barney is as excited as a kid playing cops and robbers. 'He'll have dropped worms or Trojans in your system too. They'll have destroyed most of your programs and you've probably been passing on infections as well.' He lifts the Mac off her desk.

'You should go home, Dr Chang. You're not going to see this baby Monday, or ever again. We'll order you a new computer.'

97

BEL-LA-PIZZA is a new restaurant around the corner from Mitzi's place. It's the latest in a long line in LA to badly word pun the connection between bella and LA.

She and the girls are there for several reasons. First, she has nothing in at home. Second, it's a place they've never been to before – in other words they've never been with Alfie. Most important, though, it has a half-price and free glass of wine offer until the end of the month.

A breadstick-thin teenage waitress with long black hair stands at the edge of the table as Mitzi orders. 'Two diet cokes and one glass of house red. One garlic bread. One Minestrone soup. One battered mushrooms. For mains, one medium-sized, thin-crust Neptune, no anchovies. One large stuffed-crust, Pepperoni with a cracked egg. And – ' Mitzi glances again at the card to decide what she's having, '- one small lasagne with a chopped green salad, no fries and nothing else.' As she watches the girl frantically catch up on her notepad she realises she's turning into Tyler Carter. No courtesy, just facts. 'Thanks,' she adds, hastily, as the waitress heads for the kitchen. 'Thanks for your help.'

Bad news is always best broken first and broken quickly. As soon as Jade and Amber have their drinks, Mitzi gives it to them. 'Your father's case came up in court today. They sent him to prison. Thirty days.' She curses herself, again she sounds like Carter.

Amber drops the Coke straw from her lips. 'Daddy's in jail?'

'Right now? Already?' Jade looks more annoyed than shocked.

Mitzi reaches across and takes both their hands. 'Yes. He started his sentence this afternoon.'

Jade snatches her hand away. 'Oh God. Poor Daddy.'

Poor Daddy? Mitzi has to bite her tongue.

Amber says nothing. She doesn't move. Doesn't touch her drink. Just disappears into private thoughts that her mom can only guess are horribly painful.

'So what's all *this*, then?' Jade throws her arms wide, her face reddening with anger. 'Have you brought us here to *celebrate*?'

'*No*.' Mitzi is firm but calm. 'I've brought you out to be with you. To show you that life goes on.'

'Not for Dad, though.' Jade gets up and throws her napkin at the table. 'I'm not doing this. I'm not sitting here in a restaurant while my father's in prison, probably with *nothing* to eat or drink.'

Mitzi stands up opposite her. 'Yes, you are. Sit down.'

Tables fall silent around them.

Jade glares at her mother. 'I'm leaving. I'm going home and you're not stopping me.'

'Yes, I am. Now *sit* down.' Mitzi says it in a tone that never gets disobeyed.

Jade stares defiantly then starts to move towards the door. 'What are you going to do? Beat me up? Call your cop friends? Have me locked up as well as my dad?'

Mitzi needs all her willpower not to slap the child, not to shake her and tell her to grow up.

'Go on!' Amber pulls up right in front of her. 'I know you want to hit me.' She sticks her face out. 'Do it, if that's what makes you feel better.'

A small middle-aged man in a black suit turns up in the gap between the tables. Behind him is the breadstick waitress with their coats. 'I am sorry, you have to leave.' He looks nervously at Mitzi and then motions with both hands to the door like he's shooing an unspeakably dirty animal. 'You go now, please. You go now.'

She doesn't put up a fight. She grabs their coats. He's doing her a favour. The stand-off is over. Even though they're being thrown out, they're still all together.

98

Nic turns off the bedroom light and eases back an inch of curtain. He stands at the window looking at the wet, empty street as he calls Goria. 'My room's been turned over.'

'What?'

'Someone's searched it. They haven't taken anything but I know they've been through case files, maybe even photographed stuff.'

'You're sure?'

'Positive.'

'I am still around the corner. Check out. You can stay at my place. We have to move quickly tomorrow anyway.'

Nic leaves the curtain and starts gathering his things. 'Good idea. I'll be down in a moment.'

It takes him ten minutes to pack and head downstairs. While paying the bill he thinks about asking who cleaned his room and could have messed with his personal belongings but decides against it. From the look of the half-asleep reception clerk he'd be unlikely to get a helpful answer.

Nic slips into what remains of the cold rainy night and scans the street for watching eyes as he turns the corner to find Goria's Bravo. To the best of his knowledge no one has seen him leave.

'This is like a day that never ends,' says the Italian as the detective settles into the passenger seat.

'I've had too many of those recently. Thanks again for your help.'

'Not a problem.' He starts the engine and pulls away.

'Listen, I need to call my boss. You mind?'

'Go right ahead.'

Nic dials the number. It takes a few seconds to connect, then he hears it ringing.

'Yes.'

The bluntness of the answer shocks him. It's almost like it's not her and he's got a wrong number.

'Mitzi, it's Nic.'

'Hi Nic. I'm sorry this isn't a good time.'

He can tell that from her tone. She's in a car going somewhere – there's the noise of traffic and of one of the girls shouting at her and another crying. 'Mitz, I can hardly hear you. Call me back when you can. There are some strange things happening and I need to bring you up to speed.' The line goes dead and he closes down his phone. 'Seems like my boss is having a tough time too.'

'Tough times sometimes they make for good memories,' says Goria, swerving to avoid a pothole. 'For me, the happiest time of my marriage was when our lives were tough and we had nothing. My wife and I just ate soup and went to bed to stay warm and make love.' He turns and smiles at Nic. 'You know what I mean?'

'Yeah. I know what you mean.'

They head north-west across the city to Venaria Reale, a quiet area not far from the sprawling grounds of the Strada Militare Carlo Grassi. Goria's place is a small new house protected by its own iron gates and high metal fence. He thumbs an electronic zapper. The gates open and a roller door slides up and reveals a long garage.

Nic can't help but look over his shoulder as they exit the narrow street. He sees a flash of passing headlights but no following cars.

'We are safe here. Do not worry any more tonight.' Goria turns off the car engine and steps out into the garage. 'I have security cameras and a full perimeter alarm around the house. All necessary precautions in my line of work.' He goes to a metal box set in the cinderblock wall and presses several buttons. 'It is armed now for the night, nothing can get in without it being triggered.'

'Talking of arms,' Nic follows him through a door into a cool, dark kitchen. 'Do you have a piece you can give me?'

'Of course. But you did not get it from me.' Overhead neons flicker on. He opens a large steel larder fridge, dips into the coolbox and turns around with a bottle in one hand and a gun in the other. 'Beer and a Beretta – how's that for service?'

'Perfect.' Nic's phone rings in his pocket.

Goria places the pistol and Peroni on a worktop and goes for his own beer.

Caller display says it's Mitzi. 'Hello.'

'Hi, Nic. Sorry about earlier. Hey, what time is it there?'

He glances at his wrist. 'Four a.m.'

'Gee, I'm sorry. This too late?'

'I don't even know what late is any more.' He manages a tired laugh as he picks up the beer. 'I'm just about to have a drink then crash.'

There's a pause then her voice changes. 'Alfie beat up on me again and I got him busted.'

'What?'

'He started slapping me about and coming the big I am. Then it all turned nasty and I called it in.'

'Are you okay? Did that bastard hurt you?'

She's touched to hear the anger in his voice. 'Not so much physically.'

'And the girls?'

'They're in bits. That's why I couldn't talk.'

Nic puts the bottle down. 'Listen, screw this damned job, if you need me to come back, I can be on the next plane to LA.'

She laughs. 'No way, cowboy. You finish this job.'

'Seriously—'

'No. I'm fine. Besides, Amy's looking after me.'

'Good.'

'She asked about you.'

'Yeah, sure she did. What's happening with Alfie?'

'They already put him through court. Thirty days in the Big House.'

'And then?'

'I'm not thinking of having him back, if that's what you mean.'

'That was exactly what I meant.'

'Lesson learned.'

'Glad to hear it. If I can help – in any way – let me know.'

'Thanks. I will. You can help right now by closing this freakin' case.'

'Wish I could. I just moved out the hotel. Someone turned it over while I was chasing down Craxi.'

'You sure?'

'Absolutely. Dave Burge from the FBI fixed a PI to help me chase down some leads. Good guy by the name of Fabio Goria.'

'I told you there was no money for that, Nic.'

'None spent. It's a favour. Burge owed me one. Owed me several actually.'

'Good. And Craxi?'

'Found him and lost him. It's a long story. Anyway, I'm about to go AWOL on the Carabinieri.'

'Fine by me. I'm gonna hang up now, let you get a little sleep.'

'I'll call you tomorrow – I mean later today.'

'Great. Stay in touch.'

'Oh, Mitz?'

'Yeah?'

'I'm glad you got that bum busted. You're a great cop, great mom and great lady. I hope this is the first step towards you having the great life you and the girls deserve.'

'Thanks.' She hangs up quick. Doesn't want him to hear her get emotional.

99

In the damp, fetid darkness Roberto Craxi thanks God for small mercies.

He's alive. And he knows he so easily could be dead.

His hands and feet are untied and he isn't gagged. Whoever is holding him is doing so in a secluded place, somewhere they're sure any shouts for help will go unheard. Somewhere out of the city.

Craxi rubs his wrists. He can feel a ridge on his skin where the rope was pulled tight. He reaches down and feels his ankles. The same is true down there. Whoever attacked him came prepared to tie him up. If it was a lone attacker, the guy was also strong enough to carry him unconscious to a vehicle and move him around. It's a worrying thought. He would rather not think of a single enemy with such power.

He wipes a hand across and around his mouth. It's sticky. Adhesive residue. A sign that tape has been plastered across his lips. Another sign that his foe is professional and well prepared for any eventuality. Finally, he touches his windpipe. The pain here is intense. He can feel a ridge where the wire sliced into his throat. The man choking him had known exactly how hard to pull. He understood how to control life and death. He was a man like him.

The place he's being held is pitch black – not a single speck of light. It's cold too. Craxi puts his palms flat on the floor where he's sitting. It's hard and smooth. Some form of polished stone, not earth. He knows better than to try to stand up – there's every chance he could knock himself out or fall off some unseen ledge.

He raises his hands above his head. Or at least he tries to. Sat down he has about a foot of space above him. He runs his fingers over the ceiling. It feels like the floor – cold and smooth. Stone. His heart thumps out an objection. Craxi puts his hands to his sides. There's not much room there either. Maybe a foot on one side and perhaps a little more on the other. The surfaces are also stone.

Cautiously, he lowers himself into a lying position. A shade less than six feet, his head and toes don't touch any walls. He reaches up behind him and scrapes his fingers – stone. Barely six inches away. He shuffles forward. His feet quickly reach a hard stop. More stone. So now he knows. He's being held in an airless seven-foot-by-four-foot stone block. Or, to use a more familiar description, a tomb.

100

By day the neighbourhood is a suburban boiling pot. People of all hues go about their business. Cars stick bumper-to-bumper. Noise rises like steam above the suburb. Right now it's a ghost town. Dark and deserted. Silent and spectral.

It's just the way JJ likes it. He scans for house lights and surveillance cameras as he walks slowly past the clapboard buildings that run the length of Emma Varley's street. The place she used to live. It's 3 a.m. and there's nothing to disturb him. No reason why he can't go return his queen to her domestic throne. Just one more circle around the block and then he'll do it.

He winds his way back up West 169th, swings open the front gate and crosses the worn grass to her front door. JJ stops on the doorstep. Turns. Takes a final look at the street then pulls out the ring of keys he took from her purse. Satisfied he's unwatched, he tries several. The last, a square-headed brass one, does the trick.

The place is filled with the essences of Em. Her perfumes, soaps and talcs. Her hair sprays, washing powders and fabrics. He stands in the dark and inhales them all. It is like she is here with him. The rental is small – just two downstairs rooms – a sitting area and cramped kitchen-diner. Upstairs there's an adequate enough bedroom, a much smaller spare room that has no furniture in it and a tiny bathroom with a sink that's coming loose from the wall. He picks up her toothbrush from a cracked glass shelf and runs a hand over the worn bristles. He closes his eyes and puts it to his lips, glides it into his mouth and over his tongue. The taste of her makes him tremble.

JJ lingers in every room. He takes her carefully ironed and packed clothes from a rickety chest of drawers and smells and holds them. He opens the tiny one-door wardrobe and embraces the only two dresses that she owned – one short and black, one long, flowing and hippy-like.

He lies on her unmade bed, his face in the same pillow crease she made during her last night under the covers. How he wishes he'd come here earlier, spent longer among her things, got to know her even better. Painful as it is, he drags himself away from the sensual reminiscences, leaves the house and returns to the Explorer.

He drives slowly and kills the lights fifty yards from Em's place. Ten yards away he turns off the engine and lets the big old bus glide to the kerb. With darkness pressed to breath-misted glass he sits patiently and watches the street and surrounding houses. He winds down the window and listens for approaching traffic or people.

Nothing. This is the dead of night.

JJ makes his move. Quickly. Smartly. Confidently. He opens the driver's door then the rear door. He grabs Em under the arms and hauls her out of the vehicle. 'Sorry,' he whispers as her feet thud down onto the asphalt. He shuffles backwards and drags her through the gate he left open, up the doorstep and into the house.

JJ lays her out on the hall floor. He walks calmly back to the Explorer and shuts the doors. He knows he can't delay now. Can't spend the time he'd like with her. He quickly returns to the house, shuts the door behind him and crouches down to get a good lifting grip of her. The stench of decomposition is awful but it doesn't matter. He lifts her in his arms and feels like a groom carrying his bride over a threshold.

He struggles up the stairs and almost falls when her feet bang on a wall. Moonlight is streaming through her window as he lays her on the bed. It's as though God is shining a light for him, affording him a final parting view of his beloved. He leans over her pale face and kisses her lips. Then he covers her. Wraps the bottom sheet around her. Tucks her in. Tight.

'Night, night, my queen,' he says from the doorway. 'I will see you on the other side.'

101

TURIN

A lesser man would have gone mad by now. The darkness of the tomb. The stench. The silence. The cramping of muscles. The claustrophobia. Any, or all of those things, would have broken someone who lacked Roberto Craxi's willpower and training.

He's experienced enough to know that he's being kept alive for a purpose, that right now his life isn't intentionally going to be ended. But captors make mistakes – sometimes fatal ones – and as a result hostages are abandoned and left to suffocate or starve.

He concentrates on lowering his heartbeat. The slower it thumps, the less oxygen he uses and the longer he lives. The mathematics of survival. His focus is so intense he can feel the organ's soft thuds in his chest and all but hear blood slowing in his veins.

Sixty-nine.

Fifty-two.

Forty-seven.

That's as low as he can get it. Forty-seven beats a minute. Twenty years ago he would have had it down another ten, but he's nowhere near being the athlete he was.

'Signore Craxi, are you awake?'

The voice startles him. Bumps his heartbeats per minute back over the sixty mark. It was polite and foreign. English with a strange accent. Oddly formal.

'Signore Craxi.'

It is coming out of nowhere.

'Can you hear me?'

Somewhere in the darkness is a tiny wireless loudspeaker. He has no idea where. He rubs his hands over the cold stone but can't find anything. He stays silent. The fact that his abductor has gone to the trouble of putting the device in here means the man needs to communicate with him. Well, if he wants to do that, he's going to have to come and get him out of this god forsaken place.

'Signore.' The voice is louder this time and Craxi detects an accent.

Foreign. Not European – African. No, not African. Arabic.

A bored sigh hisses like steam through the thick stone. 'Signore, there is good reason why I let your wife live. Should you not cooperate with me, I am confident that I can torture her into doing so.'

'What do you want?' Craxi's voice is thin and strained. 'I am ready to give you whatever you want.'

102

LOS ANGELES

JJ steers the Explorer through the dark backstreets of Gardena, then out into the bright lights of the freeway and over to Boyle Heights.

It is time to pay Jenny Harrison a visit. The display on the dash shows 4 a.m. He knows he has only a couple of hours before the sun comes up and the poor folk that work late-night shifts come drifting home.

He's going to have to be quick. Her big old house is in total blackness. He parks down the street in almost exactly the same position he occupied last time he was here. He sits with the window down, watching and listening, waiting to see if anyone has heard his vehicle and is stupid enough to take a closer look.

At ten after four he reaches into the passenger foot well, picks up the tyre iron he put there and slips out of the car. He walks briskly across the road, through the gate and up the path. The patchy lawn around him smells of dog shit and is peppered with discarded cigarette butts.

JJ jogs up the steps onto the porch, turns and checks the scene behind him. Nothing. No movement. No noise. No people. He puts his hand on the front door and twists the big round knob. Hopefully the lock will be old and there'll be enough movement for him to get the thin end of the iron in.

The door is unlocked. He feels a jolt of excitement. God is indeed looking after him tonight. He enters the lobby and the unmistakable stench of a doss-house hits him. It disgusts him. What a fitting place for Jenny Harrison to die. Around him are more doors than he anticipated, all brown and without numbers.

JJ moves to the foot of an uncarpeted wooden staircase. He takes out his cell phone and calls the number she gave him. The dial tone rolls into cyberspace. There's a click. From above JJ's head comes the noise of a ringing phone.

103

A repetitive thump haunts the darkness. Not a loud one. Not hoof beats on hardened earth, more a woodpecker tapping stone.

Roberto Craxi cranes his head anxiously to the right. He shouts through the walls of the tomb to the man who's imprisoned him – a man he's never seen. 'What are you doing? What's going on?'

Suddenly the stone vibrates. A loud screaming noise penetrates the casement.

'Hey!'

It feels like the whole tomb is going to collapse. Craxi's training kicks in. He calms himself. Tries to work out what's happening. His captor is drilling. Boring some kind of hole. There's a bang as the whirling steel breaks through and the chuck hits the exterior. Debris from the drill bit spatters Craxi's face. The mechanical screaming stops.

Through the hole bursts a shaft of bright light as thick as a pencil. He rolls on his right side and shuffles along so he can see outside the tomb.

An eyeball stares down at him.

Craxi's heart jumps.

'Move back.' The voice is cold and insistent.

He edges away.

Ephrem puts down the high-speed battery-powered drill. 'This hole will give you air. If what you've told me is true, I will call the police and they will come and find you. If it is not, then when I have finished with your wife, I will come back for you.'

The monk bags up the tools he'd bought in Turin after Craxi had given him the slip in the subway. He leaves the old church and returns to the rental car. He'll need different tools for the next part of the mission. Very different ones.

104

BOYLE HEIGHTS, LOS ANGELES

It takes four rings of the phone for JJ to track the tone to an upstairs room.

He places his own cell back in his trousers and examines the door in front of him. It's cheap and insubstantial. A low-quality block of painted plywood fitted with a barely decent lock. No match for the tyre iron he's brought with him. He could easily prise it open.

But not yet. He sits patiently on the floor outside and listens for movement. The phone most probably woke her. He needs her to fall back to sleep. Needs her to be in a state of rest when he takes her.

JJ is waiting for the sound of her using the bathroom. The noise of a TV being put on or a kettle being boiled.

There is nothing. Forty minutes pass. Two thousand four hundred long seconds tick away, before he's satisfied enough to wriggle the fluted end of the tyre iron into the door jamb. He lets the metal chew slowly into the soft wood, nosing deeper into the space where the edge of the door and the frame meet. The work is hard and sweat beads on his forehead. Finally, it is in the right position. He's satisfied he has enough purchase – sufficient leverage – to be able to force the door open. In one crisp movement he jerks the iron to his left while ramming his right shoulder and hip against the door.

It bursts open. Bangs noisily against the wall. Certainly loudly enough to wake Harrison. He forgets about closing it and rushes inside. The room is in darkness. There's a bed and a couch and a window and a sink. No Jenny. He swings round. Another door. He pushes it open.

A tiny bathroom. She's not there. JJ inches his way back to the splintered door and closes it. The place has paper-thin walls. Chances are people next door have heard him.

He flicks on the light. On the floor near the edge of the bed is her phone. She must have dropped it. Gone out without it. An act of forgetfulness that has saved her life. For now.

105

It's a long time since former soldier Roberto Craxi has been forced to lie in a pool of his own urine.

If memory serves him well it was twenty years ago in Naples. An anti-Camorra operation went wrong and he and his team got trapped in a landfill site for almost an entire day. He killed three people in the gun battle that followed. And he'd dearly like to kill again today.

The tomb that's holding him seems escape-proof. He rolls onto his front, gets up on his knees and presses his back against the heavy slab above him. It won't budge.

Not an inch. His captor's been gone some time now and Craxi knows exactly where he is and what he's doing. It won't take an animal like him long to crack the man he's visiting. A scientist with no guts. And when he does, he will know the truth. Know Craxi held back on him. Delayed him.

Craxi takes in a deep lungful of air and once more painfully presses his back against the unyielding stone. He has to get out. *Must* get out. Escape before it's too late.

PART FOUR

He who controls the present, controls the past.
He who controls the past, controls the future.

George Orwell

106

Since he was a child, Mario Sacconi has slept with the window open. There's something about being shut in that disturbs him and keeps him awake. He feels stifled. Claustrophobic. It's a habit that's led to countless girlfriends complaining about the freezing cold in his bedroom – but that's never been a problem the handsome geneticist hasn't been able to solve.

He went to bed last night with the elegant sash window open and a beautiful Brazilian intern grateful for his body heat. Dawn is breaking now over the lush forest surrounding his home. As he opens his eyes in the pink light he realises what a terrible mistake he's made.

'*Buongiorno,*' says a man dressed head to toe in black at the foot of his bed.

'*Vaffanculo!*' Sacconi tries to sit up. A slipknot tightens around his left wrist and then his right. He looks frantically for his lover. 'Benedetta?'

'In the bathroom,' Ephrem nods behind him. 'You'll see her in a moment.'

Sacconi has read about intruders, how they sometimes get violent or sexual when confronted. Best stay calm and not rile them. Don't turn a simple housebreaking into something much uglier. 'Look, I don't want any trouble. Take whatever you want. The keys to my Mercedes are in my trousers on the chair over there. I have a safe, jewellery and money. I'll give you anything.'

The monk laughs. 'Roberto Craxi.'

The name silences him.

'Craxi is why I am here.'

'I don't know what you mean.'

Dark eyes stare through his balaclava. 'Yes, you do. You are Mario Sacconi. Craxi paid you money to do something you shouldn't have done. You abused your power, the gifts God and science gave you.'

'No. No – you're wrong.'

The look in the monk's eyes says he's sure he isn't. He strides away from the bed and enters the bathroom. He returns seconds later with the naked girl in his arms and drops her on the bed next to Sacconi. Her hands and feet are tied together behind her back. Thick parcel tape is wrapped around her mouth. Her eyes are wide with terror.

'Roberto Craxi paid you to test samples he stole from the holy shroud. I want the results of that test and any samples you have left.'

'You're mistaken. I swear to God, I don't know what you mean.'

A punch explodes in Sacconi's face. He wails. His nose is broken. Blood is smeared across his mouth and cheeks.

'Thou shalt not take the name of the Lord Thy God in vain.' The monk reaches into black cargo pants and produces what looks like a thin, oblong case beautifully covered in mother-of-pearl. The snap of a seven-inch stiletto blade ends any ambiguity about its contents. He holds the steel in front of the geneticist's eyes, makes sure Sacconi sees its sharpness, then grabs Benedetta around the neck and hauls her body across her lover's. Ephrem pulls her hair back so her eyes stare into Sacconi's. So her fear connects with his. 'Now. Will you tell me about the tests you carried out?'

Still Sacconi hesitates.

The monk puts the tip of the blade into the soft skin below the girl's right eye. He studies the scientist's face. Sees instantly that she doesn't mean anything to him. There is no hero in the man, no bond of love between them. He pushes her away. Hears her roll off the bed and hit the hard wooden floor.

Ephrem puts a hand over Sacconi's mouth then calmly runs the point of the stiletto through his left cheek.

The scientist's muffled screams last almost a minute.

Ephrem withdraws the blade slowly. Lets a curled droplet of blood drip from the tip of the steel into Sacconi's eyes. 'I am going to ask you one final time to tell me about the tests you did for Craxi.'

107

'Wake up, my friend.'

Nic hears the voice but isn't together enough to answer.

'We need to get moving. Come on.' Fabio Goria places a hand on the detective's shoulder.

Karakandez raises himself on his elbows. Blinks at the daylight as the private investigator draws back the curtains. 'I'm awake, just give me a minute to get my shit together.'

'I am making coffee and eggs, then we run.' Goria wanders out of the room. 'We don't have long.'

Nic staggers to the bathroom, feeling half-drunk as he steps into the shower. Afterwards, he towels dry and dresses in a clean, soft cotton, baggy blue plaid shirt, plain blue fleece hoodie and blue Gap jeans. He grabs his BlackBerry from the bedside cabinet and types out a mail to Luogotenente Cappelini.

Carlotta,
I'm not going to be at the hotel this morning for you
to pick me up. I got a little drunk last night with
some guys I met and we ended up across town. I'll
give you a call this afternoon and arrange a meet.
Thanks.
Hope you have a good day.
Nic.

He hits send and then enters the open-plan kitchen where Goria is sliding scrambled eggs and fatty bacon out of a pan. 'Help yourself to coffee.' He waves a hand towards a glass jug of freshly ground brewing on its own hot plate. 'There's milk and cream in the fridge.'

'You want some?'

'*Si*. Just black.'

Nic takes two white mugs off a shelf and pours coffee. They sit on leather-topped benches at a long junk wood table, looking out on a functional garden. It's a single man's yard. No flowers, no neat areas, mainly decking and a barbecue area should there ever be opportunity for such a thing.

They didn't find time to eat last night and now Nic is hungrier than he thought. 'The eggs are good.'

'*Grazie*. Italian boys are taught to cook well.'

'One day you'll make someone an excellent wife.'

'You are very funny. Eat quickly. We need to go before we end up regretting even the short sleep.'

Both men are exhausted but they know they are in a race against time. If whoever took Craxi has obtained the same information that his wife Erica gave them, then it is only a matter of time before they get to the scientist Craxi used to analyse DNA from the Shroud.

By six forty-five Nic and Fabio are in the Fiat heading south-east down Via Antonio Sciesa and Corso Giuseppe Garibaldi. Just after seven they join the eastern stretch of the Tangenziale Nord and make decent progress until they hit the tolls on the road to Milan where a huge truck has blown a tyre. Strips of shredded black rubber cover the autostrada.

It's seven-fifteen when they come off at the Chivasso exit and twenty-five past when they quietly shut the doors of the Fiat and walk to the small detached home on the outskirts of a giant estate.

'The castle behind there,' Fabio points over hedges to a distant palace of pinkish brick and green shuttered windows. 'This is Castagneto Po, the family home of Carla Bruni.'

Nic glances into the lavish grounds. 'I guess after living somewhere like that, you have to marry a president to keep you in the manner to which you are accustomed.'

'But Sarkozy?' Goria shrugs as they walk. 'It is a mystery why a beautiful Italian should choose a French dwarf.' He swings open a black metal gate and they walk a gravelled drive of honey-coloured chips to a fine three-storey house with spectacular views across the rolling Turin hills and sur-rounding vineyards.

The Italian nods to the black Mercedes SLK parked to one side. 'The car is his. He is in.'

Nic reaches across his waistband and checks the gun he'd been given last night.

Goria lifts the giant brass ring hanging in the middle of the glossy black door and hammers it hard. He reaches inside his jacket and pulls out a false ID. 'Carabinieri! Signore Sacconi, open up!'

Nic heads round the back of the house. He peers closely through the ground-floor windows as he goes quickly round and then circles back to the front. 'There's no sign of life but there is an open window on the second floor.'

Goria pockets the ID. He looks up at the drainpipes and trellis-work. He knows what's expected of him.

108

Luogotenente Carlotta Cappelini feels like death warmed up. She's been awake most of the night – not finally turning in until she'd seen the car registered to the company of private investigator Fabio Goria pick Nic Karakandez up outside the American's hotel and enter the grounds of Goria's home.

Now she's back at work. Driving her desk. Reading reports from her surveillance team and discovering the American and his new Italian friend have just rolled out of their gated retreat and made their way to a house out near Chivasso. She looks at her computer and rereads the mail he sent her full of nonsense about a night on the town and a promise to call her later. She taps his cell number into her desk phone and dials him for a second time.

'*Buongiorno*, Nic – this is Carlotta again. Please call me as soon as you can, I have some important information I want to share with you.'

She doesn't. But she knows she has to establish contact

quickly or risk losing him completely. And that mustn't happen. Not now. Not after last night's events.

Captain Giorgio Fusco beckons her through the window of his office opposite her desk. It's one of the perils of sitting within his sight line. She drops what she's doing and plods wearily his way. Pokes her head around his door. 'Capitano?'

'Come in.' He gestures to a grey-suited man with cropped black hair sitting in the shadows of the room. 'This is Paolo. He is an ROS administrator, and a close friend.'

The man from the Raggruppamento Operativo Speciale nods and manages a polite '*Ciao.*' His unblinking brown eyes show no interest in her.

Fusco walks over to the door and makes sure it's tightly shut. 'Roberto Craxi was seen in the centre of Turin.'

'That's not news, sir. We know he and his wife recently returned to their lodge.'

Paolo dips into his jacket pocket and produces a pack of colour stills that he fans out like a hand of cards. 'We picked him up on CCTV, using facial recognition software.'

She looks at the pictures. 'What was he doing?'

'Drawing money from a bank account we didn't know he had and probably much more.' Paolo peels off several shots. 'By the time we got operatives into the area, he'd gone.'

'Back to the lodge?'

Paolo shrugs. 'Maybe. We were short on men yesterday.'

'The Prime Minister was in court,' explains the captain with a smile. 'More sex and corruption charges.'

'We checked Craxi's lodge an hour ago,' says Paolo. 'It was

306

empty but he and his wife had been there in the last twenty-four hours.'

'He'll come back onto our radar,' Carlotta tries to sound confident.

'I'm not so sure.' Paolo puts a finger on one of the stills in the Luogotenente's hand. 'Do you recognise this person?'

She stares at an athletic-looking dark-skinned man in a black coat.

'Here he is twenty minutes later, in a green coat.' Paolo hands over another print.

She holds them side by side and shakes her head. 'I have never seen him before.'

'He did not come with the American that you are handling?'

'Not to my knowledge. The LAPD officer travelled alone.'

The captain interjects, 'Though he *is* working here with a local private eye whom you do know – Fabio Goria.'

Paolo raises an eyebrow. 'Good officer. We were sorry to lose him.'

Carlotta hands the photograph back. 'So who do you think this foreigner is?'

'Trouble. That's who he is. Had he not got so close to Craxi we wouldn't have even noticed him. He was following him – of that we have no doubt.'

Her cell rings. She doesn't wait for permission to answer it. '*Sì.*'

The two men study her face and try to decipher what's happening. She covers the mouthpiece and tells her boss,

307

'Goria and the American are at the home of Mario Sacconi, a scientist in the Sezioni Investigazioni Scientifiche. It looks like they're breaking in.'

109

The black metal drainpipe proves as good as a ladder. It was fitted in an era when builders worried about downpour not security and its position is close enough for Goria to climb and then stretch out a leg to the stone lintel of the upstairs window.

As he shuffles across onto the ledge he can see a man and a woman in bed. For a second he thinks they're asleep. Then he sees the river of red separating them. He turns sideways on, leans against the frame and drops to one knee. Palms to glass he slides up the partially opened sash window and climbs through the gap into the room.

The man is closest to him. On his back. Head twisted to the left. Hands tied to the bedposts and his throat cut. The woman is to his right. Curled up on her side. Hands and feet tied behind her back. Long black hair barely masking a fatal neck wound.

Goria makes the sign of the cross. He steps over the piled quilt on the floor and looks more closely at the corpse of Mario Sacconi. There's blood all over the face. It looks like his nose has been broken but there's a more curious injury –

a deep puncture wound through the left cheek. He's experienced enough to know it's been made by a stiletto blade, probably the one responsible for a single stab wound in the windpipe. The cut is clinical. Professional.

Sacconi's legs are drawn up to his side and blood has pooled between his knees and chest. Goria moves a little. It's a bloody mess but he's pretty sure he can see that the scientist has been stabbed through the heart. He steps back and makes his way around the bed to the woman. She's young – mid-twenties at best – and pretty. Or at least she was.

Two wounds are all her beautiful body bares – one through the throat and one through the heart. Goria takes a moment to imagine how it was done. The killer would have had to pull her long hair back and look her straight in the eyes as he pushed the blade through her thorax. Then, as she gasped for air, he would have needed to steady her desperate body, position the knife and force it through her heart.

He looks between the young woman's thighs and dips low to see beneath her breasts. She doesn't seem to have been sexually interfered with in any way. Professional kills. Nothing more. Nothing less. He heads downstairs and opens the front door.

Nic is stood back, looking edgy. 'What took you so long?'

'Sacconi is dead. So too is the woman he was with. We were too late.'

Nic steps towards the doorway.

'No. You can't go inside.'

'What?'

'I'm going to have to call the police. We can't walk away from two bodies and we can't disturb the scene any more than I already have.'

'Then call them. I'm still going inside. Whoever killed these people may well have killed Tamara Jacobs.'

Reluctantly, Goria lets him pass. Nic takes the stairs two at a time. There's only one bedroom door open and he can sense death before he even steps inside. The white base sheet is soaked with blood and the girl is facing him as he enters. He pulls up short, takes out his BlackBerry and thumbs through to the camera function. Quickly and professionally he circles the room and fires off as many shots as he can. He stands on a dressing table chair and gets a range of high angles and then goes in close and captures all the wounds.

He can hear Goria downstairs talking on his cell. The polizia will soon be on the way. He pockets the BlackBerry, rushes to the en-suite bathroom and pulls the toilet roll from its holder.

The dead couple are close together on the bed – the killer must have manhandled them, probably rubbed his clothes or body hair against their bodies. On the ropes binding Sacconi he finds two short dark hairs, possibly from the killer's hands when he tied the knots. Nic rips off several sheets of toilet roll, places them carefully in the middle and then folds them protectively around his sample.

His attention falls again on the dead girl. The tape. There's an outside chance the killer's fingerprints will be on the sticky tape plastered across her mouth. Nic knows that if he removes it, a pathologist will be able to tell. He also knows that the Carabinieri will go wild if he tampers with the body.

But he does it anyway. He reaches over the girl, finds the tape's edge and peels it off. He doesn't want it to double back on itself – it could ruin the print. Quickly but carefully he attaches the tape to a make-up mirror and smoothes it out.

'Nic, come on!'

'One minute.'

He lifts a dressing table stool and smashes the mirror. As he picks up the pieces he hears footsteps on the stairs. He quickly salvages the long sliver of broken glass bearing his sample.

Goria stands aghast in the doorway, cell phone dangling from his left hand. 'What are you doing?'

'Never mind. Give me your car keys.'

110

The zombified computer is still playing on Amy Chang's mind as she finishes her morning jog along the white California sands.

Hours of labour lost. Dozens of files messed up. She hopes to God some of the documents can be rescued.

She showers, then dresses in jeans and a pink hoodie. The day is shaping up fine and she pours a glass of OJ, slides open the patio window and sits down in the ribbon of sunshine warming her balcony. Someone infected her Mac with a virus, and the last person who sent her anything was the English professor, Hasting-Smith. That just doesn't seem right. Cambridge dons don't send infected mail. Surely their own firewall would pick that kind of thing up? But there's no denying the fact that her programs all got fried after he sent her his reports. Come Monday she'll tell security and see what they make of it.

She drains her juice and remembers she still owes Mitzi the report on the Shroud. She ducks out of the sunshine and fires up her own laptop. Amy spends an hour trying to recall everything she wrote at work before the Mac crashed, then turns her attention to assembling an account of the Shroud's movements across the later centuries – history and geography always help pathologists know their victims and samples better:

Thirteenth century

Ray-sur-Saone, France: Shroud kept in a casket in a château.

Roussillon, France, 1287: Templar Knights reportedly showed a long, linen cloth imprinted with the image of a man.

Fourteenth century

Anthon, Cruseilles, Rumilly and Mornex, France/Geneva 1358–89: Shroud believed to have been kept on various estates.

Fifteenth century

Montfort, France, 1418: Kept briefly in the castle of Montbard near Montfort.

St Hippolyte sur Doubs, France, retained here from 1418 to around 1453.

Sixteenth century

Turin, Italy: Held almost continuously in Turin since 1578 (apart from during World War II when it spent seven years at the Abbey of Montevergine in Avellino).

She reviews the list. In policing terms the chain of custody is dubious, to say the least. The evidence – the Shroud itself – could have been tampered with and contaminated tens of thousands of times. More than anything, the huge absence of details about it before the thirteenth century rings investigative alarm bells with her. No court in the world – except perhaps one inside Vatican City – would rule it to be that of Jesus Christ.

From her workbag she pulls out a brown Moleskine notebook. Pasted in it is a small photograph of the Shroud. Under it are notes she made based on the assumptions that the marks showing up on the cloth were caused by blood:

- Extensive 'blood markings' on skull where a crown of thorns is reputed to have been forced into position. *Note – there are also marks on the back of the skull consistent with puncture wounds caused by deep thorns and also consistent blood flow lines.
- Hard to imagine what could have caused the ring of puncture marks if not a crown/cap of thorns.
- Possible fracture of the nose and damage to the nasal cartilage.
- Dozens of marks across torso and arms, possibly inflicted by extensive scourging. The marks seem large enough to be consistent with flesh being torn from the body.
- Pronounced 'blood mark' on left wrist, consistent with a nail being driven through Destot's Space.
- Thumbs apparently turned in and consistent with damage to median nerve.
- Apparent chest wound between the right fifth and sixth ribs – consistent with penetration by spear.

Amy looks up and down the bullet points. In her mind there's no doubt what the marks are saying to her. The victim was whipped horrendously, had some multi-pointed device pressed to his skull that caused numerous wounds and he was crucified. But none of her notes answer the big question.

Who exactly was he?

111

Jenny Harrison feels the pain of the hangover before she even opens her eyes. Only when she squints up at the cracked and cobwebbed ceiling do some of last night's events come rolling back to her. This isn't her place. She isn't in bed alone. There's a naked man next to her. She shifts onto her side and gradually recognises the slab of hairy-backed blubber as a guy in the bar she drank with. They shared a couple of joints, he bought drinks, then she ended up at his place drinking bad white wine and smoking crack.

Now she's wondering what price she paid for his generosity and companionship. One look on the floor by the side of the bed tells her. Her clothes are scattered everywhere. She heaves herself off the saggy mattress and just makes it to the bathroom before she's sick. From the vomit-splattered sink she can see that her strange bedfellow is still out for the count. She runs water and thinks about showering. She'd like to but it will only risk waking the whale and she can't be doing with talking to him. She puts her mouth to the tap and swills out strange chunks of food, splashes her face and rubs the remains of make-up on his towel.

Five minutes later she's outside the apartment block wondering where the hell she is. At first she doesn't recognise the place, then she remembers. She'd gone round to Kim's to beat on the door. Feeling depressed and annoyed she'd stopped in a bar close to Hollenbeck Park, a dive she and some of the girls go to when business is slow and they need to round up a bit of cash.

Jenny starts walking. Takes a different route. One that means she can rap on Kim's door one last time. She's feeling exhausted by the time she climbs the stairs at her friend's place. Knocking seems a waste of time so she gets down on her knees, holds the mail slot open and shouts through it at the top of her voice. Then she slumps with her back against the wall. All kinds of possibilities are flying through her head. The girl might have overdosed. Got pissed and choked on her own vomit. Fallen and whacked her head. Anything could have happened.

She turns round and screams through the slot again. Two of the three other doors around Bass's apartment now open.

'Shut the fuck up!' bawls Holly Caniffe, a compact woman in a slip and nothing else.

Jenny collapses into a heap again. 'She's in there, I know she is – and something's wrong.'

'That whore friend of yours is probably sleeping off

whatever you got wasted on,' says Caniffe. 'Why don't you vanish and let us all get some rest? I've been working nights.'

'Screw you.' Jenny gives her the bird.

Caniffe's husband Keegan appears in the doorway of their apartment, in time-greyed vest and boxers. 'What's goin' on?'

'It's my friend. I'm worried about her.'

'Whadafuck?'

'I think she's in there and has hurt herself.'

'Move out the way.' Keegan Caniffe sizes up the door. 'Gimme some room.'

Jenny bum-shuffles out of his way. He fixes his attention on the lock and takes a running kick at it. It holds firm and he bounces off, almost ends up on his ass.

'Shit.'

'Leave it, doll. She's probably in a bar somewhere.' Caniffe motions to Jenny. 'This crazy bitch has probably got it all wrong.'

But Keegan isn't for leaving it. His pride is hurt and it's not every day you get to smash someone's front door down without the cops busting you. This time he runs harder and faster. He drives his left shoulder into the door and it bangs open. Keegan tumbles inside. Falls face down on the filthy carpet. His wife races in after him, followed by Jenny and old man Dobbs who's come out to see what all the noise is about.

'Freakin' stinks in here.' Holly Caniffe holds her nose as she helps her husband to his feet.

Jenny sidesteps them and heads for the lounge. There's no sign of Kim. She checks the small kitchen and eating area, dumb bitch might be on the floor sleeping off some drug or other. Nothing. She's starting to feel embarrassed. That smart-assed cow Holly is probably right, Kim has been out clubbing somewhere and is with some guy.

She pushes open the bedroom door. On the floor is a body. A corpse. Wrapped head to toe in a white sheet from Kim's bed.

112

Two of the Carabinieri's finest show Fabio Goria through to the interview room and leave him there to stew.

He's not under arrest but he knows he so easily could be. Breaking and entering, carrying an unauthorised weapon, withholding evidence, interfering with a crime scene – they're going to throw the book at him.

It's almost thirty minutes before Carlotta Cappelini breaks the room's suffocating silence with a clunk of iron locks and a steely gaze. She doesn't speak until she settles in the black, moulded plastic chair opposite him and places a notebook and pen on the bolted down table. 'Nic Karakandez, where is he?'

Goria rests on his elbows and stares at her as he sucks up the question. It's interesting she should start with that. Not what were you doing at Mario Sacconi's house? Not even what do you know about the two dead bodies upstairs?

Nic.

The Arma dei Carabinieri is more interested in the whereabouts of the LAPD cop.

Why? What are they afraid the American will do or say?

Goria leans back. 'I don't know. He asked for my car keys, I gave them to him and he left.'

'Why?'

'Why what?'

Her face shows her annoyance. 'Why did you give them to him and why did he leave so quickly?'

'I gave them to him because he is a friend of a friend. And he left, I presume, because he did not want to stay.'

'If you continue like this you're going to make me—'

'What?' His eyes laugh at her. 'Charge me?' He shrugs. 'We both know you are either going to do that or you're not. Nothing I say now can alter that.'

Captain Fusco's voice comes from the doorway. 'How about we take away your private investigator's licence, Fabio?'

The PI stays poker faced. 'The people who hire me do not care whether I have a licence or not, Giorgio.' He smiles. 'In fact, maybe I get paid more if they know that even when persecuted by the Carabinieri I stay loyal to them.'

'You have a point.' Fusco sits on the edge of the table and

smiles down on the PI. 'But if we charge you with murder – double murder – then that's a different thing.'

'It is. That's a very wrong thing. I didn't kill Sacconi or the girl and you know the forensics will confirm that. There was rigor in both bodies – I can prove I was at home when they died.'

'How?' Fusco shrugs. 'By the time-coded security tapes from your home surveillance system, showing you entering and leaving? I think not. We have already taken those from your house.'

Goria smiles. He has to remember not to underestimate these people – they're good operators – among the best in the world. 'So what now? Where are we going with this?'

'I have a proposition.' Fusco gets up and paces. 'The American will contact you. I have no doubt about it. When he does, we will have tapped your phone.'

'He will expect that.'

'Perhaps. No matter. You can even warn him that it is possible. What is important is that from that moment onwards, you take instructions from us. You send him where we want, when we want. There's a chance that if you do exactly as we tell you then we may forget you were even in Mario Sacconi's house.'

113

The fleeting warmth of the November day has passed by the time Amy Chang crosses town and joins the crime-scene personnel at Kim Bass's apartment.

She'd hoped for a death-free weekend, her first in three months, but plainly it's not to be. She parks at the kerb in front of the rundown entrance block, pulls on her whites and slides her case out of the back. Her breath freezes in the air as she locks up and walks the pathway.

'Chang. Doctor Amy Chang,' she announces as she shows her ID to a rookie logging people in and out of the scene.

'Afternoon, Doc.' He already sounds like an old-timer as he lets her pass. 'It's up on the second floor. The lead officer is Lieutenant Carter, he's already in there.'

'Thanks.'

The stairs are full of other uniforms coming and going. Taking statements from neighbours and probably hanging around a while too long so they don't catch for another job late on a Saturday afternoon. At the apartment door a photographer is firing off approach shots of the landing and stairs. Two CSIs are dusting walls, a handrail and light switch.

The seldom-cleaned entrance to the apartment has already been exhaustively printed and photographed and dozens of male and female footprints lifted. More shoe and boot impressions have been taken from the carpet and floor tiles in every room. As usual, the whole interior of the place is bleached white by harsh forensic lights casting monstrously large shadows everywhere. Tyler Carter turns as soon as Amy's elegant silhouette joins the magic lantern show on the lounge walls. 'Dr Chang – my apologies for dragging you out at the weekend.'

'Accepted. Where's the body?'

'In the bedroom. It's tight in there so I sealed it off until you came.'

'That's a help. Thanks.'

Most cops can't help but tell the ME what they think. Right from the start they fire off their theories on how the victim died, what they might have been doing, what the cause of death could have been and how long the vic had been lying there. Not Carter. Tyler Carter doesn't say a word. Doesn't offer a single personal thought on a case until the examiner asks.

One step into the bedroom is enough to tell Amy what she's dealing with. Six times now she's witnessed the same scene. A sheet or quilt drawn over the head and toes of a victim. The work of the Creeper.

114

Nic is cursing himself.

Those couple of hours sleep that he and Goria grabbed have cost a man his life. If they'd gone straight to Mario Sacconi's house after ensuring Erica Craxi was safe, he'd still be alive and the Tamara Jacobs case might be much closer to being solved. Now all he has to go on is one final name, one last shred of information that Erica gave him: Sacconi's best friend, Édouard Broussard, a scientist who used to be his boss but is now in private practice. Roberto Craxi made some sizeable payments directly to him at Sacconi's request. He has to be involved.

As the detective drives, his eyes scan every lane and road for police cars. It won't be long before they issue widespread alerts for him. His first stop is a strange one. Certainly not what you'd expect from a man on the run. From the browser on his BlackBerry he's found a parcel firm out near the airport that will ship overnight to LA. He grabs packaging from them, bubble-wraps the broken mirror from Sacconi's bedroom and separately, the locket that Erica gave him. He fully understood the importance of it when she handed it over. Even though he said nothing to Goria, he knew it was more than just a good luck image of Saint Christopher.

He scribbles out a note, adds the envelope with the crime-scene photographs that he believes may have been gone through in his hotel room, seals the box and pays with his credit card. For good measure he gives the guy behind the desk an extra twenty euros in return for a promise his stuff will be on the next plane out of Turin.

Before he leaves he visits the restroom and cleans up. The journey ahead is long and dangerous. He looks at himself in the sink mirror as he pats the water off with paper towels. If things go wrong, this could be the last time he ever sees his own reflection.

115

WALNUT PARK, LOS ANGELES

The old green school bus is heading off and Mitzi is on the sidewalk waving an embarrassing goodbye to its tail lights and her disappearing daughters, when she gets the call from Carter telling her they have a fresh body.

The guy must be psychic. He said the Creeper was overdue and lo and behold, within twenty-four hours he's proved right. No wonder they call him the wizard. She fires up the old car and tries to keep Alfie and the girls out of her head as she drives out to Boyle Heights. Worries about the girls and the emotional blow-up in the Italian restaurant are still haunting her. She just hopes Jade forgets it all for a while when she gets out on the slopes. The kid's filled with so much anger and pain it's heartbreaking to even think about it. She was always Daddy's girl – always will be – and that's going to be hard for everyone to deal with.

Mitzi wonders if she should let her visit him. Until now it's something she'd completely ruled out. Just the thought of her daughter passing through prison gates almost makes her heave. But maybe she has to stomach it. If it's what Jade really wants – and if Alfie consents – then she'll have to be supportive and see the girl through it.

Eventually, the lieutenant shrugs off the ghosts of personal horrors and thinks about her work. Carter doesn't seem as bad as his press makes out. Not a lot of fun, granted, but there can be no doubt about his professionalism. One thing for certain, she's glad she's not the lead on the Creeper case. From what she's read in the files, this guy is grade-A sicko. A 100 per cent sociopath without a care in the world.

Mitzi spots Amy's van parked by the old stucco apartment block. It'll be good to see her friend – even though the circumstances are so wrong. She shows her ID and gets logged through. In the stairwell she suits up in Tyvek overalls and foot covers, then pads upstairs.

'Mitzi Fallon,' she announces, holding her badge as she walks in. 'Anyone know where Carter is?'

A young female CSI looks up from the couch where she's tweezing off hair strands. 'Back bedroom with the ME.'

'Gotcha.'

Carter and Amy are in the far corner of the room near the head of the body when Mitzi walks in. 'You buy a ticket for Mega Millions this week, Detective? I sure hope so, given your ability to predict the future.'

He almost smiles. 'Female, thirty-two, by the name of Kim Bass. Tenant of the house from pictures and paperwork we've found. Lived here near on two years. Been dead a couple of days. Dr Chang's about to get more specific.'

'Hi Mitz.' Amy gives her a look of genuine warmth. 'Your lady died from strangulation with a ligature. Pick your way over and see.'

Mitzi squeezes around the bed and follows her friend's pointing fingers to the bloated face of the corpse.

'Look at the marks on the neck. You can make out four lines less than two inches wide. I'd say it's a leather trouser belt rather than the kind of thick strap you'd normally associate with jeans.' Amy lifts her hands as though holding the ends of the belt in separate fists. 'The killer was stood behind her, looped the ligature around her neck like this and crossed his hands for extra leverage as he choked her.' She stops gesticulating. 'Now look back at Kim's neck.'

Mitzi leans over.

'You see these additional marks on and around the windpipe? These are made by fingers and knuckles.'

'I'm willing to bet he flipped her and finished her by hand,' says Carter. 'Flesh to flesh.'

Mitzi gets the picture. 'He wanted to see her die.'

'Not just that. He wanted to *feel* her die.' Carter points

at the corpse. 'At first I wasn't sure it was our boy, but this face-to-face finale is definitely his work.'

'Any shroud?' asks Mitzi.

Carter nods. 'Covered her head to toe. No mistake about it, the Creeper's back.'

116

Ephrem is driving when his cell phone rings. He's been expecting the call. Knows it's going to be unpleasant.

'You've left a mess.' Carlotta Cappelini sounds calm but irritated.

His mind is filled with flashbacks. The blood on the bed, endless crimson pooling out of the still pumping heart of the scientist. The girlfriend pulling her knees up to protect herself. 'I had no time to clean up.'

'I understand, but it is not good. Now more people than necessary are interested.'

'I am sorry.'

'Apologise to God not me. Did you obtain the information you came for?'

'I did.'

'*Va bene*. The detective I told you about, he has gone missing.'

Ephrem remembers the image she sent to him, the voice

327

on the phone he picked up in Craxi's lodge, the belongings he searched through at the hotel.

'*Si*. We arrested his partner but Karakandez escaped from the house. He has a car, a blue Fiat Bravo. I will text you the plate. Do not underestimate this American. He is not stupid and he has come a long way.'

'So have I.'

'Then make sure you are not the one who ends up disappointed. Finish the job and finish it quickly. *Arrivederci*.'

He'll do as she wants, but not yet. First, he has another matter to take care of.

117

Nic gets back in the car and makes sure the guy behind the desk sees him heading off towards the airport terminal. He knows the Italian border police will have his description and passport number and there is no chance he will be able to catch a flight out of Turin.

Five minutes later he pulls into the fly-drive area of a cheap hotel near the airport and pays to leave Goria's car there for two weeks. The Carabinieri will find it. Maybe even within a couple of hours. That's long enough not to be a problem. He catches a transit bus to the airport terminal and follows the signs to the rental car returns. He walks quickly to the busiest area, the one where families are losing their tempers because staff are lazy or slow and they're scared of missing flights. Nic watches the comings and goings and is soon able to identify the worst of companies and even pick out the nationalities of the returning drivers. Italians weave their way back to the bays at speed, confidently navigating lanes and honking horns for people to hurry up. Foreigners make nervous approaches, staring upwards at signs hoping they've made the right choice and are not about to be sent on a hugely time-wasting trip outside the airport roads.

He walks the longest of the backed-up lines and knocks on several drivers' windows until he finds an American. He shows a bald man in his late fifties his LAPD shield and makes sure his leather jacket is open enough for the kids in the back and Mom in the front to see the Beretta. 'Could you please step out of the car, sir, and show me your ID?'

'Sure, Officer.' The good citizen climbs out of his Renault people carrier and is a foot shorter and twenty pounds heavier than the out-of-town cop.

Nic looks carefully through the documentation of John Henry Watkins then adds, 'Sir, could you please come around the back of the vehicle with me.' En route Nic puts his finger in his ear and talks as though he were on a hands-free police radio. He turns his back on the driver, who is by now nervous, until he's done. Finally, he swings slowly round to give him the bad news. 'Mr Watkins, I am assigned to an international anti-terrorist unit working with the Carabinieri. We have information that an attack may take place at this airport and we've been asked to look out for a vehicle identical to the one you're driving.'

'Mine?'

'Yes sir, yours. I'm afraid I'm going to have to confiscate it, move you and your family from the scene and have you questioned.'

'But I have to take it back. We've got to get home, we're going to miss our flight.'

'Not my problem, sir. I'm sure the Italian police will be sympathetic and deal with your case as quickly as they can.' He looks down the long line of vehicles. 'Though you may have quite a wait for the senior officer in charge to come over. Things go a little slower over here.'

Watkins is mortified. Already he is sensing the difficulties of coping with tired children at a foreign airport, not to mention his short-fused wife. 'Aw c'mon, Officer, can't you cut us a break? We're American citizens, I've got to return to Chicago, get my family home and get to work.'

Nic rubs thoughtfully at his chin and looks around. 'Okay. Listen, I just ran a check on you and I know you're a law-abiding, family man but I've still got to do my job and take this vehicle to the pound for checks. You know how for-malities go. You say your flight is leaving soon?' Watkins nods. 'I guess I might be able to do something for you. If you give me your documentation, I can drop you, your wife and kids at the main terminal and when we've swept the car I'll take it back to the car pool. But you'd have to agree to keep this between us. It's the kind of thing that could get my ass fired.'

'I understand completely. And if we do that, we go straight home?'

'Yes, sir.'

'What about our deposit?'

Nic puts on a suitable grimace. 'You paid with a card?'

'Yeah.'

'I'll have someone do the paperwork and get it refunded.'

Watkins looks relieved. 'That would be great.'

Nic glances at his watch. 'So shall we get moving?'

John Henry Watkins grins broadly, extends his sweaty hand and gratefully passes the detective the keys.

118

Carlotta Cappelini sits back from the computer screen that takes up most of her desk. In front of her, in full shocking HD detail is Ephrem's handiwork. She's gone through every still frame, examining – or pretending to examine – the fatal crime scene at Mario Sacconi's home. The monk is an animal.

A young female officer turns up at the edge of her desk. 'For you, ma'am.' She hands over a single sheet of paper.

Cappelini sees the young brunette's eyes snag on the screen, a shot of the knife wound straight through Sacconi's

331

heart. The Luogotenente uses her mouse to shrink the image out of sight. 'Grazie. That will be all.'

The girl gets herself together and walks away.

Cappelini looks at the document. It's a trace report on the American's phone. Turns out he used it several times after fleeing the murder scene. Carried out searches from the Yahoo! browser, located a logistical services parcel delivery company out near the airport and then called it.

He's shipping something.

Something so important it has to cross a border even if he can't.

No. Cappelini picks up the untraceable phone she uses to call the monk and dials his number. 'Listen carefully, I'm going to text you the address of a parcel company near the aeroporto. You need to go there, quickly. Find whatever Nic Karakandez left to be shipped and stop it — at all costs. Do you understand?'

'I understand.'

The line goes dead and she sends the SMS. Through the window of her boss's office she sees Fusco with the Major and the Commander. She knows exactly what they're saying. And it's not going to be good news for the LAPD cop.

119

The Watkins family wave gratefully from beside their suit-cases and Nic waves guiltily back from the driver's seat of the people carrier as he leaves them at the revolving doors of the terminal.

He drives away from the drop-off zone and joins the main traffic flow. Once he clears the airport grounds he pulls over on a quiet dirt road to set the satnav for the long journey ahead. The touch screen is tiny and it takes several goes to finger in the address Erica Craxi gave him of Mario Sacconi's former boss, Édouard Broussard.

The little computer does its work and automatically announces that the journey is 366 kilometres long, will take just under four hours, involve two major motorways with toll charges and will cost forty euros in fuel.

He starts up the engine again and hopes the trip doesn't prove to be a lot costlier than the computer's promised.

120

Mitzi parks outside Jenny Harrison's place and wishes she was anywhere else other than here. Given her own personal problems, the last thing she needs professionally is to be interviewing a young woman about how she discovered the corpse of her best friend.

She knocks on the busted front door and a uniformed cop jerks it open from the other side. He's dark-haired, mid-thirties and already carrying too much weight and attitude.

'Lieutenant Fallon.' Mitzi badges him. 'You got one Jenny Harrison in here?'

'Unfortunately.' He swings the door open. 'She's quite a lady.'

'Meaning?'

'She's got a real mouth on her.'

'Good. A mouth is what she needs to be able to answer my questions.' Mitzi rolls her eyes as she walks past him. 'What happened to the door?'

He pushes it closed. 'Says she's been burglarised. The neighbourhood's full of junkies and pimps.'

Mitzi enters a room filled with smoke and struggles not to cough. Her eyes settle on a bleached blonde wreck of a

334

woman chain-smoking on an old brown Dralon two-seater. 'Jenny, I'm Mitzi Fallon. I've just come from your friend's house. I need to ask you some questions. You want to do it here or downtown?'

Harrison looks up, ash from her cigarette falling on the arm of the couch. 'What happened to Kim?' She sounds doped. 'What did they do to her?'

'That's what we need to find out, Jenny.' She moves closer and sees the girl's eyes. She's high as a kite. Probably been burning joints right from the moment she saw her girlfriend's corpse. Who could blame her? 'Go have a shower. Get your-self a change of clothes and I'll take you for some food.'

'Don't want no shower and I ain't freakin' hungry.'

Mitzi drops down so they're eye to eye. 'It's not an offer, honey. It's an instruction. I've got a murder to clear up and you're no use to me wasted.'

Harrison swears under her breath. She heaves herself up from the couch and disappears into the bathroom with a slam of the door. The uniform sidles up to Mitzi. 'The great unwashed has a temper. This'll be the first shower she's taken this year.'

'She might be dirty but you're an asshole. Ten minutes from now she'll be clean and you'll still be an asshole.'

'I was just sayin'.'

'Then don't. Your first step towards not being an A-hole is shutting the hell up.'

The uniform drifts off and pretends to inspect the damaged front door.

Mitzi walks around. There are no framed photographs, no landline, no cooker, just a small old TV, a microwave oven and a kettle. She's seen jail cells better furnished than this.

A once-white bed quilt is chequered with coffee stains and cigarette burns. The base sheets look like they've never been changed. She lifts the mattress and finds a strange stash – dozens of condoms, a vicious-looking vegetable knife and an ultrasound picture of an unborn baby. It's a sixteen-week scan, date-stamped two years ago. She guesses Harrison caught pregnant and either lost the child or aborted it. The fact she kept the photo means she harbours thoughts of being a mom.

Mitzi drops the mattress, brushes her hands clean and checks the kitchen area. On the front of the small fridge are a couple of snaps pinned by fruit-shaped magnets. There's one of Harrison and the dead girl in a nightclub, both laughing and holding big cocktails complete with straws and lots of greenery. There's another of them at the beach in bikinis, blowing kisses off their palms at the camera. Harrison looks pretty much as she does now. Mitzi guesses the beach shot was probably summer and the cocktail shot maybe New Year.

Inside the fridge is a four-stack of TV dinners, a tub of cheap spread, a stack of mouldy cheese slices, four cans of tuna and a quarter bottle of vodka. Two cupboards next to a single-drainer sink are empty bar a few non-matching cups, three bowls and two plates.

Harrison comes back in the room looking tired but a little less wasted. She's naked except for a faded green towel that barely covers her modesty. Her bleached hair has turned into brown rats' tails. Mitzi walks to the front door and opens it for the uniformed cop. 'Give us five.'

He's glad to. Harrison slides open a built-in wardrobe and pulls on a faded pink T-shirt and black jeans. She either doesn't have clean underwear or doesn't want to wear any. She pushes bare feet into filthy sneakers then uses the towel to rub her wet head. 'Dryer's screwed. I got hair like one of them wiry dogs.'

'You look fine. The cop out there says you were burgled. What they take?'

'Nothing. There wasn't nothing to take.' She downs the towel and then realises she's been too honest for her own good. 'Shit, that's not true. They stole some cash I'd been savin' – vacation money, maybe five hundred dollars, and some jewellery and stuff and my cell phone, a new one.'

'Sure they did. By the time we get downtown I bet you'll have remembered that fifty-inch 3D plasma they took as well, along with the Valentino dresses and enough Jimmy Choos to fit out a centipede.'

121

TURIN

The noise wakes Roberto Craxi.

A dull thump. Then another. He has no idea how long

he's been asleep. The air is hot and stale – and he's weak from lack of water. The ground beneath him shakes. Something heavy has been dropped nearby. There's another dull thud.

And another.

He works out what it is. Someone is moving heavy stones off the slab. In the next few moments he'll be free – or dead.

The noise is clearer now. Stone on stone. Boulders of some kind must have been heaped on the slab to secure it. Those at the top have been moved; now the last of them are being slid away. He summons all his physical and mental strength in preparation for the grand opening of the tomb. Silence.

He guesses his captor is thinking about how to oslide the lid off the tomb. The man won't want to lean over it and push it away because that would leave him off-balance and exposed. Nor will he try to pull it towards him and risk it falling on him. No, he'll probably slide it off from one end – the end above Craxi's head. It's the only way to remain positioned directly above him.

Craxi is right. Ephrem hauls the slab to his left in one powerful movement. The former soldier makes his move. Springs up as fast as he can.

The monk is knocked back. He'd expected resistance but nothing as swift and powerful as this.

Craxi's ankles buckle as soon as his feet hit the ground.

The monk's right hand twitches. A split-second move-ment – but a decisive one. Craxi sees the flash too late. He grabs his abdomen.

Ephrem watches Craxi struggle with the pointed iron railing he's impaled him on.

Craxi holds it with both hands and tries not to fall. He goes dizzy and drops to his knees.

Ephrem walks towards him. Looks indifferently at the blood blotting into his captive's shirt and makes a cold calculation.

It will take a long time for him to die like that. A very long time.

He circles Roberto. Stands behind him. Takes his head in the crook of his arm and with one violent twist breaks his neck.

122

Nic hits crawling traffic as soon as he picks up signs for the Tangenziale Ovest-Sud/Savona/Piacenza. So much for the confident predictions of the satnav. It takes more than an hour to get from the A55 to the A6. He thinks about calling Mitzi and Amy. There are things he has to tell them. Actions that must be carried out. But he has no intention of using the cell phone in his pocket. Save the brief bit of web surfing to find the parcel company, it's been turned off since he left Fabio and it's going to stay that way. Sooner or later he'll find a pay phone. From now on, the cell is for emergencies only.

Thirty miles and forty minutes further on, he struggles through another jam at a toll road rolling out to Savona. He tries to drown out blaring horns by switching on the radio. As he finally picks up speed, he realises his attention has been so focused on looking for the dark-blue cruisers of the Carabinieri or the paler blue and white ones of the Polizia that he has barely noticed the strange mix of urban and agricultural areas flashing past the Bravo's windows. The thin winter light is already fading as the satnav interrupts his thoughts to announce his estimated arrival time – he's still more than two hours away from his chosen destination.

The delay might actually be a good thing. With any luck he'll catch Broussard relaxing safely in his own home. Nic doesn't have a picture of the scientist, just Erica's description – tall and thin, elegant with silver-grey hair and an immaculately trimmed grey beard. Easy to spot. There's a Madame Broussard too – Ursula. Small and round. Dark haired with small hands like a hamster. He thought it funny how Erica described her like that.

Nic faithfully follows the navigation system's emotionless commands and comes off at the Savona toll exit. He must be about halfway there. The main question playing on his mind is whether he's ahead of or behind the man who killed Mario Sacconi and his lover – the man he believes also murdered Tamara Jacobs.

And if he is behind him – by how much? Nic glances at the upcoming signs illuminated by the stream of headlights. He's just entering France. He'll have the answers to his questions soon enough.

123

The factory runs only a skeleton staff on a Saturday. Partly because of the recession but mainly because few of the women will work weekends. Times are tough but the lure of being poor in the Californian sunshine beats being a few bucks richer inside a sweatshop any day of the week – especially Saturday.

John James finds himself in his office, unable to concentrate. He's thinking about Kim Bass. It was a clumsy kill. Maybe even an unnecessary one – a taking of life for the wrong reasons. Normally things are clear. Those needing to be helped to the other side are complete strangers. God guides him to them. Picks them out as surely as lighting a beacon over their heads.

Bass was different. She was known to him. A blatant enemy of the woman he loved. *Still loves.* He's tormented by the thought that anger and hatred were why he killed her.

Not God's will, just payback for all her bullying of Em.

Then there is Em herself. God had brought them together. Shown him that another person could stir him in ways he had never imagined. But had he misunderstood? Were those yearnings good or bad? He had certainly felt different with Em. His emotions were churned up. His

341

affection for her had made him feel different about everything – about life, and even death.

He has begun to question himself. Was it all a test of his faith? Like when Jesus fasted in the desert and Satan tempted him to turn stones into bread? *Yes.* That's what Em had been. A test of faith. And he failed. He'd read about how weak men had been diverted from their holy missions by the wiles of women. Now he understands. Satan has been at work.

He puts a hand under his shirt and feels the scabs forming over the last razor cuts. He hasn't hurt himself enough. Not paid sufficient penance for the pain he caused God. He scratches his nails repeatedly across his stomach until he sees blood on his fingertips. JJ bows his head and prays for forgiveness. Prays not only for the soul of the woman he loved, but also for that of Kim Bass, the woman he never should have killed.

124

FRANCE

A hundred miles along the A10, Nic joins the A8, then takes the exit marked Nice-Nord.

Even in the dark he can see that this is a place he'd like to spend some time. Time getting lost in the little villages spread out across the winding hillside roads. Lingering in a seafood restaurant overlooking the ocean. Time on anything other than chasing a killer.

He's more tired than he thought. The realisation comes as he takes the boat-like people carrier too quickly into a roundabout and he hears the squeal of rubber when he straightens her up. Not good. *Very* not good, given the kind of enemy who waits in the dark for him. He sharpens up his act as he loops around again to make the exit into Boulevard Paul Rémond.

The twists and turns come quickly now. Right at Boulevard Comte de Falicon, right at Avenue du Ray, left at Boulevard Cessole, onto Gambetta, left into Rue du Maréchal Joffre, right into Rue de Rivoli and out onto the Promenade des Anglais. The computerised voice announces that in three hundred metres he will arrive at his destination.

Destiny.

He parks a hundred metres from the grand house of Édouard Broussard and turns off the engine. He checks the gun Goria gave him, leaves the vehicle and makes the last part of the journey on foot.

125

Joe's Steak and Surf is painted fairground reds and racing greens and looks like a poor man's Frankie and Benny's. The place is buzzing because Joe does a three-course meal deal with a glass of wine for $10 a head.

Mitzi and Jenny Harrison sit at a red plastic banquette near the kitchen. Harrison finds her appetite and has a starter of refried potato skins, then an eight-ounce steak, skinny fries and a pile of garden peas as hard as buckshot.

'You want dessert?' The question comes from their middle-aged waitress, whose badge declares her to be Suzie. 'Pecan pie, chocolate brownie or ice cream assortment is included in the set price menu.'

Mitzi fishes a wad of single dollars out of her purse and hunts for some rare fives or tens. 'We'll skip it, thanks.'

Suzie's not used to people passing on free dessert. 'You sure? I can pack pie for you to go.'

She's about to say no again, when Jenny jumps in. 'Okay, we'll take the pie.'

Suzie cracks a thin smile and disappears.

Mitzi finishes counting out the cash. 'I saw the pictures of you and Kim on your fridge. Seems you were good friends.'

'We went to school together. She was like a sister to me. We hung out all the time.'

'You and her turn tricks together?'

For a second she thinks about lying. 'Sometimes.'

'Piss off anyone recently?'

'A john you mean?'

'Aha.'

She thinks a minute. 'Not that I can recall. Most go away more than satisfied.'

'You seen a lot of guys together over say the past two to three months?'

Now Harrison looks worried.

'This is between you and me, not the IRS or anyone else. I'm only interested in who Kim was seeing.'

'There are some regulars.' She takes a beat but doesn't have the energy to censor things like she normally does. 'We got this guy who looks after us too. Sometimes – you know – he expects us both to do him.'

Mitzi gives her a maternal look. 'Life's a shit and most times the guys in it are the reasons why. They're just shit-making machines.'

'You don't have to tell me that.'

'We get to the station house, I need names and numbers – the pimp, the johns, boyfriends, ex-lovers, okay?'

Jenny's in too deep to do anything other than nod in agreement.

Mitzi holds off the questions as Suzie the waitress returns. 'Here you go. I put pie and brownie in there. I hope you enjoy.'

345

'Sure someone will.' Mitzi gets to her feet and hands over a white saucer with the money for the meal and a $5 tip. 'Thanks for looking after us.'

'My pleasure.'

Harrison stands and takes the dessert box as the waitress drifts away. Her stomach grumbles from the shock of being fed after so long. 'Hey, will that cop leave my busted front door open when he goes?'

'No, don't worry. We'll get a new lock fitted and you can collect the key when we're at the station house.' Mitzi holds the restaurant door for her. 'Have you been broken into before?'

'Yeah. Couple of times. Most people have. Probably one of the bitches next door.'

They take the short walk up the block to the car. Mitzi zaps the central locking and goes round the driver's side. 'You lose anything?' She gives her a stern look over the roof, . 'You *really* lose anything?'

She shakes her head. 'Don't think so. Maybe my phone. I'm not sure, though. I got pretty wasted last night and could have left it or dropped it somewhere.'

Mitzi climbs in the car and waits until Harrison's inside and buckling up. 'The phone, was it contract or pay-as-you-go?'

'Contract. I got a deal – cheaper in the end than running burners. It's due an update. I thought I might get one of those adenoids.'

Mitzi laughs as she starts the engine. '*Android*. You mean

android.' She puts a finger to her face. 'Adenoids are glands at the back of your nose, near your throat.'

'Damn!' Harrison laughs. 'I've been saying adenoid for months.'

126

FRANCE

Two steps from the car, Nic smells salt and hears the roar of the Med churning foamy breakers in the darkness off to his left. The fact that his case started on the dunes of Manhattan Beach and may end on the sandy shores of the Côte d'Azur is not lost on him.

There's an uncomfortable tension in the air. One he's not felt since the day he put down the phone in his apartment and realised his wife and child had gone for a walk without him.

Death is in the air.

He's close to Tamara's killer. Close to a force that can end an innocent life without remorse.

Édouard Broussard's 1920s villa is ostentatiously lit by the golden glow of security lights and is clearly visible from the historic Promenade des Anglais. Set back on a rising corner plot behind elegant stone walls, it's a prime piece of real estate, with long, thin windows and a grand double-staircase of white steps leading to a giant mahogany entrance door.

Nic's way is blocked by black wrought-iron gates. He presses a button on a brass nameplate and waits.

A French voice – female, refined and mature – crackles out from a recessed speaker. '*Bonsoir.*' It's more a question than a greeting. '*Qui est la?*'

'Hello, I need to speak to Monsieur Broussard.'

She replies in English. 'Who is there?'

A faint light blinks high above Nic's head. He sees there's a video camera linked to the intercom. 'Ma'am, I'm Nic Karakandez from the Los Angeles Police Department.' He digs out his shield and holds it up to the lens. 'This is my identification. I'm happy to give you the phone number of my supervisor at the LAPD.'

The crackle stops and now there is only silence. Nic watches the side street and main road as he waits. Thankfully, there's no sign he's been followed. An electronic buzz releases the gates and they swing open. He walks through and hears them stop and then start to shut behind him.

By the time he reaches the bottom of the stone steps, the large entrance door has opened and a tall, distinguished man with silver-grey hair and beard is studying his approach.

He's sure it's Édouard Broussard. He allows himself a smile. He'd feared he'd be too late. Convinced himself he'd be walking in to find another butchered body – or two.

'Monsieur Broussard?'

'*Oui. Bonsoir.*' He deftly pulls the door behind him, anxious his wife doesn't hear anything she shouldn't. 'What is it you want?'

The detective shows his badge again. 'I really need to come inside and talk to you. I believe your life – and that of your wife – are in danger.'

Broussard looks sceptical.

Nic reads the doubt in his eyes. 'I've just come from Turin. Mario Sacconi has been murdered. I think both you and I know why.'

Fear falls like a shadow on the scientist's face. He swings his front door open. 'Please.'

Nic walks past him into a closed lobby floored in thick coir matting. An antique coat stand dominates one corner, like a thin, brown sentry.

Broussard locks and bolts the front door, then leads the way across a gleaming, marble-floored reception lit by a giant teardrop chandelier and lined with large, gold-framed mirrors. He twists the polished brass handle of a glossy white-panelled door and steps into a spacious windowless study. 'We can talk in here. I use this as my home office, it is secure.'

Nic glances at the oak-clad walls and imagines that behind them there are safes, cupboards and drawers filled with secrets of paternity and criminal defence cases. 'I'd really like you to ask your wife to join us.'

Broussard frowns. 'Why?'

The detective pulls open the right side of his jacket and reveals the Beretta. 'So I can protect you. If Mario's killer comes here and you're in separate rooms, at least one of you is going to die.'

127

The interview room is a whole lot less friendly than Joe's Steak and Surf but with a cigarette and a cup of coffee Harrison's still talking and writing down names of the johns. Truth be known, she quite likes this female cop. She's not as much of a ball-breaking bitch as most of them are. Probably because she's murder police and not vice or drugs. 'That's about it.' She pushes the sheet with six names on it across the melamine tabletop to Mitzi.

'You think any of these would have wanted to hurt Kim?'

Harrison rubs her fingers in her hair like she's scratching for bugs. Just thinking about Kim lying dead on the floor makes it pound. 'Marlon maybe.'

'The pimp?'

She nods and draws hard on the last inch of her cigarette.

'He beat you both up?'

'No more than most do.'

'How bad?'

'Me? Nothing – a slap here or there when I got mouthy. But one time he let loose and broke two of Kim's teeth.'

The comment makes Mitzi think of Alfie and maybe for the first time she feels truly glad to be free of him.

'He paid for the caps, though.' Harrison smiles. 'Nice set. Guess he thought he'd lose money if he didn't. I mean, no one wants to be blown by a vampire, do they?'

Mitzi thinks she'd like to blow Marlon – blow his scumbag head clean off his shoulders with a .45. 'Pimp aside, what about boyfriends or ex-boyfriends?' She pushes a clean sheet of paper across the table. 'Names and addresses of any significant others in the past two years.'

'Significant?' Harrison laughs. 'Kim should have been so lucky. Guys saw her as a dime piece.'

'Okay to toss from one friend to another.'

'You got it.'

'Was there ever anyone who meant anything to her?'

She thinks on it. 'There was one guy. She hung out with him for about six months, till his wife found out.'

Mitzi taps the paper. 'Name.'

'D'rick Watts.' She starts to write it out. 'Fell out the ugly tree and hit every branch on the way down.'

'Why she like him?'

'Dunno. He was kind to her. Bought her stuff sometimes. Not many guys do that. Lives over the tile shop at the Pomona Freeway end of East 6th. I can't remember the name of it. Watch for his old lady, she got a temper.'

'What about Kim's family, any beef there?'

'Like I told the uniform, she got no folks. Never knew her old man and her mom ran out when she was a kid in

351

Vegas. She was brought up in care homes and some fostering.'

The interview room door squeaks open and the big moonface of Deke Matthews rises through the gap. 'Fallon, step out here a minute.'

Mitzi looks towards Jenny. 'How could a girl refuse?'

The captain holds the door, then shuts it behind her once Mitzi's walked through. 'Have you heard from Karakandez?'

'Not had the pleasure.'

'Then you better call the son of a bitch and find out what the hell he's been playing at.'

'Captain?'

'I've just had a call from the Carabinieri in Turin. Nicky boy and a private investigator broke into a house today – one where two adults were subsequently found dead.'

'Dead?'

He glares at her. 'You want me to explain dead?'

'No, sir.'

'Karakandez then fled, having first interfered with the scene and removed forensic evidence.'

'This can't be as it seems, Captain.'

'You're right, Detective – it can't be.' He looks past her into the interview room. 'Sort out that low-life in there, get hold of your boy and clear this mess up before I have the Commissioner coming down here with a bat for my balls.'

Matthews storms off. Mitzi takes a beat before re-entering the interview room. She has to force herself to stop thinking about Nic and focus again on the murder. She pins

352

on a smile for Harrison and picks up the questioning. 'Was Kim working over the last few weeks?'

Harrison gives her a sideward look.

'Day job – not night work.'

Now she understands. 'Yeah. We work the same place. Pull in minimum wage at a sweat shop in the fashion district.'

'Where?'

'Fahed Fabrics, West Olympic Boulevard. I got her the job.'

'Doing what?'

'Sewing. Cutting. Piecing trash together. Mainly bed sheets, curtains, stuff like that.'

LA's fashion district covers a hundred blocks. Mitzi knows it inside out. Running a home on short purse strings means frequenting reject shops and warehouse sales. 'A lot of she cats thrown together. I guess that can lead to some fights.'

'Yeah, sometimes. Mostly we all get on.' Jenny peers into her coffee cup. 'Any chance of a refill?'

'Sure. We'll take a break in a minute. Just finish telling me about your co-workers. Did Kim pick fights with any of them?'

'No one messed with her – or me. We had some fun, you know. There was always a bit of bitching going on but no one disrespected us.'

Mitzi comes at it from another angle. 'Is there a chance you went too far with anyone – crossed the line at all?'

'What d'ya mean?'

'Gave someone reason to carry a grudge?'

Harrison scratches at an eyebrow. 'Not now. There was a girl, but she quit. Emma, Emma Varley. Teacher's pet – you know the type, worked so freakin' hard we all looked like slackers next to her. We used to roast her a bit.' Harrison puts two fingers to her left cheek. 'She's got a birthmark here and was always tryin' to hide it, so the harder she worked the cover the more we gave her.'

'She ever turn violent?'

'You're jerking me, right?' Harrison laughs. 'She wouldn't know how. Girl's a mouse.'

'Mice can be dangerous – go ask an elephant. This place, Fahed Fabrics, who runs it – a Mister Fahed, or his wife?'

'It's a mister but we don't see him much, maybe once a month. He's got a couple of places downtown, all rag shops. Factory's run by a supervisor named James. We call him Fish Face.'

'First name or last?'

Harrison frowns.

'James, not Fish or Face.'

'Last. I don't know his first name. He can't tell shit from Shinola.' She thinks for a second. 'To be fair, he's been okay the last few days. He rang you guys for me, tried to find out if Kim was in trouble and needed bail.' She touches her cup again. 'I really need that caffeine now. Either that or you let me have some weed.'

'Coffee's all you're getting.' Mitzi waves the bunch of papers that Harrison has written on. 'I'll have a pot sent

354

through while I get people working on these names and see if Robbery have had your door fixed.'

'Pot would be cool.'

'Pot of coffee.' Mitzi heads out of the room.

'Hey, can I ask you something?'

'Sure?'

'Why are you being nice to me? I mean, most people think I'm a clownbitch and they treat me like shit. So why?'

'Maybe because you're *not* shit. Maybe it's your life that's shit and you just smell of life.' Mitzi walks back to the table. 'Get through all this and start again, Jenny. Help me catch who killed your friend and you'll have done something good. Wiped the slate clean. Then you'll be able to tell yourself you deserve a new beginning.'

Harrison nods and for a second Mitzi thinks she almost made a connection. If she'd caught this kid a few years back, maybe she could have turned her life around.

128

FRANCE

Ursula Broussard is dressed modestly in a white silk blouse and ankle-length blue pleated skirt. The only real clues to her wealth are the rows of pearls around her neck, the thick gold wedding band and huge engagement diamond on her finger.

'I know this is going to sound strange,' says Nic, as they stand in the study, 'but I need you both to leave this house and I need you to do it as quickly as possible.' He locks his attention first on Édouard. 'Earlier today I saw the body of your former colleague, Monsieur Broussard. He had been tortured and killed in his bed in Turin. Murdered by a man who took his life without a second thought.' He switches his focus to Ursula. 'The young woman Sacconi had been sleeping with had also been killed – *after* she had been tied up and gagged.'

Madame Broussard covers her mouth and presses against her husband. He puts on a brave face for the sake of his wife. 'Do you know why?'

'We *both* know why.' Nic gives him a look that says it's time to cut the crap. 'You analysed DNA taken – correction, *stolen* – from the Shroud of Turin. Now someone is prepared to kill you because of what you found.'

Ursula speaks before her husband can answer. 'How did you get our address, Monsieur?'

'Erica Craxi gave it to me.'

She nods then asks, hesitantly, 'Are they all right? Erica and Roberto?'

Nic doesn't want to lie. 'Not exactly. Roberto is missing – still alive, we think. Erica, though, *is* safe. I made sure of it myself.'

Ursula cups her hand and says something quietly in French that Nic can neither properly hear nor understand.

But Édouard does. Édouard has done many foolish things

in life, mostly for money, but he seldom if ever ignores the advice of his wife of thirty years. Without speaking he walks to a wooden wall panel behind the detective and presses it hard with the palm of his right hand. A door pops open. He swings it wide, revealing a squat black safe half a metre by half a metre, with a twist dial combination. It takes the urbane scientist almost thirty seconds to twirl in a complicated sequence of numbers. Finally he pulls down on a heavy steel bar and swings the door open.

Nic checks his watch. He's been in the house almost ten minutes. Six hundred seconds for Mario Sacconi's killer to close in on them.

The Frenchman lifts out the only thing in the safe – an A4-sized envelope, sealed and taped. 'This is it.' He holds it out. 'Everything. The full results. The original transparency. The data file and the last remains of the sample.'

Nic takes it from him and rips open the top. Inside is a glossy A4 of what looks like a giant barcode. It's a genetic fingerprint. Maybe the most important one in the world. Maybe God's DNA? Or it could be just that of an unknown stranger? There's a small plastic envelope containing dark scrapings and a tiny, eight-gigabyte microchip for a USB port. There are notes and letters too. Typed and handwritten documents in Italian and French. Another in English. From Tamara Jacobs to Robert Craxi.

Nic looks up. Not at Édouard. It's clear to him now who makes the major decisions in the Broussard household. 'Madame, we need to leave here – straight away.'

357

'Then we leave.' Ursula Broussard opens the office door. 'Our lives are in your hands, Monsieur.'

129

Édouard Broussard presses the zapper on his key ring and the electronic iron gates at the rear of the villa swing open. He drives the black BMW 7 almost silently from the driveway out into the side street.

Nic is in the back, head down, gun levelled just below the window line. Ursula uses the in-car phone to make several calls as her husband takes them west along the Promenade. The ocean crashes white and noisy on their left. Grand hotels flash past on their right. Nic scans traffic on all sides. He uses the driver's rear-view and side mirrors to aid his surveillance of the front and anything that comes up alongside. 'How long will it take us to get there?' he asks.

'Ten minutes, no more,' says Ursula, leaning between the front seats.

'Don't look at me,' snaps Nic. 'Turn around. It's just you and your husband in the car, remember.'

'*Pardon*,' she says, startled by his lack of manners.

Nic doesn't care. Whoever snatched Roberto Craxi – a former special operative – needs no advantage against a middle-class married couple and a jet-lagged cop.

The car slows into a rolling jam as a large truck crosses

both carriageways. Traffic around them struggles to get through and horns blaze.

Nic grows tense. A jam is a bad place to be. They're going to be sitting ducks. The car in front comes to a standstill and Édouard is forced to halt the big BMW. Nic sees a motor-bike coming up in the rear-view – slaloming the stranded cars behind them – searching for openings. The rider is clad in black leathers and a full face helmet. Perfect cover for an assassin. Nic slides across the back seat, braces himself against a door pillar and grips the gun with both hands.

The bike weaves around the cars. Pulls level with the window of the passenger side rear door. Nic levels the Beretta at the helmeted head. The car's windows are heavily tinted and he presumes the rider can't see him. The bike edges forward. Its engine growls. Nic's finger tightens on the trigger. The rider edges level with Ursula Broussard.

Nic repositions and sizes up a shot over her shoulder. No point going for the Kevlar-protected head, it'll have to be either the neck or body. Suddenly, there's a roar. The bike dips to the right. Nic leans left. He swings his arms across. It's gone. The motorbike races off. Just the noise remains. A throaty roar to confirm an explosion of gasoline and exhaust fumes trailing through a narrow gap in traffic. Nothing more.

The guy was just being nosy. He simply wanted a gawp inside the top of the range sedan to see what it was like and what kind of person can afford a vehicle worth more than a hundred thousand euros. Nic breathes more easily as the jam frees up and they spot signs for the Côte D'Azur airport.

130

The cell phone on the passenger seat rings.

Ephrem picks it up. 'Yes.'

'Where are you?' Carlotta Cappelini asks in a brusque manner.

'I am outside the villa. Their lights are on. I can see the vehicle the American was driving.'

She knows he means Fabio Goria's Fiat. 'They're not there. Neither is the American.'

He scans the grounds. 'What do you mean?'

'Exactly what I just said. Our communications unit picked up a GPS lock on Édouard Broussard's phone. As it was moving west at a speed of fifty kilometres an hour, it is reasonable to think it is in his car and they are heading to the airport.'

He starts the engine. 'Do you still have the signal?'

'*Si.*' She looks at the map on her computer monitor and the flashing orange dot. 'Get moving and I will direct you.'

He slips off the handbrake and pulls out into the main road along the Promenade.

'Did you stop the parcel being shipped?'

He was afraid she'd ask that question. 'I was too late. It had gone.'

'Too late?'

He chooses not to explain what had delayed him. He couldn't leave Craxi to die a slow death in that tomb, nor could he afford the risk that the man might escape.

Cappelini is furious. 'What if someone in the parcel office recognised you or gives your description to anyone?'

'They will not.'

'How can you be so sure?'

'I am sure. All that is left of them are ashes. Ashes cannot speak.'

131

Édouard Broussard hands his car keys to a uniformed valet at the Sheraton Hotel, directly opposite the airport.

Too late to get flights out of the country, Nic and the Broussards have booked rooms and will leave first thing in the morning. Ursula will head to a friend's home in Switzerland –a senior diplomat with twenty-four-hour security. Nic and Édouard will fly to Paris and catch a connection to LA where full statements will be taken by the homicide squad. Or at least that's Nic's plan to keep everyone safe and get himself off the inquiry.

They collect their keys and haul the small bags they

hurriedly packed to adjoining rooms on the third floor. Nic bolts and chains Ursula's and jams a chair beneath the handle for good measure. He and Édouard retreat to the other room and Nic secures the door in the same way.

Édouard opens the mini-bar, 'I need a drink. You?'

Nic does. He wants several cold beers and then a tumbler of Jack Daniels but a restrained voice overrules his desire to unwind. 'Just some water please.'

'As you wish.' Édouard picks a couple of brandy miniatures and tosses a plastic bottle of still water to Nic. 'The man who killed Mario, I think I know something about him, where he came from.' He empties the brandy into a glass. 'Your writer, Madame Jacobs, I met her in Italy with Roberto. We saw her together when I verified the results of the DNA tests. She had been worried about the accuracy of tests carried out on something so old.'

'I can understand that. A viable sample from centuries long gone – I wouldn't have thought it was even possible.'

'No, it was very possible.' Édouard is dismissive even of the thought that he couldn't carry out such a thing. 'Mario used standard PCR processing, you know what that is?'

Nic's blooded enough rapists to have a basic understanding of the process. 'I think so – Polymerase Chain Reaction – the lab use it to build up a sample when there isn't enough of the genetic code to do a full profile.'

He smiles. 'A crude analysis of a scientific breakthrough that won its inventor the Nobel Prize in Chemistry more than twenty-five years ago, but it is accurate enough. PCR can amplify a single piece of DNA thousands or millions of times, certainly until we have enough genetic information to form a reliable profile.'

'But that wasn't sufficient in the case of the Shroud?'

'It was but we wanted verification by two techniques and two different testers. So I decided to use a new technology, something more cutting edge than standard PCR.'

'Being what?'

'Amplification of MicroRNA.'

Nic looks nonplussed.

'I don't have time to explain. Think of RNA as being like DNA, like a genetic code. But single-stranded rather than double-stranded, with a much shorter chain of nucleotides than DNA.' He stops, as if deciding something. 'Let us just say that MicroRNA, coupled with newer commercial kits like MiniFiler and Identifiler Plus, gave us a more trustworthy result, something we were certain the scientific community would feel more secure with.'

'What did Tamara Jacobs expect to prove with the results?'

'The identity of the man beneath the Shroud of Turin. She thought she could use it to prove – or disprove – that it was Jesus Christ.'

'But how?' Nic frowns deeply. 'To do that she would already have to have a DNA sample of Christ to match it to.'

'Not necessarily.'

Nic's confused. 'Yes, she would. It's a problem we face all the time. You get DNA from a crime scene, but you've got to match it to a suspect. The Shroud is essentially her crime-scene sample, but she had no subject.'

'No, but she knew there was one.'

'I don't understand.'

'Tamara believed there was another sample. Not taken from the Shroud. Taken from the cross on which Christ died.'

132

It's almost midnight by the time Mitzi has checked in with Tyler Carter and finished processing Jenny Harrison's statement. She's tried Nic's phone several times and not managed to get through. Matthews is going to go ape again tomorrow.

Even though she could get the girl a cab or have a uniform drop her, she chooses to drive her back to Boyle.

The Robbery squad has been as good as its word and Harrison gratefully slides the new key into the lock fitted to her busted-up door. 'We should have a ribbon or somethin' to cut. This place ain't never had anything new before.' She turns to Mitzi. 'You want to come in for a drink? I've got vodka.'

'No thanks, I'm kinda beat. You have my number – find a pay phone and call me Monday. Earlier if you think of anything or you're just messed up and need to talk.'

'Thanks.'

She watches the door close and listens for the lock to turn before she goes. The world is full of Jenny Harrisons – single women born on the wrong side of the tracks and stuck there. On the drive back she thinks of the scan picture she found under the mattress and wonders if one day Jenny will get her act together and be lucky enough to get married and have children. Despite all her trouble with Alfie, she'd go through it all again if that's what she had to do to have Jade and Amber.

Mitzi parks up and lets herself into the house. It feels horribly empty. No Alfie. No kids. Just her on her lonesome. Makes her wonder what life will be like when the girls finally fly the nest. She glances at her watch. It's kicking on for 1 a.m. but she's not going to be able to sleep. Her mind wanders. They'll all be locked down now out at California State. A prison built for two thousand inmates and jammed tight with more than twice that number. What the cops call *cosy*. Lights will be out. Strange noises banging and bumping in the labyrinth of stinking blackness. Thousands of guys – including the father of her girls – staring up in the dark above their bunks trying to figure out how in God's name they messed up so badly.

'Keep staring,' she says with no shake in her voice. She opens the refrigerator and realises she should have gone shopping. 'Think hard about what you've thrown away, Alfie Fallon.'

Her cell goes and she snatches it off the table where she dropped her bag. 'Hello.'

'Mitzi, it's Nic.'

Her eyes widen. 'Thank God. What the hell have you been doing? Matthews is going to tear you a new asshole.'

133

Mellow light filters through the reception windows of the Sheraton Hotel. It's 7 a.m. on the kind of morning that promises to be warmer than it should be for the time of year.

Édouard and Ursula pay the bill while Nic sits in a chair watching the hotel grind into life. This is his last week at work. The thought is uppermost in his mind. It is the beginning of an end. The drawing to a close of his life as a detective and the personal horrors that have accompanied it.

Late last night he gave Mitzi chapter and verse on everything that had happened in Turin and she promised to go straight to Matthews today and explain things, including why he had to take evidence from the Sacconi crime scene. Soon, he and Broussard will be on a flight into LAX and Ursula will be safe in Geneva. Tomorrow he'll take Broussard's statement and hand him over to someone to run the case after he's left the force. Come Tuesday, with a little luck, all the forensic will have been processed and verified. It's hard to imagine the crap that's going to fly as and when news gets out that there's a DNA profile of Christ going around. Adam Geagea and the other dorks in the Press Office are going to shit in their pants.

Nic thinks ahead to Thursday – by then the LAPD should have secured assurances from the French police that they'll protect Édouard and Ursula Broussard and the scientist could be heading back home. Friday night he'll be lifting a cold beer in a noisy bar and bidding a fond farewell to the LAPD.

The Broussards come into sight and shake him from his thoughts. They look like something's wrong.

'There is a strike.' Édouard gives a resigned shrug. 'French air traffic controllers.'

'Lightning action,' explains Ursula. 'All planes are grounded for twenty-four hours.'

Nic buries his head in his hands. 'We can't stay here, We can't just sit and wait for a day – that's inviting trouble.'

'I agree,' says Édouard, turning to his wife. 'We will drive you to Geneva and fly from there.'

Nic has no idea how far away Switzerland is. 'How long will that take?'

Édouard shrugs. 'It is Sunday, so traffic will be light. I would guess six, maybe seven hours depending upon whether we stop.'

'I will have to stop,' insists Ursula. 'Such a journey is unthinkable without stopping.'

Nic gets to his feet. 'Then let's do it. The sooner we get going the better.'

'I'll get the car brought round.' Édouard starts across the reception floor. 'We can wait outside for it.'

'No.' Nic shakes his head. '*Inside*. We wait inside until the very last moment.'

Édouard looks shocked. 'As you wish.'

Ursula Broussard moves closer to Nic as her husband heads to the valet stand. 'He is not a well man. He will not want to speak of it, but it is true.'

'What's wrong?'

She puts her hand to her chest. 'Last year he had a heart scare. Arrhythmia.'

'That's an irregular beat, right?'

'*Oui*. He has PVC – premature ventricular contractions. His doctor says it is stress-related, maybe also a little too much caffeine and cigarettes. I have made him quit the smoking but the coffee he cannot give up.'

'I'd be the same.' He tries to give her a reassuring smile. 'Madame Broussard, I'm not going to lie to you, you're not out of danger yet. I'll do everything I can to protect you and your husband, but I'm not sure I can take the stress out of things.'

'I understand. I just wanted you to be aware of his condition.'

Édouard is heading back their way.

'Thanks, I'll keep an eye out for him.'

'*Merci*.'

'The car is here,' announces the scientist with a calm smile. 'We can go.'

134

John James stands naked in his candlelit bedroom. A thin razor blade is pinched between the forefinger and thumb of his right hand. His mind is aching from the inner storm of emotion and doubt still raging.

His eyes fix on the long thin wardrobe mirror. Without flinching he cuts from his left shoulder straight down three inches. Before the blood flows he slices horizontally across the cut, an incision of two inches. He watches as a perfect cruciform of red appears.

Normally, from the first cut he can feel the pain. Outer pain matching inner pain. The perfect balance. It is a sign God is forgiving him, a signal his soul is being cleansed by the letting of blood. Just as Jesus suffered, just as the Lord bled for mankind, he must bleed for Jesus.

But in the early hours of this Sabbath day, he feels nothing. He cuts again. Still nothing. Tears fill his eyes. He is being forsaken. The rush of adrenalin that comes from the cuts, the sacrifice, the focus – they all help him to control himself, to direct himself. They subdue him. But not tonight. There is only emptiness. As though God has deserted him. He must try harder. Must prove himself more worthy.

JJ covers his entire breast in razored crosses. As the blood streams down, he works on his ribcage and abdomen. In the mirror he sees not a reflection of himself but a fleshy canvas – a portrait of his love for God. Thin rivers of red now surge from collarbone to hipbone.

It is not enough. Not nearly enough. He switches hands. He repeats the cruciform cuts across his right breast. Not as accurate with his left hand, he clumsily slices into the tender bumpy area around the nipple – the areola. At last there is a rush of endorphins, a sign of God's pleasure. The Lord expects more of him. Jesus is asking he step up and prove himself.

He cuts deeper into the pink circle with its proud fleshy monument and steps closer to the mirror. His eyes fix on those gazing back at him from the candlelit glass. He feels like he's outside his own body. Disembodied. Separated from reality.

The razor slashes back and forth until the pain hits him. Rushes him like a shock of electricity. God is pleased. JJ tilts his head back in proud delirium. His eyes are closed but his fingers and blade find his hanging nipple and slice off the last hinge of flesh.

135

They head north from the airport then after a mile join the fast-flowing river of traffic moving west. Through the BMW's tinted glass Nic sees signs to places he's only ever heard about: the ancient port of Antibes, a place dating back five centuries before Christ; Cannes, the home of the international film festival; Saint-Tropez, the jet-set playground of the world's richest people.

Édouard passes time by adding colour to the towns they're skirting. 'Do you know how Saint-Tropez got its name?'

Nic takes an educated guess. 'Some saint founded the place or took shelter there?'

'*Très bon*. A martyr named Saint Torpes was beheaded in Pisa during the reign of Nero. His body was placed in a rotten boat – along with a rooster and a dog – and it washed up here.'

Nic pulls a face. 'A rooster and a dog? I'd hoped for something a little more romantic than that.'

'Saint-Tropez has romance,' insists Ursula. 'Coco Chanel, Elsa Schiaparelli – much glamour has made its home here. And, of course, Brigitte Bardot.'

Édouard's face lights up. 'Ah, Brigitte. Proof that God created Woman.'

Nic watches husband and wife reach across the seats and hold each other's hands. For a second he thinks of Carolina. It was the kind of thing she'd do when he was driving, then they'd both peek over the seats and look at Max in his tilted-back baby seat and they'd say how beautiful he was and they'd imagine what he was going to grow up and do. 'How did you guys meet?' He asks the question more to break his own chain of thought than anything.

'Us?' Édouard laughs and whispers something in French. Nic watches their hands tighten.

'Okay,' Édouard says with a smile. 'My wife consents that I tell you. I saw her breasts and then I fell in love with her.'

'Sorry?' Nic's eyes widen.

'My father ran a cosmetic clinic in Nice and Ursula was a patient. I saw the photographs of her and I knew I wanted that beautiful woman to be part of my life.'

'So medicine runs in the family.'

'Only from my father. He ran the practice in Nice and even though my mother divorced him, he always looked after us and I stayed in touch. He was my inspiration.'

'But your mother brought you up?'

'*Oui*. We were very close. Papa was at work all the time, I barely saw him. She was Italian. Unfortunately, she is dead now, God bless her soul. So when they split she took me back to Rome where she was born and had family. I lived there from seven years old.'

Nic finds himself warming to the scientist. 'Do you consider yourself more French or Italian?'

Broussard laughs. 'French, of course, though I have a deep love for Italy. I had wonderful years at La Sapienza University in Rome and I won a place in the training school of the Arma dei Carabinieri, quite an achievement for a French boy – though by then I had dual citizenship. Back in those days speaking French and Italian made you very popular with the girls.'

'I imagine it still does.'

'I think so too.' They both laugh. 'I mastered in biological sciences and then won a scholarship to Oxford.'

'Oxford, England?'

'*Oui*. Though the English girls were not so impressed with me. Young men studying genome mapping were not nearly as interesting to them as those studying arts.'

Ursula interjects. 'You know that the English and French are not easy bedfellows?'

'I thought Europe was one big happy family.'

'Not at all. The French hate the English – we think they are vulgar. The English hate the French – they think we are arrogant. The Dutch hate the Belgians because they believe they should own their country; the Belgians loathe the Dutch because they are so blunt and make such bad food – and everyone hates the Germans.'

They all laugh now.

Édouard picks up his story. 'Most of my life was in the scientific investigations wing of the Carabinieri but I would come home and spend time with my father. It was on a visit that I met Ursula and I knew then I should spend the rest of my life with her.'

'We lived in Italy for a while,' she explains, 'but I am French and Nice is always home.'

'For me too. When my father died he left his house and business to me and we moved back.'

'So you now do cosmetic surgery?'

He looks aghast. 'No. I would be disastrous. We employ many good surgeons to do that. I just expanded the clinic to include DNA profiling for French celebrities and VIPS – the ones who are looking to avoid costly paternity cases.'

The car slows as they approach another toll.

'And you?' Ursula asks. 'What made you the man you are?'

'Death,' says Nic. 'Death of my parents. Death of my wife and child. Death shaped me more than anything else in life.'

136

OAKWOOD, LOS ANGELES

It's 3.45 a.m. and insomniac Tyler Carter is watching crap on the box, a rerun of the latest *Conan* show. The guy's nowhere near as funny as he was.

He's actually pleased when his cell phone rings. Anything to break the dullness of the dead hours between midnight and sunrise. 'Carter.'

The call takes less than a minute but by the time he hangs up he knows it's going to change every second of his life for the foreseeable future.

It's the call he's been dreaming about. He scribbles notes on a pad he keeps next to the bed and then rushes for the shower. Ten minutes later he's dressed, in his car and breaking the speed limit to get to the precinct.

137

CARABINIERI HEADQUARTERS, TURIN

It's mid-morning when Luogotenente Cappelini gets called to Giorgio Fusco's office. The forty-five-year-old is facing the wall, his hands clasped, his thoughts troubling him.

'Capitano?'

He turns and looks stern-faced. 'Sit down.'

She takes a chair on the other side of his desk.

'The body of Roberto Craxi has just been found.'

'Where?' Her voice is flat.

'In an old church on the east of the city. A couple of kids found it. It is being brought in to *patologia*.' He looks away, his eyes catching on the Carabinieri crest hung on the wall behind his desk. 'I'm told he had an iron railing sticking out of his stomach and his neck had been broken.' He looks back to her. 'This man, whatever you think of him, was once one of Italy's bravest and most trusted soldiers.'

She flinches. '*Sì*, Capitano, I understand. What of his wife?'

'No news.' Fusco starts pacing. 'Tell Fabio Goria about Craxi and see if that silent mouth of his can now find words for us.'

She nods.

'The officer at the church says an old tomb had been opened and the remains removed. Craxi's clothing was covered in dirt and mould that matches debris from inside the tomb. Someone kept him in there. Held him in that place, then let him out to kill him.'

She says nothing.

'Luogotenente, is there something about this case that I don't know? Something you should be telling me?'

'No, Capitano.'

He's not sure he believes her. 'You asked for resources some time ago, because you thought Craxi was involved in an international fraud – selling secret information, perhaps about illegal DNA samples taken from the Shroud of Turin – but now we have a murder in America and three murders here in Italy.' He moves around the desk so he is close to her. 'Carlotta, I respect that you want to protect the good name of the Arma – that is why I sanctioned your case – but I will not respect you holding back information that could prevent people from being murdered.'

She shrugs innocently. 'Capitano, I know nothing more

than I have told you. There may be much more behind Craxi's activities than I have discovered, but so far my inquiries have not revealed anything beyond his links to Mario Sacconi.'

He stares at her. Cappelini is a flyer. One of the few female lieutenants in the Carabinieri and tipped for great things. He has to give her the benefit of the doubt. 'Any news of the American detective?'

She shakes her head. 'Not yet. He will surface.'

'The Commandante spoke to his superior officer about the interference in the murder scene – do you know what he said?'

She stays silent.

'He said Karakandez would have had *good reason*. Said he was an excellent detective – one of his best.' Fusco tilts his head inquisitively. 'So why would he do that, Carlotta? Why would one of Los Angeles's most excellent detectives take evidence from a crime scene in Turin? Could it be because he didn't trust the local officer he was working with?'

'I hope not, sir.'

'Me also. Me also.' He waves her out of the office. 'Go back to work and don't end the day without bringing me good news.'

138

The monk has the luxurious black limousine in sight. He's five cars back. The optimal distance for surveillance. He's able to see any deviation from the main freeway in plenty of time but not easily be seen.

Ephrem has been behind the big car ever since it slipped out of the Sheraton Hotel valet line two hours ago. Édouard Broussard is the perfect driver to follow. He keeps an even speed – ninety – with the odd burst over a hundred when he needs to overtake.

The monk imagines how they're all sitting. Madame Broussard will be in the passenger seat, the American in the rear – jumpy and edgy like all cops are. And armed most probably. A small pistol. A gift from the Italian PI. Americans like guns. No doubt he will know how to use it.

Thoughts of the weapon make him decide against ambushing them on the open road. He's sure he could kill the cop – *easily* – but the scientist and his wife might make a run for it and out in public that could end up messy.

No, he'll be patient. They'll stop. They'll rest. They'll make mistakes. People like them always do.

139

'Where is he?' The wolf-like glare in Tyler Carter's eyes conveys his anxiety.

The desk sergeant looks up and sees a detective who seems to have forgotten his manners. 'Good morning to you too, Officer. And how are you? It's been a while since we've seen each other.'

'Don't mess with me, Jim, you know how much I want this guy.'

'He's in a single, down in lock-up. I'll take you through.' Jimmy Berg lifts the gate separating his desk from the thoroughfare where cops book in prisoners. 'Doctor Jenkins is with him right now.'

'Jim, I said no one was to go near him.'

'I know you did, but my dear hot-shot friend, it's my pension on the line if the guy dies in here, and believe me, this fruitcake needed to be looked over by the doc.'

'Why?'

'You'll see for yourself.' They walk the line of cells until they reach the one Berg wants. He opens the metal door and stands back. A broad smile breaks across his face as Carter pushes past him.

Carl Jenkins, the duty police surgeon, is bent over a man lying flat out on a low bunk.

'I'm Detective Carter, the principal investigating officer.'

'I'm sure you are.' The middle-aged medic holds up a suture needle. 'But unless you also have a degree in medicine or your hobby is needlecraft, step outside for a while and let me finish my job.'

Carter gets his first clear look at the patient. 'Holy shit, what happened to him?'

Berg shakes his head. 'Outside, Detective.'

Carter is rooted to the spot. The guy on the bed is covered in wounds. His chest is a sticky mass of clotted blood. The cuts form crucifixes and they're all over his body, his head, his face, eyelids and cheeks – even down the bridge of his nose. Carter can't believe what he sees. The crazy son of a bitch has cut off his own nipples and ear lobes.

140

FRANCE

Five hours after leaving Nice, Édouard Broussard flicks down the indicator and guides the BMW off the A7. His wife is sleeping so he speaks quietly to Nic. 'This is Malataverne. We'll stop for a quick break in Montelimar.'

'How far have we come?'

'About three hundred and fifty kilometres.'

'What's that – halfway?'

'A little further, but it is taking longer than I hoped. The road works around Aix-en-Provence delayed us badly.'

Ursula stirs. Her face is stuck to the leather seat where she cosied down. 'Are we there?'

'No, my love. We are going into Montelimar. We'll take a break for lunch.'

'Oh good.'

Nic nearly protests. He'd rather they just used a restroom in a service station and got going again.

'I know a perfect little restaurant there.' Édouard's hand comes off the wheel and finds his wife's. 'By the Palais des Bonbons et du Nougat. For ten years it has held a Michelin star.'

Nic lodges his objection. 'We really don't have time to linger. We need to get to Geneva and then to the airport.'

'Nonsense,' says Édouard, dismissively. 'We have to eat.'

'And drink,' adds Ursula, now fully awake. 'Sunday lunch is not lunch without a glass of wine or two.'

141

77TH STREET STATION, LOS ANGELES

Carter calls Mitzi and tells her to come straight in, then heads down to the bookings desk where Jimmy Berg's waiting to show him surveillance footage from the main reception area.

'Disk just came down from the video unit,' says the sergeant. 'I've cued it at the point your guy comes up the front steps.'

'Okay. Let it play.'

Berg sets it going and points a finger to the screen and a black officer manning the front desk. 'Look at Howie out for the count, sleeping his ass off.' He snorts out a laugh. 'Damn near soils his pants when your fruitcake leans on the buzzer.'

Carter watches the big old officer jerk awake. It's just like Jimmy said and it makes him smile for a second. The shot is wide-angled and covers the desk right of frame and the public door on the left. There's an electronic clunk and the door opens. A man walks in. He's barefoot and wearing what looks like a cream cape and underpants. A ridiculous sight. A kind of kick-ass superhero. Carter suddenly realises what he's got on. It's not a cape, it's a sheet. A bed sheet, like the ones the victims were covered with. He turns to the custody sergeant.

Berg answers the question before it's even asked. 'Already bagged and tagged with his other stuff.'

'We got a name for this fool?'

He nods to the footage and smiles. 'He's just about to tell you.'

Carter's attention swings back to the monitor. The man has his arms spread wide as he approaches an astonished

Howie. 'I am God's helper, I am Deliverance, the carrier of souls.'

Deliverance.

The detective's spirits sink. The guy is a shrink's wet dream. A good lawyer is going to dust off a big medico-legal casebook lying on a shelf in his rich private practice law firm and whip up an insanity plea. He just knows it.

'I am a vessel of the Lord, a messenger of the Almighty. God has sent me.'

Howie eases his sleepy ass up and out of the chair. 'Sure he has, brother, but right now the good Lord wants you to go straight home and sleep off whatever's got you buzzed.' Howie spots the cuts as the guy closes on the desk. 'Man, what you done to yourself?'

'My work is over. His work is done. *Dominus vobiscum.*'

'Shit, are you okay?' Howie presses a button under the desk to summon back-up.

'I praise the souls I have delivered.' The man falls to his knees. 'The holy souls of Kathleen Higgins, Stephanie Hayes, Lisa Griffin, Lucy Bryant, Shelly Hughes, Louise Perry, Krissy Patterson, Kylie Gray, Sally-Ann Ward, Maria Gonzales, Kim Bass and—'

Carter leans closer to the screen. He missed the last few words. Another name. 'Rewind Jimmy, does he say something there.'

'Don't think so.' The sergeant spools back.

They watch the footage again. Carter still can't hear anything. It's like the guy stops himself naming someone.

Why?

Right now it doesn't matter. The crazeball in a cape just listed all eleven victims in the serial killer case Carter's spent years working. Including the newest kill – Kim Bass.

142

FRANCE

Ephrem follows them off the A7.

He wonders for a moment if there's an airport nearby, whether they've booked a private plane. He'd be left stranded. His fears are abated as he watches the BMW cruise down the Route de Marseille and pick up signs marked Montelimar-Centre.

Within fifteen minutes the open countryside of south-eastern France has gone and they're enfolded in the concrete arms of a big city. The Broussards' limousine cruises gracefully to a roundabout and takes the first exit onto Rue Saint-Gaucher. It's a tight narrow street with tourist shops and shuttered homes leaning over a line of asphalt barely wide enough for cars to pass.

Ephrem is closer than he would like to be – just three cars away. Traffic stops while a courier pushes a tall sack trolley loaded high with bottled water from one pavement to the other. Once he's gone the BMW veers right and Ephrem follows into Place du Marche. It's a modern, paved square with cafés and shops set around a slightly recessed and pedestrianised area. There's no place to park.

To his surprise the limo pulls up outside a red-canopied restaurant and blocks the road. Édouard Broussard steps from the driver's seat and opens the door for his wife. She holds his hand as he helps her out. He closes the door, then they both enter the restaurant, leaving the car there. The two drivers in front of the monk palm their horns in objection.

The restaurant door reopens and a black-suited waiter hurries to the BMW and slides into the driver's seat. The rear door opens almost instantly and a tall, dark-haired man in black leather jacket and jeans steps out.

Karakandez.

The cop's eyes sweep the street as he stretches off several hundred miles of rear seat travelling. Ephrem wants to study him, wants to take in his size, his weight, how he walks, how he holds himself – wants to see a visible weakness in his adversary. But he knows better than to be caught staring. He looks down at the radio and plays with the tuner dial. Through his open driver's window he can hear the motorists shouting their disbelief that the rich man and his wife just left their car at the restaurant door for a waiter to park. Most Lebanese have good French and the warrior monk is no exception. He hears the sound of engines accelerating and looks up.

Karakandez has gone. A fleeting glimpse, that's all he got of the man he suspects he'll have to kill.

143

Tyler Carter is pacing impatiently when at last the cell door opens and Doctor Jenkins emerges with a worried look on his face. 'He's all yours but you'll need to tread carefully.'

'Is he going to need surgery?'

'No. It's not the physical wounds I'm worried about – they stitched up fine. It's his mental condition.'

Carter nods. 'Did he give you any details about himself – his name and address?'

'I asked but he didn't make sense. Didn't seem to be listening to me. He just kept praying, asking God for forgiveness.' Jenkins tries to remember some of the words. '"Oh my God, I am sorry for having offended you" – something like that.'

'It's the Catholic Act of Contrition.'

'You're a Catholic?'

'Lapsed. I learned it at school.'

The doctor starts to leave.

'You want to sit in on the interview? I've no trouble with that. At the moment he's here of his own volition and can walk any time he likes.'

Jenkins shakes his head. 'You do your stuff, I'll do mine.

I'm going to wash up and grab some coffee. I'll be back in half an hour or so to look in on him.'

'Okay.'

'Oh, and given the mess he's made of himself, you best treat him as at-risk.' The medic nods towards the bookings desk. 'I already told the sergeant back there, this is a suicide waiting to happen.'

'Understood.'

Carter stands for a moment and looks in through the cell eyepiece. The guy's just as he'd imagined the Creeper would be. Slight. Insignificant. Cowardly-looking. Anyone who would kill someone in their sleep was bound to lack strength – both physically and mentally.

The door behind him bangs open and he turns around. Mitzi Fallon walks in, hair looking like badly spun cotton candy. No make-up. Pupils as small and dark as rabbit droppings.

'Don't say anything. No smart cracks. I know I look like Joan Rivers on a bad day. I'm here, that should be enough for you.'

'It is. Thanks.'

She leans forward, looks through the peephole, then turns to Carter. 'This scrap of nothing did all that killing?'

'Seems that way. He turned up in reception, recited all the victims in chronological order, including Kim Bass.'

'Bastard. He got a name?'

'Deliverance.'

'Oh shit. A fruitcake. You got me out of bed and publicly

387

humiliated me for someone who's been banging his head on an idiot-stick?'

'I haven't yet met a serial killer I'd call sane.'

'Sure, but not many call themselves Deliverance and turn themselves in during the middle of the night.'

Carter grows quiet. Mitzi sees a strange look on his face, like he's just remembered something important he should have done. Then she realises the enormity of the moment. Carter is stepping off a ledge. One he's been standing on for two years. He makes the right step and the guy on the other side of the metal door goes to death row and his career resumes an unstoppable upward trajectory. He makes the wrong step and the nutjob known as Deliverance gets plead down to a psych case while Tyler Carter's chance of glory is unceremoniously flushed down the pan.

'You want to grab some coffee? Maybe an early breakfast?'

Mitzi looks startled. 'Say what?'

Carter smiles. 'I just decided I'm not ready to interview him.' He waves a hand at the cell. 'He's shown himself now. What's he going to do, ask to go home and pretend this never happened? At least if he does, we'll get to know where Deliverance lives. No, before we go in there and start laying down charges, I want to know who he is, what he's made of and what made him like he is. Now shall we get that coffee?'

144

Édouard and the stout old restaurant owner clearly go back some.

After the hugging, smiling and handshaking is over, the proprietor settles his guests at a table and has the maitre d' bring over the menus. But the feeling in Nic's gut is one more of worry than hunger. Stopping for lunch is insane. He can't believe that he agreed to it. At least the scientist and his wife look relaxed. Maybe an hour spent eating is better than a cardiac arrest later today.

'I told Jean-Paul that we are in a hurry,' says Édouard. 'He has promised us two of his finest dishes in less than the hour.'

The owner is as good as his word. Saumon d'Ecosse Tériyaki is the best fish the cop has ever tasted. The Ravioles de Roman et son émulsion de Foie-Gras Maison would convert even the most hardened vegetarian.

Édouard Broussard leaves a generous tip and after more embraces they step into a glint of sunshine. The owner hands Édouard the keys and tells him his car is parked five metres away, just around the corner in Rue Bouverie. He walks them to the corner and more embraces follow.

Nic's eyes don't leave the street and his hand doesn't stray more than an inch from Goria's Beretta.

'Would you mind?' The Frenchman offers Nic the keys. 'Could you drive for an hour?' He pats his stomach. 'I have had maybe a little too much food and wine.'

Nic's cop instincts say no. One hand on the wheel and the other on a gun is no way to fight a battle. Then again it might be safer than being driven by a drunk. 'Sure, but you'll need to direct me.'

'There is a navigation system in the dash. It is set for our destination.'

Nic takes the keys and the Broussards slip in the back looking more than pleased to be together and chauffeured. The car is an automatic and after gliding the seat back, Nic gets comfortable behind the wheel. A rear-view parking camera and over-sensitive front and back sensors usher him out from between two other parked cars. The satnav guides him out through a maze of tight streets onto the Route de Valence, where the computer diligently pings out a warning that speed cameras are coming up in three kilometres.

The big car's V12 six-litre engine is begging to be opened up but he keeps faithfully to the limit. Édouard has to help out with loose change as they join the A7 and hit a quick succession of tolls, then the Frenchman sits back and takes his wife's hand on his lap. Through the rear-view mirror Nic sees them dozing. No harm in that, they've still got two hours and around two hundred kilometres to go. *Sleep well, sleep long* – he just wishes he could do the same

The miles flash past and after more than an hour it's clear the Broussards look like they're going to snooze most of the way.

The traffic is light and Nic gets round to enjoying the big limousine. Unless he someday gets a job as a driver this is probably the last time he'll be in charge of such an expensive car.

As the first signs for Switzerland appear he starts to feel seriously tired. A tweak of the climate control directs a stream of cool air into his face and it seems to do the trick. The passing scenery is subtly altering behind the thin leafless trees that line the highways. Tantalising glimpses of forests, lakes and mountains give a feeling more of the cool ruggedness of Switzerland than the lush, green countryside of France.

Red tail lights suddenly blink on ahead. The traffic bunches for some reason. Probably Sunday drivers not used to the open road. Nic eases his foot off the accelerator and touches the brake. It goes soft. Nothing happens. He pumps it hard. There's a hiss of air then it flattens to the floor. The car isn't slowing. The brakes aren't working.

145

Mitzi watches the recording of Deliverance while she sits at her desk and drinks canteen coffee. 'He could just be a hoaxer. You thought about that?'

'He's not.'

'Wait a minute. Forget that he's weird and looks like a blind guy who tried to shave with a switchblade. All he's done is reel off the names of the Creeper's victims. Names that have all been printed.'

'Not Bass. That's not in the papers yet.'

'It's on the local radio, though. I heard it this morning.'

'Trust me, he's our guy.'

'Why? Because he's a religious nut? Let's do a sweep of LA churches and temples – I bet I can raise you a dozen by lunch.'

'Okay, listen – we have DNA from the Creeper case. Next step is we take swabs from Deliverance and see if they match. No match and he walks.'

'Logical.' Mitzi picks up the phone.

Carter stops her. 'Remember, this fruitcake came wrapped in a sheet. A bed sheet. As in the kind he covered his corpses with. We'll get that tested as well and I know we're going to find more than our boy's traces all over it. You make the Lab and Records calls. I'll get us some more man-power – and more coffee?'

'Just the manpower,' Mitzi hits a pre-dial. 'My tooth enamel won't survive a refill.'

Carter heads back to his office and pounds the phone. He manages to persuade a secretary, an admin guy and two old hands – Libowicz and Amis – to give up their Sunday lie-ins. He'll use the detectives to carry out any secondary actions that he and Fallon produce.

Mitzi finally gets through to Hix, the one forensic scientist she knows will drop whatever he's doing to help her. 'Tom, we might have a break on the Creeper case. We got a guy in central holding came in wrapped in a cloth that needs a rush job. We also need his DNA and a quick blood match.'

'Elimination screen?'

'Yep, though Carter's sure he has his man.'

Tom Hix has seen a dozen detectives assert they have their man only to be reduced to drink at the end of the day. 'I'll come right in.'

'Thanks.' She remembers Nic's call last night. 'Oh, if you check your in-tray you might find a parcel from Nic Karakandez in Italy.'

'Italy?'

'The Tamara Jacobs case. I sent him there to chase some leads. He's rushed samples to you from a crime scene in Turin, wants to know if there's a match to anything from the writer's house.'

'Sounds like I have a busy day. Actually, I was going to call you about the Jacobs case. We've completed the analysis on the cat and the carpets. You remember we had them both vacuumed?'

'Sure.'

'Well, we got a human DNA profile from the cat's paw – but that's not the good news.' He sounds animated. 'On the carpet pile we found particles of *Glyptobothrus lebanicus* and *Pogonocherus ehdenensis*.'

393

His enthusiasm is lost on her. 'Tom, it's early on a Sunday and I don't speak alien. What did you just say?'

He lets out a sigh of disappointment. If only she understood the rarity of his discovery. 'The *Glypto* is a grasshopper and the *Pogo* is a longhorned beetle. What they have in common is they don't come from America. The species is endemic to Mount Lebanon and the Anti-Lebanon Mountains.'

'Lebanon?'

'As in the Middle East. The vacuuming also produced traces of Lithosols – rocky, skeletal soils that you would certainly find on steep mountain landscapes.'

'I'm not sure where that takes us. I guess you're saying the killer must have been there recently or comes from there?'

'Exactly.'

'Okay. Will you send the genetic fingerprints over when you come in?'

'Sure. I'm on my way now.'

Mitzi puts down the phone and sees a red light flashing on the base. Missed calls. Her heart jumps a beat. Maybe her girls. She picks up again and triggers the answerphone. The automated voice says the message was left at five o'clock yesterday. She was dealing with Jenny Harrison at the time. She hopes Amber and Jade are all right, crosses her fingers that they haven't had an accident out on the slopes.

'Hi Lieutenant Fallon, it's Sarah Kenny from Anteronus Films. You said to call if I found anything new of Tamara's.

Well, I don't know if this is important but I might have something. You've got my numbers, ring any time. Have a good day.'

It's only 8 a.m. but Mitzi takes her at her word and rings.

She gets a pre-recorded message. 'This is Sarah – I can't take your call, leave your message and if I'm not out filming with Scorsese or the Coen brothers I'll get back to you. *Ciao*, darlings.'

'Sarah, it's Mitzi Fallon. You left a message on my work phone. It's Sunday morning and if—'

'Hello.' The real Sarah answers sleepily.

'Oh, hi. I just got your message.'

'Sorry, I was dozing.' It takes her a beat or two to sit up and get herself together.

'No problem.'

'I got a bill at work for a cloud.'

Mitzi's not sure she heard her right. 'A what?'

'A cloud. I didn't know Tamara had one but it seems she did. A storage cloud. It's a digital database – Apple, Google, Amazon all have them. You upload content – documents, videos, pictures, music, whatever you like. The cloud keeps it safe, so if you have your laptop stolen or your home burglarised, you can always download your content again.'

'Wow. They can really do that?'

'Yeah. You want me to mail you the details of her account?'

'That would be good.'

395

'Okay.' Sarah looks over her slim, suntanned shoulder at the handsome, naked actor stirring in his sleep. 'I can't do it right now – I'm going to have my hands full – but it'll be with you in about an hour.'

146

Nic's brain is working at warp speed as he frantically pumps the brake pedal. The V12 is doing seventy and he's only thirty feet from the car in front.

He tugs the automatic's stick down a gear and swerves into the outside lane. It makes little difference. He pulls the eight-speed transmission down another gear and zigzags violently to try to build tyre friction on the blacktop. The sudden jerking wakes Édouard and his wife. They look shocked and frightened.

Up ahead, the traffic is pulling to a sharp stop. The BMW's down to fifty but Nic's running out of road. He daren't turn off the engine, he'll lose all hydraulic power to the steering. He swerves across the lanes. Dust kicks up as he breaks out onto a thin strip of hard shoulder. There's a sickening screech like fingernails over a chalkboard as the BMW clips the side of someone's car.

Nic tugs down another gear. He's still doing forty and isn't losing speed fast enough. To make matters worse, the carriageway is sloping and curving downhill.

Édouard starts to panic. 'Slow down! Slow down!'

'I'm trying.' He tries to sound calm. 'The brakes have gone.'

There's a police traffic van up ahead, crawling along the dusty shoulder, blocking the only safe route he has. He hammers the horn and tugs down another gear. It won't be enough. He knows it won't. The giant police slug is barely moving. No way is he going to miss it.

He pulls the handbrake. The Broussards lurch forward. Rubber burns. The limousine twitches. Nic braces himself. Two policemen spill from opposite sides of their big Renault. Metal hits metal. There's a loud bang. Then another. And another.

Nic feels a punch in his shoulder. Then his face. Breath whooshes out of his lungs as the airbags pop. He loses his white-knuckled grip on the wheel. Loses all feeling in his hands. Blackness floods his brain. He can taste blood. The pain, fear and adrenalin slip away as he loses consciousness.

147

77TH STREET STATION, LOS ANGELES

Carter gathers his hurriedly assembled team in the Creeper Incident Room to brief them. He's lessened the pain of working Sunday morning by getting secretary Alice Hooper to pick up coffees and muffins on her way in.

As the lieutenant goes through the latest news, it becomes apparent to Mitzi that Kris Libowicz and Dan Amis are case vets. They're peas in a pod. Both early forties with that softened look that comes from too much fast food on too many stakeouts. The big differences between the two are that Libowicz has grey-black, razored-short hair, while Amis has a mass of jet-black curly springs, courtesy of his mother's African-American parentage. Both come with good reps – stand-up cops who have seen it all, done it all.

Tom Hix arrives and smiles at Mitzi – a little too much for her liking. Carter saves her further embarrassment by showing him the bed sheet that needs to be swabbed for DNA. Once the scientist goes about his business, the cops settle down to view the footage that ruined all their weekends.

'The sheet thing,' Libowicz points at the freeze frame on the screen, 'Why's he wearing that? Why'd the fool bring that thing in with him?'

'Emotional attachment,' answers Amis. 'He's like Linus.'

'Linus?'

'Charlie Brown. You know, the dopey kid with the blanket.'

Carter takes a spare coffee from the centre of the table. 'He chose the sheet rather than pick up a coat. There has to be a reason for that. You jokers might not remember this but Linus van Pelt was both weak and smart. Charles Schultz cast him as the strip's philosopher and theologian – he even went around quoting gospels.'

Libowicz breaks a bran muffin in half. 'Guess "Thou shalt not kill" wasn't one of his regular sayings.'

Mitzi can't take her eyes off the monitor. 'What's Deliverance holding in his left hand?' She points at the screen. 'Right there, look, he's got something hooked around his thumb and dangling.'

They all lean closer to the monitor.

Carter sees it now. 'Keys. Damn it. Car keys. Why didn't we see them before?' He knows the answer. They're all dog-tired and you miss things like that when you're running on empty. 'Mitzi, contact the desk sergeant, he'll still have them. Send a uniform to try the vehicles in the street. There can't be too many around on a Sunday morning.'

She grabs the remains of her coffee and leaves them to it. On the way down to the front desk she turns her cell phone off mute and replays a message she missed during the briefing.

'Mom, this is Jade. I'm sorry we rowed. I love you. See you soon.'

'Love you too,' shouts Amber from somewhere noisy. 'We're having a good time. Love you.'

That's all there is. But it's all there needs to be. Mitzi stops on the stairs and feels a rush of emotion. Thank God she's in the middle of a murder case – *two* murder cases – otherwise she might just have a soppy mom moment and cry her eyes out.

148

Through the blackness Nic feels something covering his mouth. Choking him.

He opens his eyes in panic. A paramedic is bent over him, pressing an oxygen mask to his face. The young man confers with a colleague in what sounds like an odd French accent. He listens, then turns back to Nic and speaks English. 'You are all right. Don't move, you'll be fine.'

The detective realises he's no longer in the car. He's outside. Lying down on damp, winter-greyed grass at the side of the road. In his peripheral vision he sees flashing lights and hears voices – but not traffic noise. Either the crash has blocked the freeway or the emergency services have shut it down. He tries to move but it feels like an anvil's on his chest.

'Stay still.' The paramedic has one hand on the mask and another on Nic's wrist.

He forces himself to sit up, and palms the guy away. Pain roars through his chest. It feels like he's cracked a rib. He pulls off the mask. 'The old couple – are they okay?'

The medic tries to ease him back down. 'They are being checked, as you should be. Now please, stay still.'

Nic tries to get to his feet.

'Whoa. Sit down. I'm not finished.'

'Thanks, but you are.' Nic tries again. This time he makes it. He staggers over to the Broussards, who are sat on the back steps of an ambulance.

Édouard forces a smile. 'I never let you drive again, *mon amis*.'

'I may never want to. The brakes completely failed. I put my foot down and there was nothing there.'

Ursula has her hand to her shoulder, nursing a bruise where the seatbelt snapped tight on impact. 'We are lucky to be alive,' she says.

'I'm sorry,' says Nic, inexplicably feeling compelled to say so because he was at the wheel at the time. 'I hope you're not badly hurt.'

'We are fine,' says Édouard. 'Bumps and bruises, that is all. It's good that others stopped to help and got the ambulance people here so quickly.'

'I think that other driver called them,' adds Ursula, gingerly rotating her arm.

'What driver?'

'He helped us out of the car,' she explains. 'Said we should move because it could catch fire.'

'He even got our luggage out,' Édouard nods to the banking where their small Louis Vuitton cases are standing.

Nic sees his bag isn't among them. The one with the DNA profile and documents the scientist gave him is missing.

149

There's a point in every investigation where all you can do is wait. Wait for tests. Wait for results. Wait for a break.

But waiting is something Tyler Carter is not good at. He drums his fingers on his desk and once more goes through all the actions in his head. Mitzi has uniforms out on the street trying to find which car fits the keys recovered from the suspect. Tom Hix has taken a swab from Deliverance and is running rush blood and DNA tests on both him and the sheet he brought in. Libowicz is chasing up fingerprints, though no one is expecting AFIS to come back with a match. Amis is running mugshots lifted from the surveillance footage through LAPD facial recognition software to see if Deliverance is flagged as a known offender. Uniforms have been sent to pick up Kim Bass's friend Jenny Harrison so she can try to ID the guy and Doc Jenkins has just completed his second review and is about to submit an official report on the subject's condition.

Mitzi's every bit as impatient as Carter. It's already gone midday and she feels they're still stuck in first gear. If she were calling the shots, they'd be in there giving the fruitcake hell. She forces herself to sit at her desk and fire up the computer.

There are a dozen new mails in her inbox, including the information that Sarah Kenny promised to send.

A cloud? Who would have thought such a thing existed?

She pastes a link in her browser and then enters the username and password Kenny's given her. There isn't much to look at – a dashboard of icons for Music, Videos, Photographs and Documents. She clicks the last one and it produces a spread of files: PDF, Excel, Word, Keynote, Pages, PowerPoint, Numbers, Contacts and something called Scriptmaster. She clicks on it and a new span of documents fans out on the desktop: 'The Age of the Rothschilds', 'The Duke and the Showgirl', and 'The Shroud (Final Draft)'.

Mitzi wonders if it really is the final draft. Any other day, she'd be excited as hell to be finding out. She opens it.

THE SHROUD

By Tamara Jacobs

FINAL DRAFT

Confidential – not to be photocopied. Only signed copies to be distributed to authorised personnel.

She flicks through the first pages. It all seems similar to what she's already read. Boringly so. This really isn't her kind of movie. She pulls up a wordsearch function and tries the new location that Hix added to the puzzle – LEBANON. A fresh page comes up. One she's not seen before.

LEBANON/BEIRUT. 1176.

EXTERIOR. Night.   **Scene 49**

Winter. Snow-capped mountains, forests of Lebanese cedars. (As the camera moves deeper through the forests day turns to night.)

The sound of hymns being sung by male voices is heard in the distance.

Torchlights flicker through the open window slats of a secret Maronite monastery.

INTERIOR.   **Scene 50**

The singing stops and hushed male voices are heard. Two Maronite monks stand together. A large blood-red crucifix sown over each man's heart uniquely distinguishes their full-length brown habits. They are as much warriors as men of God.

The first monk is called YOUSEFF. He is a senior in the order. He is stocky and in his mid-thirties. The second, KHALIL, is fifteen years younger, and is taller and thinner.

YOUSEFF

Word has come from our Holy leader: it is time for us to pray and ready our brave knights for their tasks. Satan has been hard at work. He has bestowed the blackest of his evil blessings on the foulest of his bastard offspring – the monster Salahuddin.

KHALIL

Foulest and fiercest. The whole of the Muslim world is
gathering behind Salahuddin's bloody sword.

Bells ring out. It is the call to evening prayer. YOUSEFF and KHALIL
walk the dark passageways of the monastery. Wall torches flicker
as they pass. Their shadows grow eerily long on the stone
slabbed floors.

YOUSEFF

The infidel Muslim mocks our Lord, Jesus Christ. He generates
grandly the pretence of peacekeeper among those hoards of
heathens.

KHALIL

I pray for his downfall. Daily and nightly I pray with all my heart
and soul that the great army of Franks, with the proud Templars
and Hospitallers at their head, will burn his camps and ensure
the shadow of the True Cross falls upon his sinful soul.

YOUSEFF

I fear it is not to be. Judging from the request that has come
down to us, so too does the Holy Father.

They cross an inner courtyard, where a statue of Saint Maroun
stands in the middle of a fountain. Flower petals are scattered on
the water and it is ringed with tall, lit candles. YOUSEFF stops to
dip his hand in the water and bless himself in front of the statue
of their patron saint.

Do not be afraid, young Khalil, we will not ride alone. The spirit of Maroun will be with us at all times. He will guide our eyes and our swords.

He gestures past the statue to the wall opposite. It contains a giant crucifix of Christ and a number of kneelers cut into the hard stones.

YOUSEFF

It is time to unchain the Knights of the Darkness. Time for them to wield the wrath of God.

On the other side of the fountain they both cross themselves again. They kneel side by side and slide back small iron plates fitted in the wall. The stench from inside the cramped cells makes both monks wince.

YOUSEFF

Brother, our Holy Father has sent us to you.

The camera slowly zooms over YOUSEFF'S shoulder into the darkness of the cell. For seconds there is only blackness. Gradually a man's red staring eyes grow larger and larger until they fill the frame.

YOUSEFF (cont.)

We are here to take down your stones and release you. It is the moment for you to raise the sword of God and slay the greatest of his enemies.

150

Two miles from the crash site, Ephrem pulls over and puts on his rental's hazard lights. He descends the steep banking and in a thicket at the bottom busts open Nic's cheap case. On top of the crushed clothes he sees what he wants.

What he crossed continents for.

What he killed for.

He holds the glossy, black-and-white DNA print in his hand and marvels at it. Ten rows of dark and light columns, dozens of blocks of magic stacked on each other, the ultimate historic tracer, a unique treasure.

He takes out his phone and dials a number long ago memorised and seldom called. The tone blips out into cyberspace. It crosses countries and comes to rest in the handset of Nabih Hayek. The Lebanese cleric answers on the second ring.

'It is Ephrem. I have the profile, the original transparency and the data file it came from.'

Hayek heaves a sigh of relief. 'You are sure?'

'I am. I have just taken them from the scientist who conducted the tests and the American who was trying to protect him.'

Hayek doesn't ask if they are still alive. He wants to avoid *explicit knowledge*, wants to be able to talk to Andreas Pathykos truthfully and in return have him speak openly to the Pontiff. 'You have done well, my brother.'

'You wish me to destroy them?'

Hayek hesitates. Destroying something so historically important is still hard to sanction. 'Yes.' He swallows hard.

'Very well.'

The cleric thinks a moment, then adds pointedly, 'We would all sleep better knowing this never happened – knowing such a thing could never be repeated, and could never be spoken of.'

'I understand, Father.'

And Ephrem does. He *fully* understands what is expected of him. His mission is not yet complete.

151

77TH STREET STATION, LOS ANGELES

Mitzi scans another page of the script. Searches every scene, every sentence of dialogue for clues that might help her solve the Tamara Jacobs murder.

The movie's action has moved to Damascus, the ancient city sited in the shadows of the Eastern Lebanon mountain range. The year is 1187, soon after Salahuddin recaptured the city of Jerusalem.

DAMASCUS: THE PALACE OF SALAHUDDIN (SALADIN):

EXTERIOR. Late evening.   **Scene 74**

Two crimson-cloaked guards on black horses cross each other's
paths as they patrol the circumference of the palace. Closer to
the towering walls are foot-soldiers, posted no more than an
arm's length from each other.

INTERIOR.   **Scene 75**

In the grand hall there is loud music and excited celebration.
SALAHUDDIN is staging a lavish feast and night of entertainment
for his most trusted men. They are marking their great victory at
Hattin. As well as jugs of wine, pipes of hashish are being
smoked and exotic women dance tantalisingly close to the
soldiers.

SOLDIER ONE (taking hash pipe from friend)
Revenge is so sweet. The Holy City of Jerusalem – the place
the Christians slaughtered our ancestors – is painted in their
blood. It is rightfully ours again and will now remain so until the
end of time.

SOLDIER TWO (shouting excitedly)
We praise you and salute you! Our greatest of generals –
Salahuddin!

The lone cry from the soldier sparks a spontaneous and intoxicating
chorus from the mass of soldiers.

MEN

Salahuddin! Salahuddin! Salahuddin!

SALAHUDDIN modestly acknowledges the refrain with a raised hand. To his right is NOUREDDINE, one of his most-valued generals. He is older and smaller than his master. An angry red scar, still unhealed from the last conflict, runs from his left ear down his cheek and across to where the tip of his nose used to be.

NOUREDDINE

Behold, master – these are your men, men who would die a thousand times for you. We have taken Egypt, Syria, Arabia and now Jerusalem. All of the world could soon be ours.

SALAHUDDIN (starting to walk away)
God's, Noureddine. Not ours – God's.

NOUREDDINE (ignoring the reproach)
Stay with us, master. Share with us the moment when the blessed light of morning rises over Islam's blossoming empire.

SALAHUDDIN (smiling)
Enjoy yourself – you have earned it. I am fit now only for my scribes, my prayers and my rest. May God be with you.

NOUREDDINE

And with you.

SALAHUDDIN exits.

The Sultan is flanked by two bodyguards – both the tallest of all his soldiers. They march with shields aloft and swords drawn. As they climb a winding stone staircase one soldier advances a step, while the other drops behind.

En route to the general's chambers they pass great treasures looted from the countries his armies have conquered – giant statues, bronzes and pottery from the palaces of Syria and Arabia. More guards stand in pairs at each turn of corridor and a new hallway.

SALAHUDDIN pauses as the foremost soldier opens the door to his rooms. Inside stands another armed guard and two learned scribes.

SALAHUDDIN (to his escorts)

Leave me now. Return to the feasting and revive yourselves. Make the most of the last embers of celebration. May God be with you.

SOLDIERS (responding together)

And with you.

The antechamber is vast and filled with personal trophies from battle – flags, shields and pennants of those who dared stand and fight against him. Upside down, gathering dust, is a large wooden crucifix made from the wood of the so-called 'True

411

Cross', the one upon which the Christians claimed their Lord Jesus died. It was prised from the hands of a slain bishop in the aftermath of the Battle of Hattin and is spattered with blood. The arms of the cross had been used as a resting block to behead captured Christian soldiers who would not convert to Islam or were not worth releasing for ransom.

SALAHUDDIN unfastens a gold breast clasp bearing his crest and removes his cloak. He walks into an adjoining chamber where his two personal scribes are sat working. These are men who for more than a decade have travelled at his side, chronicled his rise to power and described his philosophies. The scribes stand and bow as he approaches. Both look tired but dare not yawn. They know their master's dictation may take hours.

SALAHUDDIN
Come my wordsmiths, muster a little more life – I need your penmanship to convey the excitement of the history we are creating.

As SALAHUDDIN begins a monologue about the battles he still faces and the Jihad still to come, the camera zooms in to the flowing ink curves of the ornate Arabic writing the scribes begin to create. The lines of dictation then fade into a wide shot of sand dunes cresting a heat-shimmering horizon.

152

Neither of the Broussards can give a good description of the man who took Nic's suitcase. Thin not fat. Olive-skinned – no beard. Short hair – very short. That's the best the detective can get out of them. It could match millions of males in France and tens of millions across the Med region.

The scientist looks crestfallen. 'If he has taken your case, then both my work and your time have been wasted.'

'No, not completely. Erica Craxi gave me a Saint Christopher – a locket on a chain. Inside it, behind a picture of the saint, were fragments of the Shroud – I guess Craxi wanted back-up in the event something went wrong. I have sent them to Los Angeles for our lab to examine.'

Édouard sees a problem. 'But still – you have nothing to compare them with. It is impossible for me to remember all the sequencing.'

Nic produces his BlackBerry. 'This isn't the best camera in the world, but I think its imaging is good enough for you to recognise the Shroud's DNA profile.' He opens up the media files and plays a saved video. 'I made this footage of your profile when I was in my room at the Sheraton. I've already mailed it as a digital file to my own AOL account.'

The scientist squints at the tiny screen. 'Yes, I can confirm that it is the profile I produced.'

'Good.' Nic shuts down the file. 'It's not as powerful as having the original prints but if you come back with me, you'll be able to examine the LAPD tests and compare the results with those you produced.'

Édouard thinks it through. 'It is possible. Yes, I am willing to do this.'

Nic thumbs through the BlackBerry's contacts. 'I'll call the lab in LA and set the wheels in motion.'

153

THE SHROUD – TAMARA JACOBS   Scene 76

DAMASCUS: SALAHUDDIN'S PALACE. 1187.

EXTERIOR. Morning.
The morning after the night before. The soft pink light of dawn falls on the sand outside the palace gates. Horses' hooves kick up dust as we see the now-familiar sight of patrolling guards riding slowly.

CUT TO

INTERIOR.   **Scene 77**

The grand hall is littered with men and women sleeping at long tables, on floors and entwined in seats. The remains of the great feast still strewn around them.

As the wide-angle camera tracks low, up the winding stone staircase, a dull thumping sound can be heard with increasing urgency. It is the banging of a clenched fist on wood. The sound becomes louder as the camera swoops between pairs of guards standing at each corner of the twisting corridors that lead to SALAHUDDIN'S chambers.

The giant oak and iron-studded doors to his rooms are closed. DHUL FIQAR, the Commander of the Guards, is shouting through the panels. More men hurriedly arrive. Pushing his way through the middle is GENERAL NOUREDDINE. He has come straight from bed, his garments are in disarray and he is still robing as he arrives.

NOUREDDINE

Force an entry! What are you fools waiting for? Our master could be in danger – break down the doors! Call for his surgeon.

FIQAR

Do as he says.

He looks around and then points to a stone statue of Isis taken from an Egyptian tomb.

FIQAR (cont.)

Use that false god to open the way.

415

It takes six soldiers to lift the giant granite representation of the Egyptian goddess. They let out a mighty cry as they run at the double doors. With a thunderous crash they break through. Several soldiers fall on impact.

NOUREDDINE
Wait!

He holds a commanding hand aloft and stops the men.

NOUREDDINE (cont.)
I, alone, will enter first.

NOUREDDINE takes a sword from the belt of a guard and steps through the splintered wood and gaping doorway into the antechamber. He pushes open the doors to the inner room.

NOUREDDINE
Sweet Muhammad! This cannot be.

The camera tilts from NOUREDDINE to the floor. It pans over the corpse of a guard – his throat has been slit and his heart punctured by a single knife wound. It focuses on the dead face, then the body of a scribe – his intestines spilled through a deep sword wound. The camera moves on and stops on the iconic and now dead face of SALAHUDDIN. The shot pulls out and widens to reveal the sultan's corpse – only now do we see the full horror that has NOUREDDINE transfixed. SALAHUDDIN has

416

been stripped and nailed to the captured crucifix made from the wood of the True Cross. His body is a chequerboard of cuts, slashes from a knife or sword, and shards of broken glass have been beaten into his skull to create a bloody crown.

NOUREDDINE rushes to the antechamber door to prevent soldiers entering. He holds it closed and shouts through it for the Commander of the Guards.

NOUREDDINE
Dhul! Dhul, come into the chamber. The Sultan is unwell, he is asking for you.

DHUL pushes through the door. NOUREDDINE quickly closes it behind him.

NOUREDDINE (visibly shaken)
Salahuddin is dead.

FIQAR
What?

NOUREDDINE
Assassins have killed him in his chamber.

FIQAR
It is not so. *Swear* it is not.

NOUREDDINE

I swear by God's holy name that it is. Come.

The General leads the Commander of the Guards through to the inner chamber. For a moment both men stand in mournful silence.

FIQAR

How can this have happened?

NOUREDDINE

A scribe is missing. He will have been an Ismaili or Christian plant. I can still smell his stench.

He looks around the room at the pools of blood and mutilated bodies.

NOUREDDINE (cont.)

He must be wounded and cannot have got far.

His eyes fall on bloody hand prints on the wall, near an open shutter the Sultan's bed. FIQAR can tell that the General thinks this is the escape route the assassin took.

FIQAR

I will send my best men to capture him.

FIQAR starts to the door.

NOUREDDINE

Wait. Do *not* do that.

FIQAR stops and turns.

NOUREDDINE

There is a matter of *greater* urgency.

He paces before he speaks.

NOUREDDINE

We must feign an illness of our master. The Christians cannot
know he is dead. The world must not know. Bring Salahuddin's
physician – we need his complicity to add face to our
deception.

FIQAR leaves. NOUREDDINE picks up a sword and prises out the
nails pinning Salahuddin to the crucifix. He lays the great sultan
on the floor and pulls a sheet from the bed to cover the corpse.
Then he kneels and prays.

FIQAR returns with physician ADHAM BAHIR. The Commander
once more shuts the door to the chambers. Having done so, he
pulls a dagger from behind his robe and holds it to the doctor's
throat.

FIQAR

You will do as General NOUREDDINE commands or I will cut any
unwillingness from your insolent body. Do you understand me?

419

BAHIR tentatively nods over the blade of the knife.

FIQAR
Good.

DHUL pushes him through to where NOUREDDINE is knelt beside the corpse of SALAHUDDIN.

NOUREDDINE
Physician, bring proper linen, attend to our master's body personally, see he is treated fittingly.

He stands aside and lets the doctor inspect SALAHUDDIN.

NOUREDDINE (cont.)
He is with God already, I know he is. I only pray I live long enough to wreak vengeance on all those who orchestrated this evil.

DHUL strides over to the body of the dead scribe, spits on him and then kicks at his head. NOUREDDINE pulls him away.

NOUREDDINE
Vent your rage another day – I need your calmness of mind this very moment. There is much work to be done.

He looks towards the doctor.

NOUREDDINE (cont.)

What say you about our Sultan? How shall we make his
courtiers believe he is alive but so ill he need be confined to
rest?

BAHIR

Some years ago the master was struck with afflictions of the
heart. We may say with sadness that the same malady has
surfaced. To avoid infection, only I must enter his chamber.

NOUREDDINE (looking pleased)
How long can this pretence be perpetrated?

BAHIR

Ten days. No more. Salahuddin is known of old to be a poor
patient. Beyond such time, it is not conceivable he would not
seek to rule from his chamber even if I forbade it.

NOUREDDINE
This will have to be sufficient.

He moves close to FIQAR and talks in hushed and confidential
tones behind a cupped hand held to the ear of the Commander.

NOUREDDINE (cont.)
I will need to ride to Salahuddin's wife and speak with his
brothers. Their complicity must be secured as a matter of
urgency.

FIQAR

I will have my most trusted men ride with you.

NOUREDDINE nods.

NOUREDDINE

And the unworthy body of this treacherous scribe?

BAHIR

I will personally see to his disposal.

NOUREDDINE

Make sure you cut his stinking soul from his body. He must spend eternity without it, burning in the fires of eternal damnation.

Mitzi's desk phone rings. Reluctantly, she looks away from the script and hits the hands-free button.

'Fallon.'

'Detective, it's Officer Fisher – Andy Fisher. I found your suspect's car around the corner. There was a licence inside and he matches the photo ID. We have a name and address for your guy. You want me to give it you over the phone?'

'No. Great job, Andy. I'm coming straight down.'

154

COINTRIN AIRPORT, GENEVA, SWITZERLAND

Nic's badge is enough to swing a ride in a Swiss police car
to the airport and another to take Ursula safely to the home
of her diplomat friend in Geneva.

After collecting tickets from the Lufthansa desk, the detective goes straight to the restroom. He locks himself in a
cubicle, lifts the ceramic toilet lid and reluctantly drops the
emptied Beretta into the tank. As much as he'd like to hang
on to the weapon there's no way he can get it through the
scanners. He adjusts the floating ball, checks the toilet still
flushes, then heads out to the concourse.

He and Edouard barely have time to speak as they rush
through check-in and then get processed in the security, customs and passport areas. They reach the departure gate and join
the hundreds of passengers on the thirteen-hour flight to LA,
via a connection at JFK in New York. Eventually, the 747 lum-
bers down the runway and levers itself into the evening sky.
Once the flight has levelled out and the seatbelt signs go off,
Nic will find the chief steward and get a copy of the passenger list. He wants to walk the plane and check names
against faces. Only then will he feel safe and be able to think
about going home and the new life awaiting him. He's going
to sail north first, up to San Francisco, then past Fort Bragg

and skirt along the forest edges of Crescent City, Gold Beach and Florence. Maybe he'll scoot across to Neah Bay and do Victoria, Richmond and Vancouver. He'll pick up work along the way. Lose himself. Reinvent himself. Who knows?

Broussard touches his arm and brings him back to the present. 'Do you think you will ever catch the man who murdered your writer and tried to kill us?'

Normally, Nic would be upbeat and positive. He'd toe the standard detective line and say in the end the bad guys always fall. But those days are almost all behind him. 'Probably not. This guy kills in both the US and Europe – he's a professional assassin. Pros vanish in the way that street gangsters don't. You cross borders, you throw police off your trail – you cross continents, the trail itself gets lost.'

'But you have clues, forensic evidence, days and dates of movement. These things all help, no?'

'They do, but they mean a whole lot more if you have a really good description of the guy – and we don't. He's a ghost.'

155

Mitzi collects the driver's licence from Andy the traffic cop and heads back upstairs knowing they've got a break.

There's a hot crackle of electricity jumping in her head, lighting up all kinds of possibilities, making connections. She also knows this is the time to keep cool and go slow. You have to treasure a breakthrough, position it right and build on it carefully. If you don't, it turns to sand in your hand.

'We got something,' she says, throwing open the door to Tyler Carter's office and slapping the ID on his desk. 'Deliverance is John James and unless I'm mistaken he's Jenny Harrison's boss – Kim Bass's former employer.'

Carter's eyes drift from his spread of case papers to the licence. 'John James. The name of a nobody.'

'I know, but I got bells going off on this guy.' She flips open her notebook. 'When I interviewed Jenny, she mentioned the factory being run by a supervisor called James. She said he even rang a local precinct to find out if Kim was in trouble and needed bail.' She flips the book closed. 'What do you think about that?'

Carter muses on it. 'Could be he was trying to divert Harrison from calling in the local cops – then again, he might just have genuinely been helping out.'

'Sure he was.'

'Get someone to pull his home and cell numbers and see if any of the stations received a call.'

She nods.

'Harrison's on her way in, isn't she?'

'We couldn't raise her. I've got uniforms trawling the neighbourhood, won't be long before they find her.'

'Okay. Let me know when you've spoken to her and had her ID James.'

'Will do.'

'Meantime, I'm gonna send Libowicz to check out his home.'

'You got a warrant?'

Carter gives her a *don't ask* look.

She heads for the door. 'I need an hour of personal time – I'll be back ASAP to interview Harrison.'

'You've got it.'

'I'm on my cell if you need me.'

156

BEVERLY HILLS, LOS ANGELES

Matthias Svenson rushes down the stairs of his rented mansion. Some idiot's been pressing the bell for the past five minutes and he's going to tear their head off. He fastens the belt of the short white towelling robe that does little to hide his tanned body and yanks open the door.

'Detective Fallon?' The Swede looks startled.

Mitzi slaps the final draft of *The Shroud* in the middle of the director's broad chest. 'I'm coming in. We need to talk about this.'

'I'm not sure I—'

'Believe me, you're sure.' Mitzi pushes her way into a cool reception area of dazzling white and grey veined marble. Sunlight pours into an airy reception room to her right and she wanders in and looks around. 'Nice place. Much snazzier than the cell I've got on hold for you.'

'What's this about, Lieutenant? I've told you everything I know.'

'Just so you know, I don't have the time or patience for you to lie to me.' She sits on a plush white sofa and slaps her hands on the rich cushions. 'I should get one of these. Wouldn't cost more than my year's pay, I guess.'

Svenson picks a phone off a glass table. 'I'm calling my lawyer.'

'Feel free. Only, have him meet us downtown. Tell him you've been arrested in connection with perverting the course of justice in a homicide.'

The director slots the phone back into its base station and takes the seat opposite her.

'Good decision. That script I gave you, it shows you've been holding out on me. You never mentioned the DNA samples taken of the Shroud, the Muslim links, the storyline about Saladin or the Maronite monks. Now why would you forget all that, Mr Svenson?'

'Why is this relevant?'

'Because it's why Tamara got killed. But you've known that all along, haven't you?' She points at the script he put on the arm of the chair. 'Tell me the end of the movie. The scenes that are not in there.'

He picks up the draft and looks thoughtfully at it. 'Tamara was a remarkable writer. Her passion for the written or spoken word was only matched by her love of history and its mysteries. Before *The Shroud* she'd been researching an ancient group of warrior monks, crusaders who fought the Muslims in the Holy Land.'

'Hang on – I feel complicated coming along and I'm not good with complicated. I'm going to need to write this down.' Mitzi pulls a notebook and pen from her bag. 'Okay. Fire away.'

'You have heard of the Knights Templar?'

'Sure. An ancient order of fighting monks, right?'

'Right. Well, the Knights of the Mountain are the same, but more secretive and ruthless. They began back in Lebanon in the fifth century, disciples of Saint Maroun, the hermit monk who founded the Maronite Church.'

She remembers Hix's forensic report and his insistence that Tamara's killer had been in the Lebanon. 'What's the Maronite Church?'

'Catholicism by another name. It operates parallel to the Church of Rome. The Knights of the Mountain are its ultimate protectors. Suicide warriors. A bloodline of highly trained soldiers who fought secret crusades.'

'Black ops assassins in the Holy Wars?'

'If you like. But they were also devout monks. When they weren't killing, they fasted and prayed on a saintly scale.'

'And these are the knights in *The Shroud*, the ones responsible for killing Saladin?'

'The same.' He puts a hand on the script. 'We printed off scenes only as far as the cover-up of Saladin's death. What happened next was that the assassin – a monk called Ephrem, wounded by Saladin's guards – fell from his horse crossing the mountains and died. As a result, for many years the Maronites didn't know that the assassination had been successful.'

Mitzi is intrigued. 'Then how did they ever find out?'

'Rumours spread around the Muslim camps. Somehow their great leader just didn't seem the same. He was less decisive. Different. Unusually uncertain. Spies picked up on this and when Muslim soldiers were captured some even volunteered the information in attempts to stop the Christians executing them.'

'So just hearsay?'

'Isn't most of history? I mean, what proof is there of Jesus Christ's *miracles* outside of any religious writings?'

'I'm not a historian, but I get your drift. How's all this connected to Christ's shroud?'

'*Saladin's* shroud.' He lets the words sink in. 'The imprint on the linen is that of Christianity's nemesis.'

157

Force press officer Adam Geagea sits at Mitzi Fallon's empty desk and writes a polite note asking her to call him when she gets a chance.

He knows she'll ignore it, all the cops do. He casually swings her swivel chair left and right, then takes advantage of the fact that there's no one else nearby. He opens the bottom drawers first and works his way up. There's not much of interest. A faxed contract from a lawyer engaging the firm to handle her divorce. Good luck to him, he'll earn every dime representing a ballbreaker like Fallon. There are pictures of her daughters, a hidden stash of candy, hand cream, spare tampons, a celebrity gossip magazine, cup of loose change and a couple of stacks of old notebooks.

The top drawer has the good stuff. A copy of *The Shroud* and a more recently filled notepad. Geagea turns to the back of the pad and examines the final entry. It seems to be some kind of forensic checklist:

- Possible fingerprints from intruder at Nic's hotel (on photographs)
- DNA sample from locket
- DNA from Tamara's cat

- Hairs from Sacconi's bed
- Tape from mouth of dead girl (possibly prints on edges)
- Shroud analysis report/Amy

Geagea feels his heart quicken. He looks around the room. There are voices in the corridor. No time to write down everything he's seen. He stares at the page and tries hard to commit it all to memory. The press officer shuts the drawer and stands, just as a couple of sergeants roll in. They glare at him as he beats a hasty retreat to the corridor. He takes the stairs two at a time and locks himself in the safety of his office.

From the bottom drawer of his own desk he gets out an untraceable cell phone. Geagea's fingers are trembling as he dials the number of his Maronite contact. The monk was supposed to be good. The best. Undetectable. Well, it doesn't seem like that to him.

158

BEVERLY HILLS, LOS ANGELES

Mitzi stares across the spacious lounge of the millionaire movie director and weighs up what he just said. 'You're saying the Shroud of Turin bears the outline of the Muslim warlord Saladin, not Jesus Christ?'

'That was one of Tamara's shock points in the movie. Plus, of course, the revelation that the Catholic and Maronite churches have been trying to cover up the fact for centuries.'

'Sounds like BS to me.'

Svenson looks amused. 'Tamara's version is actually more credible than the one we've been led to believe by centuries of propaganda from historians.'

'How so?'

'Surely, if Christ's followers had found the Shroud in his empty tomb, they would have shown this miraculous image all around the ancient world in order to convert people and spread his word?' Svenson ticks off more key questions on his fingers. 'Why wasn't the discovery independently documented back then? Why does the Shroud disappear for hundreds of years and then pop up in the hands of rich Western dynasties like the Savoys?'

'Good questions, but I still don't get how the Catholics came to possess and venerate the Muslim shroud.'

'They stole it.'

'What?'

'Simple as that. Back in those days, both Christian and Muslim armies sacked each other's cities and temples. When they came across a protected case containing a shroud of a bearded man, they had the arrogance to assume it was that of Christ. They took it thinking they were actually reclaiming one of their own religious artefacts.'

'And of course the Muslims wouldn't be too keen to

admit Saladin had been assassinated and generations of people deceived by his replacement.'

'Exactly. Historians even reported Saladin as though he were two separate people. Some chronicled him as blood-curdlingly vicious. Others said he was a great statesman.'

Mitzi's cell phone buzzes. She glances down at a text message from Carter: Hix has forensics. Harrison's here – where are you? She pulls herself out of the comfy chair and addresses Svenson. 'I gotta go, but we're not done.'

He gets up and walks her to the door. 'Please keep the lawyers and press off my back. I'll cooperate any way you want.'

She steps out onto the driveway. 'I'll try.' She glances down at his short robe. 'By the way, you either need a longer robe or lessons in how to sit in it without showing all you've got.'

159

77TH STREET STATION, LOS ANGELES

Crime Scene Investigator Tom Hix lives for moments like this. The point in the grand play of homicide when science takes centre stage and cops are rightfully reduced to mere supporting acts.

He hurries across the squad room floor as soon as he

sees Mitzi heading to her desk. 'Hi there. I've got some reports—'

'Jeez, Tom. I ain't even put my bag down yet.' She picks up the note left by Geagea. 'Little prick.' She balls it and tosses it in the waste bin.

Hix looks offended.

'Not you. Our freakin' press officer. Now what you got?'

He lays a manila file on her desk 'I'm flat-out running samples on the Creeper case, but I thought you'd want to see *this*.'

She flips open the front of the folder. '*This* being what?' Then she remembers her call to him. 'The Tamara Jacobs case?'

'Let me talk you through it.' He pulls two transparent sheets out and puts them side by side on the desk. 'I've got a DNA match.'

'Which samples are these?'

'The first is hair we took from the headrest on the Lexus traced out to the rental at LAX. The second is from skin we recovered on the claw of the dead cat at the writer's house.'

'Kitty's revenge.' She overlays the transparencies. 'One and the same. You're right, you've got a matching pair, but to win the game you have to also have the name of a perp to pin to the samples.'

His face says he hasn't. 'Ran Profiler, no hit. Didn't expect there to be. I already told you, your guy is an out-of-towner.'

'Way out. You said Lebanon.'

'Mount Lebanon to be precise.'

Mitzi looks across at the photograph of Tamara Jacobs pinned to a board, the one reproduced every time *Variety* or *Hollywood Reporter* ran a story on her. 'Her script contains whole scenes set in the Middle East. Historic scenes not modern. Svenson told me a tale about Maronite—'

The phone on her desk rings.

She snatches it. 'Fallon.' After a slight pause she adds, 'Okay, tell her I'll be right down.' She drops the receiver back on the cradle and looks pissed at the distraction. 'Sorry. My other case calls. Jenny Harrison is acting up downstairs. The uniform minding her says she's going to walk if I don't get my ass down there quick.'

'I understand.' He shuffles the transparencies back in his file. 'You know where to find me when you want to come back to this.'

160

GENEVA–NEW YORK

An hour out from Geneva the seatbelt lights are still on. Storms and high winds are blowing in from the Atlantic and the Bay of Biscay. France and Spain are getting a savage whipping and the turbulence is tossing the plane as it heads west.

'I hate flying.' Broussard pulls down the window blind,

hoping to shut out the misery. 'As a young man I had phobias. Now I can cope, but I still do not like it.'

'Unnatural, isn't it?' Nic agrees. 'So much heavy metal and so many people, floating through the air, defying science. But you know, statistically—'

Broussard holds up a hand. 'Science it does not defy. It only flies because of the science.' His tension makes him sound curt. 'And I know all the statistics, *merci*. It is safer than crossing a road, smoking a cigarette, etc. but I still do not like it.'

'The storm will pass,' says Nic, reassuringly. 'And when it does, I'm going to walk the plane. It's routine, that's all. I just want to make sure the only people we're up here with are friends.'

'Surely, you can't think the man who attacked us is on this flight?'

'I *have* to think that. It's incredibly unlikely. But I *have* to think it. Don't worry. Let me do my job. Everything will be fine.'

Broussard distracts himself by pulling out dreary magazines from the seat pocket in front of him. He wishes none of this was happening, that he'd never met Roberto Craxi and wasn't leaving his wife thousands of miles behind.

Finally, the turbulence passes and Nic hits the call button above his head. A heavy-hipped brunette is soon bending over him. She introduces herself as Glenda and asks how she can help. Conscious of others watching, Nic unfolds his ID wallet on his lap and answers in hushed tones. 'Miss, I'm a

Los Angeles police officer and I need to see both the chief steward and the air marshal. Can you fix that for me?'

Glenda's experienced enough to take it all in her stride. A ten-year transatlantic veteran, she's dealt with everything from heart attacks to terrorist alerts. 'Certainly, Officer. If you come with me to my station, I'll call them both.'

He follows her to the curtains and glances back at the scientist as he goes. Broussard has his head in some magazine article and looks happy enough. Nic stands in the galley kitchen while Glenda calls the steward, then makes a discreet announcement only the air marshal would understand. 'Could any passengers who forgot to pick up duty-free when boarding the plane in Geneva please identify themselves to a member of the cabin crew. We have a bottle of very nice brandy here that doesn't *yet* have an owner. Thank you.'

A prim middle-aged steward with dyed black hair appears through the curtains, eyes wide as he addresses Glenda. 'What's wrong?'

She nods to Nic. 'This is Detective Karakandez from the LAPD. He wanted to see you and the marshal.'

The steward pulls his tie straight. 'My name is Brian. May I see your identification, please?'

'Sure.' Nic pulls it from his back pocket and hands it over.

Brian is reading as a stocky, blond-haired guy with gingery stubble comes into the galley. He's mid-thirties, in a baggy grey sweat top over black Levis and, if Nic is right, is packing a standard-issue Taser.

The steward hands him the ID. 'This is Officer Karakandez.'

The man glances at the wallet and passes it back to Nic. 'Gerry Brookes. What's going on?'

'I've been working a case that brought me to Europe.' Nic nods beyond the curtain. 'Man back there in 48A is an important witness, connected to a homicide. I want to walk the plane and check there's no threat to him. Would you babysit while I do the rounds?'

'Sure thing. What's his name?'

'Édouard Broussard.'

'When do you want to do this?'

'Now would be good.' Nic turns to the chief steward. 'Do you have a copy of the passenger manifest? I need to put faces to names as I do the sweep.'

'Certainly.' The steward unfastens a list hanging from a clip board on the galley wall. 'That's everyone.'

'Any way you can identify late bookings?'

Brian shakes his head. 'Not from this list. We could have done it at the gate.' He glances to Glenda. 'Do you have any prelim sheets?'

Her face says she hasn't.

'Sorry,' says the steward.

'One thing,' adds Glenda. 'Even when we're coming in to land we always find empty seats. People who've snuck off to the washrooms or they've swapped places with other passengers or just moved to a spare seat for a bit more space. You want we order everyone back to their own places?'

438

Nic thinks about it for a second. He doesn't want to frighten passengers after the storm – or, if the assassin *is* on board, make him edgy and aware that someone is looking for him. 'No, leave it for now. Let me do a circuit and see how many people I miss. If necessary we could make your announcement.'

161

'You look like shit, Jenny. What the hell have you been taking?' Mitzi holds the door of the interview room for the uniform to leave. 'Thanks,' she says, as he escapes into the corridor.

Harrison looks up sulky-faced from the interview room table. 'I ain't taken nothin' – that's why I look like shit.'

Mitzi pulls up a chair. 'Where you been today?'

'Walkin'. Tryin' to get my head straight. I didn't sleep none last night.'

Mitzi's not surprised. The kid's world is upside down and she knows how sleep is the first thing that goes out of the window when that happens. 'I'll get you coffee and a smoke.'

'Coffee and cigarettes?' she says, disparagingly. 'Big freakin deal.'

'Hey, watch your tongue. I'm trying to help.'

Mitzi ducks out and bums a couple of Marlboro Ultra Lites and a box of matches from a traffic cop near the vending machine. On the way back she grabs two mugs of black crap that might be coffee and returns to the interview room. 'Here you go, best I can do.'

'Thanks.' Harrison's face says she's thought about behaving better. 'Sorry I snapped.'

'You should be. Today I feel almost as bad as you do.' She slides across the matches. 'You're not supposed to smoke in here – then again people aren't supposed to be in police stations on Sundays, so what the hell.'

Harrison lights up. Pulls hard and draws in a big hit of nicotine.

Mitzi watches her fingers shake. The girl's in a bad way. She waits until she's exhaled and taken a second drag. 'We've got a guy in a holding cell down the corridor. I want you to take a look at him.'

Harrison's eyes pulse wide. 'You got him? Kim's killer?'

'Calm down. I just want you to look and tell me if you recognise him.'

Harrison bangs her fist on the table. 'I want to kill the fucking bastard.'

'Hey. I said calm down. Now cool it. This guy isn't even under arrest. He came in here voluntarily.'

'It ain't him?'

'I just want you to take a look, Jenny. Can you do that?'

She is close to tears. Anger. Sorrow. Rage. Grief. Her

emotions are about as mixed as they can be. 'Yeah.' She pinches the end of the cigarette. 'I can do it.'

'You can bring your coffee.'

Harrison picks up the paper mug and follows the lieutenant into the grey corridor.

Mitzi leads the way into the holding area. Jimmy Berg has gone home and a new sergeant is now working the desk. 'Witness in the Bass case,' shouts Mitzi to the officer, who looks like a bald Tiger Woods. 'I need her to take an unofficial squint at our guy in cell one.'

'Be my guest.' He waves them through.

Mitzi uses her ID pass to swipe an electronic plate. She pulls open a heavy door of iron bars, lets Harrison through and bangs it shut again. 'Don't say anything. Just put your eye to the peep hole. Take a long look then step away and tell me if you recognise the man in there.' She nods to a grey door to her right.

Harrison steps forward. She rests her cheek against the cold metal and peers through the thick glass into the bright ugly light of the room. At first she doesn't see anything. Then she spots the man in orange detention clothes lying down. It's hard to see his face. He rolls over. Adjusts a pillow on the bunk.

Her heart thunders. She steps away from the door.

Mitzi reads the shock on her face. 'Do you recognise him, Jenny?'

She nods but can't speak.

Mitzi takes her by the hand and guides her from the door. 'Who is it?'

441

Harrison takes a breath. 'Fish . . . it's Fish Face.'

'The guy from the factory, the supervisor?'

She nods. 'Yeah. Mr James. Emma's friend.'

162

GENEVA–NEW YORK

Nic reads the passenger manifest as he walks into the first of the business-class cabins. It's made up of nine rows of seats, configured in three sets of two. All the usual corporate suspects are hanging out. Lean and mean-looking ladder-climbers with iPads and MacBooks already open. A couple of middle-aged senior execs with grey hair and spreading waistlines have passed out through too much free champagne and fatty food. A chic, long-legged woman is in the process of dropping her seat and curling up beneath a blanket. Their eyes briefly catch. Passing ships. A moment gone.

Emergency exits divide the next two rows of three, then there are four main economy-class sections. Nic takes a long slow look down the endless aisle and then tries to match male faces to his list of those connecting to LAX. Reto Ruhr and Stefan Sauber sound Swiss. They're both young-looking guys, slim and of average build. Nic shifts to one side and takes a closer look.

They're holding hands. Reto puts his head on his friend's shoulder.

Nic ticks them off his list. Not because of their homosexuality, but because hitmen don't mix business with pleasure.

A couple of young kids break from their seats and paw their way from one side of the plane to the other. Looks like they're swapping Mom and Dad's laps for those of Grandpa and Grandma. Nic can't help but think of himself, Carolina and his son doing a trip like this. Squashed up, full up, loved-up, heading home after a couple of weeks of showing Max Europe. They never got to take him on a plane. Never got further than messing in the sand at Point Dume.

He forces himself to concentrate. Give or take an empty seat or two, the plane's carrying about three hundred men, women and children. He takes it slow. Real slow.

A guy travelling alone in 24A interests him. Thirty to forty, short dark hair, dressed in blue track pants and grey hoodie. He's slim, fit and relaxed, with three-day stubble and a look that says he travels light and is ready for anything life throws at him. His eyes lock on Nic and for a second the two mentally interrogate each other. Nic checks the manifest. Steve Bryant. He looks down at the list and sees Kelly Bryant occupies 24B. Man and wife. Another write-off.

Painstakingly, he works his way to the back, relentlessly checking men's looks against listed names, filtering out the fat senior citizens, the weedy teenagers and physically disabled. Midway through the return leg, he stops and sits in a spare seat next to a guy called Rico Aguero. Rico's mixed race, broad-shouldered and somewhere in his thirties. Looks like he could handle himself in a skirmish. After five minutes of chat he discovers Rico's a systems analyst from Manhattan and could bore a saint to death.

It takes close to forty minutes for the detective to complete his tour and make it back to his seat. 'Anything to worry about?' asks Brookes, the air marshal, as he gets up and swaps places with Nic.

'Don't think so.'

Gerry nods to Broussard. 'Old guy's been sleeping like a baby. Give me a shout if you need any help.'

'I think we're good now.' Nic shakes his hand.

The scientist is out for the count, snoring peacefully. The poor guy must be beat. Nic opens the courtesy blanket, reclines his seat and settles down. Finally, he can relax.

163

77TH STREET STATION, LOS ANGELES

Mitzi leaves Harrison in the interview room and heads to Carter's office to update him.

He's hunched over stacks of paperwork and looks like an accountant chasing year-end. 'You ever think about knocking?'

'Nope, nasty habit. Harrison's ID'd your fruitcake. She's

a hundred per cent certain he *is* John James, her supervisor.' She perches on the edge of his desk and frowns at all the Excel sheets. 'On top of that, she says that very recently said fruitcake has been close with a co-worker called Emma Varley.'

'It happens.' He pulls the papers out from under her leg. 'Stay open-minded, Mitzi. Many people – even fruitcakes – meet future spouses at work.'

'Or *future victims*. Varley went missing last week. She just didn't turn up one day.'

Now she has his attention. 'No reason?'

'None that he mentioned. James told the factory floor she simply handed in her notice.'

'You get an address for Varley?'

'Not exactly. Harrison didn't know it but says she lives out Gardena way.'

'I'll get Dan to pin it down and take a ride out there.' Carter's desk phone rings. 'Yes?'

'Boss, it's Kris. I'm in James's house in Carson and I can tell you it's seriously weird.'

'Whatcha got?' He switches it to speakerphone so Mitzi can hear.

'There's no furniture. No carpets. Newspaper sheets all over the floor. It's like nothing human's ever been here. Ain't no lights in the place either.' He works his way through with a flashlight. 'It's more of a squat than a home. I'm just going in the bedroom and man it stinks in here.' The beam plays over the ceiling, down the walls and across the floor. 'There are burned-out candles all over the place. It feels ritualistic, you know. Satanic. Scrub that, there's a holy big Jeez-us crucifix on the wall.' The light pools in the far corner on a stack of white cloth.

'He's got linen sheets here.'

'Check them out,' says Carter. 'But don't touch them.'

Libowicz bends over the stack. 'I ain't no bed expert – as Mrs L will testify – but this looks strange stuff.' He runs the light up and down the cloth. 'There are freakin' yards of sheet here, enough to wind round a mummy.'

'Probably took it from the factory where he works,' says Mitzi.

Something glints in the beam of the cop's flashlight. 'Man, there are hundreds of blades here – the old double-edged types that you screw down.' He leans in close. 'Lots of blood on them too and a bottle of disinfectant and an old handkerchief by the look of it.'

'He's a self-cutter,' explains Carter. 'That's his kit. Don't touch the things, he may well be Positive.'

'No intention of doing so, Boss.' Libowicz goes quiet for a second. He stands up and shines the beam across the far wall. Dull marks appear. He steps forward and takes a closer look.

Blood.

He moves the light around, then turns and sees behind him. 'Oh, shit.'

'What?' asks Carter.

'He's scrawled something on the wall. In blood. It says, 'I AM THE WAR THAT WILL NEVER END. DELIVERANCE..'

164

During the changeover to the LAX plane, Nic charms the desk crew into an upgrade for him and Broussard and asks for a fresh manifest and details of any late bookings made at Geneva. No last-minuters come up on the terminal screens – not even him or Broussard. Seems data systems the world over let you down just when you need them most.

By the time the plane takes off Nic's met the new steward and the air marshal, a tough-looking former soldier called Ike, who has settled into a seat across the aisle from him and Édouard. The scientist is more relaxed this time, as the belts-free signal pings down the aisles and Nic gets up to do another sweep.

Glenda, the attendant on the first leg, was right then and is right now – people are all over the place. At times no one seems to match the manifest. Women are sitting in men's seats. Kids are missing. Queues trail from all the bathrooms and kitchen galleys. By the time Nic makes it back to his seat he thinks there are more than a dozen male names he's not managed to put faces to – about twice as many as on the Geneva leg. As he muses over the missing men, Broussard eases himself into the aisle.

'I need the *toilette*,' he explains, reading the critical look on his companion's face.

Nic doesn't take his eyes off the Frenchman. He tells himself he's being stupid. He should relax. They left any threat back on the freeway near Geneva. But old police habits die hard and he can't help but watch the washroom door and wait for the scientist to reappear. His nerves twitch when a young guy in a cream T-shirt and blue jeans crosses from the other side of the plane and tries the locked cubicle. He's lean and a shade under six feet, tanned and fit. The backs of his arms show grazes and bruises. There's a healing cut on his jaw below the right ear.

He gives the door a second rattle. Nic doesn't recognise the face – not from Geneva and not from his latest round of checks. The detective gets out of his seat and nods to Ike. The big air marshal drops his book and circles down the other end of the aisle. Nic scans the stranger for any sign of a gun and prays one isn't going to be drawn up here in the sky. A flight attendant points the man to another restroom down near the far curtain.

Nic follows. He studies every inch of him as he approaches. Looks at the fall of his denims; any chance a concealed weapon – or explosives – are stuffed in a sock or shin strap. The stranger pulls up and tries the washroom door. There are raw cuts and some swelling on his right knuckles, like a punch has been thrown within the last few days. Nic checks Ike is parallel with him over the other side of the aisle and then clumsily stumbles into the guy in front of him.

The man turns around and flat-hands the detective. 'Hey man, look where you're going.'

'Sorry there. I was just trying to reset my watch and didn't see you. Did you catch how many hours the attendant said New York was behind Switzerland?'

The guy checks him over. 'Six.'

'Thanks.' Nic adjusts his timepiece. 'You heading to LA for work or fun?'

'Fun. And right now you're ruining it.' He turns away.

Ike edges through the galley curtain and comes round so he is close to Nic, with the stranger caught between the two of them.

Nic turns him back again. His eyes show he's not afraid of any repercussions. 'I'm not finished talking to you.'

The guy glares at him. 'What are you, a cop?'

'Matter of fact I am.' Nic flips out his ID. 'What's your name and seat number?'

The marshal leans against a wall and slips his hand round the back of his belt and feels for the Taser tucked beneath his jacket.

'Manton. Jimmy D.' He fishes in his pocket and pulls out a ticket stub.

Nic takes it and checks it again the manifest. It tallies. He passes it back and nods at the guy's grazed hand. 'You been in a fight recently?'

He touches his grazed knuckles. 'No way. I ain't hit anyone since high school. I knocked myself up skateboarding. It's

449

what I do. Fun and work. I skate and surf. Get pretty well paid for it too. Any laws against that?'

'Not yet. I know a little about surfing, but educate me, Mr Manton, who do *you* think are the best boarders?'

The guy's eyes light up. 'For me Mick Fanning – all the way. Though I like that Hawaiian, Torrey Meister. My style's more like his.'

Nic looks again at the manifest. He's convinced the guy's who he says he is – another cocksure idiot who can earn a living getting sponsorship deals out in Malibu.

Down the aisle, Édouard appears from the restroom and returns to his seat. Ike catches the cop's eye and drifts away to cover the scientist.

Nic's done asking questions. 'Enjoy yourself in California, Jimmy D. and stay safe.' He playfully punches him on the arm and wanders back to Broussard.

165

GARDENA, LOS ANGELES

Dan Amis still has a handkerchief to his mouth as he walks out of the shadows and stench of the old clapboard house. He takes a long, clear breath of early evening air and calls in what he just saw. 'We need the ME, boss. Body of a white female laid out Creeper-style in the bedroom of Emma Varley's house. Our guy's been here.'

Carter is listening on the speakerphone with Mitzi. He covers his head with his hands. Another death – another killing he failed to prevent. 'You think it's her?'

'Yeah. Decomp has already made a mess but there's a picture of her in the living room – looks enough like her.'

'Okay. Stay there. Act as primary on that scene. I'll turn out forensics as well.'

'You got it.'

Carter calls Amy Chang's cell. She's worked all the previous Creeper bodies, so he wants her on this one too.

She picks up after a couple of rings. 'Dr Chang.'

'Hi, this is Tyler Carter. Sorry to screw up your Sunday night but we've got another Creeper killing. Might even have the perp as well.'

'I'll get my kit.'

'Vic is a woman by the name of Emma Varley. Twenty-something. Found in her home over in Gardena. I'll have Mitzi email you details. Amis is out there – says she's already started to ripen.'

'Tell Mitzi not to mail me – my desk computer fried the other night and I'm having trouble logging on through the external VPN link. Text me the address.'

'I'll do it myself. Thanks.' He puts down the desk phone, picks up his own cell, thumbs in the crime scene's address and hits send. 'Mitzi, will you get Tom to send the CSIs out there?'

'Sure. Can I share something with you?'

'Shoot.'

'A couple things been playing on my mind.'

'Like?'

'Jenny Harrison's break-in and her missing phone.'

'You're thinking what?'

'Maybe the Creeper killed Kim Bass and was planning to kill Jenny too. Only luckily for Jenny, she wasn't there that night. She was out getting high and ended up in a strange man's bed.'

'A moment of sexual promiscuity that for once bettered her life?'

'Maybe even the Harrisons of this world get a break some time.'

'A search team is going out to meet Kris at James's house. I'll have him look for the phone.'

Mitzi's still thinking things through. 'If James did go to Harrison's house, then he might have left prints and DNA. There's so much soil and dog shit over the path, you might even still be able to get boot prints.'

'Matthews said your legendary right hook was merely a distraction from a brilliant brain.'

'Matthews should shut the hell up and pay me more.'

'What else?'

'I checked the local precincts. They have no records of anyone but Harrison calling about Kim Bass. James told Jenny he'd called the police – he clearly hadn't.'

'Or they missed his number on their logs. We'll have all his home, work and cell-phone call details in the next hour.

Get one of the clerks to cross check them with station house numbers.'

'Will do.'

'Anything else?'

'I'm done.'

'Then make those follow-up calls and come meet me downstairs. I'm going to check with the doctor, then we're going to interview Mr James and see what he's got to say for himself.'

Mitzi glances at her watch. She's been on shift more than twelve hours and it feels like the day is never going to stop. 'Let's hope it begins with "I confess" and ends with his signature.'

166

The police doctor gives Tyler Carter news he doesn't want to hear. 'My medical opinion is that he's not fit for you to interview.'

'What?' Carter spits the word out. 'Don't tell me you've bought into that faked lunacy act.'

'I'm not sure it is faked. But that's not why you can't have your pound of flesh.'

'Then why?'

'He's opened up his wounds.' Carl Jenkins illustrates with his hand. 'He just dug his thumbnails into the razor cuts and pulled apart the stitches. It's a painful mess. He should have been in a straitjacket.'

'No way. He's prepping an insanity plea.'

'As maybe. But I've still got to send him to the hospital.'

'Not happening.' Carter paces away. 'I let him inside a public hospital, hundreds of people are going to be at risk. Get him treatment here.'

'You mean *your case* is at risk.'

'Oh pardon me – yes, I do mean that too. My *serial murder case* is at risk. There's a chance a man who we are pretty damned sure has killed a lot of women will be slipping through our hands.'

'Tyler, I don't have a choice, and neither do you. Self-harming on this scale means I've got to refer him to hospital, and to fully qualified mental health practitioners. And you have to fully support that or someone's going to take your badge away.'

'God give me strength.'

'I hope he does. Meanwhile, it's been a long day and I have to effect this man's transfer as quickly as possible.'

Carter points to Mitzi. 'We charge him first and Lieutenant Fallon goes with him.'

'Not my call,' says Jenkins. 'She can ride with him, unless he objects – which I guess he won't. Let's face it, he could have walked out on you any time in the last twelve hours. But you maybe want to think twice about charging a man you have reason to believe is mentally ill.'

Carter wants to punch the wall.

'We can charge him later,' says Mitzi, in a tone of

conciliation. 'The guy's cut to ribbons. I'll ride with him, maybe he'll give something up in the ambulance. Like you said, there's no need to rush this one.'

'Fine,' says Carter. 'But you don't take a single chance with this jerk-off. I'm putting a uniform with you. Despite what he looks like, not for one minute do you forget he's a killer – a *serial* killer.'

167

John James – aka Deliverance – aka Fish Face – is all parcelled up when Mitzi steps on the backboard and climbs into the rear of the paramedic's wagon. A footstep behind her is the giant frame of Joey di Matteo, a tough young uniform, one of a rare breed who grew up in Compton and Paramount without a rap sheet. He blocks most of the light as the medic bangs the door shut.

Mitzi shuffles along the bench opposite the gurney where James is laid out. A bag drips blood into his left arm. There are red safety belts around his waist to stop him falling off. 'I'm Lieutenant Fallon,' she says, gently. 'I'm going to ride with you and stay with you. You okay with that?'

He opens his eyes and manages only a dazed look.

She knows that whatever she says now is going to set the tone. It'll either open him up or shut him down like a clam. 'You been to hospital before?'

His head rocks from the motion of the ambulance but he still doesn't speak.

'There's nothing to be afraid of. They'll clean you up proper, sort out those cuts.' She puts on an understanding face. 'A friend of mine hurts herself. She's got it in her head that she has to be punished. That what you think?'

He licks his dry lips and whispers, 'I have sinned.'

'Sure you have. Me too. None of us are perfect, right?'

He mumbles something: '... mawaz ...'

'Sorry? Say that again.'

'Emma was.'

The name blows a hole in Mitzi's calm front. 'Emma? You mean Emma Varley?'

'My Emma.' His voice is still only a decibel above a whisper.

'You said was. *Was* not *is*.'

'She is with the Lord now.' He tries to sit up. 'No more pain. She is in Paradise.'

A paramedic leans over and puts a restraining hand across him. 'Lie back, take things easy.'

'How?' Mitzi presses. 'How did your Emma get to Paradise?'

He looks content. 'I helped her.'

'And the others – did you help them too?'

'My mission is to help.' He reflects on what he's said, then adds, 'I am a soldier of the Lord.'

'And Kim Bass – did you help her?'

His face changes. The calmness goes. Tension ripples

across his brow. 'A mistake. She was evil – but it was a mistake to take her. She needed time to redeem herself. It was wrong of me to take her before she'd done that.'

'Take her?'

'I thought the Lord had chosen her but I was mistaken. Her soul is burning in hell and it is my fault.'

The paramedic takes JJ's wrist and checks his pulse. 'I think he's done enough talking now, Detective. His heart-beat's racing and he's still in trauma.'

Mitzi backs off. She needs to absorb what he said. Needs to get out of the ambulance and tell Carter that James has confessed in front of witnesses to at least one of the murders.

JJ closes his eyes. Shuts them tight and begins to pray softly. '*Deus meus, ex toto corde paenitet me omnium meorum peccatorum, eaque detestor. . .*'

'It's Latin,' interjects di Matteo. 'He's saying an act of contrition.'

'You know an act of contrition?' Mitzi floats him a look of surprise.

'I was an altar boy. The Catholic Church kept me off the corners.'

'What does it mean in English?'

'It means "God, I am heartily sorry for having offended Thee and I detest all my sins because of thy just punishments, but most of all because they offend Thee, my God, who art all good and deserving of all my love. I firmly resolve, with the help of thy grace, to sin no more and avoid the near occasions of sin. Amen."'

'Impressive.'

'We had to learn it off by heart.'

Mitzi looks across at Deliverance. He's certainly going to *sin no more*. With a little luck, an execution team at San Quentin is going to make damned sure of it.

168

It's late evening and hospital staff looked stretched to breaking point as Deliverance is wheeled into the secure side ward administrators keep for LAPD cases.

More than an hour passes before a doctor sees him and a further forty minutes before he gets stitched up.

Joey di Matteo fetches coffee and sandwiches, while Mitzi approaches the blue-uniformed ward sister, a slim woman with well-cut, shoulder-length auburn hair.

'Any idea how long before I get my prisoner back?'

Stephanie Dawson produces a well-practised, professional smile. 'You mean our *patient*. From what Doctor Jenkins told us, he's not technically a prisoner. And in answer to your question, some time.'

'We're paying the bill, lady. That means he's ours. And for the record, he will be charged just as soon as we haul his murdering ass out of here.'

Dawson gets the point. 'His surgical care is all but done. However, the psychiatrist won't be round to assess him for another hour or so.'

'You're kidding me, right?'

'That's not the kind of thing we do.'

Mitzi looks at her watch. 'It's nearly nine now. You're saying you can't get a shrink here until ten, maybe eleven?'

'It's Sunday night. Doctors have lives, normal lives.'

'I've seen their pay slips – that's not what I call a normal life.'

The sister almost smiles. 'Money's got nothing to do with it. Truth is, if this wasn't a special case, we'd just keep him under observation tonight and have him seen in the morning.'

'Can I at least go talk to him?'

'Afraid not. He's been given a sedative and is asleep. I suggest you just take a break. We'll tell you as soon as the psychiatrist arrives.'

To ward off boredom and the onset of madness, Mitzi calls Carter and updates him. 'It's going to be gone ten, maybe even later, when we get James seen by the shrink.'

'Not James,' says Carter. 'He was born Jibril Walud Saleh walud Khalid Al-Fulan.'

'Man, that's a lot of Waluds. I can see why he changed it.'

'Probably not for the reason you think. His all-American, Delaware mom Madison changed it first. Right after his all-Muslim father Saleh tried to blow himself up in a New York subway.'

'Oh God.'

459

'Kid grew up under her maiden name of Moore and would probably have stayed Moore, had the papers not got hold of the story when he was six. Madison overdosed and the boy found her dead in bed the next morning.'

'Died in bed in her sleep. There's something awful familiar about that.'

'Shrinks will see it as causal to his crimes. As a kid he got told Mom had gone to heaven. God had apparently called her name.'

'Taken before her time.'

'Defence lawyers are going to go to town with our boy. I'm going to bet he never sees the inside of a jail in his life.'

169

LAX, LOS ANGELES

The A340 tips its wings and starts a gradual descent into the sixth busiest airport in the world. Through the window Nic sees the grid of lights sparkling beneath him like he's flying over a giant computer motherboard.

Broussard stirs from his slumber as the cabin crew do their rounds and the captain announces that thanks to good flying weather they're twenty minutes ahead of schedule at the end of a fine Californian day.

'Did you sleep well?'

'*Comme ci comme ça.*' He puts his hand to his neck and shifts his head gently to the left and right. 'I am a little stiff and still tired.'

Nic checks his watch. 'Coming up to midnight, you've got a whole night's rest still ahead.'

The pilot brings the big bus in for a textbook landing. Smooth as silk. No jolt. A cheer goes up from back in coach. Nic guesses it's the school athletes – probably the only ones with that much life left in them at this time of day.

The crew stand by the doors to thank them for travelling Lufthansa and wish them a good stay. Nic nods to Ike the marshal as the officer stays behind to make sure everyone's off and the aircraft is safe.

As they walk the air bridge to the terminal he turns to Broussard. 'I called our admin desk from JFK and they've booked you into a hotel, but if you like you can stay at my place tonight. There's a spare room, nothing as grand as your villa, but you're very welcome.'

Édouard understands that Nic is still being cautious. 'That's very kind of you, I appreciate it.'

'Not at all. One day I'll come sailing to the south of France and maybe you and Ursula can show me Nice?'

'That would be our extreme pleasure.'

Ten minutes later they're approaching the roped-off pits where Homeland Security carry out their checks. They drop a flight of stairs into the security zone and prepare to briefly go their separate ways briefly – Nic to the fast-flowing US residents line and Édouard to the heavily congested visitors section.

'See you on the other side,' he tells the scientist. 'I'll be waiting for you just behind the line.'

Nic's queue moves quickly and he's soon called forward by a sour-faced official in a glass booth. The guy scans his documents and processes him without a hint of warmth.

As promised, he wanders along the back of the booths and waits for Édouard. The Frenchman looked pretty white coming down the steps and he hopes his heart condition isn't slowing him up and giving him problems.

Familiar faces filter through the check lines – Steve Bryant through the US gate, Rico Aguero and the Swiss guys Stefan and Reto through the non-residents route. Nic walks up and down behind the booths. He can see the full length of the visitors lines from here.

Surfer Jimmy Manton drifts through the checkpoint, his eyes briefly catching Nic's as he passes into the baggage area. The cop looks back to the lines on the other side of the booths. He still can't see Broussard.

There's no sign of him anywhere. And by now there really should be.

170

Sister Dawson is as good as her word. Ten minutes past eleven she stirs Mitzi from her daydreaming. 'Mr Weinstock is here. He's just coming up.'

Forty-year-old Robert Weinstock rounds the corner and heads straight to the ward desk. Stephanie flits away like a navy-coloured butterfly, drawn to the two thousand dollar suit and the small, immaculately groomed, dark-haired man wearing it.

Mitzi watches them and wonders whether to mention that Deliverance, aka John James, aka George Moore, actually started life as Jibril Walud Saleh walud Khalid Al-Fulan? That he is the son of a terrorist, a fanatical 'sleeper' who was ready to murder as many innocent people as a vest of explosives can manage. She decides not to. Then feels guilty. She knows she's holding back solely because she doesn't want the smart-suited shrink to say the Creeper's insane and therefore entitled to spend the rest of his days in hospital watching TV or eyeing up nurses.

Weinstock drifts towards where the cops are sitting. Mitzi creaks her way up from the hard chair that's rendered most of her body numb.

'Robert Weinstock.' He offers a well-manicured hand and

463

smells of fresh cologne. 'I'm sorry to have kept you waiting. I was at a charity dinner with the Mayor.'

'Lieutenant Fallon. Do you know why my friend and I are here?' She nods to di Matteo. 'Have you any idea what this guy has done?'

'I know enough.' He treats her to a smile as rich as his suit. 'And I promise I will be as prompt as professionalism will allow.'

'Doctor.' Mitzi can't help herself. Despite all her instincts, she can't hold back. 'I have to tell you something. We just found out details, facts about his childhood that you really should know.'

171

LAX, LOS ANGELES

Ephrem makes a final check.

He puts two fingers to the scientist's neck and searches patiently for a pulse. There is nothing. Broussard is dead. His job is done. He repositions the corpse on the seat in the cubicle where he dragged him and pulls the garrotte wire from a deep cut around the target's neck. He wipes it free of flesh and blood, threads it back into a soft leather bracelet-like holder and refastens it around his wrist.

The monk stands on the toilet and looks over the stalls.

They're empty. He pulls himself up and over the partition, slips down the other side, opens the cubicle door and walks out of the restroom.

The hall is still full of tired passengers standing impatiently in lines. He walks slowly and confidently to the short US residents line. It had been amusing to him to see Karakandez working the plane, checking names against the manifest, not noticing him as he disappeared down one aisle while the cop went up the other.

There are only five people ahead of him. The guard is methodical and efficient, moving people swiftly on but taking long, hard looks at their faces.

Ephrem reaches the head of the line. He takes the passport from his pocket and waits to be called forward. Five minutes from now, he knows he'll be free.

172

Nic shows his badge to the guard working the last Homeland booth and the official calls airport security.

Across the glass cubicles word spreads quickly. One by one the border officers shut their windows and walk from the gates. No one's getting through until the cop's reunited with his travelling companion. Passengers in the queues start to complain. It's late. They're tired. A delay of any kind, let alone a big security sweep, is the last thing they want.

465

Nic and the guard walk the lines. Broussard isn't in them.

Where the hell is the guy?

He sees a restroom to the left and remembers how pale the Frenchman had looked. He doubles his pace and strides over there, towing the border guard behind him. As they go inside the guard unholsters his gun. Nic shows his badge to a couple of guys stood at the latrines. 'LAPD, finish up and stand back against the far wall.'

'Do as he says.' The guard raises the gun.

'Keep them there while I check the stalls.' Nic looks down the line of doors and pushes the first. It swings wide and reveals an empty cubicle. He does the same with door two. Empty.

So are the next three.

Door six is locked. He steps inside the fifth cubicle and climbs on the toilet. Over the panel he sees a body slumped forward, head against the partition.

'Édouard . . .'

Nic vaults the partition and drops into the stall.

He pulls the scientist upright.

Broussard's shirt is soaked in blood. There's a gaping wound in his neck.

Nic lets the body slump and steps out of the cubicle feeling sick to the pit of his stomach. Édouard's murderer is gone.

The only question is – how far has he got?

173

Ephrem stands at the front of the line.

The whole area is in lockdown and he's only a step from getting away with murder. He looks at the empty space beckoning to him from beyond the booths. Freedom. He knows his false passport will survive extra scrutiny. Knows he can tough out *any* questions the border police throw at him. But Karakandez is different. A wild card. He looks for him. There are two hundred, maybe two hundred and fifty people, still standing in the roped lines. More coming from the arrival gates. And it's hot. The aircon must be out. He watches the cops and guards slowly working the lines, inspecting passports, visas and asking questions.

Way over at the back, he sees paramedics pushing a blanket-covered emergency trolley out of the restrooms.

The scientist.

Now he sees Karakandez. He's walking away from the rest, moving quickly, scanning every face. Running on instinct not logic. Ephrem turns away. A border guard is at the front of his line, asking questions. 'Can I see your documents, sir?'

He hands over the passport without speaking.

'Where you from, Mr Blake?'

'New York.'

The official's eyes flick from the photo to Alvin Corri Blake. 'Which part?'

'Brooklyn. Out near the Navy Yard.' He looks the official straight in the eyes. The jerk is trying to guess his ethnicity – struggling to pigeonhole him as Hispanic, African-American – maybe Arabic and therefore by default a Muslim terrorist. 'Case you're wondering, I get my perma-tan from my Christian Lebanese mom and my youthful good looks from my Catholic longshoreman dad.'

'Is that so?' The guard shakes his head and hands the passport back. There's always a smart-ass in the lines. 'Enjoy your stay in LA.'

'Thanks.' Ephrem returns the passport to his jacket and the guard moves on. He notices Karakandez with another cop. He's close now, just a few yards away. For a split second their eyes catch. He looks away. The face of a fat woman to his right is beaded with sweat and she looks ready to faint. He pretends to help her. So does a female cop.

Nic peels away and discreetly shows his shield to the guard who checked Ephrem's credentials. 'Where was that last guy from?'

'New York, out Brooklyn. Caught me eyeballing his skin colour, says his old man is American but mom is Lebanese or something.'

'*Lebanese,* that's what I thought he said.'

The fat lady falls like a big round pine tree and brings gasps from the passenger lines. She goes down face first. A lady cop stoops to see if she's all right.

Ephrem goes to help too. Help himself to the gun on the officer's belt.

174

CENTURY HOSPITAL, INGLEWOOD

Just before midnight Robert Weinstock emerges from the secure side ward and Mitzi tries unsuccessfully to read his face as he steps toward her and di Matteo. Sister Dawson predictably flutters from her station to his side.

'Hello, Lieutenant. Again my apologies for keeping you waiting.' He turns to the sister. 'Do you have somewhere more private that I may talk to the officers?'

'My office. Please follow me.'

'Thank you.'

'I'll stay here.' Di Matteo gestures at the Creeper's room.

The three of them make the brief trek from the open area around the corner into a small ten by ten office.

'Thank you, Sister. That will be all.' Weinstock shuts the door after her. 'Okay, please sit down.'

Mitzi looks depressed. 'Am I going to need to?'

'I think you are.'

Mitzi takes another bum-numbing plastic chair and he pulls up one opposite her.

'You know what the M'Naghten Rules are?'

Her heart sinks. 'Not guilty by reason of insanity, right? Gift from the good old British to our wonderful mess of a judicial system.'

'You're right. And according to those rules, the man I just saw *is* mentally ill. There is no question about that. He is lucid enough to know his own name, address, age and job, but his spontaneous lapses into Latin, his intermittent dialogue with God and his profound and persistent self-mutilation are clear signs of extreme mental instability. I have little option but to begin the process that will admit him into institutionalised medical care.'

Mitzi covers her face with her hands. Carter is going to be suicidal when he hears this.

'I have only done a preliminary examination tonight, but it's already sufficient to determine that he is delusional and would easily meet the M'Naghten criteria of temporary mental impairment. Put simply, at moments when he kills, Mr James doesn't believe it is wrong to do it. He is a danger to both society and himself.'

'What about the "Policeman at the Elbow" test? This guy crept into women's houses and killed them in their sleep. Would he have taken their lives if there'd been a police officer in the room?'

Weinstock forces out a thin sympathetic smile. 'Maybe. But Mr James's case isn't as simple as I've made out.'

Mitzi flinches. 'Nothing I've heard sounds simple. So something in his brain, in his genes, in his upbringing drove him to do it – anything except the fact that he just *wanted* to.'

'Lieutenant, please. I understand your frustration, but this won't help.'

'I'm sorry.'

'Mr James is completely aware of what he has done. He understands why you are here and that I intend to have him admitted into psychiatric care. Nevertheless, he has asked to see you.'

175

LAX

Nic isn't distracted by the woman's fall. His eyes never leave the lithe-looking guy at her side, bundling into the cop and going for her gun.

Ephrem turns and lets off a shot into the roof of the hall before anyone closes on him.

Screams break out and people hit the ground. He scoops up a young girl in a yellow dress, wraps his left arm tight around her. The kid's no more than four and for now she's going to be his shield.

'Stay away!' His shout is aimed at two guards with drawn weapons ten metres away. 'Drop the guns and stay back or I'll shoot her.'

Pistols clatter to the ground and Ephrem edges back

between the glass booths. They'll come after him, he knows that. He has to slow them down. He snakes the gun around the terrified girl and fires two shots into the huddle of petrified passengers. The first hits a teenager in the back. The second spurts blood from the head of an old man in a wheelchair.

The monk bolts into the luggage area, still carrying the kid.

Nic is first after him; most of the cops and guards are sorting out the wounded and the mayhem. Someone will be on a radio calling for back-up but it might be too late. Up ahead are unsuspecting customs guys. They're lazily waiting to do final card checks before passengers wriggle free of all the border bureaucracy and disappear into the main terminal.

'He's got a gun!' shouts Nic. 'The guy's got a gun and a hostage!'

Too late. Shots bark. The guard to Nic's left goes down. Then his buddy on the right.

More screams erupt from passengers. Nic grabs a Smith and Wesson from an injured guard and unclips the safety. He clears the automatic doors. The arrivals hall is packed.

A wave of people crashes into him. The shooter is gone. Nic can't see beyond the flotsam of white name cards held aloft by waiting drivers. He spots a flash of black jacket slipping through one of the exits. It has to be the guy.

He pushes his way to the exit. Outside he turns right. The shooter is facing him.

In a blink Nic checks for the little girl. She's not there. He sights his gun.

472

Too late.

A bullet tears into his left shoulder. Rocks him. Sends his senses racing.

Years of training kick in. He keeps focus. Breathes slow. Squeezes the trigger. Blood spurts in the distance. There's a bang. Like a clap of applause. He sees a hazy figure stagger. A second bullet rips into Nic. He never saw it coming. Never expected this.

His legs buckle. No pain. Not yet – it's still being trucked in, lorry loads of the stuff. He can't breathe. Shock freezes his lungs. He can't get a whisper of air into his body. A wave of cold trauma drowns his nerves and brain. Nic *sees* his hands but he can't move them. Can't *feel* them. Blood puddles through his fingers.

He's hit in the stomach. It's a bad one. That much he knows. He's caught a real bleeder.

176

CENTURY HOSPITAL, INGLEWOOD

Mitzi can't believe how peaceful James looks. Despite the mass of crusting red crucifixes on his face and chest, there even seems to be a smile lying smugly on the soft hammock of his lips as he rests against a pile of pillows.

Anyone who's done what he's done should never be

allowed to rest. Goddamn animal should be kept awake until his dying day and Mitzi hopes that's sooner rather than later.

Weinstock closes the door behind them and the Creeper's lids shutter.

Mitzi swallows hard. She doesn't want her rage to show. Not yet. Not until the evil-crazy-psycho-nutjob has said whatever it is he wants to say.

John James looks sleepily from the lieutenant to the psychiatrist as he fights the effect of the sedatives.

Mitzi pulls up a chair alongside the bed. 'Mr Weinstock here says you want to talk to me.'

He nods slowly. 'I do.'

She tries to take the hate out of her eyes, tries not to think of all the crime scene pictures she's seen of women covered in sheets, of holes left in people's lives.

'I know what I did, Detective.' His voice is weak. He reaches for a glass of water on a bedside cabinet. 'I took the lives of other human beings. I need you to understand that they wanted to be taken.'

'Sure they did.'

'They did. All but Bass and Emma – my Emma.'

'I don't understand.'

He takes a sip of water. 'I killed Bass because she and Harrison made Emma's life hell. God didn't tell me to. I just wanted to. I would have killed Harrison too had she been there when I broke into her home.'

Seems to Mitzi that she was right about Jenny's phone. 'To be clear,' she glances at Weinstock, making it understood that he's a witness to what's being said, 'you admit to the premeditated murder of Kim Bass and attempted murder of Jennifer Harrison?'

'And the murder of Em – Emma Varley.' He looks away.

He's crying. Unbelievably, the man who slaughtered a dozen or more women is actually weeping.

He uses the edge of the pillow to wipe away tears. 'I thought that God had chosen her, had wanted me to help her go to him. But I was mistaken.'

'Mistaken?'

'My feelings for her confused me. I've never felt like that before.'

'You loved her.'

'Still do. That's why I know it's wrong. It felt wrong when I did it. But I still did it.'

'And you're telling me this now, why? Presumably, only because you know you're safe from prosecution, and the death penalty.' She looks toward Weinstock. 'You're rock-solid certain that the good doctor here is going to insist on you being hospitalised so there's no risk of you ever going to trial.'

'No – you're wrong! I'm telling you, because God wants me to stand trial.' He takes a slow breath and calms himself. 'The Lord wants me to face up to what I've done. He's not ashamed of how He guided me, nor I of how I was guided. The world must know the errors made were mortal not divine.'

Weinstock bends close to his patient and whispers, 'May I explain a little more to the officer?'

The Creeper nods.

'With respect, Lieutenant, I don't think you understand the enormity of what is being said to you. A landmark case some years back ruled that an insanity defence cannot be imposed upon an intelligent defendant who wishes to forgo such a defence. Mr James is just such a person.'

'That's right.' His face is filled with contentment. 'I wish to *forgo such a defence*. I confess to the murders of Kim Bass and Emma Varley and I demand I be punished for them.'

177

Sirens blare. Voices fade in and out. Lights flash.

Nic Karakandez knows from the chaos around him that he's in an ambulance and is dying. The pain comes now. Comes with a fanfare. A big brass band of agony booms out the message that his body can't survive this level of trauma.

Strangers mop blood from his gut. They press pads with desperate hands and shout about hydrostatic shock, haemorrhaging, BP levels and Christ knows what else.

Their tones give away that they're in a race to save his life – and they're losing.

A cop's face swims into view.

'Hang on, buddy.' A forced smile. 'We're nearly there. Keep looking at me, you hear.'

Nic tries his best but his eyelids are heavy. He can't hold out any more.

Blackness.

'He's going. Quick. Come on, *do something*.'

'Keep him awake. For God's sake just keep him awake.'

Distant voices. The world bumping. Sirens. Incredible heat and then waves of cold.

'Come on, buddy, you're going to be all right.'

Nic opens his eyes and sees the cop again.

'Good, that's good. Keep staring at me.'

He recognises the look. The one he's worn often enough. Pulled it out on street corners when gangbangers, kids too young to even drink, are bleeding out. He's knelt beside them, given them that look and lied away their last minutes.

He closes his eyes again.

'No. No. Come on buddy!'

The darkness is restful. This is where the peace is. This is where the pain can be locked out.

He thinks of Carolina and Max. The three of them flying off for the holiday they never took. Running in the sand and sea together, holding hands, splashing and laughing as they jump waves.

'We're *losing* him.'

The brass band stops now.

The pain rages no more.

PART FIVE

I believe in God, the Father Almighty, Creator of Heaven and Earth. I believe in Jesus Christ, His only Son, our Lord.

178

Mitzi walks in at 8 a.m. to an office already close to full.

She scans the desks suspiciously as she slips off her coat. 'So what happened, guys? You all get tossed out by your wives as part of some class action?'

A stone-faced sergeant by the photocopier catches her eye. 'Go see the captain. Said he wanted to know when you came in.'

She spins her coat around the top of a chair. 'Matthews, at eight on a Monday?'

'Your phone's off. He's been calling you.'

'Shit.' She hasn't paid the last bill. They finally disconnected her. She digs in her purse for her cell. It's dead. Has been since she called Carter going home last night. She'd been too tired to remember to put it on charge.

Mitzi heads to the boss's office. If she's in trouble, it's probably to do with the legal mumbo jumbo at the hospital. What the hell. She did the best she could. They can't ask more than that.

Matthews' secretary isn't at her guard post. Through the door she can see him talking to Tyler Carter. Doesn't look too friendly.

She knocks and walks in. 'You wanted me, sir.' Her heart skips a beat.

'Come in, shut the door.' He waves her over.

She doesn't like the look on their faces. 'What is it?'

'Nic Karakandez was shot last night at LAX, a gunfight with a man fleeing border guards.'

She takes a deep breath.

'He died on the way to County. A bullet through the gut and another in the shoulder—'

'Oh Jesus.' Her legs go shaky.

He puts a hand up. 'Let me finish. They brought him round in the ER. He's alive but in a coma.' Matthews guides her into a chair. 'He shot dead a guy running away, the son of a bitch who'd pinned him with two .45s.'

Carter touches her shoulder. 'Broussard, the scientist you said he was bringing back, he's dead too. Plus a disabled guy who caught a headshot. A teenage boy is going to be paralysed for life.'

Mitzi is speechless.

'Broussard was found murdered in a LAX restroom – airside of the border line. It's what sparked the shoot-out.'

'I thought they were home and dry,' she finally says. 'Nic rang from JFK and said everything was fine.'

'Well, it wasn't.' Matthews tries to be practical. 'Tyler's got a couple of his men processing the scene and the two bodies are down at the morgue.'

'I'd like to go to the hospital.' She looks to Carter. 'If that's okay? I'll try to wrap up my stuff on the Creeper when I come back.'

'Sure. Watch yourself down there. The press have got wind of the shootings and they're crawling over the local ER rooms.'

The office door is opened by Amy Chang, her face full of sympathy. 'I came straight over when I heard.'

Mitzi's glad to see her. 'Thanks.'

Matthews can't let her leave without spelling things out, bracing her for the worst. 'Things don't look good with Nic. The docs last night said it was sixty-forty against him pulling through.'

'Screw the docs.' Mitzi pulls the door open. 'He's got a boat to sail and I'm gonna damn well make sure he does.'

179

COUNTY HOSPITAL, LOS ANGELES

The trip out to County almost breaks the lieutenant's job-hardened heart.

She'd hoped that turning up at his bedside would have some magical effect – like it does in films. But it hasn't. Nic Karakandez is as pale as a ghost.

She looks across the tubes, the blood and plasma bags and the beeping monitors to Amy Chang. 'Can you go talk to them – you know, doctor to doctor? Tell me what his chances really are?'

'Of course.' The ME heads out.

Mitzi stares at Nic. Shit, he really looks dead. 'Four days, you dope.' She takes his hand in hers. 'Four freakin' days. How can you go screw things up with just *four* days to go? I should kick your ass. Fact is, when I get you outta here *I will* kick your ass.'

She studies the monitor then locks his fingers between both her hands and just holds on. Amy opens the door and the movement makes her turn.

'Good and bad news, Mitz. The gut wound was a through-and-through. He bled out badly but no vital organs were hit. That's a big plus. Bad news is he cracked his head going down and that caused intracerebral haemorrhaging and edema that they didn't find until they CT-scanned him. Add the shoulder wound, major blood loss and trauma and you can see why he flatlined. Paramedics did an incredible job bringing him round and keeping him ticking until they got him in surgery.'

'What are his chances, Amy?'

'Really hard to say.'

'Don't doctorise me. Friend to friend. Are we booking a party or fixing for a funeral?'

Amy pushes out a smile. 'The next few hours will tell us.'

180

Sixty-forty against.

The odds roll like dice in Mitzi's head. Surely Nic's beaten stats worse than that out on the street? She bites at a nail and stares out of the passenger window as Amy drives back to the precinct. If she hadn't sent him to Italy, none of this would have happened. But she knows there's no use beating herself up – it ain't gonna make him better. She pulls off the last of the hangnail and turns to her friend. 'The guy Nic shot, did you do the exam on him?'

'Terri Jones got him. I was still finishing up on Emma Varley when they called it in.'

'You see him at all? See what he looked like?'

She knows why she's asking. 'Just a glimpse. He was nothing out of the ordinary. Arabic. Athletic. Late-thirties, I guess. I didn't pay too much attention.'

Mitzi can't help but ask. 'Where'd Nic shoot him?'

'Head.' She taps a finger just above her nose.

'Shame. Bastard would have died quick from that.'

They park up and swipe themselves in. 'I'll call you later,' says Amy. 'I've still got stuff to do. I finished that report on the Shroud. Let me know if or when you want it.'

'Thanks. It doesn't seem important right now.'

'It isn't. Anyway, I'll stick it in the internal mail for you.'

'Thanks.' Mitzi smiles. 'What do you think? Faked or not?'

'Ignoring what all the sceptics and nutjobs claim – and believe me, there are hundreds of them who've written on this – I'd say the marks on the Shroud are consistent with someone crucified and stabbed.'

'You'd stand up in court and say that?'

'Probably would – but I'd want a big fat fee to do so.'

They both laugh. Amy waves as she turns away. 'Don't go home without calling me.'

'Wouldn't dream of it.' Mitzi walks back into Homicide and through to Carter's office. She's going to keep busy. Stay involved. Not think about those monitors, tubes and unfavourable odds.

Carter is with Tom Hix, hands on his desk, bent over folders, papers and transparencies. He looks up as soon as Mitzi walks in. 'What's the latest?'

'They say he's stable but still critical.'

'Out of the coma?'

'No. Amy Chang reckons the next couple of hours will be decisive.'

Hix nods. 'We used to think that all the brain damage came at the moment of injury. Now we know the time afterwards is even more dangerous. You're talking brain swelling and complications like spastic hemiplegia, hyper-reflexia, quadrispasticity—'

'No, we're not, Tom.' Carter interrupts. 'We're absolutely *not* talking that kind of trash.'

'Sorry, Tyler, I wasn't thinking.'

Mitzi gestures to the desk. 'What you looking at?'

486

Carter takes a beat. 'Tom's discovered something unusual. Unusual and disturbing.' He spreads out three sets of DNA codes. 'You're the scientist, you explain it.'

Hix is keen to do so. 'The first transparent printout is the DNA of the offender who left trace at Tamara Jacobs's house and in the rented Lexus. We've already blood-matched it to the man Nic shot dead last night. It's one and the same.'

Mitzi looks pleased. 'So we have Tamara's killer.'

'And,' adds Carter, 'Édouard Broussard's.'

Tom qualifies it. 'Yes. Subject to a fuller DNA test, but that's really only a formality. Now look at this second pro-file.' He slides the transparency from its folder. 'This is the sample Nic FedExed from Italy – trace from the killer of sci-entist Mario Sacconi.' He lays it over the top of the first print. 'One and the same.'

'His prints match too,' adds Carter. 'We got partials from the sticky tape used on the female victim in Italy – they're good enough to show a conclusive match. This guy was a pro. A professional assassin.'

Hix produces another three transparencies. 'Let's move on to the Creeper case. Here things get even more intriguing. Do you know whose genetic fingerprints these are?'

'Not a clue.'

'The first is the DNA profile of the Creeper himself. We've had it on file for more than a year. The second is from swabs John James voluntarily gave us yesterday. The third is

from hair root samples found on the body of Emma Varley.'
He lays all three on top of each other.

'Perfect matches,' announces Carter. 'If we can get the DA
to prosecute, we have an open and closed case on James.'

Carter and Hix exchange looks.

'What?' asks Mitzi. 'This is good news, isn't it? We got
two separate killers and two separate DNA profiles that link
them to their crimes. Is there more than that?'

'Show her,' says Carter.

The scientist carefully slides a transparency out of a plastic cover. 'This is DNA from the blood that Nic shipped us
and said came from the Shroud of Turin, samples Erica Craxi
gave him inside a Saint Christopher locket.'

She looks at the printout. It's just a mass of shaded boxes
but even she can tell it's not the same as the others. 'So what?
What's the connection?'

Hix pulls away two of the other transparencies. 'The one
here on the left is the man Nic shot. The one on the right is
John James aka the Creeper.' He pauses and lets Carter and
Mitzi take a good long look. 'The print in my hand is of the
DNA from the Shroud.' He lays it first on top of the left-hand
profile, the man Nic killed. 'Here, you see similarities. Not
total matches in all columns, only familial matches. Distant
relations, diluted through the generations, maybe even
through centuries, but nonetheless matches.' He lifts it off and
then places it over the second profile, the one of the Creeper.
'Again you see matches. Not a complete match but nonetheless another conclusive indication of distant family links.'

Mitzi's not sure she understands. 'You mean the Creeper and the man Nic shot are descendants of the same bloodline as Shroudman?'

'That's exactly what I mean.' Hix places the two profiles over each other. 'Here, in these boxes, you see it. Distant paternal links, a genetic chain crossing countries and centuries.'

'The *criminal* gene.' Carter scoffs at the idea of it. 'This is a gift to all the do-gooders who believe cold-blooded murdering bastards like the Creeper simply can't help themselves – oh no, no, they're just poor victims of a genetic defect, unavoidably and inevitably passed from father to son – they simply can't help their urge to kill.' He lifts a wastebasket from the floor. 'Our case against James just turned into garbage.'

181

ROME

Andreas Pathykos thought he would never see his old friend again. Now here they are face to face. But there is no reason for celebration.

Nabih Hayek drives the papal advisor a short way down Via della Conciliazione before turning into an unlit side street. The two men sit in the battered Fiat that the Lebanese priest has owned for more than a decade. Moonlight falls on their faces as he explains the reason for the hasty liaison. 'The monk is dead. Shot by a policeman in Los Angeles.'

'Dear God.'

Hayek determines to tell the rest of it before the questions come. 'Others were hurt. Two airport guards, a teenage boy and the policeman who killed Ephrem.' He takes a beat. 'And I'm afraid an elderly man was shot dead as well.'

Pathykos is grey with shock. 'How is this so?'

Hayek holds back much of what he knows. 'It is unclear. I am informed the monk had all but completed his task when the police cornered him at the airport. It seems he had no choice but to fight until his last breath.'

The adviser lowers his head in thought for the dead, the injured and their loved ones. So much pain, so much suffering has been caused. 'Is this the end of it now, Nabih?'

The face of his friend says it isn't. 'Craxi and the scientist, Broussard, are dead but all the DNA taken from the Shroud may not have been destroyed.'

'What? The whole purpose of the monk's mission was to eradicate the findings of those sacrilegiously stolen samples.'

'I know, but it seems the original source was split and a sample has found its way back to the laboratories of the Los Angeles Police department.'

'Then we must ensure that it is never tested or its results never known. It is our duty to guarantee that any connection to the Holy Shroud is always unverifiable.'

'I agree – but *you* must do this, Andreas. You must use the name of the Holy Father and reach out to friends of ours.'

Pathykos nods.

'But that alone will not be enough. You understand, don't you?'

'Don't lecture me on responsibilities, Nabih. Take me back to the Vatican. I know what has to be done.'

182

The long and awful day ends on an unexpected low – another call to Deke Matthews's room.

Mitzi feels drained as she drags herself down the long corridors to the captain's office. All the trauma has left her running on empty. His secretary smiles up from her desk and waves Mitzi through. She opens the door and immediately wishes she hadn't. Matthews is at the head of his small conference table, next to him is Carter and Tom Hix. Opposite them – beautifully dressed in a black Armani suit – is Deputy District Attorney Maria Sanchez.

Maria is everything one woman can possibly hate in another.

Mitzi can maybe forgive that she's a cold-hearted, self-centred, egomaniacal bitch who used a child murder last year as a personal publicity platform. But what she can *never* forgive is the fact that no matter what godawful time of day it is, the raven-haired lawyer – who is almost fifty – always manages to look half her age.

That is beyond forgiveness.

'Captain.' Mitzi stands at the far end of the table.

'Take a seat.' He gestures to the conference table. 'We're discussing the Creeper case and in particular the DNA evidence Tom pulled together.'

'*Been* discussing.' Sanchez shoots Matthews a courtroom look as she emphasises the past tense.

Mitzi just can't bring herself to sit alongside the lawyer. She takes a place opposite Matthews. 'How can I help?'

'We're not going to prosecute James.' Matthews pauses to let the point sink in. 'He's going to be committed into psychiatric care.'

Sanchez clears her throat. 'Captain, if your team can properly tie up James's confessions to the murders of Varley and Bass, Commissioner Bradley will make a public statement about those crimes being linked to James and explain he is not fit for trial. He'll also state publicly that you've now closed the Creeper files and are not looking for anyone else.'

Matthews turns to Carter. 'Public-wise, it has the same effect as winning at trial. Case closed.'

'The commissioner would like that,' Sanchez smiles. 'It would also be done without any of the risk of *improper* disclosure or further cost to the taxpayer.'

Carter looks furious. 'By "improper" you mean Tom's scientific evidence – science American citizens have a right to know.'

She waves a hand at him. 'Don't be immature. Ninety per cent of them wouldn't understand if he visited them all in person and spent a day explaining it.'

'Why?' Mitzi barks. 'Why are you trying to sweep all these findings under the carpet?'

Sanchez sighs. 'You really have to think this through.' She gives Mitzi a condescending stare. 'Think about the implications of full disclosure. If we go public, we risk arming defence attorneys nationwide with a new plea of genetic mitigation.'

'Bullshit.' The word tumbles out of the lieutenant's mouth. 'There are examples worldwide of fine, upstanding, law-abiding citizens – men, women and children – who are closely, never mind *distantly,* related to rapists, murderers and terrorists. They're not *bad* people. Their genes don't possess badness.'

'Mitzi's right,' snaps Carter. 'Bad people are bad because they make the choice to be bad.'

'We can't open this can of worms,' Sanchez starts to pack her leather document case. 'We're done discussing it.'

Silence floats like a poison cloud. Mitzi reaches to the middle of the table, grabs a glass and pours water from a jug. 'There's something else, isn't there?'

No one answers.

She looks at their faces. 'C'mon, I'm a big girl, I can take it. After all, that's why I'm in here. You need me to come in line, nod nicely and agree to some other grade-A political horseshit, don't you?'

Matthews waits until she's settled down. 'Mitzi, this whole business with the Shroud is a problem. A real problem. Messy as a dropped wedding cake for both us and the Italians.'

She throws back a gulp of water. 'You mean the Carabinieri?'

He nods. 'The commissioner had diplomats on his ass all afternoon. Embassy guys. Ambassadors. They don't want anything made public about the Shroud being interfered with, about samples being taken illegally.' He looks across at Hix. 'Especially about unauthorised tests in foreign countries and links to serial murder cases.'

'Man, I bet they don't,' says Mitzi, her anger rising.

He tries to reason with her. 'Italian–American relations have always been good – and important to both countries.'

She shakes her head. 'Are we missing out the Mafia here?'

Maria Sanchez glowers at her. 'Decisions have been made, Lieutenant. Captain Matthews got you in here out of courtesy, that's all. The DA and the commissioner have already given assurances that no comment will be made on the Tamara Jacobs case or anything to do with the Shroud of Turin without them approving it.' She pushes back her chair and readies to leave. 'Anyone breaks that rule they'll find themselves jobless and pensionless. Good day to you all.'

Mitzi stares at the floor, heart thumping like she just ran a mile. 'Hey, Councillor.'

Sanchez stops, her hand on the door handle. 'What?'

'When you go to Catholic Mass this Sunday – as I'm sure

494

all good Spanish girls do – I hope to hell the whole church gets up and gives you the huge round of applause you so obviously deserve.'

Matthews's door slams so hard the glass almost breaks.

183

ROME

It is not a problem for Andreas Pathykos to take the key from the pontiff's antechamber. The Holy Father has been long asleep and the guards at his door are accustomed to admitting the old Greek at late hours to leave documents and carry out chores.

As he enters the darkened room, his mind floods with a disturbing mix of science, religion and history. Over the course of centuries the Church has venerated artefacts presented as the crown of thorns and the lance that pierced the side of Christ. But none have ever produced samples that scientists can reliably attest is blood – the blood of a man, the blood of Jesus Christ, the son of God.

Even the Shroud of Turin had refused to yield biological evidence of life – until, that is, a sample had been stolen and tested with methods more advanced than the Vatican has ever used. And now comparison is possible. Science can use its modern trickery to crush the beliefs and goodness of

Christian faith. Worse still, it can open up the old stories of Saladin and reignite the Muslim groups.

Pathykos cannot let that happen. If the police in America are to defy political pressures and disclose the stolen DNA, they must have nothing to compare it with. The pontiff's most trusted adviser and oldest friend lets himself into the Holy Father's bedchamber. The room is cool and smells of lavender. He treads gently towards the large bed that holds the divine representation of God on earth. Less than six inches from the sleeping pontiff is a small silver-gilt casket and in it a splinter of wood that has yielded the most precious drop of blood on earth.

Christ's blood. Taken from the True Cross. Preserved and protected by Holy Knights before the warlord Saladin took the True Cross in the Battle of Hattin.

Pathykos feels his heart beat so fast he thinks he will collapse before he steals his way out of the chambers. Every step from the pontiff's bed takes an age. Every yard the Greek achieves brings him an agonising pain. Was this how Judas felt in his hour of betrayal? There are tears in his eyes as he makes it to his own chamber. He locks the door and looks out of the window across the Eternal City. Daybreak will come soon. Church bells will ring out across the rooftops and the faithful will make their way to morning prayer.

He will not be among them.

A fire is still burning in the grate. He has sat here many hours, contemplating his life and beliefs, staring into the flames and being comforted by their ephemeral warmth.

He takes a poker and stokes the coals, then uses it to break open the casket. Soot smudges his hands and he kneels and places the fragment of blessed wood gently on the flames.

It takes a second for it to catch. The dry wood throws off a bright flame and a crisp crackle. Pathykos feels a stab in his heart. He keeps his hands over the fire and lets the flames scorch his skin. As the cuffs of his robe catch alight he bows his head into the burst of orange light. The last words he manages before the fire engulfs him are 'Bless me, Father, for I have sinned.'

184

COUNTY HOSPITAL, LOS ANGELES

Sixty-forty is now eighty-twenty. Against.

The doctors give Mitzi the bad news soon after she arrives. There's a chance he won't even make it through the night. And if he does, then he could be in a vegetative state for the rest of his life.

Eighty-twenty.

Vegetative state.

Some choice. Some odds.

Mitzi wanders the corridors feeling lost. Right now she's regretting telling Amy not to come in with her. She sent her home, told her to get some rest, said she'd be all right. She's not. Most definitely not.

The hospital drink dispenser produces the worst chicken soup she's ever tasted. But it's all she can manage. Muffins in Carter's office were her last meal and that seems weeks ago. She takes the plastic cup back to Nic's bedside and sits there in a daze. Waiting is something cops do better than most people, but Mitzi's always struggled to pull it off. Especially when she's waiting for someone to die.

She stares at his grey face. His eyes used to be bright with adventure and he was just about the cutest of rookie cops she'd ever seen. She'd denied all her natural feelings for him. Thrown water on the fires within, just as soon as they started to flicker into life. She'd been nothing but professional. Shown him the ropes. Wiped his nose. Walked him through his first domestic murder. Stood next to him when he almost hurled at his first autopsy. Got him blind drunk after he lost his first case in court.

She'd done anything and everything except loved him.

She bends her lips to the fingers entwined in hers and kisses the back of his hand. It's the most meaningful contact they've ever had. Until now they never exchanged more than a peck on the cheek. The thought almost makes her laugh and cry at the same time. How had she managed to bury her feelings? *Alfie*, she supposes.

Alfie and the twins.

She'd been the good wife and mother. Been determined not to be the cop other women pick out as the one having an affair with their partner. She wishes she had. My God she does. She wishes it had been long and mad and passionate. Full of life. That's what being close to death does for you. It makes you want to live to the fullest – makes you regret every wasted second of your precious time on earth. Mitzi stands up and tugs a tissue from a box on the bedside cabinet. She blows her nose and dabs her eyes. It's 11 p.m. She'll stay until midnight, maybe one, then turn in for the night. Even as she thinks it, she knows she's still likely to be in the same chair in the morning, nursing a stiff neck, wondering how much coffee she'll need to stay awake through another shift.

Screw them. Tomorrow she might not even go in. Being here is more important than all their political accommodations. She looks round the room for anything to distract her from the monotonous bleep of the machines.

There's nothing.

She's read the place dry. Even the signs on the wall – about visiting hours, the importance of hand washing, the danger of infections and all their rules on not using cell phones. Re-reading the last one makes her decide to call the girls.

Tapping in Jade's number brings back a smile to her face. At least they're talking again. The rift is healing, the bond is being strengthened.

A loud and intense beep startles her. At first she thinks it's the phone and almost drops it out of surprise. Then she realises what it is. An alert from a monitor. The door opens and a nurse walks briskly in. The kind of stride cops and medics have when they're disguising a moment of panic.

This is it. She knows it is. *Feels* it is.

'What's happening?' Mitzi moves closer to Nic's bed. 'What was that noise?'

'Stand back please.'

She feels a hand on her shoulder. A white-coated doctor eases her out of the way. He guides a stethoscope to his ears and bends over Nic's body.

He's dying. Right this minute. Cop instinct makes her look again at her watch – one of the first things she was taught was the importance of keeping track of the time that things happen. The moment everything changes. The precious second that life becomes death. More white coats fill the room. Mitzi drifts back to the wall, out to the periphery of the action, as though thrown there by centrifugal force.

Through the melee of bodies and the forest of arms spread over the bed, she sees Nic's body spasm.

Death throes.

His feet jerk up and down. He's being shocked. A last effort to bump-start his broken heart.

Standing and watching, she feels lost. Stranded like a helpless wife or sister. Not like a cop, not like any other professional in the room. The medical talk is all just a meaningless mumble. She's treading water. Waiting for them to back off and tell her the news.

The bad news.

They shift the crash paddles and study the monitors.

Something moves Mitzi's legs and she becomes a cop again. She walks around the bed and finds a gap. If he's going to die, it's not going to be without the touch of a friend, someone who loves him.

A doctor glances at the monitor. Nic's body heaves again. She takes his hand. Squeezes it. Stays strong.

He coughs.

'Stable,' shouts a nurse. 'Pulse normal.'

Nic coughs again. His eyes flicker open.

She stares at him. The dying often have a last gasp. Body full of fluids and juices, jolted by enough electricity to light up Vegas – the signs are meaningless.

'Mit-zi.'

The slowly whispered word tears her apart.

Medics shuffle tubes and check fluid bags. The nurse who first came in adjusts a finger-monitor and checks his pulse again.

Mitzi's eyes are locked on Nic. If she looks away or even blinks, he'll die. She knows he will.

He can't force out a smile. His voice is a soft, painful croak. 'Where am I?'

She lifts his hand and kisses it again. 'Where'd you think you are? The freakin' boatyard?'

ACKNOWLEDGEMENTS

First and foremost the biggest possible thanks to Luigi Bonomi and his team at LBA for invaluable guidance, encouragement and fun. Big, big gratitude to all at Little,Brown/Sphere – especially David Shelley for faith and support, Daniel Mallory for inspiration and energy, and Iain Hunt for perspiration and imagination. Behind all great men are great ladies and they don't come greater than Andy Hine, Kate Hibbert and Helena Doree in international rights and Kate Webster and Hannah Hargrave in marketing and publicity. I'm hugely indebted to Professor Guy Rutty, MBE, Head of Forensic Pathology, East Midlands Forensic Pathology Unit, University of Leicester, for his guidance and patience over the crime scenes – any deviations from fact are down to me and not him. Special thanks to 'Scary Jack' at Everett Baldwin Barclay for knowing what Donna and I never know. Finally to everyone who read *The Stonehenge Legacy* and wrote or posted on www.facebook.com/samchrister.

LIKE ACTION, INTRIGUE AND RELENTLESS SUSPENSE?

 / samchrister

JOIN THE CONVERSATION AT
WWW.FACEBOOK.COM/SAMCHRISTER